A Very Satisfactory Manner

JOHN LITTLE

© 2023 John Little

All rights reserved

No part of this publication may be reproduced, stored in a retrieval system, stored in a database and/or published in any form or by any means, electronic, mechanical, photocopying, recording or otherwise, without the prior written permission of the publisher.

ISBN 9798861597128

A Very Satisfactory Manner

Preface

It is possible for human beings to develop into something that they perhaps never intended to when they were young. Some become great sages, others artists, generals, leaders and all kinds of things not thought of when they were babies in their mother's arms. There are also those who become thieves and murderers. Some become these things and also transmute into "monsters." Hitler was a monster; so was Attila the Hun, Vlad the Impaler, Pol Pot, Robespierre, Caligula and many other figures in history who have earned that same label. So what is a monster?

My own definition has to be that it is someone who moves away from and beyond the normal morality that governs a compassionate and civilised society. They no longer think as a caring and everyday human being but have acquired a set of norms that suit them and the pursuit of their own aims to the exclusion of their own humanity. Stalin could watch films of his opponents begging for mercy as they were shot; yet the young Stalin trained as a priest. Hitler reportedly cackled watching the July bomb plotters hanging on meat hooks; this was a man who wanted to be an artist. Terrorists might be called 'monsters' because they blow up and kill innocent people in pursuit of their own ends and regard the suffering and death of other human beings as mere collateral damage. Yet physically the person thought of as a monster, is still, a human being; they have wives, husbands, aunts, uncles, children, friends and so on.

Perhaps in some ways we label such people as monsters because we are uncomfortable with them being human, because that means that they are like us. And if they are like us then we too have the capacity to do what they have done; and that thought we both hate and fear. It is difficult to escape the idea that monsters in the human race are not born; they are made; manufactured by social forces into something society cannot tolerate. And yet, as society keeps on doing it, we have to ask if the creation of monsters is a necessary evil in that they distract people from where their attention would otherwise be.

In Cumberland in 1885 three or four men carried out a spree of robbery, callous and calculated violence, and ultimately murder, ending in one of the most famous trials that has ever taken place in the county. They were portrayed as monsters in the press right across the world, and in Cumberland they stirred genuine and visceral hatred in ordinary people. This novel is my attempt to understand why they did what they did. They were human beings; I present them as such.

To state the obvious, this is not a history book; it is an historical novel. The novelist is allowed to make things up where the historical record has gaps; a history textbook cannot do this. Having said that, this story has a solid foundation of evidence and fact underpinning it. Where I have strayed from actual history I have tried to include only that which is possible, plausible, or probable. My version of events may even be the truth; but there is not one person alive today who can say that, or otherwise.

I wish to thank my wife Ruth for her help and patience in listening to my chapters, and David Banks of Beechville, Nova Scotia, for the eagle-eyed proofing that he always does so well. To my beta readers, Betty Telford, Irene Martin and Eunice Small, I also owe a debt of gratitude. Especial thanks must go to Gerald Smith, who gave me a very informative tour of Netherby Hall, and to Kim Capstick, Netherby's Operations Manager, for setting up my visit. That made quite a difference. I must observe that the concluding chapter would not have been possible without the help of David Banks and his contact with Sarah Manchon of The Canadian Museum of Immigration at Pier 21; I am most grateful to both of them. Likewise I must also thank the British Newspaper Archive, an incomparable resource, Whitehaven Archives, and Carlisle Archives for their assistance. To you, the reader I send my good wishes and the hope that you enjoyed reading this as much as I did writing it.

John Little 2023

Glossary of slang, late Victorian England

Flash pull	A showy job
Bang up	Fine sort
Foozle	A mess
Swag	Loot from a theft
Barker	Pistol
Crushers	Police
Mobsman	High ranking villain
Stretch	A year in prison
Bludger	Muscleman armed with club
Jack	Detective
Red	A gold watch
Jug	Prison
Grassed	Informed
Peach/ grass	To inform upon
Rozzers	Police
Topped	Hanged
Oliver widdling	Moon shining
Browns	Copper coins
Black Boys	Priests, Clergymen
Taters	Freezing
Lob-lolly	A mess
Click	Pick a pocket
Bottle	Courage

1

Rich Pickings

Anthony Benjamin Rudge was on holiday, or so he thought of what he was doing at this current time. Although a Londoner born and bred, being in London for the last few months had been rather 'hot' and he was not thinking of the temperature. The capital had been in an uproar, at least the strata and circles that he moved in. An honest thief could hardly put his nose out of the door these days before being pounced on or followed by a local crusher or some Jack trying not to look like a Jack, but they all did. There had been a murder down in Essex of a police inspector and the man the crushers wanted to question lived in London. They were turning the place upside down to try to find him.

Making a living in the capital was very hard right now, but of course there was a solution to this. Rudge was not averse to a bit of travel, and although he was an East Ender, he liked a change. He would occasionally sally forth to other parts of the country too. In Rudge's case, a love of variety existed in him because of Mr Ned Buntline. The American writer, who had made Buffalo Bill famous, produced many cheap 'dime novels' which were easily available in England for a halfpenny. Young Rudge had been an avid reader and soaked in whatever he could get. Like most self-taught men, his reading was not picked for balance but by opportunity. He had absorbed page after page of cowboys, Indians, fast-guns, quick draws and all kinds of escapades with gamblers, sharp-shooters and the like. In his early teens the young Rudge had left his home in London and worked his way to America as a deckhand on a cargo ship, and when there, down to Texas, the place he really wanted to see.

If this sounds unlikely for a lad of tender years, young Mr Rudge's background must be borne in mind. Anthony had not lived with mum and dad, but was brought up by his grandfather, a fact significant because the old man lived by his wits. This is a euphemism in reality because grandfather made a living by frequenting race meetings all over the country, gambling, acting as a bookie's runner, picking the odd pocket, stealing what he could, and so on. Young Rudge learned to be a very adept disciple, knew his way round, and was nobody's fool. He wanted to see Texas, so he went to Texas, where everybody carried a gun. At some point he began to use the name Anthony Benjamin Rudge as an alias instead of his real name, which was William Fennell; his reasons for doing this were never clear. This is of no matter, for a man may call himself whatever he likes. Texas was not to his taste. Apart from being hot and dusty, he soon realised that there were many people living there who were far more vicious and venal than he was, and that in a place where there was so little law, his survival to any age was unlikely, especially as what passed for law was enforced by sheriffs and marshals who would just as soon shoot you as look at you. In Britain, the law, as a rule, did not carry pistols, which meant that a man who did, was at a certain advantage.

In the country of the blind the one-eyed man is king, so back in England Rudge carried a pistol at all times, but it was a proper one, with stopping power, firing a large and heavy bullet. The threat of it had got him out of some nasty scrapes. Many mobsmen carried something lighter that fired a tiny round, but Rudge was well armed, so unsurprisingly he soon got himself a name. He made a good living from thieving, wore the clothes, carried a fine 'Red' on a chain, hung round the proper mobsman haunts, and, having an outgoing sort of personality, was on good terms with most of his fellows. Unfortunately he was clobbered by a householder when he climbed through a window in October 1870 and did not have time to draw his pistol by reason of being unconscious. He woke up in Clerkenwell cells and ended up with five years in the jug, particularly Portland. His memories of his time in prison were somewhat mixed, but more of that later.

For now Anthony Rudge was out at work, and he stood on a street corner on the edge of Hilly Fields in South London, far from his usual haunts. In the street the gas lights were yellow and a slight fog had rolled up from the Thames, lending a pleasing invisibility along the pavements. This was a well to do sort of area where managers and city types lived with their families. Much of the housing was terraced, but a bit further out were streets of large three storey villas where lived those who had more than a bit of money, right on the edge of London, where the countryside began. Gaslit downstairs, they were well made with fancy plasterwork, roses in the centres of the large high ceilings, and moulded cornices adorning the edges of the rooms. The prosperous and aspiring middle class people who lived here aped their betters in having dinner at eight, with the cook-maid waiting on them. While they ate their food in splendour in the dining room at the front, the back parlour was empty and so was upstairs. This was the burglar's favourite time of day.

Behind the row of houses was a back lane, with a line of doors leading into the various yards and gardens down the row. The people in the first house, Rudge's target, which he had picked out on a Sunday stroll the previous week, had very kindly left it unbarred which made life much simpler. He quietly lifted the sneck, opened the wooden gate, and passed through. He found himself standing in a garden, laid to grass with two narrow flowerbeds, one on each side. Ahead of him was the window of the back parlour, curtains drawn, and to his side was the window to the back kitchen which a flowered Scotch Holland roller blind concealed from the outside. The architects who designed the building had been very considerate in their provision of heavy cast iron downpipes which a child could shin up with ease, let alone a practiced cat burglar like Rudge. Out of consideration for his victims, he slipped a mask over his face, and almost scampered up the pipes, wedging one of his buttocks on the window ledge. From his pocket he pulled a thin strip of steel and inserted it between the frames of the sash window. Moving it smoothly across he disengaged the central catch and gently pulled the lower sash upwards. Good; it had no side screw-locks. It also slid very smoothly, probably thanks to a regular application of wax to its runners. He approved of this, for it meant a good and well ordered household where the maid did her job properly; in doing so she made his job much easier.

Pushing the window up, he slid through into the bedroom and stopped, listening. Although he had observed the house for a couple of days, along with some others, he knew there were no children there, but the sound of breathing would quickly alert him if there was someone in the room he had just entered. It was, of course, pitch black, as gas lights were not situated upstairs in most houses for fear of fire. When the family retired for the night they would use candles or oil lamps. For the moment, this floor was his domain. The floor above did not concern him for it was normally servants' quarters. From downstairs he heard the chink of cutlery and voices as the family ate their evening meal; the maid was fully engaged in seeing to them. He then pulled from his pocket a box of the burglar's friend, courtesy of Messrs Bryant and May, removed a match and struck it. Excellent! He would not have to go any further than the room he was in, because beside him was a dressing table with several boxes on it, and best of all, a lady's purse, which looked rather well stuffed. No need to be greedy by going out onto the landing and looking at other rooms. Golden rule number one; take what was easy and get out quick.

First things first though; safety at work was important. From his pocket he took a small wooden wedge. It was not a workmanlike thing, but could be whittled from a suitable twig in a few minutes. This did not detract one bit from its usefulness. He stuck it under the door which now could not be opened from outside without force.

Taking a stub of candle from his 'useful' pocket, he lit it. Padding quietly over to the dressing table, he found the purse to be well stuffed with banknotes and not a few sovereigns which he put into his pocket, replacing the purse where it had rested. Money is universal and hard to identify as a personal possession, whereas a purse clearly had an owner, and he was not her, so did not wish to be found with it on him. Now for the boxes; ah most satisfactory. There was nothing too fancy in this sort of house of course, but a nice little selection of brooches, necklaces, ear-rings and pendants, along with a couple of pin-on watches set with small diamonds. A nice haul, and quite enough; he loaded them into a deep pocket inside his jacket and turned to leave, blowing out his candle, pouring off the liquid wax and replacing the stub in his pocket. Out of the window he went, foot reaching over to the drainpipe, solid and reliable against the wall, and down he went into the yard. Without pausing, he walked across the yard and out of the gate, closing it behind him. He took off his mask and slipped it into his pocket. The small wooden wedge he left under the door of the room he had robbed, for it would waste some time when anybody tried to enter, and increase the distance that he could put between himself and the scene of his operations.

All in all, it was as neat a little job as he had ever pulled, and Rudge gained a certain professional satisfaction from the smoothness of the operation. All he had to do now was to transport his takings to a certain address in Stepney where the gold would be melted, the jewels extracted, the watches sold or exported to Amsterdam, and all expenses and tolls would be taken care of. His own portion would be noted in a ledger and the amount set against his name, as safe as if in the Bank of England. Most importantly, the Nabob would get his share and this meant that Rudge could continue his business with all the advantages proffered by that payment. In other words he was safe from having the life beaten out of him by the Nabob's enforcers.

It was highly amusing that a large number of newspaper editors thought that many of the robberies up and down the country were carried out by one gang. They had dubbed them 'The Ladder Gang' and speculated about who was behind them, for they were evidently a highly skilled bunch of villains. Rudge sometimes had a quiet chortle at what these gentlemen might think if they realised that the robberies were actually done by freelancers, but all using an organisation that provided what they needed. The Nabob's system was ingenious. Rudge, or any other London mobsman could go anywhere he liked in the country, doing jobs wherever he pleased and all he had to do with his takings was to place them in a box and send them to Stepney by way of Her Majesty's Royal Mail. That way he did not have to carry any incriminating swag about with him and his earnings were assured by the Nabob. Rudge had used the modern conveniences of railway and postal services to travel round the country several times and had never been found with anything on him. It was quite a laugh that the gangs so feared by the newspaper editors did not actually exist. Mind you, if ever someone did organise such a gang, what rich pickings they might have!

Rudge's daytime activities provided recreation much to his liking as well, because he was fond of the horses and often took himself off to race meetings all round the country. Rudge had always been a bookie's runner when he was a kid, but now he was a grown-up he did it on a much larger scale. He took bets, large and small from all comers and noted them down in a black book. This was highly illegal for he was not a licensed book keeper. But a licensed bookie was only one man and could only attend to the wishes of so many sporting men in a given period of time. Rudge was doing them a favour if he gave them a nice book stuffed with bets. The bookie gave him a cut of the money he collected, and paid him the money that his customers had won. Rudge then paid them and kept a cut of the winnings for himself so he got paid twice. It was a nice little earner so all in all he was coining it by day (during race days) and by night. It was nicer that the Nabob did not demand a cut of this money. Of course if there were no races on, there were other things; dogfights he liked in particular because he himself had trained and owned fighting dogs. He had been arrested a few times in his career and had described himself on occasions as a dog trainer, but in the absence of dog fights there was bare knuckle prizefighting, cock fighting and if you knew where to go, badger baiting. And at all of these, there was beer. At the age of forty-five (though he claimed to be thirty-nine) Anthony Rudge was very fond of beer, though his prosperity also gave him a growing taste for wine. Inclining towards being stocky, round faced and with thinning hair, Rudge looked and behaved rather like a commercial traveller, which it was most convenient for him to be. Indeed if asked, he could claim to be acting on behalf of a company in Hoxton that manufactured hardware. The company did exist, but it was a front owned by a mobsman and provided cover for men such as he who needed a respectable reason to be travelling round. It must be added here that the term 'commercial traveller' in this case did not mean one of these men who hawked suitcases of goods round doorsteps! That would be demeaning for a man like Rudge. No, he was the respected and respectable representative of a respected and respectable company with *bona fides* that were unimpeachable.

The night was young yet though and Rudge was not finished. His night had been incident free so why not do more? Not far from Hillyfields lay the district of Brockley and it was semi-rural, containing several large houses set in their own grounds, and many of them looked prosperous. One of these, in Brockley Rise, appeared to be very promising, and Rudge had observed that at night, the windows had no lights showing. Although the place was occupied, the owners seemed to be away, which was very tempting, and very convenient. Habit and a humane nature made him put on his mask, and he was not very put out when he found that the windows downstairs at the back had locks. Taking a sheet of thick brown paper from a pocket, folded into a four layer square, he placed it against a window pane and punched it sharply but not too hard. The glass broke, and some fell inside with little noise, but it was enough. Rudge began to remove the splinters but then froze as a footstep sounded behind him.

'What the bloody hell…?'

Turning quickly Rudge saw a man staring at him in disbelief; he was dressed as a gamekeeper, and under his arm he carried a shotgun. Coolly but quickly and without pause for thought, Rudge pulled his revolver out of his right hand inner breast pocket and pointed it straight at the man's head.

'Drop the gun,' he whispered loudly. He had learned long ago that if a man whispers then it is very hard to distinguish an accent in his voice or to identify it if heard again. It is also rather intimidating. Whisper it might be, but to the man with the shotgun, in the still dark night air, it sounded demonic. Rudge could not see his face well, but he might have gone very pale. He dropped the shotgun.

'That was wisely done,' whispered Rudge. 'Now I'm going to walk away in that direction and you are going to go that way.' He gestured across the garden towards the hedge and the fields beyond. 'If I see you again I will shoot you. Do you understand me?'

The man nodded.

'Then go now. And don't look back.'

The man departed, his relief at being away from the pistol written all over his face. Rudge watched as he went towards the hedge over which were fields with cows in them, bordering the railway, then turned and picked up the fallen shotgun. He ejected the cartridges and threw the gun into a flower bed before calmly walking out of the garden. As he exited the gate he removed his mask. The reason he wore it was for the protection of people who saw him about his work. If he thought the man would know his face again, then he would have shot him. Rudge's five years in prison were not the end of his experiences as a guest of Her Majesty. By 1874 he had been let out of his five stretch on a ticket of leave, but of course an ex con could not get a job. He was caught in the act whilst doing a house in South London and was arrested and taken away in a cab by a policeman. Seeing a chance to escape he attacked the policeman and leaped out of the cab window, thinking to get away in the maze of alleys nearby. Unfortunately a carpenter was passing and Rudge stumbled out of the cab almost at his feet. The policeman leaned out of the window and shouted that a prisoner was escaping and told the carpenter to hit him on the head with his hammer, which he did; enthusiastically. Rudge woke up in gaol again. He got ten years penal servitude. In Portland.

Later he described those ten years as a living death. He was determined that he would never go back into prison, where he had now spent over a third of his life, but would rather die. That meant that any threat to him had to be removed; he would quite happily kill to avoid prison, and he was not alone in this; thousands of his fellow travellers on the criminal way thought the same.

After the encounter with the game-keeper Rudge cursed his own stupidity because he had set the man walking across the fields towards Honor Oak Station, therefore he himself could not go that way. Instead, he headed north in the autumnal chill of the evening air; a few minutes after leaving Brockley Rise, Rudge turned into Arabin Road and walked the back streets to Brockley Station and caught a train to New Cross from where a train ran north under the river. Shortly afterwards he emerged into the bustle of Stepney and was soon safe in his rented room. He had not been there five minutes before a knock came on the door. Opening it he saw a man he knew well, a Mr James Brindle.

'The Nabob wants to see you at 10 tomorrow morning. Sharp.'

'Right'.

Brindle nodded and left.

Rudge would be there; nobody ignored an appointment with the Nabob. He wondered what the man wanted, but of course, he had to go.

2

The Shareholder

The house was, as James Baker admitted to himself, out of his normal experience, and as he approached it, he felt like a fish out of water. Barnsbury was fashionable, and this part was predominantly stately town houses, the front of each having a white colonnaded entrance facing onto the square, dazzling in the autumn sunlight. They were solidly respectable, the home ground of professional men and their families, the sort that had servants in the attic rooms, and a carriage in the mews at the back. Baker was not a physically brave man, and although he had been instructed to attend at one of these impressive dwellings, he had lost sleep over it for several nights since he had received the message. The Nabob wanted to see him at 11.00. You did not say no to such a summons, and the taste of fear rose in his throat as he pulled the bell at the address he had been given.

Baker was a professional burglar, and what was known throughout London as a mobsman. In the hierarchy of the London criminal classes he had a certain amount of status in that he had prospered enough to sport the symbols of success. He wore a natty brown check suit, a felt brimmed hat, and that ultimate sign of prowess, a gold watch and chain at his waistcoat pocket. In his heart though, Baker knew that he was a follower; he did not aspire to become a high mobsman, because he quite simply did not have the guts. Most of the high mobsmen carried guns and were quite happy to use violence in the pursuit of their trade. James Baker did not, and he knew that he never would. He was quite happy to hang round the pubs where others of his kind gathered at weekends and holidays, and to accept the respect and adulation of the numerous petty thieves, pickpockets and assorted villains who admired mobsmen and wanted to be like them. There were some men that he did not approach, for he knew they looked down on such as he as men with no bottom, and that was fair enough. He knew his place and not to offend his betters. Yet the Nabob had sent for him.

The door opened and a smooth faced man in his thirties asked who was calling.

'My name is Baker. Mr Walker asked me to call.'

'Yes, you are expected Mr Baker. Please walk in; I shall tell Mr Walker that you are here. He is with his family at the moment.'

Sounds of a man and woman laughing could be heard through an adjoining door, and the manservant knocked softly on its oak panels. Baker looked around curiously. The entrance hall was hung with paintings, and furniture which looked expensive; an umbrella stand, a small table on which stood a post box and tray, a couple of elegant eighteenth century chairs with brocade, and Greek style vases in niches on the wall. Up the stairs ran a Turkey carpet which screamed out 'King's ransom'; the *toute ensemble* looked like the home of a prosperous banker. The voices stopped as Mr Walker was told of his visitor, and then the man himself came out.

He was not very tall, but was squat, his head covered with grizzled wiry hair, and his face with a large black beard. If a bull mastiff had been turned into a human being, thought Baker, then this would be him; he looked as if he could tear people's arms off and eat them. James Baker repressed a shudder because if some of the stories he had heard of the Nabob were true, then he had done far worse. For now though, the man had an affable smile on his face and he came forward, and gripped Baker's hand with a firm hold, shaking it in a friendly manner.

'Mr Baker, I am pleased to see that you are punctual. I like that in a man and it backs up what I have heard of you. Please come into my study, for we have much to talk about, and I hope that we may do some business of mutual benefit. There is already a gentleman in there who I believe you know. William, we are not to be disturbed.'

The man servant nodded; there would be no disturbance. Baker and the Nabob entered a room lined with books and the visitor looked round impressed. There was a man sitting on a sofa who he recognised immediately.

'Mr Rudge!'

'Mr Baker.' Rudge nodded condescendingly to a man years younger than himself but got up to shake hands.

The two men had known each other for some years, having shared a cell as guests of Her Majesty.

The Nabob waved a hand around proudly. 'Quite a library ain't it?'

The remnants of an East End twang could be heard in his voice, but many years of mingling with the prosperous locals had modulated it to a vague London accent.

'Yes sir. I don't think I've ever seen so many books together.'

The Nabob laughed. 'I ain't read any of 'em but a man has to impress you know. If the men I do business with got the notion that I was just some thick barrow boy, they'd try to take advantage of me, and I ain't having that. Sharks the lot of 'em. Give 'em 'arf a chance and they'd do me down proper. But they think I'm a reading man and that helps put 'em at a disadvantage, you see. Right James, sit down; Anthony, you too. I have a proposition for you. Wanna glass of something?'

Baker hesitated.

'Whisky ain't it? Not too much and no water.'

Baker looked up at Walker. This was always his drink of choice.

'Oh yes. I know a bit about you James; you ain't been pointed out for my interest for no reason. There you go; sip on that and listen. Anthony will have rum I know. He is very fond of it.'

Baker sipped at his glass and knew it instantly for an excellent quality malt such as he could never afford to drink regularly.

'Good stuff innit? Yeah well I can afford it, and if you two take me up on my offer, you'll be able to afford it as well. Now then…'

The Nabob sat behind his desk and lit up a fat cigar.

'I'm a businessman Mr Baker and you may believe it or not, but most of my income these days is legitimate. I have a man of affairs who handles my dealings in the city and makes me a fortune in stocks and shares. This is not to say that I do not derive a fine income from my other activities, because I do.'

He paused for a moment. 'Yes, by God I do. I have fingers in many pies Mr Baker, too many to mention, and lots of strings that I keep a tight hold on. On occasion I pull them. By and large my other business runs very smoothly, though sometimes I have to take direct action to keep it so, and I am generally satisfied with what it yields.'

Baker listened intently because he knew full well that Walker was speaking in euphemisms. 'Fingers in pies' meant that he had protection rackets, drug dealing and shares of burglaries all over London. A thief in London had to 'show respect' to Mr Walker, or bad things could happen, the mildest of which was ending up dead, drowned in the river. 'Lots of strings' meant an intelligence network that spanned the Metropolis, which kept Walker informed of everything that was going on. He also wondered why Walker was speaking primarily to him, because Rudge was a much higher grade of mobsman than he was.

'I like to think of myself as a philanthropist sometimes Mr Baker, for I stand at the top of a vast organisation that puts bread on tables, clothes on backs and pays for all sorts of things for many thousands of people.'

Baker thought of the abject misery of thousands of beggars, petty thieves and small time burglars who were forced by fear to share what they stole with Walker's enforcers, but kept his mouth well shut. The Nabob was the highest of high mobsmen, and he ruled London as surely as an Amir ruled in Afghanistan. Walker was becoming expansive.

'I have shares in the railways Mr Baker, and it is a reproach to me that I did not think until recently of the opportunities that might be offered to a man like me, and his associates. We do not, in our line use the advantages offered by the railways sufficiently to maximise our profits.'

'In what way sir?'

'Ah now there you have it James. It is becoming more difficult to carry out burglary in London, and the police are more difficult to bribe, though I do own many of them. You do not mind me speaking so frankly I hope; we are both in the same line after all. I am sure that Mr Rudge would agree.'

Rudge, who had been listening intently but not saying anything, now interjected.

'Not at all sir. I know that what you say is true. I find it so myself.'

'Many of the people whose jewels or money we appropriate do not live in London. They come down here for the season, they sport their jewellery, and then they disappear back to the country. Take Lady Hermione Graham for example.'

Baker's eyes shot up to meet those of the Nabob.

'Ah now that got your attention didn't it! Don't be surprised James, I told you I know a lot, and I know a lot about you too.'

Walker got up from his desk and padded round the room waving his cigar.

'Estimates vary but I have heard that she has jewels worth between one and ten thousand pounds, depending on who you talk to. It seems to me that is an awful lot, and that men in our profession might wish to relieve her of some of that weight.'

The Nabob grinned.

'Nellie,' said Baker.

'Nellie,' replied Walker. 'I said I know a bit about you, but it's not just Nellie. I heard other things that I find worthy of note and a recommendation to me. The Silverdale job was quite something.'

Baker winced. 'But I got arrested.'

'Yes, you did, but the manner of it showed guts James. The manner of it.'

In 1876, Baker had forced the window of a solicitor, Edwin Howard, at Silverdale in Lewisham after climbing a ladder at the back of the house. He had just managed to grab a few jewels off a dressing table when he was discovered. Going out of the window with a burly and angry solicitor in pursuit, he had attempted a 'plasterer's slide' down the ladder, something he had done many times, but on this occasion he slipped and fell, breaking an arm and injuring his head. Somehow he managed to escape and later made his way home to Montague Street, Bethnal Green where he and his wife, Eliza, ran a greengrocer's shop. It wasn't much of a business, but it served as a cover for his real profession.

'Now that took sand,' said the Nabob. 'To get home with those injuries. That's resourceful.'

'I heard about that job,' said Rudge. 'I agree. Dunno how you did it.'

Baker was flattered. 'But they got me.'

'Yes; you was arrested a few days later,' said the Nabob. 'I do declare that if you had managed to fence the stuff they found, you might have got away with it. You got a five stretch for that I believe?'

'I did sir. Portland for the most part. That is where I met Anthony. We were cellmates.'

Baker's memory winced again at the thought of five years penal servitude at one of the worst prisons in the country. He and other convicts had been put to hard labour in the stone quarries there, sawing limestone for London's great houses, carrying it round like slaves, and being beaten by warders just as brutal and vicious as the worst of the men in their charge. Hell on earth. The worst was the silent system, for during the hours of work and round the prison, men were not allowed to talk to each other. Only in cells after work was over did men whisper and communicate with their fellows. Many said that they would sooner die than ever do another stretch in such a place.

'Eliza left you when you were in Portland, and took up with another bloke. You did not try to get her back?'

'No,' said Baker. 'Her choice.'

'That and the fact that the geezer she's with is twice your size.' The Nabob looked at him shrewdly.

'That as well.'

'Honesty is a good thing among thieves Mr Baker. That's a strange paradox but I have often found it to be true. Honour is important.'

Baker nodded but said nothing.

'You got ticket of leave in 1881 but they took you back in when you were caught picking pockets. Bit of a comedown that James; you must have been desperate; hungry.'

Baker nodded.

'And when you got out, you resumed a favourite activity of yours; you went to Carlisle races. You've been there before.'

'My dad used to take me up there every year and see what we could get. A sort of holiday.'

'Lots of profitable stuff at the races James. That's where you met Nellie. A Carlisle girl I believe. And she had a job that interests me greatly.'

'I can see why you've asked me here sir. Yes, she used to be a maid at Netherby Hall.'

'Indeed, and whilst Sir Frederick and Lady Hermione's house at number forty Park Lane is nigh impregnable, Netherby Hall is not. Quite the opposite I hear. Opportunity Mr Baker. Opportunity. And you are very good at what you do up to a point; imagine if you had some professional assistance.'

'It's a long way out of our usual area sir.'

'Indeed it is, but no longer.'

'Sir?'

'I was much taken with the policy of our government in both Afghanistan and Zululand in recent years. You know, in sending an expeditionary force to carry out their will. I have in mind to send a group of men to certain destinations with the purpose of our mutual enrichment. I should finance such a group, pay their fare, their subsistence and their expenses, and of course I should expect a good return on my investment. I had in mind a fifty-fifty split of the proceeds once all expenses have been deducted, including the fence's share when the goods are disposed of. Burglary by the railway timetable you might say. And I become the major shareholder in a new and speculative adventure.'

'That sounds very fair sir, all things considered, and a very interesting idea. I take it that Netherby Hall would be one of the destinations you had in mind?'

'It is, Mr Baker. Your Nellie would be able to supply you with many valuable details about how to do the job and how to get away. Local knowledge is always an asset in these affairs.'

'These affairs? This will not be the first of its type?'

'Not at all. I had some gentlemen attempt something of the sort earlier this year down in Essex, but it all went rather wrong. They were clumsy away from home and bungled it. Now that things have quietened down I wish to try it again, but with a little more *finesse*, shall we say?'

'Apart from me sir, who else would be in the group?'

'As you may gather James, I am not a man to leave things to chance. I had in mind Mr Rudge and another gentleman. In case you were wondering why I have been speaking primarily to you, it is because I had Mr Rudge here for an hour before you arrived and he is in perfect agreement with my proposals.'

Baker could not but ask. 'Who is the other gentleman sir?'

'John Martin.'

Baker could not resist his eyebrows shooting upwards.

'You find some objection to the man?'

Baker's mind whirled. You did not want to disgruntle the Nabob.

'No sir, it's just that he is...' and here he hesitated, looking for words.

'Very formidable. A great exponent of his craft and prone to violence should the situation warrant it?'

'Exactly so sir,' said Baker weakly. He had been about to say 'trigger happy' which was a description of Martin that came more readily to most men's lips, but decided not to articulate the thought.

To his surprise the Nabob smiled.

'I am quite aware James, that you are not in his league when it comes to heavy stuff, or that of Mr Rudge. We may be frank I think.'

'I would not put it that way,' said Rudge, looking mildly embarrassed.

'Ah, but I would Tony because it is so.'

The Nabob laughed inwardly as he watched Rudge wince. As he well knew, Rudge hated being called Tony and his use of it was quite deliberate.

'I do not think, begging your pardon sir, that Mr Rudge and Mr Martin would see me as quite on the same level as them professionally.'

The Nabob laughed. 'That is so, I will allow, and very diplomatically put, but they will work with you, for as they know, you have skills they do not possess. Do they Tony?'

Rudge reddened but dared not contradict him.

'And I have to say that you are not without a name yourself. Apart from your unfortunate run-ins with the gentlemen of Scotland Yard, you have had quite a lucrative time as a one man band. You know them both. Mr Rudge and Mr Martin quite well I know.'

'Met them in Portland sir, and laboured beside them for years.' He looked at Rudge. 'Martin don't take nothing from nobody.'

'True enough,' said Rudge. 'He's his own man.'

'He will from me James.'

This last remark was said in dead flat tones, but when Baker looked up at the dark brown eyes that had appeared so friendly, he looked deeper, and inside them lurked a demon of such fury that he became afraid. The Nabob knew the effect he could have; no harm in showing what lay behind the veil of his urbane exterior, but he was not out to frighten James Baker. Rudge saw it too, and he had the good sense to feel fear.

'You are right. He is too easily a man of violence, but that is the trouble with a lot of men in our line of work. They smash things, even when on a job. That is where your particular skills as a cabinet maker come in. You still have your tools?'

'I do. I might be a greengrocer but I still have the trade my dad taught me and I practice it occasionally.'

'Excellent, so I shall impress on Mr Martin that he and Mr Rudge must make it easy for you. Instead of forcing drawers open and smashing cupboards, I send a man who can do things subtly and without a harsh and crashing din alerting the house. A more gentlemanly style if you like, but with two men of force and proven expertise backing him up, the chances of success become higher and my investment is safer.'

The Nabob finished speaking, and fished out a solid gold watch that looked to Baker as if it was the size of a turnip.
'Well James, I think we are done. May I take it that you are convinced to become part of my northern expedition?'

'You are sir. I think it a magnificent conception.'

The Nabob looked pleased. 'Very well then. My representatives will be in touch with you shortly about ways and means. I look forward to a long and profitable association. Anthony; as we discussed earlier, the same goes for you.'

He shook Rudge's hand and then James Baker's, and he turned to leave.

'Oh James…'

'Sir?'

'You're a good and respectful chap and I like that; but don't come here again unless invited. I asked you to come here because this particular operation is one by which I set great store; it could be most profitable, but even more, it will bring me great prestige, but not among the respectable community.'

He paused and looked at Baker with deep meaning, a look that stirred fear in the very depths of his soul.

'This meeting never took place. If I had not been determined that this railway scheme should succeed, I would have set my deputies to it. So my name never comes into anything that may happen; that would be a most unfortunate thing. Oh dear yes, a most unfortunate thing. Understand?'

Baker looked into the Nabob's eyes again, and this time he could not repress a shudder of horror and fear though the man was smiling.

'Yes sir. Completely.'

The Nabob chuckled softly, the sound sending shivers down Baker's spine.

'I know you do, so all will be well. Right; off you toddle. You're one of my lads now, and don't forget it.'

James Baker left Barnsbury and did not look back. He never wanted to go there again; ever. Rudge looked rather more devil may care about it, but Baker knew him to be afraid too. They walked together to Highbury Station and caught a train back to the East End where they went to Webb's Bar for a much needed stiff drink.

3

Lying Low

A few months prior to James Baker's conversation with the Nabob, a very different discussion had taken place between Mr Brindle, the Nabob's chief enforcer, and a tall pale man with a wispy moustache.

'Are you bloody mad? What was you thinking of? A simple job like that. You was sent to Romford to do a flash pull and you made a complete and utter foozle of it! You were sent because you's supposed to be a knowing sort of cove, The governor thought he could rely on you but you ended up shooting a crusher, and for bloody what? Did you know this Inspector Simmons? 'Ad you and him any grudge or something?'

The tall man with the moustache had the grace to shuffle his feet and murmur.

'What did you say?' shouted his questioner.

'I'm sorry Mr Brindle. I saw the uniform and I kind of lost my head.'

'Lost your head! For Christ's sake, people look up to you. They think you a bang-up sort of bloke that knows what's what! You shot him because you lost your head? Is that it? I can just see me saying that to the Nabob. I know what he'll think; he'll think you've lost your bottle, and if that's the case sonny Jim then you're no use to him. In fact you might have made yourself a liability. The man is dead and they're tearing the place apart trying to find who done it. A bloody inspector for Christ's sake! You might as well put a rope round your neck and get it over with!'

The tall man swallowed hard. If the Nabob thought him a danger, and had no purpose for him, then he could be got rid of, like the trash.

'I thought he was going to arrest us Mr Brindle.'

'Oh yes? And what for. You hadn't done the job so there was no swag on you. You hadn't broken the law in any way, had you?'

'I was carrying a barker. So was Adams.'

'And why would he pull you in for that? Lots of people carry barkers. Even cyclists carry them to protect themselves against mad dogs. Since when was carrying a barker against the law?'

'It ain't Mr Brindle. Sorry.'

'Sorry don't cut no ice. I'll tell the Nabob that you lost your head if you want, and see what he does then! But I would think that a lot depends on what happens in the next few weeks. The crushers are going to be all over us for killing one of their own, until they get someone for doing it, and they won't particularly mind who it is.'

The tall man knew this would be so, but listened intently to what Brindle was saying. This was the Nabob's chief butcher in the East End, and although he looked like a shop keeper, it would be difficult to find a harder or more murderous lieutenant in the United Kingdom. He was right too. This sort of thing brought the police out in force, raiding mobsmen haunts, searching buildings and whole blocks of houses for evidence, arresting people on the smallest of charges and generally clamping down on criminal activity in a most unfortunate way. It was bad for business and cost a lot of money.

'Anyway, what you just told me ain't true is it?'

'How do you mean Mr Brindle?'

'You didn't panic. You shot 'im because of Portland. That's right innit?'

The tall man did not answer.

'You got done in 1877 for that job in Greenwich. Five years in Portland as I remember. You'd do anything rather than go back there; I know, I've felt it myself. A man would murder his own mother rather than go through that again. You didn't panic; you just froze didn't ya?'

'Sort of. Everything went blank.'

'That's it! Felt it myself a few times. Been told by enough blokes they'd rather hang than go back there. The Nabob will understand that. He knows how that feels.'

'What should I do Mr Brindle?'

'Do? Well you can pray that you're still alive this time next week, but in your case matey I would advise you go to ground, you and your partner. Find a deep hole to hide in and don't show your faces round here no more, at least not for a few months. A lot depends on what Dredge says.'

'Have they got him then?'

'No. They ain't got him yet, but they will. They have a name, a face and they know him. He'll be got, and best for him that he is, or he might just disappear; that would probably be more convenient.'

Brindle grinned, but it was not a nice sight.

'Thinking about it, it might be best if we got him first, but he's hiding right now.'

'Do you know where he is?'

'Now that's the thing; I do not, so he's well hid. He must be changing his address every now and then, but nobody has narked on him yet. Either we find him, or the crushers will. The governor thinks you might still be of use, for you have skills. Dredge is just another bludger and we have plenty of those.'

'A lot depends on events.'

Brindle stopped and thought for a minute or two.

'Right. Get out of here now. When I want to speak to you again, I'll put the word out. Try not to be found, nor your footman neither. Oh and grow a beard. Next time I see you I don't want to recognise you.'

'Yes sir, right sir,' said the tall man, and left hurriedly, full in the knowledge that the interview had ended.

....

Detective Sergeant William Rolfe had a reputation to uphold, ever since a newspaper had described him as one of the cleverest detectives in the East End of London. He also had a task to carry out, on which his reputation and that of the Metropolitan Police depended. He had to find and arrest one David Dredge who was apparently a witness or a party to the shooting to death of Inspector Simmons of Romford Police. Working out of Commercial Street Police Station, he had developed a network of his own; narks, snitches and professional grasses. Each one of these took their lives in their hands by making a living from informing on others in their game, but the criminal classes were so numerous in East London that it was a dog eat dog sort of place. If you could earn a sovereign or ten bob by telling Rolfe where somebody was, then that was fair enough. One evening late in January, Doggy Bill, a breeder of canines and bookmaker for illegal dogfights, bumped into Rolfe in the throngs along Whitechapel Road. The detective did nothing obvious, but as he returned to the station he felt in his pocket and brought out a dirty piece of paper on which was written "3 Copperfield Road". He needed no more; taking Detective Constable Bolton with him, he raided the premises. It must be understood that ordinary policemen would not have done this, save in greater numbers, but both Rolfe and Bolton were known to be able to give a very good account of themselves if violence became an issue; nobody interfered. On this occasion though, their efforts came to naught because there was no-one in the house. Rolfe's instincts told him that the information was good, though he had used it at the wrong moment, so he and Bolton kept the house under observation for the next few days. It was on Tuesday 3 February, a fortnight after Simmons had been shot, that Rolfe saw a man come out of the house in Copperfield Street. He did not know Dredge but had a photograph; stepping forward he stopped in front of the man.

'I am a detective officer of the Metropolitan Police. You are David Dredge, wanted, with two others, for the murder of Inspector Simmons of the Essex Constabulary on 20 January.'

'Alright,' said Dredge, and Rolfe handcuffed him, he and Bolton taking him to the police cells. At the station Dredge insisted on making a statement to the effect that he had not seen Inspector Simmons on 20 January. He had left a train at Rainham and was walking down a lane when two men asked him to show them the road towards Romford. He left the men to go through a gate because he needed to piss. As he finished what he was doing, a policeman came through the hedge and said 'David Dredge, what are you doing?'

'You can see what I'm doing.'

The officer had assumed that he was with the two men, but he was not.

Eventually Dredge was taken by train to Romford with Rolfe and Bolton. He continued to insist that the two men he had been seen with prior to the shooting of Inspector Simmons, were complete strangers to him. When Rolfe was at Romford, he asked PC Marden, a witness to the murder of his inspector, to describe the man who had shot Simmons. Marden then told of a tall man with a moustache, perhaps with a sallow complexion, and Rolfe said 'I know his identity. His name is Jim Adams.'

Facial hair was a very common thing in Britain, and had been since the Crimean War. Images of Britain's brave soldiers battling the Russians, sternly holding back the Tsar's hordes whilst sporting bushy beards, sideburns and moustaches looked very heroic. Hirsute faces became associated with ideas of strength and virility; army regulations made it compulsory for all ranks to wear a moustache at the very least. Products such as 'Harlene' promised the user a luxuriant growth in the desired area; a fierce and brutal set of follicles that would make anyone think twice before taking you on. How Rolfe jumped to his immediate conclusion out of the five and a half million people living in London is an interesting question, since half of them were potential moustache wearers; that figure is before taking into consideration the population of the Home Counties in addition. Jim Adams was a tall man, and a professional burglar. It would be a very good thing if he could be put away and out of circulation, but to identify him as a murderer based on Marden's description of a man he had seen in failing light from sixty yards away was rather a stretch.

Jim Adams had "form". He was suspected of being one of two men accused of shooting a police officer in the knee whilst escaping from a burglary in Gloucestershire in 1878. For seven years DS Rolfe had regarded Adams as unfinished business, and it is hardly surprising. Adams's name kept coming up in a series of daring crimes, which included shootings and stabbings; he was a nasty piece of work. Rolfe was obsessed;

he wanted to feel Adams's collar more than anything. All he had to do now was find him.

On Tuesday 10 March James Adams was in a pawn shop in Euston Square when two uniformed policemen walked in and arrested him. When told it was for the shooting of Inspector Simmons in Essex, he said to them 'You must be mad!' When they got him outside he attempted to escape. There was a furious struggle and he ran off, only stopped because he collided with a passer-by who held on to him until the policemen handcuffed him. When he got to the police station he was put into a charge room to await the arrival of Rolfe, but managed to get some bullets out of his pocket and throw them into the fire. He tried to escape during the panic but several officers managed to overpower him and cuff him again. When Rolfe came, he told him that he would be charged with the murder of Inspector Simmons, but Adams consistently denied having anything to do with it.

'I don't know anything about it in any shape or form. It is the dirty dogs that know me that have got me into this.'

....

'Are we going to do anything about Dredge Gov?'

'I had thought we might,' said the Nabob, 'But Rolfe got him first and he seems to have grassed. I don't think it's a bother to us. He's small fry and knows nothing.'

'I had two bludgers ready to do him in for forty quid; I was just gonna ask you.'

'Really?' replied the Nabob, interested. 'How was they going to do it?'

'Go for a ride in a train, shoot him and dump the body through the window in a tunnel.'

'Hmmmph,' grunted his boss. 'Not very imaginative, but I suppose effective. Lucky for him that the crushers found him before you did. Bit slack that Mr Brindle.'

'Yes, I'm sorry about that Gov. Trouble is that the crushers are all over the place and everyone is on edge. It's hard to get good information right now; no one wants to be seen as a nark. And now they've gone and arrested Adams.'

'The problem is,' said the Nabob, 'that Jim is such a villain. He plays up to it. Have you read this in the paper?'

'Nah Gov. I don't get much time to read the papers.'

'Fair enough, but there's a lot of useful information to be gleaned from these rags Brindle me lad. It says here that he was grimacing at the crowd when they took him down to Romford. He was sneering and shaking his fist at 'em.'

'He's been fitted up.'

'Well, yes. You know that. And I know that. The trouble is that he does fit the frame so beautifully, and he insists on adjusting it so it fits better.'

'Do think Rolfe has fitted him up on purpose?'

'I don't think he has. Let's put it this way. Sergeant Rolfe has been after Adams for a long time. In his mind he fits the Simmons job, because he is perfectly qualified to be the man who did it. Adams is a high mobsman, known to shoot in a corner, and he's a vicious sort of cove anyway. I am certain as I sit here that Rolfe thinks he has the right man. But we know he doesn't. It can't be denied that Adams has given a few people an earth bath, just not this one.'

'They're gonna hang 'im.'

'I think they probably are.'

'We gonna do anything about it Gov? Give 'im an alibi or somefink?'

The Nabob grew serious, leaned forward on his desk and laced his fingers together, thinking hard.

'No. We will not. For one thing, we do not help crushers, ever. Secondly, we are not narks; it would be a very damaging thing to us if people got that idea into their heads.'

'Seems a bit off to let a man hang for a murder he didn't do.'

'Getting a conscience Mr Brindle?' The Nabob chuckled unpleasantly. 'He's done things that he deserves to swing for well enough. For that matter, so have I; and so have you. True?'

'True enough Gov. But he has been very profitable for us, and might be again.'

'He has. But our other asset, the one who really did the Simmons job has also been useful to us, and he's not in gaol. If they hang Adams then things will go quiet, and our man will get off scot free. A bird in the hand is worth two in the bush eh?'

'I see that Gov.'

'It is very inconvenient at the moment, all this police activity. It is having a damping effect on the operations of many of our associates, and hitting our profits; I imagine things will quieten down now that they have Adams, and that normal proceedings will resume. Anyway Mr Brindle, there are two other considerations to bear in mind about this, which you have not referred to.'

'What's that Gov?'

'The first is that I am disinclined to help Mr Adams because I do not like him. He's flash and cocky, and entirely above himself; I am fairly sure he's been holding out on our dues this last couple of years. I do not find him trustworthy.'

'You won't find many that are that way in our line Gov.'

The Nabob looked up sharply.

'I take your point, but you understand me I think.'

'Oh yes Gov; entirely.'

'The second point Mr Brindle is our courts.'

Brindle's brow furrowed in puzzlement.

'I have faith in the processes of British justice. If Adams is innocent, and we know he is, they will find him not guilty, will they not?'

Brindle looked at his boss, trying to decide if he was being ironic, but you could never really read what the Nabob was thinking.

'Otherwise he'll swing for it.'

'Exactly Mr Brindle; and things will be well quiet again, and as we know, quiet is good for business.'

....

James Adams, despite his consistent avowals that he had not done the killing of Inspector Simmons and that Rolfe was uttering complete falsehoods, was sentenced to death. On 18 May, James Berry, the official hangman carried out the sentence. Adams displayed considerable courage, avowing his innocence to the end, vehemently denying that he had not shot Simmons. One of the witnesses to the execution was Sir Claude Champion de Crespigny, a newly appointed magistrate, who was determined to find out all he could about the business of justice, so seriously did he take his responsibility. Now all that remained was to find out who had the third man been with Adams and Dredge in order to serve out his own portion of justice. All the country wondered where the villain might be found and looked to the brave Detective Inspector Rolfe to find him. If he was wise, he would have made himself scarce.

4

Planning a Journey

Detective Sergeant Rolfe was a man of strong convictions. Adams had hanged, because his face fitted the frame which Rolfe had prepared for him, and he fitted it beautifully. There was another man who Rolfe had been wanting to put away for a very long time, and that was John Martin. It was now August 1885; the newspapers, the public, and Rolfe's superiors wanted results; he had to get them. He badly wanted to see John Martin, or as Rolfe knew him, John White, his real name. Martin/White had been a regular drinking companion of the hanged man Adams, but for weeks he had not been seen and Rolfe knew why; he was the third man who had been present when Inspector Simmons was shot.

Martin, of course, knew that Rolfe would be after him and that he was convinced that he was involved in the shooting. Evidence did not matter with Rolfe as far as Martin was concerned; he knew he had done it. Once in the sergeant's clutches, he was done for, and at the least he would be looking at a long term of imprisonment or a hanging. That being so, Martin made it his business not to be found. For weeks he lay low, only going out at night and being supplied by cronies with the necessities of life. Eventually however, he grew restless and started to think that now Adams had been hanged, the heat would be off him. He decided to take a walk along the Commercial Road in the bright summer sun. Suddenly he heard a West Country accent behind him that he knew well.

'White. I want you.'

When Martin turned he saw DS Rolfe standing not far away on the pavement looking at him. The game seemed to be up, but Martin shoved a hand into his pocket.

'Take a step closer and I'll put a bullet through your eye.'

Rolfe knew better than to ignore this warning. He knew Martin's reputation sufficiently well to know that he might die in the next second. He spread his hands out in a negative kind of gesture and stepped backwards. Martin laughed scornfully, then went down an alleyway into a maze of side streets where the police never walked alone. It was no matter to Rolfe because Martin was one of the most easily identifiable men, having a large lump in the shape of a darkish wart or mole right between his eyes. He could be picked up easily any time he showed his nose out on the streets again; it was only a matter of time, and no-one knew this better than Martin himself. Like a rat cornered by an army of cats, he needed a way out, and ultimately he did not have one. A quiet taciturn man, who did not say much, he was, nonetheless at his wits end when James Brindle found him.

'It seems to me John, that you are in more than a spot of bother and that you need a way out of it. Rolfe is after you.'

'I ain't done nothing.'

'Whatever you say. I know better, but my respected employer has a proposition for you which I think you may find to your advantage.'

'I'm listening.'

'He is sending two gentlemen north on an expedition which he hopes will net him great gains. He would like you to go with them and add your expertise to theirs. That gets you out of London.'

'That would be a fine trick. I'm a bit obvious and the first rozzer that sees my face is gonna grab my collar.'

'Yes. I have to agree you are a bit obvious. Ever thought of having that thing removed? I could do it for you real quick; I have a suitable instrument in my pocket.'

Martin looked at Brindle, but he did not appear as if he was joking.

'I'll bet you could. If it's all the same to you I'll not bother.'

'Probably wise. I might take an eye with it. Anyway, there is another part to the proposition. If we get you out of London, you would not be coming back. There is no future for you here.'

'How do you mean?'

'Well with Rolfe and the whole Met after you, what can you hope to do? It's time for a new start for you John. The Nabob is prepared to help you.'

'Why should he?'

'You're an object lesson that he looks after his people. You've been a source of great profit to him this last twenty years. How would it look now if he abandoned you to your fate? It's a much better idea to help you get the hell out of here. Then everybody knows that if you work for the Nabob, then you get help if you need it.'

'Didn't work with Adams though did it?'

'Nah well that was different. The Nabob hated his guts. He might have had to finish Adams himself; he was getting ideas above his station, if you see what I mean.'

'He was a flash git.'

'Now we don't speak ill of the dead John, but you ain't wrong.'

'The Nabob don't do something for nothing. What does he want?'

Brindle grinned. 'You're what now? Forty? Been round the houses a bit ain't ya? But yes, you're right. He wants you to help with one last job.'

'What sort of job?'

'He wants you to go north with two other blokes and nick Lady Netherby's jewels. You've heard about them I suppose?'

'Yes. Difficult one.'

'Nah; should be straightforward enough. Up to her Ladyship's country mansion, get the jewellery and out. We have inside information that will be of great assistance.'

'What happens to me after that?'

'You will receive a letter addressed to *poste restante* in Liverpool with full instructions, but basically the idea is that in return for your able assistance with this job, you get a berth on board of a certain ship at Liverpool Docks and you head for the United States. There will be a small stake to help you in New York and a letter of introduction to some gentlemen there who may find your skills useful.'

'Like I said, it's very generous. You're pretty sure that I want to get out of Britain!'

'You're forty, no wife, no family or at least none that I know of, and you'd be an idiot to stay here with only a rope round your neck to look forward to. What else you gonna do?'

Martin thought, but very quickly.

'You're right. I know it. Alright, I accept. Big problem is getting out of London. How do I do that, with every station and main road being watched?'

'You just leave that to us. For the moment you stay hid, right? I'll be in touch; just have your bag packed and ready to go; one bag and that is all.'

....

Nellie was particular about detail. It was she who packed James Baker's bag, because he would be away for a while on this special job. It was not so much the clothes that took up space; one set of underwear and a spare shirt were all that Baker was taking, and a couple of pairs of socks. There was a cloth roll of chisels, and another roll of various tools, such as awls, augers, a few screwdrivers of varying sizes, a picklock, a bunch of skeleton keys and so on.

'If anyone opens this they'll know you're on a job,' she said.

'No they won't. I'm a journeyman cabinet maker and I take my tools where I go. There will not be a problem Nell, so stop fretting.'

She looked at him fondly but with the worrying despair that some women have towards their bad boys. He was not, in everyday life the deferential underling that he had presented to the Nabob. Baker was a thief, good at his work, and like many mobsmen he had a swagger and arrogance to him that she found highly attractive. It was partly that which had drawn her to him in the first place. She had been a scullery maid at Netherby Hall when they met, for just down the road, and every year, was held one of the biggest hare coursing events in the whole of the United Kingdom. It attracted sporting men from all over the place, as well as a thriving market, side shows and all sorts of amusements. Sir Frederick Graham and Lady Hermione always attended, with their children, and always gave leave to their staff to do likewise. It was done in shifts so that the life of Netherby Hall went on uninterrupted, but it was a most enjoyable place to be.

It cannot be said that Nellie was beautiful, for she was not; in fact by most definitions of female beauty, she was plain of face, and certainly not delicately made. Sometimes she described herself laughingly as a solid peasant girl with good shoulders and muscles, but there was something about her that caught the eye of James Baker. He had seen her in a pretty cotton print dress heaving wooden balls at a coconut shy, and not having much success. There were people round her who were hooting at her efforts as she became pink in the face, but he did not join in.

'I think that one you knocked before is about ready to go miss. If you slow down and take your time with that last ball, I reckon it might go.'

Sure enough; she stopped trying too hard, aimed the last ball and won the nut.

He had then invited her to take a glass of beer with him, and had very quickly fallen in love. Lest this seem strange it must be remembered that his wife was now living with another man, having taken herself off whilst James was in prison. James was at that time twenty-eight and Nellie twenty-two. He had a huge and gaping void in his life where a woman should be, and in Nellie he had found one who appeared to appreciate his company. He had hung around for a few weeks, made some money at Carlisle race meetings, and shown her another way of life. To Nellie, the scullery maid, hands red and dry from constant dish washing, James Baker was an envoy from another world and one where she ardently desired to be; a world with money and where she might, ultimately, be able to have her own maid. She was no fool and knew very quickly what he was; the sort of man her mother had warned her against in some ways, but she did not care. She also knew that Baker had a wife who had run off, but that did not bother her either; indeed this was a phenomenon very common in her class, and, in the absence of accessible divorce law, not unusual at all. When he asked her to come back to London with him, she had very quickly given her notice and left Netherby Hall. She did not miss it at all.

For over a year now she had helped James to run a greengrocer's shop in Bethnal Green, but she well knew that it was not his main business, though she hoped that it might be one day if the shop prospered. She was very happy that her man always had a lot of cash, that he was respected in the neighbourhood and among his peers, but there was always the shadow of prison if he got caught plying his trade. He never brought any of his 'colleagues' home, so although she had heard him speak of Rudge and Martin, who he had been in prison with, she had never met them.

Of course she knew Netherby Hall and its environs very well indeed so it was not difficult for her to brief Baker on the best way to reach the house unseen, which rooms would hold the valuables he was after, and how to get away quickly afterwards. She also knew where there would be a handy ladder to reach the bedroom where Lady Graham kept her jewels, and the layout of the various chambers making up the suite of rooms where she slept, performed her *toilette* and dressed.

'I think these are good enough,' said Baker, waving some papers at her, 'You've drawn the scene very well here. I'll let the others have a look at them on the train if we are not disturbed. They'll be able to see we are well prepared.'

Nellie looked at him with a quizzical expression.

'They are not strictly necessary though are they? I mean, all things considered.'

A look was exchanged, and he snorted.

'But yes, they are Nellie. These supply answers to questions, and beyond that, they need to know nothing else.'

'So you'll be up north for a few days with those two before you go to Netherby.'

'Yes. As we are going so far, Mr Rudge and myself thought we might pull off a few small jobs while we are up there.'

'That's fine so long as you don't get caught. The Nabob would not be best pleased if you did not pull off his star job.'

'No. He wouldn't, but we are not talking London coppers Nell. These are Cumbrian bobbies; hardly a brain between them, and that they probably share around.'

That made her giggle.

'I can just see them now at the station, "Here Joe, it's your shift so you'd better 'ave the brain. Lift up yer hat and I'll slip it into place for you."'

Baker laughed. 'Nothing would surprise me up there, but yes, they do find some of the big city types a little bit out of their understanding. Lots of gormless coppers and very few knowing types.'

'And you'll meet Mr Smith at the coursing.'

'Yes; I look forward to that.'

Nellie smiled. 'Will the other two mind a fourth man? Are you going to tell them he's my brother or something?'

'No. I'll just tell them he's a local man I know who will guide us to the Hall and help us to leave the area quickly for a small consideration. It's best they have no name for him so if things go wrong they cannot identify him.'

'We must protect Mr Smith.'

'Yes, we must.' Baker put his arms round Nellie's waist.

'Now my girl, give me a kiss. I'll see you again before too long, and hopefully with enough profit to allow us to move and set up shop in a nicer area.'

'I'd like that. Stay safe James. I love you, you know.'

'And I you. Now give me a kiss, 'cos I'm off.'

So with fond farewells, James Baker left the apartment above the shop at 106 Musgrove Street, Bethnal Green, and made his way to King's Cross, where Anthony Rudge was waiting for him. Soon they boarded a train that was due to depart for Newcastle.

'Where's Martin?' Baker said to Rudge.

'He'll be along directly I should think.'

'I don't see how. The station is full of rozzers looking at everyone. Made me feel fairly uneasy.'

Rudge laughed. 'I wouldn't worry about it. There's a lot of us sporting men heading north for a few events coming up. I expect they're quite glad to see us go for a while, and they'll be sorry when we come back.'

Baker glanced at his watch. 'Well if he don't hurry up, he'll miss the train. Could he be getting on further up the line?'

'Nah. First stop is Peterborough, then Grantham, Doncaster, York, Darlington and Newcastle. Brindle said he'd be on this train and he will be. They have their minds set on him, so he's got to get out.'

'Rolfe you mean?'

'Yes. Once that bastard has an idea in his head he's like a bloody bulldog. He thinks Martin did the Essex murder.'

'Did he?'

Rudge shrugged. 'Dunno. Don't care. But if Rolfe gets him. he'll end up being fitted and topped. If he's got the sense he was born with, he'll be on this train.'

John Martin was, at this time, making his way underneath the platform where the train stood, in company with the guard, a bearded gentleman in a thick jacket and a portentous manner. Railway servants were not paid on a lavish scale, and he was quite happy to smuggle Martin onto the train because he had a legitimate ticket. If he wished to avoid certain people in the station, why then that was his privilege and the guard did not wish to know more. John Martin wore a railwayman's coat, carried two flags, one red, one green, and a whistle in addition to his own bag. He also wore a railwayman's peaked cap whose visor came down to the top of his nose, effectively hiding the area between his eyes. In the staff subway, accompanied by a well known figure, nobody gave him a second glance. Emerging past the police at the barrier, from a door halfway down the platform, Martin stepped a few paces and boarded the Guards' van where he stopped and dropped his bag.

'Thank you Mr Wright. I am quite past the gentleman I wished to avoid seeing, and I shall let my guvnor know how accommodating you have been.'

'A pleasure sir. Let him know that if he needs the same service for other gentlemen wishing to travel discreetly, then Wright is his man for the same consideration as this time.'

Martin grinned at him rather wolfishly.

'I bet you are. Now which direction is my compartment?'

'One moment sir. You are a legitimate traveller and if you had come through the barrier in the normal way, you would have had your ticket clipped. It might look odd if it were not. May I? Thank you. Now follow me sir.'

Martin took off his uniform jacket and returned it to its owner, along with the rest of his disguise. Underneath he had his own jacket from which he pulled a Crimean style cap with a glazed peak, and put it on. Once again the lump between his eyes was not obvious. Exiting the Guards' van he followed his guide down towards the front of the train to where the man stopped by a second class compartment whose blind was down.

'This should be the one sir.'

He opened the door, and sitting inside were Rudge and Baker; the air was already thick with smoke and stink.

'Bon voyage sir,' said the guard and closed the door.

'Just in time by my watch,' said Rudge 'Sit down and have a bottle of this.'

Rudge had contrived to have a case of beer brought on board.

'You're a brave man. It's miles to Peterborough.'

'Wouldn't be the first time I've pissed out of a train window,' replied Rudge. 'Get your choppers round that as well.'

With an air of amiable hospitality, he pushed over a pork pie. Martin looked round the rest of the compartment and five unoccupied seats.

'How come you managed to get this to yourself?'

'Got here first.'

'No-one else tried to get in?'

Rudged guffawed, puffed smoke copiously from a fat cigar and farted loudly. 'Would you?' he asked.

'Probably not,' said Martin.

'That's what I thought. Now let's get the cards out. We've a long way to go.'

Chuffing with determination, the train pulled out of the station; seven hours and forty minutes would take them to Newcastle, away from Rolfe, the Met, the Nabob, Mr Brindle and all the rest of it. It would be just like a holiday.

5

A Few Small Jobs

From the Reverend Theophilus Bennett, Newton Hall Rectory, Stocksfield on Tyne to the editor, The Newcastle Chronicle:

'*On 9 October 1885 a burglary was committed at Newton Hall, about 8.30 and jewellery taken to the value of £10. Being all comfortably seated at a dinner party at Newton Hall, we were led to believe that the burglars were locked in the large bedroom through the window of which they had entered. So all we gentlemen at once rose from the dinner table and proceeded to the bedroom door, which we found locked. Being assured that they must be in the room, as the windows were all down, and a gamekeeper and an assistant posted in the grounds to watch them, I challenged the burglars to come out and surrender themselves peaceably, otherwise we should break in the door. As there was no answer, the word was given and the door was forced, and we all rushed in prepared to tackle anyone we faced, but our birds were flown. On our first alarm they had hurriedly scrambled through the window and shut it down after they had made their exit, and removed the ladder and carried it to some distance in the grounds. But had they remained it would have been worse for us as undoubtedly they would have shot most of us down, and to many of us it would have been our last dinner party...*'

'Bugger me, but that was too close for my liking,' panted Rudge as the three men bundled sweatily onto a train at Ovingham, having fled three miles across the fields, to find, as good luck would have it, that a Newcastle bound train was just entering the station. They had not headed for Stocksfield Halt because it was too obvious a place for pursuers to look.

'Not much to show for it neither,' said James Baker. 'What we've got here might pay a few days' lodging, but not a lot more.'

'Well they was having a dinner. She was wearing the bloody jewels downstairs wasn't she?' Rudge was not happy. 'How was we to know they was having friends over?'

'Nothing to be done,' grunted John Martin. 'Chalk it up and forget it.'

'We're not doing bad all in all,' said Baker. 'What that bloke at the races said was right enough; we just picked the wrong night, that's all.'

'We're still showing a profit though,' replied Rudge. 'If you add in what we made from the bookies I reckon we're twenty quid up on when we left London. We've got time to do a few things before the coursing starts at Longtown.'

'You got a few more suggestions don't you Anthony?'

'I do. As we are gentlemen of leisure seeking to profit by our time away from home, I suggest we go to Edinburgh for a few days and then Glasgow. I have been there a few times, and there are a few streets that look very promising.'

....

'That's mine,' said Rudge, showing his cards. 'Vingt-et-un!'

He then swept his winnings, three pennies over to his side of the seat. The three men were heading for Glasgow on the train from Edinburgh, still having a few days to kill before the job that the Nabob set special store by. They had not had much luck in the Scottish capital, netting a grand total of fifteen pounds for their trouble in two different houses, and having to flee from two others. The last had been horrendous, for as they forced the back window of a prosperous looking villa in Morningside, the owner had appeared in the room with a very large pistol and had let fly at them. They might have been tempted to fire back, but for the fact that he had two large mastiffs with him, slavering savagely for blood, thankfully on a lead and they lunged across the room baying. They looked like hounds from Hell. James Baker shouted 'Jesus bloody Christ!' and they all fled as the owner loosed the dogs from their leads. As Rudge cleared the garden wall, he felt the hot breath of the dogs at his ankle, but thankfully it was too high for them to jump. After this debacle they decided to try their luck elsewhere and Rudge had declared that they were to go to Glasgow.

'The cards are with you mate, I'll give you that,' commented John Martin. 'You always was a lucky dog.'

'Not always. If I was, then I wouldn't have ended up with you in a cell at Portland would I?'

Martin stared at him for a moment. 'Don't speak of that place. Gives me the bloody horrors just remembering.'

'Alright. I'm the same. I sometimes have nightmares that I'm back there.'

'Only thing I'd like to be back there with is a gun. I'd shoot the lot of them. Only thing them screws are good for; shooting.'

James Baker was diffident in his talk with these two men. Rudge was thirty-nine supposedly, Martin forty, and Baker at twenty-nine felt by far their junior. They did however, have a condescending regard for him, because he had been their cell mate, and though they did not rank him as highly as they might, in some ways he could speak to them as an equal because of their shared experience.

'You said you'd rather die than go back. I know what you mean. I've spent enough of my life in places like that.'

The older men looked at him without saying anything for a few moments, then Rudge, in serious mood, which was not always his way, mused, 'I've spent a third of my life in the jug. Think of that. A third. It's too much. I ain't doing any more.'

'Nor me,' said Martin. 'I'll shoot anybody that looks like taking me back. Yes. I said it and I meant it; I'd rather be topped than go back inside. It's a living death.'

'That's the way to put it,' agreed Rudge. 'Hell can be no worse than what we have already seen.'

'What about life though,' asked Baker. 'Do you want to settle down, have a house, and kids?'

'Wife and family you mean? Nice little house,' scoffed Rudge. 'How's that going to work eh? Men like us?'

'Well lots do,' responded Baker, rather defensively.

'How many blokes in our line do you know like that then?' asked Martin, with something of a sneer.

'Well the Nabob…'

'The Nabob!' Martin laughed derisively.

'Well it's true ain't it? He's married, nice house, kids…'

'Somehow James I can't see you doing likewise.' laughed Rudge. 'The Nabob is a bit of a special case. You and that girl of yours got any yet?'

'Well, no; but we have plans.'

'Plans! Oh well, plans are a very fine thing, but though you got plans, you have no kids. As I recall you've been married for a few years.'

Baker was annoyed now. 'You know bloody fine that I was put in the jug for five years, just three months after I was married.'

'Well that's right. Can't make kids if you're in the jug can you James? Still you're young enough; you might have them yet I suppose, but I hope if you do they'll get a better chance in life than what we have.'

'What do you mean?'

'I mean our life is planned for us ain't it? Coming from where we do, what else were we ever going to do?'

'You two playing cards or what?' demanded John Martin.

'No!' said Rudge, flinging his cards down. 'I ain't playing cards. You think about it. What was we ever going to do other than this? Now John here was on the knock wasn't you?'

'I was,' replied Martin, 'And my dad before me; it was an honest trade.'

'But a poor one I think.'

Rudge knew he was right. The 'knock' was an occupation that engaged hundreds of tailors across the East End of London, who would take old clothes and refurbish them for sale, many of the poorer classes being unable to afford new.

'You was never going to get anywhere doing that were you?'

'True enough,' admitted Martin. 'This lark pays more.'

'And people look up to you don't they? You're a mobsman, and you get admiration and rank.'

'Rank?'

'Yes. You're seen as a cut above, an object of respect.'

'You've been reading too much Anthony.'

It was probably true; Rudge was very well read. Part of the prison rehabilitation routine was to provide books for convicts, which for most, did little good at all. Rudge however, had turned into quite a bibliophile and was versed in Milton, Shakespeare, Dickens, Thackeray, the Brontes, and Edgar Allen Poe. At the drop of a hat he would talk about these people and their work, and had acquired himself a name amongst his fellows as a man of learning, and something of an orator. It also made him think rather deeply about why he was the way he was, and why he had little choice but to be how he was. But as Rudge well knew, being well read can also make you unhappy with your lot; he shrugged.

'That may be so, but it broadens the mind don't it? Makes you think about things.'

'Like what?'

'Like you're forty and you ain't married or got kids. Why's that do you think?'

'I don't want none of that malarkey,' retorted Martin. 'Wife, kids, house. Sounds like prison to me. I do what I want, when I please, and no-one to tell me different.'

'Don't you like women then?'

'I like women well enough,' said Martin defensively. 'I just don't see any reason to set up house with one, that's all. Anyway I can't see why I should bring any more poor bastards into this world. Why should I put some innocent nipper through this grind? I keep my dealings with women on a commercial level.'

'You can catch nasty things from whores John,' observed Rudge. 'Good Catholic boy like you, you should be hitched mate.'

'You can bloody well talk. You're as Catholic as me; but I don't see you going to mass with a trail of kids behind you. You ain't married either are you? Spent too much time banged up.'

'Well that's true enough,' said Rudge, 'But I hope to be one day.'

'And you ain't got any kids.'

'Maybe,' said Rudge.

'What the hell does that mean?'

'Leave it,' said Rudge, 'I don't want to talk about it.'

'The devil you don't!' said Martin, riled at Rudge starting a conversation then clamming up. 'What do you mean maybe? How can you say maybe you got kids? You either know or you don't.'

'It ain't that simple.' Rudge was nettled.

'What do you mean Anthony?' asked James Baker. 'I confess that I am a little bit intrigued by the idea of you "maybe" having kids. Won't you tell us?'

If there was anything Rudge liked, it was being the centre of attention, and he certainly had that from his colleagues right now. He basked in it, and unwound.

'Alright. I'll tell you. It's like this, and it goes back twenty years.'

'Before your first spell in Portland?'

'That's right. Anyway I knew this girl; fancied her something rotten and even wanted to tie the knot you know. We were together a few times if you get my meaning, then I got my collar felt. I got a letter from her a few months later telling me she was in the family way, but that it wasn't mine.'

'She'd taken up with someone else after you got banged up?'

'Nah. She'd been seeing him at the same time as me, only I didn't know that.'

'Doesn't sound the sort to marry really.'

'I didn't own her James. It was up to her what she did with her life.'

'Fair enough, but how did she know it wasn't yours? I mean it might have been mightn't it?'

'Well she said she'd had her time of month after she'd been with me, so it couldn't be mine. So that was that. Woman says you're not the dad and that's the end of the story.'

'So she had a kid and it's not yours.'

'I haven't finished John. Of course I accepted what she said; what else could I do? Then I got out of Portland last year and came back to the East End.'

'You took up with her again?'

'No. I was walking down Burdett Road and I saw her. I do not think she recognised me, for my appearance has changed somewhat, due no doubt to my fondness for beer.'

'You mean you're getting stout.'

'Thank you for that John. I agree that I am somewhat thicker in the body than I used to be, but that is not the point I wished to make. She had a girl with her and when I looked at that young woman I was…' Rudge searched for a word from his wide reading vocabulary. 'Thunderstruck. That's it; I was thunderstruck. I swear to you that girl is the spit and image of my sister Hannah.'

'You think she is your daughter then?'

'I dunno. I think there is a good chance that she is.'

'But you said that she could not be; that the woman you was with had her time of month.'

'Yes,' replied Rudge grimly, 'But I am older and wiser than I was. I did not know that if a woman is in the family way, she can bleed a few weeks after she conceives, and it is not her time of month, neither is it a miscarriage. It is, apparently a common thing and in the nature of child bearing. The unborn child is not affected by the bleeding.'

'So it could be your child?'

'She could be, but I do not know.'

'What's her name? Have you enquired?'

'I have. Her name is Rebecca.'

'You think you've been lied to by this woman?'

'No.' Rudge's tone was definite. 'I think she believed what she told me. But I think she might well have had her wonderings in recent times; she did meet Hannah on a couple of occasions. The doubt must be there sometimes, for the likeness is striking.'

'You going to do anything about it?'

'No James, I am not. What would be the point?'

'Well if I thought I had a child of mine running round the place I think I'd want her to know.'

'Well so would I. But I don't actually know do I?'

'You could just ask the woman.'

'What? Ask her what?' Rudge was visibly irritated. 'She told me the nipper wasn't mine. What am I supposed to do? Go and tell her she's wrong and it is mine? Who knows better whose baby it was eh? Her or me? There's no way of showing either way, and what would be the point unless I'm certain? Eh? What difference does it make to the world? The other geezer's dead now, and this girl has seen him as her dad all her life. What's her reaction if another dad turns up now? We turn the world upside down? For what? The fact is that I'll never know the truth of it so I ain't gonna bother myself about it. You haven't thought this through mate, so stop with your easy advice. There's nothing easy about it.'

'They might find a way of telling one day; whose kid belongs to who,' said Martin, who was not in the least afraid of Rudge and would not be told what to talk about.

'That's as may be,' snapped Rudge. 'But I think that's quite enough of my life thank you. Change the subject.'

'Alright. Why are we going to Glasgow? You said Brindle mentioned we might go there but what for? Can't be for the racing. Flat season's over. No coursing that I know.'

'No. We ain't going there for sport. Business is what Mr Brindle had in mind. Lots of money in Glasgow; some very well off people live there.'

'So we might exercise our trade as it were?'

'Yes James. It is, after all, what we do best.'

'Any lodgings in mind?'

'Yes. I have stayed in the Bridgeton area before now, and it is our sort of place.'

'Our sort of place?'

'Yes. It is a low kind of area with old housing, people with no money, full of thieves and villains of all descriptions.'

'Just our sort of thing then,' said Martin. 'You have an address in mind?'

'I do. A very reasonably priced lodging house for travelling gentlemen like ourselves.'

'You mean a low dirty workmen's place.'

'I do. And it must be cheap. Our funds are running low since we have not had a lot of luck.'

'I thought Brindle gave you a sub from the Nabob.'

'He did that, but we were expected to be self funding and what Mr Brindle gave me was in the nature of a float.'

'We'd better do some work then, and the sooner the better.'

Arriving at the impressive and very new Glasgow Central Station on the cold and frosty afternoon of Saturday 24 October, the three men made their way towards Bridgeton, but since they were all feeling the chill, they decided to warm up with a drink in a bar. They walked into a fairly crowded pub, snug with a smelly warmth, flaring gaslights, sawdust on the floor, and instantly knew they had made a mistake, especially Baker in his mobsman brown check suit when he opened his coat. They looked what they were; London flash lads. The buzz of conversation died down momentarily, but the resentment could be cut with a knife in the smoky fug.

'Do you think we should leave?' muttered Baker. 'They don't like us. This is the wrong place to be.'

'I don't give a damn,' said Martin. 'I came in here for a warm and a drink. Sit down and I'll get 'em in.'

Baker knew that what John Martin said was true. He really did not give a damn; he was not a man to cross, and it was written in his face, long, bony and with thick side whiskers joining to a moustache arching over a clean shaven chin; he had not followed Brindle's instruction to grow a beard. He walked to the bar and came back with three whiskeys and sat down.

'Get that down you.'

'I don't like this,' whispered Baker. 'There's something wrong here. Have you drunk in this place before?'

The room did have a strange look to it. All the men in it were in black trousers, black jackets, black waistcoats, and identical check caps; every single one of them wore a white neckcloth which appeared to be silk.

'Never have,' replied Rudge, 'and don't care if I never do again but this is just what the doctor ordered.' He smacked his lips over his glass. 'Look James, stop worrying about the Jocks. I ain't so you don't be either.'

They were sat at a table with four chairs, but all of them looked blankly at a man who came over to them and calmly sat down with them.

'Got lost have you lads? We don't get many English in here.'

'Fine by me,' replied Martin in his East London twang. 'I'm Irish. So are my pals here.'

This assertion caused James Baker to sweat because he was London born and bred.

'Is that so? And where in Ireland was you born?'

'I wasn't. My mam and dad were from County Cork.' said Martin levelly. 'I'm as English as you are.'

'Ye'er a Catholic then?'

'I am. What does that matter?'

'Oh it matters a lot round here pal.' The Scotsman grinned wolfishly. 'You don't know where you are do ye?'

'In a pub. Pubs is open to everyone.'

'Aye they are. But this is Norman Street and this bar is for Conks.'

'Conks?'

'Ask your friend here; Mr Rudge.'

'Do I know you?' said Rudge.

'No. You don't know me. But we know you, because you've stayed in this area before, and ye didnae pay any dues last time you were here.'

'Dues? What dues?'

The stranger's eyes slanted almost shut, and the atmosphere turned nasty.

'Now then Mr Rudge, do not come the innocent with me or you might find yourself with a new mouth under the old one if you ken my meaning.'

'What's this about Rudge?' snarled Martin. He was looking wild about the eyes, and James Baker saw it and got worried.

'The Norman Conks they call themselves. A razor gang based round Norman Street. They never gave me no trouble when I was here before.'

'That's right Mr Rudge; we didnae; because we thought you'd pay your fees afore you left.'

'What fees?' scoffed Rudge.

'Now let's not be pretending we don't know what is due? If I was in London plying my trade, Mr Brindle would get very cross if I did not pay my dues. The Nabob must have his fees must he not?'

'The Nabob doesn't run Glasgow,' said Rudge.

'That's right. The Priest does. And you always pay the Priest.'

'Why do you call him the priest?' asked Baker, rather nervously.

'Because he always lets you say your prayers before he sees you off,' came the deadpan reply.

'I ain't paying no fucking priest,' snarled Martin. 'Fuck off you Jock bastard.'

'Ach well it's a shame that you take that attitude,' said the Scotsman. 'I had hoped that we could come to some amicable arrangement.'

'Amicable be damned,' growled Martin. 'Bugger off before I put a bullet through your brain.'

To his surprise the Scotsman laughed.

'We are the Conks. This is our bar; we drink here. There's at least twelve guns on you right now.'

'What?' gasped Baker, looking round. Everywhere he looked he saw men looking at his group with smirks on their faces and hands in their pockets.

'John,' said Rudge. 'Don't do nothing rash John. He ain't bluffing.'

Martin looked round as if making up his mind, then subsided into a sullen silence.

'Now we understand each other,' said the Scotsman. 'Let us turn to the question of your fees. You will understand gentlemen than we have some characters in here who are mortally offended by your attitude right now. But you are not

Sassenachs and are decent Catholics so you may walk out of here, all being well.'

'What do you want?'

'Put your pocket books on the table. You too ma wee mannie,' this last to Martin who looked as if he was about to resist.

'John. Don't!' said Rudge, who pulled his wallet out and put it on the table. Baker did likewise, and, after a momentary pause, and swearing, so did Martin.

The Scotsman opened them and pulled out what was inside.

'Fifteen pounds, twelve shillings and tuppence-halfpenny. You're not doing so well are you boys? Well, as it's all you have, we shall accept it in full settlement of your dues.' His manner now changed.

'Get the fuck out of here you London scum and consider yourself lucky that you're not face down in the Clyde. Walking into our place like ye was God A'mighty; the nerve of you. If you were Proddies your lives would not be worth a bawbee. Go on, fuck off.'

The three Englishmen got up and left the bar. Standing in the street as the frost came down, Martin shouted at Rudge, 'What do we do now Brainbox? We got no lodgings, no money nothing!'

'Do?' said Rudge. 'We get some dosh. We know how to do that.'

'Yes, like they just took from us!' Martin was steaming with rage. 'I've a good mind to go back in there and blow the brains out of them.'

'With that peashooter of yours? Don't be a nutter John. They'll blow your head off.'

'So what do we do?'

'We walk away. It's the only sensible thing to do; you know it and I know it.'

'And money? To pay for lodgings, food and trains?'

'We get some. Now. And I know just the place; but not in this area. Follow me.'

6

Preparations for Some Sport

'I do not approve of it Tomer. I do not approve of it at all.'

Police Constable Tomer was, to say the least, rather surprised.

'Of the hare coursing sir?'

'Exactly Tomer. If I had my way I would abolish it, cancel the upcoming meet, and prosecute anyone caught doing it.'

Tomer was puzzled. He had been called into Carlisle ten miles from home because Superintendent Sempill wished to see him, but the telegram summoning him had not explained why. Tomer was one of two constables and one sergeant stationed at Longtown, a largish village right on the border of England and Scotland and was usually kept very busy carrying out the duties of a rural policeman. He was, however, rather more than that, for as Sempill knew very well, Tomer had one of 'those' faces. The fact is that if you dressed Tomer as a policeman, he looked like one. If you dressed him as an aristocrat, he was one to a tee. If you dressed him as a villain, then other villains would take him as a villain. Tomer could probably have been a great actor, but Sempill had noticed him and with the cheese-pared resources of Cumberland County Police Force, he used the constable as a detective. One of his favourite ruses was to dress Tomer as a rough and have him thrown into a cell with another man, a real criminal who was being held on remand. It was Tomer's job to be accepted as a bona fide prisoner by his cell mate and wheedle useful information from him. This had succeeded on several occasions, but in 1884 had backfired when Tomer was put into the cells with Patrick France, the man accused of setting off a dynamite bomb at Cleator Moor. France had rumbled him, and had complained to his lawyer about being set up in such a way. Such was the fuss that it had hit the papers nationally and Sempill had to admit that France's cellmate was a policeman. He stated that France had appeared agitated and that Tomer had been placed in the cell to 'safeguard' him, the implication being, from himself. Tomer had returned home, but it had been over a year since Sempill had required his services in a plain clothes job, and now here he was, waiting to hear what his boss required of him.

'You do not like the hare coursing sir?'

'I do not; I think that is clear.'

'Is it on account of it being a nuisance sir?'

Sempill looked at Tomer wearily.

'It is a nuisance, and I would rather not have to deal with it year on year, but I do not like it because it is a cruel and barbaric practice which masquerades as sport and brings out the basest instincts and behaviour in men, and in women too I might add. Blood lust and avarice are not qualities I would wish to encourage in civilised people.'

Tomer said nothing; Sempill noticed.

'I take it you disagree Constable? Speak freely if you will.'

'Well sir, I do not agree with you. It provides a good sport which many enjoy, and it keeps down the numbers of hares which are destructive of crops. It seems to me to be a harmless spectacle for people to enjoy.'

Sempill looked at the constable with a jaundiced eye.

'I fear that you are in the majority there but I think there might be more humane ways of controlling the numbers of hares without setting them free in terror and having them ripped to pieces by dogs.'

'It's not quite like that sir. They do have a chance to escape.'

'Oh? And how often do you see that happen?'

'Not often sir,' admitted the constable, 'But that's nature isn't it sir? Nature is red in tooth and claw. Dogs attack hares even in the wild I should think.'

'That may be so,' grunted Sempill, 'But here we have dogs bred for speed and savagery set upon poor beasts that have been trapped for the purpose. They turn them loose across a field and they die horribly under the slavering jaws of hounds. If the purpose was control of hares, they could just shoot them after they have trapped them.'

'Most die very quickly sir. One twist of the neck and they are dead.'

'It's beside the point,' said Sempill. 'The fact is that they die for the pleasure of the spectators.'

'Nothing wrong with a bit of pleasure sir. And a flutter on the outcome.'

'Oh you do that do you?'

'Well yes sir. Of course. The Longtown meet is one of the biggest in the country. They expect around three thousand people this year and more on the last day for the Netherby Cup.'

'The Netherby Cup,' repeated Sempill. 'Does that not strike you as a bit odd?'

'What sir?'

'That where the deaths of hares are sanctioned by the likes of Sir Frederick Graham and other gentleman, they are referred to as good sport, the proceedings reported in the newspaper, and the people who own the dogs admired for what they have bred?'

'It's an old country sport sir; one of our traditional pastimes. It's all done on Sir Frederick's land and with his hares. Can't see that is odd sir.'

'The oddness comes when you remember that if a group of working men take dogs and course hares, betting on the outcome of the chase, they will be arrested and sent to prison.'

'Not their land sir. Not their hares.'

'But they were surely, by your reasoning, doing the landlord a favour by reducing the numbers of hares?'

'Question of property sir.'

'That's as maybe,' retorted Sempill. 'However, I did not invite you here to debate the event. I want to talk to you about your role.'

'My role sir?'

'We are thinly stretched Tomer. I can send ten constables, two sergeants and an inspector to police the Longtown meet.'

'That's not many sir, for three thousand people.'

Tomer's eyebrows had gone up above the rim of his helmet.

'No it's not,' said Sempill, 'and that's where you come in. Some of the most incorrigible rogues, gamblers, villains and tricksters of all kinds will be flooding into Gretna Station this coming weekend, and any officer in uniform is not going to see what is going on. The instant they see him, everything stops.'

'You want me there in plain clothes sir.'

'Exactly. You'll blend in perfectly. Illegal books, runners, whores, gamblers, pickpockets, obscenities; you'll see them but not act on them. Keep blending in and quietly inform a uniformed officer as soon as it can be done discreetly.'

'I can do that sir, with no problems at all.'

'I know you can Tomer, and that's why I'm relying on you. I don't want these characters to think it's open season for any dodges they want to get up to. A fair arrest count sends a clear message; that we are on the case and if they get up to mischief, they have a chance of being caught. You are the cutting edge of

Cumberland Police here Constable Tomer; I know I can rely on you.'

Tomer was flattered by the confidence of his superintendent and left for home feeling uplifted and full of determination that nothing untoward at the upcoming Border Union Hare Coursing would escape his eagle eye.

....

Sir Frederick Graham gazed at the Netherby Cup with that certain admiration that he had always felt for it ever since he had first seen it as a boy. It was sterling silver and stood just over fourteen inches high, weighing about five and a half pounds. Made by Barnard Brothers, the last word in silver craftsmanship, it was a stunning piece of work. A shallow lid of silver, fluted and scalloped was surmounted by a sleek greyhound, sitting alert, ready to spring up and dash away in pursuit of prey. Underneath this remarkable lid was the cup itself, the top entwined with vine-leaves and laurels, all in silver, their stems forming beautiful and ornamental handles of breathtaking artistry, descending to a crinkled floral base sitting upon a massy square of the pure metal. It had been made in 1839 and was inscribed 'Newmarket Coursing Meeting' which was its former incarnation. Sir Frederick's grandfather had won it outright by being victor at Newmarket for three years in succession. Rather than let it gather dust on a shelf, he had the other side engraved with 'Netherby Cup' for it was now his to use as he wished. It had become possibly the most sought after trophy in the hound coursing world, though it never left Longtown. If anyone did win three times in succession again, then it would become their property, but no-one ever had. Instead, each year the victor at the coursing event held the cup aloft and was recognised as that year's winner of the Netherby Cup. What they actually took home was a solid silver plate worth thirty guineas inscribed with their name and honouring them as the winner of that year's cup, along with three hundred guineas.

George Farron, the butler at Netherby Hall, had burnished the cup to a glittering and almost luminous sheen, and it was ready to play its part in the forthcoming events of the weekend. The Longtown meeting of the Border Union Hare Coursing was a grand society event as well as anything else, and Sir Frederick had invited enough friends and family to fill his great house for the whole three days of the meeting. Several would be staying on afterwards. The Grahams, it was well known, were not extraordinarily rich, but they were prosperous enough to be able to hold their heads up in the very best of society. Lady Hermione, Sir Frederick's wife, was a highly regarded society hostess, inviting many people during the season to balls at forty Park Lane, their London House. She was, of course, a daughter of the twelfth Duke of Somerset, so was very much regarded as being in the top drawer. Invitations to Netherby Hall were highly prized, largely because of its romantic associations.

The Grahams were not just any other family in the border area, but the hereditary heads of Clan Graham, one of the largest and most powerful families on the frontier. They had been influential for centuries, and Sir Walter Scott had been a friend of the family, staying at Netherby on many occasions. The house was a scant few minutes stroll from the River Esk, and it was over this stream that brave young Lochinvar swam his horse to swagger into Netherby Hall and snatch his bride away from her groom and ride away with her into Scotland. Many sightseers, thrilled by Scott's *Marmion* would have loved to saunter along the great driveway that approached the house a mile or so outside Longtown. It skirted along the base of a hill, a lawn sloping up to the long frontage of red sandstone, with towers, tall windows and antiquity in every course; the driveway circled round behind the house to the great door. By design, there was no doorway in the front of the house and thus any visitor had no choice but to circle round to the rear, viewing the whole house as they went.

Sir Frederick was a man who liked his comforts at home and appreciated informality, so his guests for the great meeting were appropriate enough. Guendolen would be coming, Mione's sister and with her would be her husband John Ramsden. Fabulously rich of course, and owners of vast acres of England and Scotland, but what counted was that he also owned most of Huddersfield with all that entailed. Mr and Mrs Aglionby would be present, representing an old county family and the majesty of the law. Mr Aglionby was a barrister who cut quite a figure in his appearances Carlisle Assizes, and he was good company. The Vicar and his wife would be present, and of course George Faber, who would soon be his son in law. Hilda was now twenty-five, and as Sir Frederick well knew, a daughter of that age should be married and soon if she did not wish to be left on the shelf. Faber was a barrister and well in with many leading politicians; he would go far. He also had a lot of money; it was a fine match. A handful of local friends completed the roll of guests at Sir Frederick's table. He looked forward to it immensely.

Sir Frederick himself had been a dashing young man, a cornet in the Life Guards, a captain of cavalry, and had gone on an expedition into the remote Canadian West with fur trappers. As he had grown older and settled into married life he became a magistrate, a Justice of the Peace and High Sheriff of Cumberland.

It was time for him to stretch his legs; at his time of life he found that regular walking kept him feeling fit. At sixty-five years of age, long periods of sitting doing nothing but read could make a man feel seedy and liverish, so a stroll down towards the village and back was something to banish the blues. Sometimes he actually did go into the village by the lane, some fifty minutes on foot, buy his own tobacco and return along the west bank of the Esk, recrossing by the suspension bridge at Kirkandrews Tower. It being a crisp and cold afternoon, Sir Frederick whistled up his two dogs and set off down towards Longtown. Having obtained his favourite pipe tobacco from the Longtown Co-operative shop, he set out along Bridge Street to cross the Esk and take the footpath homewards, when he saw a face he knew.

'Christopher Gaddes! How are you doing? I was thinking of you just the other day.'

'I'm doing well thank you sir. Just got made guard. I hope one day to be able to drive the engines myself.'

'I'm very glad to hear it. We were sorry to see you go you know; best under-coachman we ever had, but of course I'd never hold a man back from getting on in life. You still living in Longtown?'

He liked Gaddes, but knew the man could not have progressed to coachman at Netherby Hall, because that position was filled and would be for many years. Nonetheless, as an under coachman Gaddes drew comments in many quarters, especially from ladies. Tall, fair haired, muscular and with a fearless blue eyed glance, Gaddes had been an ornament to his profession, until he discovered the rates of pay on the railways.

'I am sir, though based in Carlisle for work. They send me on goods trains all over the country, but always back to Carlisle, so it's an easy step home from there.'

'I imagine they pay you rather more than we could?'

'I'm afraid so sir. It's about double the going rate for a coachman, and of course there's always the chance of promotion.'

'Well I should think that a man of your proven abilities would rise quickly in the service of the railways. I'm delighted to see you getting on so well.'

'Thank you sir, and a very good day to you.'

Sir Frederick nodded and moved on across the bridge. He was genuinely pleased that Gaddes was prospering, for he had always thought highly of him. He little knew that before very long he would think even more highly of him, and that the nation would know Gaddes's name and speak it with admiration.

As Sir Frederick walked home along the west bank of the Esk he looked across the river to his own land, to the fields where the great meeting would take place the following week. His agent had the matter in hand; stewards were appointed, refreshment stalls rented, and soon areas would be roped off for spectators, competitors, judges and so on. Money would be spent, and made, spectacle would be seen and sport would be had. His gamekeepers had been trapping hares for weeks now and had over forty, with days to go yet. Before long, special trains would be disgorging thousands of spectators at both Longtown and Gretna stations, mostly the former. They were a mixed blessing of course; the locals welcomed the trade and the open purses that came with the crowds, but there were other matters that were not quite so welcome. Some of those who came were from a class of people not so desirable, many of whom were no more than petty crooks. They relieved themselves everywhere and left their dung dotting the hedgerows; many of them slept rough, and were not above helping themselves to game to feed themselves. There was by no imagination, enough accommodation in the area to lodge all those who wished to watch the sport, so local people tended to lock their doors and make sure there was nothing left lying around loose for the duration of the coursing. Some locals would have liked to see the end of the coursing for the nuisance it caused, but most saw it as a tradition which they must, and did accept.

    As a sport the event was simple enough, and went on all day as pairs of dogs were matched against each other in chasing the hares. The hares would be released on the coursing field and ten seconds later two dogs would be set after them. Keen eyed judges would watch the chase closely and count the number of times each dog managed to make the hare turn, so many points for each check. The one who turned the hare most would be the winner if the hare escaped, which did happen occasionally, but usually a dog killed the hare quickly by snapping its neck, and that made the killer the outright winner. Sir Frederick himself had a few dogs in the competition, but did not expect to win this year as there were so many champion dogs from all over the United Kingdom competing. It did not matter; what counted for him was the keeping up of a long family tradition which must not be allowed to disappear from the countryside calendar. He might not be the richest man in the county, and it was well known that the Grahams were not rich, but he was Graham of Netherby, and that title was worth something; yes by God it was! The great coursing event at Longtown was as much a matter of family honour as anything else, and as long as he was alive, he would keep it up. As Sir Frederick strolled back up towards his great house, seated like a jewel among the ancient Graham acres, he might have been excused a feeling of quiet pride in the maintenance of his estate, his house, and the customs of his clan.

7

Fundraising

'I'm bloody freezing,' said John Martin. 'What the hell are we doing here anyway? It's past midnight and I want to be in bed.'

'That would be a fine thing,' replied Rudge. 'There's only one problem.'

'What's that?' snarled Martin, who was out of temper.

'On account of the fact we ain't got no cash, we can't afford no lodgings.'

'What's happened to the money Brindle gave you? Twenty quid wasn't it?'

'All gone matey. We got to get our hands on some more, that's all. Now stop worrying about it. We've arrived.'

'Where have we arrived?' ventured James Baker.

'It's a bloody station. Crookston Station,' said Martin. 'We catching another train are we? With money we ain't got?'

'I swear John, if I wasn't used to your little ways,' said Rudge, 'I'd think you was a miserable carping bastard. Now why don't you shut up and think?'

'Think what?' replied Martin sullenly.

'Stations has got ticket offices ain't they? And ticket offices have got safes ain't they?'

'And the station is shut,' said Baker, his face lighting up. 'There's no-one here.'

'Thank God for someone with half a brain.' Rudge's sarcasm was lost on Baker who dumped his bag on the floor, whipped out a flat steel bar, and had the station door open and was on his way through it almost before the older man had finished speaking.

'Now that's what I call nifty,' said Rudge admiringly. 'Gawd but it's dark in here.'

'Shall we risk a light?' queried Martin.

'Nah. A match will do. Let's find the safe and carry it out. There's a field over the road and there's enough light for what we got to do. Full moon last night and almost as good tonight.'

It was easier said than done. They located the safe quickly enough but it was heavy, weighing between three and four hundredweight. It took all three of them cursing and groaning a lot, but they managed to get it onto a station trolley, wheel it out of the station and through a gate into a nearby field. Crookston was a semi-rural area and there were no residences in the immediate vicinity.

'Right, let's get this thing open. What have we got?' said Rudge.

'I got this!' said Martin and attacked the safe with a small hatchet. It made no impression, but bounced off it, each impact making a loud metallic bang.

'What are you doing John? Some bloody professional you are!'

Rudge angrily took the hatchet from Martin. 'Is that what you got? Muscle and ignorance?'

'Let me have a go,' said Baker.

Rudge handed him the hatchet, but he did not hit the safe.

'I've seen these before. Hold on a minute.'

Baker rummaged around in his bag and pulled out a wedge shaped chisel. He held it in the join of the door where the knob of the lock was located, and hit it sharply with the flat back of the hatchet blade, several times. To Rudge's delight, he then pulled the door of the safe open.

'How d'you do that?'

'Cheap safe. The outer body is made of steel right enough, but the bar is made of wrought iron.'

'So?'

'It's softer than steel. If you hit it enough times it bends inwards and disengages from the other side of the latch enough to get it open.'

Baker having shown his proficiency, threw the hatchet and the chisel to the ground and peered at the opened safe.

'See John?' crowed Rudge. 'Bit of *finesse*; that's what's needed. None of your banging the damned thing fit to wake the dead. Now let's see what we've got.'

Reaching into the safe he pulled out a small cashbox. It was not locked; being inside a safe there was not need for it.

'Come on; that's all there is. Let's find a streetlight and see what we've got.'

'Oliver's widdling enough for that,' said Martin. 'Let's have a look now.'

With some reluctance, for he had seen the inside, Rudge handed the box over. There were a lot of farthings, halfpennies, pennies and silver threepenny bits, a few florins and half crowns, but no notes at all. Feverishly Martin counted it into his hat then snarled at his companions.

'Three pounds, two shillings and sixpence halfpenny. For all that! Hardly worth the effort was it?'

'Now then John. You know how it is in our game; you got to take the rough with the smooth. Sometimes you win. Sometimes you don't. It's cash, and we had hardly any. It's a start; that's two week's wages for a skilled working man! The night is young.'

Rudge had a way of talking to Martin that Baker could not imitate. Truth to tell, Baker was a little afraid of Martin, because there was something in him that the man himself appeared to only just have under control. If Baker had been religious, he might have thought that Martin had a devil inside him. Some of his outbursts had an almost demonic flavour, barely restrained, and Baker did not want to be on the receiving end if he let it out. Rudge however, appeared to treat Martin almost as an older brother would treat a slightly wayward younger sibling. If Rudge had not been in the bar with the Conks, Baker was absolutely sure that Martin would have started blazing away rather than hand his wallet over. As it was, Martin shrugged and fell in behind Rudge as he set off down the road.

'Where we going now?' he asked.

'Just 'cos one station office is skint don't mean that the next one is. Cardonald Station is not far away across these fields. I suggest we go and do that one as well.'

'I want some kip.'

'The hours of darkness is our playtime John. We have enough dosh for you to snore all day tomorrow. For now my old pal, we must work. And we have a dab hand at cracking safes along with us. Let's go and do some plundering me lad.'

The three men struck out across the frosty fields until they came to the Paisley Road. Baker had left the hatchet and chisel lying by the open safe; they had completely slipped his mind. There they turned east and walked along until they came to Berryknowes Road.

'Not too far now,' said Rudge. 'The station is just along here a bit; God but it's bloody cold. Hey matey, where are you off to?'

John Martin had crossed the road and was climbing a wall.

'It's a school. No-one is in it so I'm gonna have a look at what we can get.'

'What? You are joking,' snorted Rudge. 'It's a school!'

'So?' retorted Martin and swung over the wall, followed by Baker.

'Right Jimmy me lad; let's see you open that window,' said Martin.

Baker did not answer, but pulled a flat steel ruler from his bag and slid it into the frame. He had the window open in seconds.

'John. Use your head,' said Rudge.

Martin was too busy to answer, slipping through the open window like an eel, followed by Baker. With a sigh, Rudge followed them. The school was not big, being just one of those small rural schools that catered for perhaps thirty or forty children. At the front of each of its two classrooms was a desk. Martin entered each room, and in the bright moonlight streaming through the windows, he opened the desks. They contained nothing but books and papers. Martin, frustrated, began to swear under his breath, and to lose his temper, a thing which he did very easily.

'I tried to tell you John,' said Rudge.

'Tell me what?'

'It's a bloody school. Not exactly renowned for being places where cash gets stored are they?'

'I thought they might have a cashbox.'

'What for?'

'I dunno. It just seemed an easy mark.'

'And so it was, but the most you was ever gonna find was a few browns, and that was always doubtful. Now I suggest that we get on with the main job.'

'Alright then. No need to lay it on. Let's go and do the station.'

Exiting Cardonald School the three men walked up the bright moonlit road once again.

'I hate boneyards,' said Martin, nodding towards the large cemetery that they were passing. 'Never know what you might see over there, especially on a night like this.'

'Probably what you see right now,' said Rudge. 'Loads of headstones in the moonlight with frost on them. You don't believe in spooks do you John?'

'I dunno. I hear things but I ain't never seen one.'

'Nor you won't,' said Rudge 'On account of the fact they don't exist. What about you James?'

'I have never seen one. I would have thought that men in our line might have come across at least one in our careers. You know, creeping into houses in the dark; we are creatures of the dark.'

'Creatures of the dark. I like that. Yes; we are creatures of the dark.' Rudge rolled the phrase round his mouth like a sweet that he liked.

'You're not a believer then?'

'Me? Nah.' Rudge did not quite sneer. 'I've heard enough black boys preaching at me, but I never took to their stuff about Jesus and all that.'

'You believe we shall rise again?'

'What? Life after death? Nah mate. When you're dead, you're dead and that's an end to it.'

'I still don't like boneyards.'

'Well my old lad,' laughed Rudge, patting Martin on the back. 'I wouldn't worry about it. We all end up there sooner or later. Just let yourself think that it'll be many a long year before you grace one with your presence eh?'

Martin looked at him, then he gave a short bark of laughter and everyone relaxed. Their mood grew lighter, and now they approached Cardonald Station. They were on the very edge of Glasgow now, but there were no houses anywhere near them, the closest being on the other side of the cemetery. The station existed because of the cemetery and could only be described as remote. It did not take the three men long to be inside the station office, and once again they were confronted by a large safe.

'Same as before,' said Baker by the light of a sputtering match. 'Fireproof, but not very proof against the likes of us. Let's get it out into the light.'

Once again the three men managed to lift a heavy safe out of the station building and across the road into the corner of a field. It was then that Baker realised that he had left the hatchet and chisel behind.

'Well that's a blot on your copy book James,' said Rudge. 'What else you got on that bag of yours eh?'

'Small hammer, chisel. What you got?'

'Jemmy, a few chisels.'

'They'll have to do,' said James Baker. 'Sorry about that but I can get it open with these.'

'Shouldn't lose your tools James. Not very professional that you know'.

'I know Anthony. Now, cold or not, I'm sweating like a pig after carrying that over here. I'll take my coat off before I start on it.'

'Me too,' said Martin. 'Come on. Let's get to it.'

Both men laid their coats on the ground and knelt on them. As before, Baker aimed to bend the bar inwards to open the safe, but the hammer was lighter than the hatchet had been, and the chisel was narrower than the wedge shaped one he had left at Crookston. They made a ringing sound that echoed round the welkin.'

'Bloody hell you two. That is making enough noise to waken the dead!' expostulated Rudge.

The three men stopped for a moment and their eyes went over towards the cemetery.

'I damned well hope not!' said Martin. 'Or I'm out of here like Rolfe himself was on me tail!'

The ringing of the hammer on the chisel was joined by shouts of laughter.

The night, and the area, were not quite as deserted as the three men thought. Every part of the United Kingdom had its own rural policeman, and at this very moment Police Constables McLeod and McLaren of Lanarkshire Constabulary met outside Cardonald Station, which was where their beats overlapped. Both had been attracted by the same things.

'Did you hear that banging?'

'Aye, I did. Where's it coming from?'

'Over there somewhere. Let's have a look.'

Baker had just managed to open the safe and pull out the cashbox when the heads of two policemen appeared over the hedge. It was McLeod who spoke.

'Hullo. What are you chaps doing?'

The constable knew very well what they were doing. There were three men in front of him in the moonlight, very obviously breaking open a safe with a lot of noise and swearing. Now however there was a lot more swearing, as three men, who had recently been speaking of death and cemeteries almost shot out of their boots. Rudge and Martin were completely taken aback but jumped up and instinctively put their hands into their inside breast pockets. Baker, weaponless, instantly took to his heels, fleeing off across the field and leaving his coat. The police officers suddenly found themselves looking into the muzzles of two revolvers.

'Fuck! Run Fergus!'

The two police officers ducked and ran as Rudge and Martin both fired, and the bullets missed. After firing one shot, Rudge ran like a hare after Baker; he had not aimed to hit the policemen. Martin, true to form, was not inclined to run, but fired two more shots, then, seeing his companions at the far end of the field, ran after them; catching their panic; he also left his coat.

The two policemen had retreated to the station and had drawn their truncheons. Although they knew that they were no match for men with guns, the possession of a weapon did steel them, for they were both men of duty. Now they looked across the road and, the moon still being bright, they saw three men across the far side of the field running away.

'I'm thinking that it would not be prudent to follow them,' ventured Constable McLaren.

'I am of the very same thought myself,' replied McLeod. 'I have no wish to make my wife a widow this night. If they would give us guns, then of course we could fire back, but we are outmatched, and I agree with you. We shall not pursue, but will notify the superintendent. Armed officers can be sent out if need be.'

'Those men will be in Glasgow in a few minutes. It will be like a needle in a haystack.'

'I agree, but it does not fall to us to find them.'

'You think we should be given revolvers then?'

'I do. They have been arming officers down in Essex after the killing of Inspector Simmons. This is Glasgow and we have some very nasty and hard customers up here. Just as many as down there I should think. Do you not agree?'

'I'm not so sure. If we have guns I think that more and more criminals will have guns. It will be like the wild west.'

'We have just been shot at. I felt the bullet whistle past me. It's rather like the wild west already. Shall we go and see what they were doing?'

Returning to the hedge, the officers found their way to the gate and round to the corner where they found the safe which had been cracked open, and two coats lying on the ground.

'Well at least we have the satisfaction of knowing that two of those bastards are shivering,' said McLeod.

'I will stay here Fergus. I suggest that you find the Sergeant on his rounds and inform him of what has happened here.'

Two fields away, three men had slowed down, seeing they were not pursued, and two of them were indeed shivering.

'Here's a fine to-do!' said Rudge. 'We've lost a hatchet, a chisel, and now two coats. Seems to me that whatever we make this night is going to be spent on making good our losses. Better see what we've got.'

Opening the cashbox they found a better haul than at Crookston, for there were four one pound notes and some silver coins.

'That's not bad. About eight pounds altogether then,' said Rudge.

'Not particularly good neither.'

'God but you are a miserable bugger John. Consider that your average wage in this country for a working man is a pound a week. Yes? Right, so count yourself lucky. We have enough for food, lodging, to replace your coats and to pay for transport down to Gretna.'

'I suppose if you look at it that way, then it ain't so bad.'

'No. It ain't. A few minutes of work, a bit of heavy lifting, a couple of bullets, and we have what we need. Beats working on the docks don't it?'

'I dunno. Sometimes I think a nice little job would be just the thing,' ventured Baker.

'Nah.' said Rudge. 'Admit it; you'd miss it. The excitement I mean. It makes you feel alive.' He paused for a moment.

'Was you aiming at those rozzers John?'

'Course not,' said Martin, though his expression did not match his words. "I wanted to make them shit themselves.'

'Oh they did that right enough. And so did you James.'

Rudge laughed. 'Oh I don't blame you but blimey, you can't half shift! If you was a dog I'd put you in for the hare coursing when we get to Gretna.'

'If you carried a barker they wouldn't mess with you,' asserted Martin.

'Yes, that's as may be,' said Baker, 'but if you kill one of them, you hang for it. I don't want to run the risk.'

'Risk,' sneered Martin. 'Risk? There ain't no risk. Just shoot them and walk away.'

'And you've done that have you?' asked Baker. 'I mean, you have experience of such a thing?'

Martin went quiet. It was Rudge who spoke. 'Of course he ain't. Like he said, the point is to scare the bastards into leaving you alone. Anyway they don't respect nothing except force. Show 'em what you've got and they leave you alone.'

'But what happens if you do kill one?'

'Nothing,' said Rudge. 'Unless they catch you.'

'Then you hang.'

'Yes. You hang; if you kill one.' Rudge's tone was stoic and accepting.

'And you face that quite happily?'

'I've said it before James. I'd sooner swing than go back inside. It's a living death anyway, and I'd sooner be dead than have any more of it, so there's an end to it. That goes for John too I think.'

Martin said nothing but grunted agreement.

'Well I don't agree,' said Baker, 'And that's why I'll never carry a gun. I want to get back to Nell, have kids and live a long life.'

'I fear, my son,' said Rudge, clapping him on the back, that you are in the wrong profession. However, like the rest of us, you have no choice but to make the most of it. Perhaps a little more time in the jug will make you see things our way.'

'Maybe,' replied Baker, 'But for the moment I want no guns.'

'Fair enough,' replied Rudge. 'Now you and 'im are shaking like leaves and it is proper taters! I suggest we walk into the city and find somewhere warm. Then we should get you some coats and find a place to sleep for the day. It's nearly time to go coursing and we will have a train to catch.'

8

An Interlude in Carlisle

Rudge looked out of the train window as the countryside passed by slowly, because the driver did not appear to be in any hurry to reach Carlisle. It looked cold and wintery, as if a long hard spell was about to begin.

'I just hope this place you're taking us has good fires,' he spoke to Baker. 'I'm fed up being cold. You been there before?'

'I have,' replied Baker. 'I have been to Carlisle races more times than I can think of. That's where I met Nellie.'

'I remember,' grunted Rudge. 'Bowman Street you said?'

'That's right. They let rooms to travelling men and they're not greedy about it.'

'Depends how you look at it. London is more expensive than the sticks, wherever you go. When do we meet this contact of yours? This Mister Smith?'

'Wednesday afternoon, after the coursing. I'll go off and see him tonight when we get to Carlisle.'

'It's all a bit mysterious this,' said John Martin. 'I'm not sure I like the idea of doing something like this with a bloke I don't know.'

'He's a guide, that's all. We don't know the country round Netherby and he does. It'll be dark.'

'So this Smith is gonna guide us in, watch while we do the job, then guide us out. All for what? A fiver?'

'A bit more than that, but basically, yes.'

'How do you know he's not a nark?'

Baker actually laughed out loud.

'He's no nark. He's worked at Netherby and knows his way round, but I trust him completely. I've known him a long time and he's a good friend.'

'Why's he not meeting us before the time we do the job?'

''Cos he's got business of his own to attend to and can't take time off. Alright?'

'Alright' grumbled Martin, 'But you're responsible for him right?'

'Fine by me my friend; I will answer for him.'

'Can't say any fairer,' said Rudge. 'A bloke's got to earn a crust and if he can't get off till then, it makes sense. Now ain't that Netherby Hall over there? You've been to the coursing before ain't you James?'

It was true. The train had reached the valley of the Esk, and away over the river could be seen the great red frontage of Sir Frederick's ancestral pile.

'Looks like there's some dosh there,' breathed Martin.

'Oh yes,' said Rudge. 'And before too long, quite a bit of it will be ours. Just be patient John, and your pockets will be well lined.'

'Enough to get me going in America I hope.'

'What will you do over there,' asked Baker. 'Will you go straight?'

'I don't know. I might give it a go.'

'You're a skilled tailor. Can't see why you couldn't.'

'There's not a lot of money in that game Jimmy. I chose another path to try to get some decent living.'

'But there could be in America. They still need clothes wherever you go.'

'True enough, but there's a lot of us about; like fleas on a dog.'

'There's plenty of scope for a man with a gun too,' observed Rudge. 'You could go west.'

'The thought had crossed my mind,' said Martin.

'You'll have to get yourself a decent pistol though. They'll laugh at that pea shooter you got there. That's a pimp's gun that is.'

'Leave it out! This is a good gun this; I swear by it.'

'It ain't got no stopping power. Now this,' and here Rudge fished out his own revolver. 'This is a piece with stopping power. Your little popgun fires a slug less than half an inch in diameter; mine fires nearly three-quarters of an inch. Now I ask you, which bullet has more weight and stops a man more effectively?'

'Mine stops a man well enough,' shouted Baker. 'It's proved it to my satisfaction!'

'Has it though?' Rudge whistled. 'You want to tell us something John? Something we ought to know perhaps?'

Martin subsided. 'Nothing to tell,' he said. 'My gun's good enough for me.'

'Fair enough,' said Rudge. 'No offence.'

There was a monetary pause.

'None taken.'

At the Citadel Station the three men, each humping a portmanteau, walked down Botchergate and checked in to the small boarding house that Baker had used before at Bowman Street. It was Saturday night, 24 October, and that night Rudge and Martin drank beer and sang songs in some of the numerous, and notorious pubs down Botchergate. Both got rather more than mildly drunk; Baker had gone off on his own to meet his mysterious Mr Smith who was going to guide them on Wednesday. He did not return until the small hours of Sunday morning. When he entered the room they were sharing, the style of this lodging house being mattresses on the floor, Martin continued snoring, but Rudge woke up, and sensed that it was late.

'Took your time didn't you? All set is he?'

'Yes; he's ready and willing to help.'

'S'not all you did tonight though is it,' said Rudge with a drunken titter.

'What do you mean?' returned Baker.

Rudge was inclined to coarse humour, for all his reading and obvious intelligence.

'Some woman's been all over you tonight mate. You can't pull the wool over Rudgey's eyes.'

'Rubbish,' said Baker. 'I told you, I was seeing Smith and squaring things for Wednesday.'

'Yeah well you can tell that to the marines. I got a nose you know. Naughty boy!'

It was dark so Rudge could not see that Baker's face had gone bright red.

'Oh don't worry Jimmy boy. We are all men of the world ain't we? I won't breathe a word to Nellie. A man's business is his own, and especially when playing away from home.'

Then he guffawed loudly, waking Martin, who turned over, farted, and went back to sleep.

'He's got the right idea. We need to be rested. Late shift on Wednesday night Jimmy. Better get some kip.'

Baker said nothing, but he felt like a small boy caught stealing sweets. What he had been doing was none of Rudge's business. These two just did not see him as a grown-up.

The following morning Rudge said nothing about Baker's night time lateness, but was in a cheerful mood. The three men had slept late, as was common in their chosen profession, so it was getting well on towards noon when they finally dragged themselves out of their foetid lair, and breakfasted on bread, cheese and hot tea.

'Well gentleman, I have found out that the railway line from Carlisle to Newcastle is one which operates on Sundays.'

'So what?' grunted Martin.

'I think we should stretch our legs is what; get out into the country, see some sights and walk back to the city, perhaps partaking of some refreshments on the way.'

'You mean you've heard of somewhere that sounds interesting, where there might be possibilities of doing some business, and you want to go and look it over.'

Amused, Rudge looked at Baker. 'James my lad, you have an uncanny knack of knowing my thoughts. Yes; I heard something in the pub last night. Does the idea appeal to you?'

'It does, but not before the Netherby job.'

'Of course not, but if Netherby proves successful, which it will because I'm involved in it, then we will have done the Nabob's wishes, and will be free to venture on an enterprise of our own.'

'Sounds reasonable to me,' said Martin. 'The more I can get to help me on my way, the better. Where is the place you're interested in?'

'A place called Warwick Hall, in a village called Warwick Bridge. That's all I know except that it is apparently a large and rich looking sort of house.'

'We need to find out more then.'

'Yes James. We do. You game?'

'I am. Is it near a station?'

'Regrettably, no. However there is a station at Wetheral and it is no more than a couple of miles to walk; nothing to men of our healthy constitutions.'

'Which is your fancy talk meaning we're fit enough. Why don't you just say so?'

'Because John, I like the sound of the language, having, through much reading, arrived at a love of words and the use of them.'

'You just like the sound of your own voice.'

'That as well,' smiled Rudge beatifically, which made them all laugh. 'We'd best set off now if we are to get back before dark; and we'll see how those "new" coats of yours are, because it is most damnable cold.'

The "new" coats were very distinctive, being the sort worn by 'sportsmen' and came down to the ankles of the wearers. They tended to be noticed.

It was on the road between Wetheral Station and Warwick Bridge that Rudge voiced his doubts about what Baker had planned for Netherby.

'I've been thinking this thing over and I have a notion that I might change my mind about this Mr Smith. The way I see it James, is that you are asking John and me to put our trust in someone we don't know and have never met. This Mr Smith of yours is going to guide us to Netherby in the dark and then back to Longtown, from where we make our own way. Presumably we get a train from there or Gretna and leave the area as soon as we can.'

'That's about it, but I trust Smith. I'd trust him with my life.'

'That's easy to say, but how do you know that?'

'I can't say, but believe me, I do, and I have good reasons to.'

'That you will not divulge.'

'That's right.'

'Well I don't like it. He could be a nark, a copper, or could cheat on us. I don't like the unknown James.'

'I can see that. What would you do instead?'

'Me? I'd go in there, just us three. I'd give this Smith a few bob to tell us where a ladder can be found, and I'd do the job and get out there without any outside involvement at all. Didn't your Nellie say where a ladder could be found anyway? She used to work there didn't she. She must have told you stuff.'

'She did. And she did say where the ladder can be found.'

'So what do we need this Smith bloke for then?'

'It'll be dark. We don't know the estate or the house. We don't know the best way to approach the place. We don't know what room to go for and we don't know the best route to get out of there quick. Oh I'm sure we could find our way if we had time, but to have a local man who knows all this stuff so that we don't get lost but can get in there and out again quick, well that's just pure gold isn't it? I mean in the dark and the cold, isn't it better to have a guide?'

There was a moment of quiet, then, 'Sorry Anthony. I'm with James on this one,' said Martin.

'Are you so?' asked Rudge. 'Then I give in. A majority of two to one means we go with the Baker plan; the three musketeers and D'Artagnan, rather than just us on our own.'

Seeing the puzzled looks of the other two men, Rudge laughed.

'Do you two not read at all? Ain't you heard of the Three Musketeers?'

'Course I can bloody read,' snarled Martin. 'My dad taught me. Can't hardly be a tailor without reading and writing can you? Just 'cos I don't read books don't mean I'm ignorant.'

'I went to school,' said Baker, defensively. 'I can read and write and do my numbers too. Where did you learn to read, and why do you read books? There's a lot more to do than that to earn a living.'

'True enough,' replied Rudge. 'Grandad sent me to the City Mission to do reading, writing and 'rithmatic. As soon as I had it figured, he pulled me out to work for him at the races. I guess he thought I had all I needed.'

'But you read a lot of books,' said Baker. 'Why do you do that? Ain't it just a waste of time?'

'No. It ain't. When you two was staring into space or snoring away in Portland because you was bored out of your skulls, I was escaping into other worlds. That bastard judge gave me ten years for nicking a coat and a bag of schoolbooks, but I didn't spend all my time there. I escaped to the Chateau d'If, to The Old Curiosity Shop, to Mr Rochester's house, to Mr Darcy's palace and to Barchester.'

'You were in Portland all the time,' sneered Martin.

Rudge was unfazed. 'But my mind wasn't John. I was far far away. That's the power of books on the imagination. Anyway these three musketeers was three blokes who swore to stick together through thick and thin to carry out what they was doing. Not unlike us.' He paused and looked round. 'We don't need a fourth bloke coming in and mucking things up.'

'I don't agree,' said Martin. 'I think James's plan is sensible and if he trusts this bloke enough then a guide does us no harm at all.'

'Alright. Alright. I'll go along with it. Just don't blame me if it all goes lob lolly on us.'

The three men had been walking a pleasant country lane alongside the River Eden for a couple of miles before they emerged up a steep turn onto the run-up to Warwick Bridge, a well built and warm red sandstone structure that crossed the river. They turned across the bridge and stopped halfway across to look downstream at the vista that opened up in front of them. Across a verdant, if wintery parkland, was a large mansion, red stone, covered in ivy, and obviously the seat of someone with a lot of money.

Rudge was never shy, and most Cumbrians were friendly people, so he did not hesitate to stop a passing local, out walking a dog.

'Excuse me pal; that's an impressive looking place over there. Who does it belong to?'

'That's Mr Thomas Holme Parker's place. It's a very fine house, you're right.'

'He must be a very rich gentleman to own such a house,'

'Oh he is. I don't know how many acres he owns, but he has a huge estate and owns I don't know how many farms. I have not seen inside but they tell me it's stuffed with artwork and the very best of stuff you can get.'

'Is he one of these gentlemen who live part of the time in London and a part of the time here?'

'Not at all. He lives here. He's a magistrate and plays his part in all manner of things. A very busy man.'

'He's a lucky man. I envy him his house.'

'There's many that do,' smiled the stranger. 'Good afternoon now.'

When the dog walker had gone, Rudge said conversationally, 'I don't know about you two, but after Netherby I'm going to come back and do this place.'

The other two signified their agreement to this proposal.

'It might be a good idea to stay in Carlisle for a while as well,' ventured Rudge. 'There's Brayton Hall to consider.'

'Sir Wilfred Lawson's place,' said Baker. 'You're getting a bit ambitious. They'd really be after us if we did that!'

'What? Because he's an MP,' scoffed Rudge. 'They have to catch us first. Come on; let's have a look at how you get to this place.'

Walking a little way over the bridge, the three men found themselves standing beside two stubby and castellated sandstone pillars which marked the entrance to a driveway. There was also a substantial porter's lodge and a small sign proclaiming "Holme Eden Hall".

'This is not the same place,' said Baker.

'No. It ain't,' said Rudge, 'but it's a fine big house. I wonder who this one belongs to.'

'It belongs to Mr William Watson,' said a deep bass voice from just inside the gate. 'Sightseers are you gentlemen?'

'Yes,' affirmed Rudge to the gate porter, who now emerged from his place of work, a rake in his hand. 'And admirers of great houses. Who is this Mr Watson then that he can afford a fine place like this?'

'Mr Watson? He's a nabob.'

'You what?' said Martin, visibly shaken.

'A nabob. The gentleman made his fortune in India and he came home and bought this house for the rarity of it.'

'How is it rare?' asked Baker.

'It's a calendar house. The only one in Cumberland. It has 365 windows for the days of the year, twelve corridors to represent the months, seven entrances for the days of the week and four floors to represent the seasons. Very unusual.'

'And a lot of window cleaning for someone,' remarked Rudge. 'He must be very rich.'

'As Croesus,' said the porter.

'Thank you,' said Rudge. 'Very interesting.'

He then moved away back to the bridge, because John Martin was hesitating to move.'

'It's an omen Anthony. The Nabob sent us up here to do a job and we find a house lived in by a real live nabob. I ain't touching it I tell you. It's a sign.'

'Superstitious sort of fellow aren't you?'

'I don't bloody care. We've just had a warning; hands off and I ain't having nothing to do with it.'

'Alright, alright. But Warwick Hall?'

'That's different. I'll do that.'

'So will I,' said Baker. 'But who's Croesus?'

'It's an old story about a bloke that touched stuff, anything, and it turned to gold.'

'For real?'

'Nah. It's complete bollocks. Now let's find the way in for the Hall.'

Walking back over the bridge towards Carlisle, it did not take them long to come to the beginning of another driveway, the entry fantailed in towards a gate in a low sandstone wall, where a nameplate stated soberly "Warwick Hall". Just inside the gate was a low, and rather small, gatekeeper's cottage.

'Now that's more like it,' said John Martin. 'A one legged man could hop over that easy.'

'And it would not be hard to do it without being seen.'

'All true,' said Rudge. 'And in a week or so when things have quietened down after Netherby, I suggest that we do just that. Now, it is getting on and it is freezing. Back to Carlisle I think.'

'How far is it to walk?'

'About five miles?'

'Five bloody miles! My breath is just about freezing solid and it's gonna be dark soon and you want to walk five miles?'

'Not necessarily mate. Just be patient. This is a main road.'

Before too long, and after the exchange of a few pennies to a carter, the three men were seated on a hay wagon heading back towards Carlisle, and glad to be back somewhere warm;

as well they might, this being the first intimations of a very cold winter.

9

A Sporting Event

The Independent and United Order of Mechanics had their meeting place in Albert Street, Longtown, but all charitable or social activity was suspended for the night of Friday 23 October. Here was the venue for the great dinner which was held to signify the beginning of the prestigious Border Union Coursing event which would commence on Tuesday. The Chief Steward was present, Lord Haddington, a great sporting man, with seven other gentleman to assist him, as well as Sir Frederick Graham. The Secretary of the association, Mr Carruthers of Guards Farm was also there, with Mr Hedley as judge and Mr Wilkinson as slipper. The event was to be held on the Netherby estate, and all entries were completed by five o'clock. A hundred gentlemen sat down to table, with Mr Thomas Gibbons of Carlisle presiding, and Mr James Little as his vice. Mr Gibbons proposed the health of the Queen, whilst Mr Carruthers proposed the health of Sir Frederick Graham for the use of his estate. The weather had changed from cold over the weekend, to rainy and blustery and consequently the number of entries fell short of what was hoped for. It had been hoped that sixty-five dogs would be entered for the Netherby Cup, the main event, but they were five short. Nonetheless it was thought that so many crack prospects had been entered that the event would make up in quality what it lacked in numbers.

Tuesday morning broke, dark and stormy with a rasping frost early on, then a strong gale blowing up the Solway Firth, bringing bleak and thick penetrating drizzle, to the great discomfort of the spectators who flocked out of Gretna Station to the large field at Guards Farm where the event was to begin.

Because of the weather, the number of people attending was well down on what had been expected. Rudge, Martin and Baker were not there.

Martin looked out of the window at 7 am when he woke up, saw the black clouds scudding overhead, the horizontal drizzle skittering onto Carlisle's cobbles, and people's hats being bowled off their heads by the storm. It's sole merit was that it removed the frost which had brought bone-chilling cold overnight.

'Sporting man I might be, but I ain't going out in that. Not yet anyway. Anyone out at Longtown now will be soaked to the bloody skin, and I don't intend to be among their number.'

Rudge also looked out and did not like what he saw.

'I'm staying here, at least for now. Might go out there later if it clears up a bit.'

'That's the voice of experience,' said James Baker. 'I've been there a few times when it's been pelting down straight off the sea and it ain't nice.'

'Too right,' replied Rudge, 'which is why I intend to lie here right where I am and smoke my breakfast. It's only half an hour on the train and I'm minded to go later if things improve; but I ain't no fanatic, though I do like the doggies.'

'You've trained a few I recall,' said Martin.

'Oh I have that,' said Rudge, 'And done alright with them too. There's money to be made from a well trained pup.'

'More than by nicking stuff?'

'Undoubtedly if you go in for it serious like, but you need a bit of cash behind you to go in for it big time. But a good fast dog can keep you in the readies with a bit of luck behind you.'

'Why do you need the cash?' asked Baker. 'Surely if you win, you're quids in.'

'Small scale wins, yes, I will allow,' replied Rudge. 'But the real money is from the wagering against the nobs who have got the funds to do it. They bet thousands; I ain't never gonna have that sort of money but if I did I'd have my own carriage in no time. I do know dogs.'

'What it is to be born to cash!' exclaimed Martin.

Rudge looked at him queerly.

'Well you've put your finger on it right there and no mistake.'

'What d'you mean Anthony?' demanded Martin. 'You're a funny bleeder sometimes. What have I put my finger on eh?'

Rudge looked pensive for a moment.

'I mean that there are men out there in Longtown that have proper money. They've never been short of it and they never will be; they were born to it. Then there's other men who will tell you they're self made men who got what they've got through hard work. There's all sorts of people who have varying levels of money; then right at the bottom of the heap there's you and me.'

'I ain't at the bottom of no fucking heap. I got money, I dress well and I ain't short of cash. Don't nobody tell me different!'

Rudge looked at him morosely.

'What do you do for a living John? How do you earn your crust eh?'

'Any way I can. I get by.'

'Yes. You do. 'Cos you're a thief John. A bloody thief just like me.'

'So what? I don't care. It's a dog eat dog world out there Anthony, and I aim to be with the top dogs. As a dog man you should appreciate that!'

'I do; and that's the bloody tragedy of it. I was never going to be anything else, and neither was you or James there. You was always going to be a thief.'

'No I wasn't!' expostulated Baker. 'I was trained as a cabinet maker.'

'A lowly trade that pays a pittance, and especially where you come from.'

'Same place as you; the East End of London, and proud of it.'

'Proud of it? Proud of what? What the bloody hell is there to be proud of there? Proud of the slums? Don't give me that old flannel. You was brought up the same as me, running wild on the street, mum and dad drunk out of their skulls, never enough to eat, and rags rotting off your back till they dropped off when the stitches finally decayed enough and then you had to find some more.'

Baker was silent. Rudge had accurately described his childhood, though his parents did not drink that much.

'I wasn't like that,' growled Martin. 'I wore proper clothes.'

'Of course you did! Your dad is a tailor. You was never gonna been seen in rags 'cos he could stitch them together to look like proper clobber. But you weren't rich were you? Didn't have two pennies to rub together did you?'

Martin did not reply.

'Yes; it's true though ain't it? You know what we are don't you? You tell me I read too much, and maybe you're right. But you know what we are in books? We're scum. That's what we are. I've read Oliver Twist; you know, Charles Dickens; even you've heard of him eh John?'

'I have,' said Martin.

'You know the story? You know about the Artful Dodger, and Bill Sykes and Fagin? You know who they were John? Eh James?'

'Yes,' said Baker, while Martin just nodded.

'They're us lads. We are Bill Sykes. We started out as Fagin's boys. I'm the bloody Artful Dodger! Don't tell me you don't see what I see. They was all East End kids, and nicking stuff was all they could do. And because of where they came from, nobody wanted them. You ever hear of Henry Mayhew?'

'Never heard of 'im and don't care if I never do,' growled Martin.

Rudge bounced right back at him.

'Well that's your loss ain't it John, because he wrote about men like you, and me.'

'Never knew the bleeder so he didn't write about me.'

'He wrote a book about people in London who make a living from nicking stuff, particularly Irish cockneys. That's me; and you. Irish cockneys. That's right ain't it?'

'So bloody what?'

'It's mapped out for us John. We can't avoid being what we are. It's all there; a raggedy arsed kid nicking an apple or a bread roll for his lunch 'cos his mum and dad have no food in the house. Looking to click someone in a crowd and take it home so as we don't get a thump round the ear. The slums, the fleas, the filth. It's all there.'

'I don't go for that,' said James Baker. 'I could have set up in trade as a cabinet maker, but I chose to do different.'

'Yeah? And why was that,' asked Rudge.

'Because there ain't enough money in cabinet making. I want more than I can get from that, but it was my choice.'

'Was it though? You work hard as a cabinet maker and you get lucky; what you going to get if you are one of the happy few who live by that trade? A hundred a year?'

'About that; but it's good money that.'

'Yes,' said Rudge. 'And how many get that eh? How many craftsmen in your line actually get that? Not many I should think. What do most get? What do they get for turning out cheap wash stands, chairs, tables and so on? And that's working for an owner; someone who has enough to open a shed and put men like you in it to profit from their labours. How much a week if you chose to turn an honest penny eh?'

'About one pound five shillings a week,' replied Baker.

'One pound and five shillings a week,' repeated Rudge. 'And you John. How much for turning back to your needle and refreshing other people's cast-offs for the poor beggars of East London to wear?'

'About the same,' grunted Martin. 'Precious thin pickings.'

'Could you live on that?'

'Live on it Anthony? Yes; I could live on that,' said Baker.

'With a wife, and a kid?'

'Just about. It would be short commons.'

'And with more kids?'

'Not a chance,' snorted Martin. 'You'd be starving.'

'And yet,' said Rudge, 'The average working man in this country earns one pound and five shillings a week. That's just enough to live on. Below that and you're a pauper. Who's got all the money? Tell me that, 'cos we ain't got it and neither does anyone I know. This is supposed to be a rich country with a huge empire. Where's all the dosh?'

'Well the rich people have it.'

'Yes John. The rich people have it. We do not have it, and that, my son, is why we have people like you and me.'

'What d'ye mean?' asked Martin.

'I mean that there is no legitimate way for the likes of you and me to rise in the world. There is no legal avenue whereby a street urchin like you and me, as he becomes a man, can rise to a decent station in life. I was born in the Old Nichol, and that's one of the worst areas of London; children brought up there have a life in poverty and want charted out for them, plain as day. That's why we have to make our own opportunities and nick things.'

'And if you do, they bang you up for it.'

'They do!' pronounced Rudge. 'Through their paid enforcers, who receive, for their pains, little more than you or I in an honest trade; but enough to live on.'

'The Rozzers!'

'Yes James. The Rozzers. Just paid servants; working men like you and me, but given rewards to keep the rest of us in line. That's why I don't like them. They're like traitors.'

'Sold out you mean? Like paid guard dogs, bribed to keep the other dogs in order?'

'Exactly so, and that is why, if any of the bastards tried to take me in, I'd have no mercy on them.'

'You'd shoot them even if it meant that you hang for it?'

'Without hesitation. Ten years in Hell for a coat and a bag of schoolbooks taught me to have no mercy on the servants of our lords and masters. More time in the jug would kill me. I ain't doing it.'

'You make it sound like a kind of war.'

'So it is James. That's exactly what it is. It's a battle for survival against them as would try to keep you down and in your place, poor and mean and servile. In that war, I would kill to avoid what would be visited on me if I were caught.'

'Let's hope you never have to then,' said Baker. 'If we do the job well, it won't happen.'

'Fine. Now, despite what John said, it seems to me that the rain is slackening somewhat, and we are, after all, sportsman ourselves. Let's be off to the meeting and see what is going on. Bring your bags and we shall deposit them at Gretna Station.'

Lugging their bags to the Citadel Station, the three men took an excursion train, provided for patrons of the Longtown meet, and soon arrived at Gretna Station. There they checked the luggage in with Alexander Maclean, the station master and made their way to Guards Farm to see what was happening. It was not possible to see much, the drizzle blurring visibility, but there was no doubt that it was slackening. Groups of men hung around the edges of the coursing ground, discussing the merits of the various dogs which had come from all over the United Kingdom to take part. How would Skinkle fare against Powfoot? Or Prince Charming versus Jock o' the Knowe? They huddled, waiting for the sport to commence, their backs to the rain, seeking what shelter they could in the company of others.

As the three Londoners joined one of these huddles, a tall man, about sixty years old, craggy faced with clean shaven chin but an excellent set of white side whiskers spoke up.

'John Martin. A good day to you. I have not seen you for a few months. How are you doing?'

Rudge and Baker said nothing, but looked on with some surprise as Martin replied, but it was a rather different Martin to the one they knew.

'I am well thank you my lord. I trust I find you the same?'

'I am indeed, and looking forward to the sport today. I suppose you will be here on business. Who are you working for today?'

'No one at the moment my lord. The crowd is a bit thin and I do not think there will be much for a man in my line to do if the weather does not clear.'

'True true. A thin field means a lean day for the bookies. Still, if you are on hand and find a chap that needs a runner, I'd be glad of your help placing my wagers.'

'Thank you my lord. I shall bear that in mind.'

Martin touched his cap, for the interview was plainly over as Lord Haddington nodded and turned back to his companions. Impelled by a look from Rudge the other two moved with him away from the main group.

'A fucking lord for Christ's sake? How do you know a bloody lord?'

Rudge was fizzing.

'Known him for years,' replied Martin defensively. 'I've made quite a few commissions running his bets for him.'

'You was like butter wouldn't melt in your mouth. Is he a wealthy man?'

'Filthy stinking rich; a proper lord he is.'

'A proper lord!' mocked Rudge. 'Where does he live then?'

'He's got a place called Tyninghame House not too far from Edinburgh,' admitted Martin. 'He owns most of Haddingtonshire.'

'Near Edinburgh! Why the hell did you not mention this when we were up there?'

'Because I ain't doing his house.'

'Ain't doing his house,' mimicked Rudge. 'What? Is he your brother or something? You know this lord, rich and with a house full of stuff, and you ain't gonna do his house? Why the hell not? And what you mean, "proper lord" eh? One with loads of dosh to throw at us peasants?'

There was a long and awkward pause as Rudge, incensed by a lost opportunity, glared at Martin and James Baker looked on, his mouth slightly open, just staring. Finally, Martin spoke, the words almost dragging themselves out of his mouth.

'I like him. He's a good bloke. So I ain't doing his house. Alright?'

Rudge could scarcely believe his ears.

'You let a chance like that go, and from your mates as well,' here he gestured towards Baker, 'because you like him! Now I've heard everything! John Martin, sewer rat of Dogshit Lane, Bishopsgate, London, kindly declines to nick stuff off Lord bloody Haddington who owns most of a fucking county because you like him! What the hell for?'

'Look,' snarled Martin. 'I've know the bloke for years, and he's a sportsman, like me, and like you. He likes the dogs, a bet, a drink, spends freely and he's a good sort. I ain't doing his place and if you don't like it, you can lump it. I'm allowed to like a bloke ain't I.'

Rudge knew the expression in Martin's eyes. The man had a very brittle nature, and now he was in a corner, fighting it and doing so as he knew; the savagery of him was just below the surface. If Rudge pushed him into outright defiance then the Netherby Hall expedition might not happen because Martin might just flounce off in a huff. It was time to mollify him.

'Alright John. Alright. You will have to excuse my professional interest, but if you like the man, then fine. We shall drop the matter. Fair enough?'

Martin, on his guard, hesitated a moment, then nodded.

'Alright.'

'On nodding terms with a lord though,' said James Baker. 'Ain't that something!'

A faint smile crossed Martin's face. The danger of his flying off the handle was over.

A few hares were run at Guards Farm just after eleven o'clock but then the mass of spectators moved down the way towards Moss Band Hall. One after another the 'courses' took place and the three Londoners placed a few bets themselves for small sums, which always made for more interest. Anthony Rudge was happy at the end of the day, having made two pounds and ten shillings, though his companions had not been so lucky. Sixty-one hares had been run that day, as had the first heats of the Netherby Cup and the Border Union Stakes, an event for puppies. The last courses had been run in virtual darkness, but as the three men returned to Carlisle for the night, they left their bags with all necessary equipment at Gretna Station left-luggage. They would not have to lug it about on the following day, which was going to be even more eventful.

10

Smith

On Wednesday the dawn came with a gorgeous blaze of sun, a complete contrast to the previous day. A sharp overnight frost had driven the moisture from the air and ushered in one of those bright cold and exhilarating autumnal days that lift the spirits and clear the head. The effect on the numbers of people attending the coursing was marked, and floods of spectators descended from the special trains to gather at Longtown, ready for a day's sport that promised greatness. They were not to be disappointed.

Just before nine o'clock the crowd moved along the Carlisle road towards Fauld Farm and a long low hill known, perhaps ironically, as Arthuret Heights. This served as a grandstand for the field just across the railway where the courses were to be run. Rudge, Baker and Martin were among the crowd; their interest in the dogs was unfeigned, but even so they found it hard to keep their mind on the 'sport', because today was 'the day'. Knowing this, and perhaps because of this, none of them had slept particularly well the previous night, and maybe this single fact, their exhaustion, had some bearing on the events of the next few days.

The coursing was, by all accounts, rare sport, such as is seldom seen. Twenty-four courses were held before the crowd moved further along the ridge, though remaining on the Fauld Farm. They only moved a short distance to where twenty-eight further courses were run, and the day was done so smartly that everything was over by half past two.

Rudge turned to his companions.

'A good day's sport that. I have been entertained, and I have to say that there's nothing like it for getting a man's spirits up. However, now my lads we have other business to attend to. I suggest that we get to it. The Nabob expects and all that!'

'Expects?' said Baker, 'I should think he does, and if we don't deliver, then I should not like what he might do.'

'I ain't scared of that bastard,' said Martin. 'Just let him try any of the heavy stuff, and he'll see, that's all.'

'Then you're a fool,' said Rudge, 'For if there is a man in London, or even England, that you should be scared of, it's the Nabob. Anyway, he's giving you a helping hand ain't he? Helping you out of the country. Don't be so bloody ungrateful John.'

'Fair point,' admitted Martin. 'Let's get on with it then.'

'First of all, let us imbibe some courage,' declared Rudge. 'I am fairly frozen through. Let's get the necessary and then some warming drink. I fancy a good stiff rum myself.'

'I never drink before a job, said Baker.

'Your loss mate; been listening to General Booth have you?'

'No; I just like a clear head at work. Here, are you laughing at me?'

'No,' said Rudge. 'Your caution does you credit; I was just remembering when I was a raggedy arsed little gutter rat, me and a bunch of pals threw stones and fireworks in the windows of some of the Salvation Army meetings. God what a laugh we had at all the screaming and yells.'

'But they're good people Anthony!' protested Baker.

'Oh I know that, and they do a lot of good, but they are just a plaster over a gaping wound; they can barely touch the sheer size of the problem.'

'At least they try.'

'Are you two gonna spend the afternoon talking about holy Joes, or are we going to get on with stuff?'

'Sorry John. You are right. Let's get to the station now.'

On the way into town they stopped, and Rudge asked a woman who was sweeping leaves in the lane, clearly an estate worker, if this was the lane that led to Netherby Hall. She replied that it was, and also that Sir Frederick was at home. As they left her, Baker remarked, 'I see you still have a thought of doing this job by ourselves Anthony. You don't need to know the way; Smith will guide us in, and out.'

'Yes; so you have said, but I ain't met this Smith, don't know him, and he might not actually turn up. Just getting myself a bit of insurance James. Any problems with that?'

'None at all; but Smith will be here, you'll see.'

So saying, the three men walked into Longtown and Rudge, with Martin, went into the Graham Arms. Strangely, it was not crowded, which Martin remarked upon.

'Not so very strange if you think about it,' said Rudge. 'This is a little backwater of a place and the events are over for the day. Most people have either gone home or headed into Carlisle, so this place is deserted. I should think it spends a lot of its time that way. Let's try this door.'

At this juncture, a young man appeared.

'Oh no sir. You'd better not go in there; step right in here please. That door is our private parlour. Is there anything you wish to order sir?'

'Yes please,' said Rudge. 'A large glass of rum for me, and a good warm room. Can you supply those?'

'I certainly can sir,' said the young man, who was David Johnstone, son in law to the landlord. 'Just through that door is the public room and there's a grand coal fire in there right now.'

'Just the job' said Rudge, entering the side room, which was not the public bar, and was completely deserted. 'You'd better fetch a pot of tea as well if you please; a friend will be joining us. And you John?'

'I suppose a pint of mild would do not harm.'

'Coming right up,' sirs.

'I see what you mean about not drinking before a job,' said Rudge when the waiter had gone. 'That piss is no good for man nor beast.'

'I like the taste,' said Martin defensively. 'And it don't go to my head.'

It was not long before James Baker rejoined them from the station, where he had retrieved one of the bags they had deposited there earlier. Coming in, he sat down, plonked the bag onto the next table, and drank gratefully at a steaming mug of tea.

'All right at the station?' asked Martin. 'You was longer than I thought.'

'Just some talk with the station master and an old bloke wanting directions. I got the bag.'

'Right then,' said Rudge. 'Let's have a look at it.'

'In here? Anyone could walk in through the door.'

'I doubt it. The place is like the grave; it's late afternoon Wednesday James. Mid week. The place might fill up later but I have my doubts. So stop fussing about like your grandma and let's have a look at it.'

'Alright,' said Baker and opened the bag. He fished out a bunch of keys, then another and then another, removed one key and handed it to Rudge, who grunted his thanks. The bunches of keys were then placed back into the bag.

'So this is it eh? And Nellie said that it will fit the door?'

'To the best of her memory that is a master key as close as makes no difference.'

'Fair enough. It's a far better way of securing a door than wedges. Let me just check something though.'

'What's that?'

In reply Rudge flexed the key slightly with both hands.

'Here! You'll break it!'

'Exactly James. Like a lot of these keys it is made of a softish sort of inferior iron. We do not wish it to break, so what do we do?'

'I haven't the faintest idea.'

'Well watch and learn pal. Just watch Rudgey and learn.'

Rudge placed the key among the coals of the fire.

'You'll melt it!'

'No James. I will not melt it. It takes a fire a lot hotter than that to melt iron. Let it get red, and I will tell you a miracle.'

'A miracle!' hooted Martin. 'Listen to the words of Saint Rudgey James, and behold the holy key!'

'You can laugh, but being an object of amusement to ignoramuses bounces off me my friends. I know that key is absorbing carbon from the coal. Not much, it is true, but enough to harden it up considerably.'

'How do you know all this?'

'Got a pal James. A mate, who works at the bell foundry in Whitechapel. He knows a lot about metal, and he told me stuff. Now this is called "case hardening".'

So saying, Rudge took the tongs, fished the cherry red key from the fire, and plunged it into his large glass of rum where it hissed, and the spirit caught fire. The metal of the key cooled quickly on contact with the liquid, and Rudge blew out the blue flame on his glass and looked at his companions sheepishly.

'Of course I should have used water, or John's beer, but the effect is the same. Quick cooling, or quenching as it is called, does the job nicely.'

So saying, he hooked the key into the teapot where it lost more of its heat, and then he laid it on the table and picked it up.

'Now James, try and bend that.'

Baker picked it up and tried to bend the key. He couldn't.

'There you are,' said Rudge in triumph. 'Now that's a key that won't bend or break in a lock.'

'And that's worth remembering,' said Baker, somewhat admiringly.

'I wouldn't have let you use my beer anyway,' said Martin. 'It makes it taste of flatirons. I never did take to mulled ale.'

'I will admit that it is an acquired taste,' replied Rudge, 'But I am partial to it at the correct season. It always reminds me of Christmas.'

'We have a bunch of thieves in the house,' thought David Johnstone, who had been listening and peering at the men through a crack in the door. He had not liked the look of these flashy 'sportsmen' and had decided to keep an eye on them. Now he walked rapidly to the kitchen and told his father in law that everyone should be alert because he thought there were thieves in the house, which the older man pooh-poohed as a fancy. Feeling the need to tell someone else, Johnstone crossed the road to the station and spoke to McLean, the station master, who was a crony of his.

'Aye well I think I know the ones you mean. Flashy looking sportsman types. Dodgy; very dodgy.'

'That's the ones!'

'There's been a lot like that round here this last few days David. Have they actually done anything?'

'Not that I know of.'

'Why then all we can do is make a mental note of them, and get on with our lives. There's no arresting folk for what they look like. Who knows? For all you know the men might be locksmiths or some such. But until they actually do something, what can you say? Judge not a book by its cover Davie, but what lies in it.'

In the meantime, Baker had looked at his watch.

'It's time to go. Smith will be waiting.'

'Why don't he come in here?'

'He didn't know where we was going to be. I arranged to meet outside the Bush Inn.'

Before going to the meeting place, Baker re-entered the station and deposited his bag once more with the station master. He then instructed that all three bags were to be sent on to left luggage at Carlisle in the name of "A Smith," to be called for, a service for which he was charged three pence. The men then walked along English Street to the junction of Netherby Lane where, outside the Bush Inn, stood a figure muffled against the cold, scarf swathed around his neck and a brown hat, drawn well down on his head. He had a full beard and a pair of spectacles; the moon being in its third quarter, there was not enough light to see the colour of his eyes, or of his hair, save that it was dark. His shape was hidden by a voluminous and warm looking light coloured coat though he seemed to have a considerable bulge around his middle; he was not a tall man.

'This is Smith,' introduced James Baker.

'Just Smith?' asked Rudge. 'Ain't you got a first name?'

'Just Smith,' came the reply. 'Everyone just calls me Smith.'

The voice was low, with a gruffness that might be feigned so as the speaker would appear to be tougher and more formidable than he actually was; a small man trying to appear on a level with bigger ones.

'Fair enough,' said Rudge. 'I've gone by several names in my time, and it's right that a man calls himself by what he feels comfortable with. You can call me Ralph Rackstraw; he (indicating Martin) is Koko, the Lord High executioner and this (indicating Baker) is Sir Joseph Porter who rules the Queen's Navee. So you're going to show us the best way to approach the Hall then?'

'Yes,' said Smith, without humour and unmoved by Rudge's pleasantries. 'If you'll follow me, we can get along there now.'

'It's a bit early ain't it?' said Martin. 'Nobs usually don't sit down till about eight o'clock.'

'It's two miles in the dark,' came back the low, smooth reply. 'And we won't be walking down the driveway you know.'

The gruffness was wearing off it seemed, and Martin did not like what he heard. As the four men set off down the lane towards Netherby Hall, he hung back and caught Rudge by the arm.

'What do you want John? What you grabbing me for?'

'That bloke; he's not right.'

'What do you mean he's not right?'

'He sounds like a fucking nancy boy.'

Rudge was unimpressed.

'So?'

'Well don't you mind? I mean having a bloke like that around? It ain't natural.'

'Look John; I don't care about that. It's a load of shit. Good God man! You've done enough time in the jug to have met loads of his type, and to meet the men who liked them that way. You think any the less of them? You know as well as I do that there's hundreds of them on the game in London, and that they number many important figures in this great country of ours; priests, members of Parliament and the like among their customers.'

'Do you like men like that Anthony?'

Rudge stopped in the road.

'What you trying to say John?'

'You ain't that way yourself are you?'

Rudge looked at him, and though the light was dim, Martin could sense the force of his gaze, and feel his anger. The easy going and erudite Rudge had a head of steam in his brain and might blow.

'No John. I ain't. But if I was, I would think it none of your fucking business and tell you to keep your shabby little nose out of my affairs.'

'Easy Anthony,' said Martin, who had some regard for Rudge, one of the few people he knew who treated him as a friend. 'I was only asking.'

'Only asking my arse. If I'd said I was queer your entire attitude towards me would have changed quicker than a bishop necking a glass of port. What do you bloody care anyway? Of all the villains, wife beaters, thieves, bully boys and stinkers you have met in your career, why do you find yourself going all prissy like a school mistress over a nancy boy? What you got against them?'

'It's against the laws of nature,' muttered Martin.

Rudge looked at him disbelievingly, then laughed bitterly.

'The laws of bloody nature? What the fuck are you talking about? Smoking opium in Limehouse; is that alright with the laws of bloody nature? Climbing through a window to nick stuff? Beating up a whore 'cos you don't want to pay her; is that alright? Laws of nature indeed!'

Being scoffed at by Rudge was something that made Martin feel distinctly uncomfortable.

'I would recommend John, that you take a more professional attitude. This bloke Smith has one purpose in this lark; he is to show us to our work, and then lead us out and without getting nicked. Apart from that I am not interested in the least in him. My only negative observation would be that he's got quite a gut on him; he likes his pies that one.'

'But if he's a wrong 'un…'

'If he's a wrong 'un then it ain't because he may or may not be a nancy boy. It would be because he peaches on us, narks, grasses; betrays us in some way.'

'And what would you do if he did?'

'I'd whack a bullet right through his noggin; that's what I'd do. But he ain't gonna. So let's get on shall we?'

'Oi! came the shout from two hundred yards down the road. 'You two coming?'

'Yes James; on our way. Just having a small discussion on philosophy,' called Rudge.

'I think you might keep your voices down,' said Smith when they had caught up. 'We might be heard and the first of the lodges is not too far ahead. Sound carries a long way at night. Can we speak lower please?'

'No problems pal,' said Rudge, clapping Smith on the back. 'Lead on!'

Walking on in silence, the group passed the entrance to a driveway, beside which was a well built red brick lodge. Large gates stood open. When they were well past it, Smith stopped.

'That driveway is the main entrance to Netherby Hall, but we should not go in that way.'

'Why not?' asked Martin.

'Because Sir Frederick has guests tonight. If you look through the woods you can see lights. There are flambeaux all along the driveway up to the house.'

'What's flambo?'

'Flaming torches to light the route of the driveway; it's to welcome his guests.'

'So we'd be seen.'

'Yes. Besides that, the flambeaux will go out unless they are tended so there will be a couple of men seeing to them and lighting fresh ones until all the guests have arrived. They may see you for sure.'

'And when the guests leave?'

'They probably will not leave, but stay the night. If they do go, the flambeaux will be lit again.'

'You've seen this before?'

'Many times.'

Martin grunted. 'So how do we get in then?'

'We go along the road a bit then we turn in along a path.'

'In the dark?'

'Yes. That's why we need the time, to get through in the dark.'

A little further on, they came to where a track met the road on the right. On the left was a thick, dark wood.

'This wood is Cleughfoot plantation. There is a path; it's very thin and very dark. We go slowly and we speak only in whispers.'

Smith turned off to the left and into the darkness of the wood, leaving the meagre moonlight behind. It was not quite pitch black but progress in the dark was slow and there were quite a few trips and cursing *sotto-voce* before the men managed to thread their way through the trees until they came to the edge of the parkland that surrounded Netherby Hall. There Smith stopped, and hunkered down.

'What now?' asked Rudge.

'We wait,' replied Smith. 'We could go round to the front of the house, but we are in cover at the moment.'

As he spoke a carriage came up the driveway from the road whose entrance they had just passed, and made its way along past the great front of the house, sweeping round to the rear where the main door was situated.

'If we'd have been on the driveway…'

'Yes James,' said Smith 'They'd have seen us. So we wait. When it's the right time we go out onto the lawn and round to the front, but not quite yet.'

'We wait,' agreed Rudge.

They sat, and waited.

11

A Dinner at Netherby Hall

At a quarter to eight, Smith stood up; no carriages had been along the driveway for the best part of an hour and the flaming torches marking the route had died down.

'Follow me,' he said, and made his way directly towards the house. Rudge, Baker and Martin followed, keeping to the shadows and making a fast pace between each tree to make it more difficult for them to be seen. Inside the house of course, no-one was looking out, for the curtains were closed and dinner was about to be served in the dining room. All the staff were in a flurry of making food, serving drinks, and catering for the needs of a house full of guests who all wanted hot water, maids and valets, and were making ready to come down to dinner. Outside was a cold dark night and nothing could be seen beyond the bright and warm of the house. There was only one exception to the closed curtains. Upstairs was one window where the curtains were not closed, and the sash stood open.

By now the gang were on the lawn in front of the house looking up a shallow slope to their objective.

'That's Lady Hermione's room,' said Smith. 'She likes to have fresh air and for the curtains to be left open.'

'Don't she care if anyone sees her dressing,' asked Rudge.

'Her maid did ask her that once,' said Smith, 'And she said that there was no-one out there to see, only the squirrels and they could look if they wanted. She just likes the smell of the country air I think.'

'I'm guessing that you know this maid fairly well,' leered Rudge.

Smith was not put out, 'Fairly well,' he said wryly.

'Well I won't pry,' said Rudge. 'But it's obvious that we need a ladder to get up there. You know where there is one I think?'

'I do,' said Smith. 'We'll go there in a minute; just a couple of things first.'

'What things?' growled Martin suspiciously.

'First; the room below the bedroom is the dining room. They'll all be in there having dinner. You'll have to do this in complete silence.'

Rudge gave a low whistle. 'That's risky, but they'll all have their minds on filling their faces and nattering. Once we are in there we must tread soft and drop nothing. Will she leave the lights on?'

'Yes. That's the usual practice. The maid will turn the lamps down, but one will be left on full.'

'How do you know all this,' asked Martin. 'You used to work here or something?'

'Yes,' said Smith shortly. 'A lot of locals have worked here, and many still do.'

'Did you ever meet Baker's missis, Nellie?'

'I know her, yes.'

'Ah,' said Martin. 'So that's how Jimmy here knew who to contact.'

'That's right,' said Smith. 'Now there's no doors on this side of the house and the stables are on the other side. No-one should disturb us. When the light in the room goes dim it means that Lady Hermione has gone down and there's no-one there.'

'Anything else we need to know?' asked Rudge.

'Yes. When you go in through the window you'll be in the dressing room. There's a wardrobe in there, but if you go into it, you find it's actually a door leading into the bedroom. Just outside the door is a little lobby, and a smaller room where there is a bath. These three rooms all have doors, but they make up a suite which is separated from the landing outside by another door.'

'So if we lock that one door onto the landing, we have the run of three rooms?'

'That's right. If you go through that door you are on a landing at the top of a flight of stairs leading directly down to just outside the dining room.'

'It's a bit bloody close,' muttered Martin.

'I dare do all that may become a man. Who dares do more, is none,' said Rudge.

'What?'

'Macbeth ain't it.' Rudge saw total incomprehension in Martin's face. 'I am surrounded by a sea of men who know nothing. You not got the bottle for it then John?'

'Who you asking if he's got no bottle? Just you watch!'

'Right,' said Rudge. 'You on the ladder John. We need that ladder. If anyone comes while Jimmy and me are in that room, you deal with them alright?'

'I'll do that right enough.'

'James, you got your tools?'

'All set.'

'Smith. You're a spectator but when we go, we want to go fast so no hanging about when we come out.'

'Right.'

'Now where's this ladder? It's nearly time.'

'In the shrubbery; they use it for trimming hedges; this way.'

Rudge stayed on the lawn, watching developments at the house whilst Baker and Martin went with Smith to get the ladder.

'Anything happen?' said Martin on his return.

'They've turned the lights down. I guess she's gone down to dinner.'

'More than likely,' grunted Martin, 'But we have a problem.'

'What problem?'

'The bloody ladder's too short.'

'How much short?'

'Couple of feet.'

'That's not so much; is it long enough to reach just below the window?'

'No. By my reckoning it'll just about reach above the top of the dining room window. It'd be a scrabble to get into the room.'

Rudge pondered.

'And that would be noisy; and we don't want noise now do we eh? James, any ideas?'

'I have one,' said Smith.

'Spill it out then.'

'Just over there is a garden bench. You could put the ladder on it. That would raise it a bit.'

Rudge looked at the bench, fifty yards from where he crouched. 'John; let's have a look at it.'

Quickly the two men ran to the bench, bent low to minimise their profiles.

'Will it do?'

'I think it will. Let's take it over there.'

Rudge and Martin carried the bench over to the bay window of the dining room. Light showed through a chink in the curtains; there was a noise of many voices and the chiming of glasses being touched. Champagne was being drunk.

'They're having a beano in there,' said Martin in a whisper.

'I could use some of that, but maybe later,' replied Rudge, beckoning to Smith and Baker, who came up carrying the wooden ladder which they lifted up onto the bench. The top of the ladder came to about six inches below the sill of the bedroom window.

'John, you'd better put your arse against that to make sure it don't slip. Ready James? Then let's go.'

Rudge, despite being forty-five and inclining to roundness, was still nimble enough when motivated, and the thought of a thousand pounds worth of jewellery just above his head was certainly that. He went up the ladder like a squirrel. When he reached the top, he stopped and looked into a chamber, well lit by gas which was full on, though the adjoining bedroom lights had been turned down by a maid at about eight o'clock. The window was open and it was now ten minutes past eight.

'Very considerate,' he said to himself and went smoothly over the sill into the room. As soon as he vacated the top of the ladder, James Baker was after him and up in a trice; Rudge had not hung about, but had locked the outer door. No-one could get into these three rooms unless they broke it down now. Dimly through the carpet under their feet they heard the faint noises of dinner in progress. Rudge motioned Baker over towards a chest of drawers, whilst he went to a dressing table where his heart leapt. In plain sight on the mahogany top were some very expensive looking diamond ear-drops, and a small wooden box. Rudge broke it open in a few seconds, finding three hair ornaments set with diamonds, a jewelled ring, a small gold coloured watch key, which was actually brass, and a silver picture frame. There was more on the dressing table, but Rudge grabbed these objects and put them into his pockets.

Baker had found the chest of drawers locked and was fishing in his pocket for a lever which he could use to open it.

He was not to know it, but inside the locked top drawer was approximately seven hundred pounds worth of jewels.

Lady Hermione had been irritated the previous evening because the fire in her dressing room had been smoking. She thought it was probably due to some damp or inferior house coal, and had determined that something should be done; maybe the chimney needed sweeping. Her ladyship was a great believer in the benefits of fresh air, and though it was cold outside, she detested coming up to her room for bed and finding it smoky. She had therefore given strict instructions to Margaret Watson, the head housemaid, that she should check the room several times during the evening and open all the windows if it was smoky. If it was not then the windows could be closed before her ladyship came up, so as to warm the room.

Earlier that evening, her ladyship had felt unwell, and had indicated that she might not be able to go down to dinner with the company, but eat in her room. Although she had recovered enough to join her guests at eight o'clock, some items had already been carried up to her suite from the kitchen.

At 8.15 Margaret bustled up the stairs to tend the fire, accompanied by Mrs McKie, the cook who wished to retrieve such items as cutlery, salvers and napkins. The housemaid turned the knob of the outer door to go in. Odd. It was locked.

If Margaret could have observed the effect of her turning the doorknob on the inhabitants of the dressing room, she might well have laughed. They instantly froze in horror and then they panicked. Both of them had spent considerable time in prisons and fear of a return was embedded in their very marrow. Outside the door, Margaret fished her pass key out of her pinafore pocket and tried to put it in the lock. She could not because there was a key in it from the other side. Then she knocked, but Rudge was already at the window and hissed one word at Baker.

'Scarper!'

James Baker did not need telling but ran across the room, a few soft footfalls, but Margaret, outside, heard them and realised there were people inside a room where there should be none. Quick on the uptake, she started down the stairs, followed by Mrs McKie calling loudly

'Mr Farron! Mr Farron!'

Rudge had not climbed down the ladder; he executed a perfect plasterer's slide, and Baker copied his exit so quickly that he almost landed on his head.

'We're blown! Run like stink!'

Inside the house, Sir Frederick and his guests heard a woman shouting outside the door of the dining room, and raised an eyebrow, but the dinner went on. Whatever it was, Farron would deal with it. The butler was actually in the room and he needed no hint, but crossed to the door immediately and closed it behind him as he stood at the bottom of the stairs.

'Burglars Mr Farron! There's burglars in my lady's rooms.'

'What?' Farron ran up the long single flight to the door at the top and tried to open it. It did not budge.'

'It's locked from inside Mr Farron.'

'Right Margaret, rouse the staff and get the men out and round the house. I'll inform Sir Frederick.'

As every second passed, Rudge, Martin, Baker and Smith were running themselves almost breathless down the driveway. Caution was thrown to the winds, but the main gate was open, the lodge keeper being at dinner with his family. They pounded out onto the lane leading back to Longtown just as the first male staff at Netherby Hall ran round to the front brandishing sticks and various offensive tools, shortly followed by Mrs McKie, a woman of strong character, wielding a rolling pin.

'I fear, sir, that there are burglars upstairs in Lady Hermione's dressing room.'

Farron's urbane and very quiet delivery of information was received by Sir Frederick with disbelief as the conversation flowed around his dinner table. It was not helped by it being a coursing day and all the gentlemen had taken more than a few drinks during the evening; they thought it all a tremendous joke, probably staged by their host for their entertainment. Sir Frederick, an ex-cavalry officer, saw no reason to be quiet in his response.

'Burglars upstairs?' he exclaimed. 'In the room above this one? I rather think Farron that you are being made the victim of some sort of practical joke! Who told you this?'

'One of the housemaids sir.'

'Well I fancy that she is exaggerating matters Farron. A flight of fancy. I'd rather not disturb my guests; find out what the matter is and pray calm that woman down.'

His guests were now laughing merrily at the idea of there being burglars upstairs.

'Yes sir.'

At the top of the stairs, Sir Frederick's valet Joseph Plenderleath put his shoulder to the bedroom door and tried unsuccessfully to break it open. Seeing that it was useless without an axe, he ran down the stairs and joined the other male servants in running round the house. When he reached the front he found a few men standing by the bottom of a ladder which went up to her ladyship's bedroom window, but no-one had gone up it.

'Has anyone gone up there?'

'No Mr Plenderleath.'

'Why not?'

'They might still be up there. If they are, they're trapped.'

'I hope they are still there!' said Plenderleath, a man of sanguine and rather aggressive disposition, and with a glint in his eye he set off up the ladder and was soon going through the window looking for trouble. Somewhat to his disappointment there was no-one there; the birds had flown. It was obvious that there had been a burglary though and he crossed the room and opened the door to let Mr Farron in.

Sir Frederick was now told that the burglary was real and not down to a housemaid's over-active imagination. The whole company sobered up rather quickly.

'I do apologise,' said Sir Frederick, to his guests. 'It appears that whilst we have been sitting here, we have actually been having uninvited guests in the shape of burglars, who have now made off with whatever they could. Mione, could you join me for a few minutes. I think we must find out if they have taken anything. Hilda, you must play hostess.'

'Should we not come also?' said Mr Aglionby. 'They might still be here and there might be trouble.'

'No no; Farron tells me that they have left in some haste, and whatever else I refuse to allow them to spoil what I find to be a very pleasant evening. If they took anything, all is insured. There are enough men around to deal with any malcontents I assure you.'

The dinner continued, though the topic of conversation changed from dogs, coursing and sport to more immediate concerns of law and order. Sir Frederick and his wife ascertained that some of her belongings had been taken, and with her lady's maid she was able to supply a small list within a few minutes.

'I suppose that part of the baggage that comes with the sporting event is that a number of undesirable characters come into the area, and these things happen occasionally. They do not seem to have gained very much for their trouble. However I think we must send someone to inform the police at Longtown.'

'I will do that sir,' volunteered Plenderleath.

'Will you Joseph? I am obliged to you.'

'If I go now sir, it may be that the police can get them.'

'Very well; take a good horse and let me know when you get back.'

Plenderleath was soon on his way with the news. Out along the lane, four figures walked rapidly towards Longtown.

'What a bloody mess!'

'A mess it might be John, but I've got some good stuff in my pockets.'

'That's as may be Anthony, but it ain't the pay-off we was looking for is it now? It ain't gonna get me to America.'

'No. That is true enough, but nor is it the end of our little game. You may recall that there are other houses of interest to us in this area. We can recoup our losses in those.'

'The Nabob ain't gonna be happy,' ventured James Baker.

'The Nabob,' said Rudge, 'Is a man of the world. He is not inexperienced in these matters and knows how things can go wrong. Provided we take him enough of a return on his investment, he will be philosophical about it. If he wants the Graham's jewels then remember they do have a London house as well.'

'In the meantime we'd better get back to Carlisle and get rid of what we've got unless we get nicked with it on us.'

'Telegraph offices close at eight remember,' said Rudge. 'Bit difficult for them to send a message ahead. We shouldn't have no bother.'

'Unless they knock the postmaster up.'

'Much good might it do them if the office at the other end closes at eight as well James.'

'I hadn't thought of that.'

'But I had. Rudgey thinks of everything Jimmy boy.'

'Someone's coming!' said Martin grimly. 'On an 'orse.'

Joseph Plenderleath had risen high in the hierarchy of domestic servants. A gentleman's valet had to be bright, sharp and adaptable. Riding from Netherby Hall towards Longtown, in the dim moonlight in front of him he saw four men walking towards the town and knew instantly that they were the burglars. He could not tackle them on his own and he certainly did not want to go back to Netherby so his agile mind found a solution straight away. Skewing his cap on his head and taking one foot out of a stirrup, he rolled about in his saddle and walked his horse towards the men.

'Good evning chentlemen,' he said. Then he let out a soft burp. 'I do beg yer parding. Can ye tell me whatsch the time pleash?'

'Just before nine,' said Rudge. 'You been having a good time pal?'

'Ho yesh. Grand day's schport. Won a few bob. Fine turn out washn't it?'

'Certainly was. You been celebrating?'

'I have!' declared Plenderleath, drawing himself up. 'Now I gotta get home.'

'Sure you can make it?' asked Martin.

'Yesh. Doan worry about that! The horsh knows the way.'

'You'd be best off in bed mate,' asserted Rudge.

'You are right. Thank you gentilemen; I bid you a very good night.'

Plenderleath raised his hat, nudged his horse with his foot and walked past them on the way to town. Once he was round the bend out of sight he set his mount to a canter.

The four men now behind him heard the sound of hurrying hooves.

'You thinking what I'm thinking,' asked Martin.

'Yes,' said Rudge. 'Smith; there's a good chance there will be coppers waiting in Longtown. Can we get off this road and onto the Carlisle road without going through town?'

'Yes we can. Just past this farm, Scarbank, there's a lane we can use to get to Longtownmoor; from there we go to Low Hallburn, over to Brisco Hill and then over to the Carlisle road at Hopesike Wood.'

'I don't know where any of those are,' said Rudge, glancing at Martin, 'but I am ready to admit James, that you was right. A bit of local knowledge is a good thing on jaunts like this. Right. Lead on Macduff!'

'My name's Smith,' came the reply.

'I bloody know what yer name is!' Rudge rolled his eyes in despair. 'Oh never mind.'

Plenderleath delivered his news to the police station at Longtown and they immediately turned out onto the road, because the burglars would have to come right past them to get into town. Rudge had been wrong; the telegraph was still functioning. Normally, like most rural post offices, it did close at eight. However, because a great sporting event was going on in Longtown, it was staying open until ten. PC Tomer sent a message to Carlisle, where city telegraphs were manned round the clock, alerting the city and county police that a burglary had taken place and the robbers were thought to be making for

Carlisle along the main road. Then he joined his colleagues on the road waiting for a group of men who never appeared.

By a combination of fast walking and trotting Rudge and his companions bypassed Longtown, and, the danger behind them, set out to walk the nine miles into the city. They thought they had all night; a storm was gathering ahead of them as they marched silently in the now bright moonlight, southwards towards safety.

12

Desperate Deeds

When the message from PC Tomer arrived at the telegraph office in Carlisle, a boy was sent with it to the headquarters of the Cumberland County Police; he was instructed to be quick because the matter was urgent. The message was then handed to the desk sergeant who read it, gave a low whistle and immediately summoned a constable and instructed him to take it to Superintendent Sempill's house a few streets away. The superintendent was on the case as soon as he saw the message that four suspected burglars were approaching Carlisle from the north, and rapped out instructions to have his gig made ready. It was especially important in view of where they had struck; Sir Frederick was a power in the county and much respected. On reaching the station, Sempill ordered Sergeant Michael Handley to relay instructions to forty year old Sergeant John Roche, a man of experience and sense, to proceed along the road towards Netherby with instructions to rouse the constables stationed on that route and to apprehend the suspects as they came towards the city. Handley set off at once to find Roche, who was out in Carlisle, doing his rounds. A telegram was sent to PC Tomer in Longtown: FOLLOW SUSPECTS TOWARDS CARLISLE. IF THEY TURN BACK, APPREHEND. SEMPILL. He lingered in his office for a few moments before setting out himself, looking at a large map on the wall and musing to himself. When he mounted the gig he told his driver, 'Rockcliffe.'

'Rockcliffe sir?' The driver was not sure he had heard right. This small village was miles away, off the road to Netherby, and far from where any altercation might take place.

'Yes Constable. Rockcliffe. These men are not stupid; if they have an ounce of sense between them, they will know that we have been alerted and I think they will very likely try to go round Carlisle and enter from another direction. Rockcliffe!'

'Yes sir!' The constable hesitated. 'Just us two sir? There's supposed to be four of them sir.'

'Just follow your orders Constable.'

On the way north out of Carlisle Sempill passed Sergeants Roche and Handley and informed them that he thought the suspects might have gone by way of Rockcliffe and he was going to circle round in case they had diverted and come on them from behind, thus trapping them. He had been looking at the map and thought that the burglars might just decide to leave the road and approach Carlisle down the railway line. He ordered Sergeant Handley to return to Carlisle and alert the police at Citadel Station to watch for men coming down the line. Sempill then turned his gig down Etterby Street and headed for Rockcliffe, whilst the now solitary Roche headed for the hamlet of Kingstown where there was a police house. A few short miles to the north, four figures marched hurriedly towards Carlisle.

'I will confess to you Anthony, that I had not bargained for a nine mile walk this evening. My feet are not very happy.'

'Well I don't think they're gonna get any happier for your grumbling about it John, so just put one in front of the other and in a couple of hours you'll be safe in bed and fast asleep. You can drink them numb tomorrow.'

'I think we should split up,' said Smith in that low well modulated voice of his. Did he have a trace of a Carlisle accent? Rudge could not tell, but there was something about the voice that he could not place.

'Why's that Smith?'

'Because a group of four blokes marching down the road at this time of night from somewhere there's been a break-in looks a bit suspicious.'

'No doubt that is true,' replied Rudge, 'But the people ahead of us will not have heard; we have come so fast that we are ahead of the news. It's all fine.'

'I hope you're right.'

'How else they gonna have heard eh? You think someone's flown over us and told them? Anyway it's just four sporting men who've had a day at the coursing and missed their train. Chin up Smith; it's all good.'

Blithely the four marched on, ever nearer to a warm bed in Bowman Street, and safety among the thousands of inhabitants of Carlisle.

Sergeant Roche, by eleven o'clock, was at the police station at Kingstown, a small group of houses two miles north of Carlisle. Handley had begun the walk back to Carlisle and was by now at Moorville, a scant half a mile away. Jacob Johnstone, village constable at Kingstown, a Scotsman in his early thirties, had gone to bed. When he heard thumping on his front door, he appeared at a bedroom window and demanded to know what was going on.

'It's Sergeant Roche; get up Johnstone, we have orders to watch the road. There's four burglars coming down from Netherby. Get dressed now.'

Johnstone managed to get on his shirt and trousers when he heard Roche call out 'Come out at once. Come whether you are ready or not; there is no time to be lost. The men are here.'

Johnstone ran out onto the road in his stocking feet to see Roche confronting the four men; what happened was so quick that he barely had time to react. The three Londoners were wearing long dark coats and black hats; Smith was slightly apart from them in a light coat and brown hat. Constable Johnstone heard Roche call out in a rich Irish accent, 'Where have you come from gentlemen, and what are you?'

Rudge immediately came back at him, 'What business is that of yours?'

'I am a police officer.'

'We are just sporting men coming back from Longtown,' replied Rudge.

James Baker took Smith's arm and tried to walk round Roche, but the sergeant stood in the way.

'Well as I said, I am a police officer. A serious robbery has been committed; this is the police station and all of you will have to go in there and be searched. Then you may go on your way.'

Roche was wearing a plain dark blue coat, but now he opened it to show his uniform. The sight of it sent James Baker completely over the edge.

'I'll be your policeman!' he spat, and pulled a short jemmy out of his coat pocket and aimed a blow at Roche's head. The sergeant had been in fights before, and saw it coming so he blocked it with his left arm; it knocked his hat off and impacted his arm. His right hand was already in his truncheon pocket; now he drew it and gave Baker a shrewd blow over the head. Baker staggered, and fell on the ground, though his hat absorbed much of the blow. Now Roche, his blood up, turned to face the other two. They were eight yards away from him and both had pistols out and pointing at him. As he looked, they fired. A pistol bullet took him in the left shoulder as the other nicked the same arm and he staggered. As he did so he felt a blow on his shoulders, turned and received several more blows as he grappled with James Baker who, for some reason was now up and fighting like a devil. Baker broke from

Roche's grasp and he, along with his three companions, ran off down the road, now pursued by Constable Johnstone, who was completely unarmed. Johnstone, without a hope of stopping the burglars, nonetheless ran after them and got about twenty yards when one of them turned. As Johnstone ran towards him, the man deliberately took aim and shot the constable in the chest; he fell instantly on his hands and knees, calling out, 'Oh Sergeant I am shot!'

Roche picked himself up off the ground and found that something had passed through the flesh of his upper left arm, but that it was a clean hole with not too much damage showing. He was oozing blood but his mind was clear. He managed to get Johnstone onto his feet and they staggered into the police house where Roche laid him down and walked as fast as he could to the house of Mr Jackson, a neighbour to ask him to look after Johnstone and raise other neighbours, which he did.

Down the road, all was consternation as four now desperate men walked on towards Carlisle.

'Fucking Hell Jimmy! What the Hell was you thinking of, kicking off like that?' demanded Rudge.

'I ain't going back inside. I just ain't, alright?'

'You was trying to kill him,' asserted Martin.

'No I wasn't. I was gonna knock him out so as we could get away.'

'I don't believe you Jimmy boy. I saw your eyes. You wanted to kill that man; I know that look. That's why you don't carry a gun. You're a killer and the thought of that scares you.'

'I ain't no killer!' shouted Baker.

'Makes no difference whether you are or not pal. Whatever you did, Anthony has done us up proper.'

Rudge had been quiet, and he remained so.

'What do you mean?'

'I mean Jimmy, that your little outburst was child's play to what I saw Anthony do. You didn't look round after you ran didya?'

'No. What did he do?'

'Only pulled that cannon of his out and shot a copper right through the chest. There's no chance of a bloke surviving one of those through his heart, and I reckon that's where he got it.'

'You mean that bloke's dead now?'

'I reckon so. And if such is the case...'

'We hang.'

'Spot on Jimmy. So what was you doing Anthony?'

'I've told you before. I ain't going back inside. If they'd have searched us... well they gave me ten years for some books and a coat. What will they give me for hundreds of quid's worth of jewels? Just means we got to get the hell out of here damned quick!'

'Well Anthony,' said Baker, 'that's two of you have shot rozzers. I might as well be hung for a sheep as a goat. Can I borrow your gun please?'

'Why?' asked Rudge.

''Cos the next copper that tries to stop us is gonna face me.'

Rudge thought for a moment, then nodded. 'Fair enough. We're all in this together.'

He handed his pistol to Baker who put it into his pocket.

Sergeant Handley was less than half a mile from the incident with Sergeant Roche and PC Johnstone and heard the firing of pistols up the road. He instantly knew that there was trouble, and that he would need help. Happily he knew two men in Moorville who could be depended on, so he ran to Mr Armstrong's house and asked him to come out. If he had a firearm, could he bring it because he thought there had been murder done up the road. He then ran to Mr Hetherington's, just across the road and repeated his message. Both men immediately came out, but neither was armed, though Armstrong, a nurseryman, brought a lanthorn. Although both had shotguns in their houses, at present they had no ammunition. The three men started up the road towards Kingstown; they had gone less than a quarter of a mile when they saw four men approaching them, all on one side of the road. However, as the four men approached, they split into pairs and came towards Handley on either side of the road. Smith attempted to walk past, but Handley grabbed him.

'What's all the row about back there?'

It was Baker who answered, 'Some men tried to assault us back there.'

'I shall have to detain you until the matter of that assault is cleared up.'

Baker immediately pulled Rudge's gun from his pocket and pointed it at Handley.

'Will you, you bastard?'

The gun was pointing at Handley's chest, and Baker was a yard away; he could not miss. He then pointed the pistol at Mr Armstrong, who had shone his lanthorn at him, 'I will have a go at you too!'

Armstrong froze. By now Rudge had moved past Handley and was three yards down, but he neither spoke nor did anything. Martin had his hand in his pocket and drew his pistol, though he did not point it. Handley still had hold of Smith; the tension could have been cut with a knife as Baker continued to point his gun, now at Handley.

It was cut by Mr Armstrong exclaiming in a broad Cumbrian accent, 'Leave go Handley, at once, and let us be out of this.'

It was the common sense thing to do, for any other course would have led to murder.

It was Rudge, amused by Armstrong's accent, who replied, 'I think you'd do well to get out of this.'

Handley had a clear choice between common sense and suicide; the men could be caught later; he let go of Smith. Handley, Armstrong and Hetherington backed off as the four burglars walked past them and down the road in the now bright moonlight. Handley ran with his two companions towards Kingstown and soon met Sergeant Roche and a Mr Haugh who were running towards Carlisle; it was there that they heard that Johnstone had been shot.

Down the road towards Carlisle the mood was changed.

'Bloody Hell James. I never saw you like that before! What got into you?'

'I'm not being taken; I told you. I've had enough time in the jug, same as you.'

'Nay, it was more than that. I mean I feel that way myself, but this! It was more like a bitch protecting her pups.'

Baker momentarily looked confused.

'Well I don't want you to get caught either; the three of you.'

''Cos we're your pals?'

'Not so much, but you've shot a copper. If he's dead and we get caught, they'll say that we are guilty by association and hang all of us. We have to get away.'

'Now on that we all agree. All the same, I'd like my pistol back now please. I feel strange without it.'

'Fair enough,' said Baker, handing over the gun.

Rudge turned to Smith.

'We have to get off this road. It's quite obvious that they knew we were coming and if we try to get into Carlisle this way we are going to get nabbed. What time is it?'

'About eleven-thirty,' said Martin.

'The city will be deserted now except for a few drunks. If we try to cross the bridge over the river, they'll be waiting I'd put money on it.'

Rudge turned to Smith.

'Is there any other way to get into Carlisle across the river?'

Smith thought for a moment, then replied slowly. 'Yes, there is, but we have to go along the railway line to do it.'

'You know the way?'

'Yes I do, and it's a good job you said it now, because we are at Gosling Bridge and we must turn right here.'

'Where does it go?'

'Edentown, then Etterby. We can get onto the railway there.'

The four fugitives walked on as fast as they could, and just over twenty minutes later they came to Etterby Junction where they descended a steep bank and onto the permanent way and commenced their walk towards Carlisle. With the possible exception of Smith, they were tired, having been up since early that morning. They had walked something in the order of ten miles or more during the evening and had not eaten or drunk since lunchtime. Possibly their wits were fuddled by lack of sleep, but it would, at this point, have been far better for them to throw their guns away, hide their loot and split up. Instead they stayed as a group of four; and the County and City Police were looking for a group of four. They marched on, now in silence and, oddly, they did not walk in a line abreast talking, but behind each other looking around to keep an eye on their surroundings. Animal instinct had taken over now, and like rats, cornered, they knew that they might have to fight their way through.

The group was walking down the Caledonian Railway, now led by Smith, who evidently knew where he was going, as a local man. The moonlight was still quite bright, but of course there were no streetlights, and no-one was watching the rail bridge over the River Eden. Past the dye works, past the great dark glowering mass of the castle, and past the cathedral, they trudged; until Rudge stopped.

'Here; does this go through the station?'

'Not the way I'm going to take you,' replied Smith. 'We'll take the canal branch which loops past the station, then go through the goods yard and round. We won't go through the station at all.'

Perhaps it was a herd instinct; something to do with safety in numbers, but at this point they could have split up and made their way to lodgings, or somewhere in the city to sleep under an arch until morning. They were passing over and under streets, but no longer thinking straight, so PC Christopher Fortune looked over Caldew Bridge and saw four men walking where they should not be; on the railway line. It was illegal to walk on the railway, and PC Fortune's duty was to apprehend them. If Fortune had known what had happened earlier that evening, he might have been rather more cautious, but he had been on duty for several hours and knew nothing of the burglary or the shooting of two policemen at Kingstown. His beat was the Shaddongate area, and his job was to uphold the law, which included trespassers on the railway. He found his way down from the street onto the railway line by the Dalston Road level crossing box.

John Strong, gatekeeper at the level crossing was used to the monotony of his work, and tended to use his spare time to read. The canal branch at half past two in the morning was very busy with goods trains and traffic would pick up even more in another couple of hours when the first of the milk trains began to run. His routine was disturbed by the sound of footsteps going past his box, so he took a lanthorn and looked up the line towards Rome Street gasworks. Fifty yards away, and striding rapidly, were three men walking abreast. He did not see a fourth, who could have been in the shadow of a wall. They evidently heard the signalman because they rearranged themselves and crossed over to walk in the shadow, away from the moonlight. Strong had to remain in his box, but a few minutes later, Constable Christopher Fortune arrived and asked if he had seen some men on the line. When Strong said that he had, Fortune decided to go after them, and set off, walking fast to catch up with them; he approached the group of men from behind. As he drew near to them, just by Iredale's Brewery he called out in a friendly Irish brogue, 'Hullo chaps. What's up here at this time of night?'

The group stopped and turned round; they saw a solitary policeman standing looking at them and for a moment they exchanged glances. Then, without a word they rushed him; he did not even have time to draw his truncheon to defend himself before Baker, the youngest of the men, reached him and hit him on the head with a jemmy. It squashed his helmet in and impacted his head; then Baker went berserk, striking repeatedly whilst making incoherent noises; Rudge and Martin joined in, kicking PC Fortune until he stopped moving, but Baker carried on striking, apparently in a psychotic frenzy. By the time his associates dragged him off the policeman, Fortune had been hit on the head eighteen or nineteen times, and lay unconscious across the tracks. His head was a mass of blood and hair; it looked as if his skull had been shattered into pieces.

Smith looked horrified, at least as much as they could see of his face.

'What've you done James? Once was enough I should think.'

'You want to get nicked?' asked Baker, shaking off the restraining arms of Rudge and Martin.

'No; but I think you've killed him.'

'I was making sure we were safe Smith. I was making sure we were all safe, including you.'

'I know that. Well we're safe enough from him; that's for sure.'

Baker had calmed down now, and shook off Rudge and Martin.

'I think you should go now Smith. You live not far from here.'

'What about you?'

'We need to keep going. We need to leave Carlisle way behind us.'

'You'd be safer coming and staying at my lodgings.'

'No. They'll turn the city upside down looking for us tomorrow. We got to get out.'

Rudge, who looked done in, interjected, 'He's right. This whole place will be an upturned anthill tomorrow. We got to put as many miles as possible between here and us. There's too many here who can identify us now. But you ain't in this Smith; you should push off.'

'And keep your mouth shut,' growled Martin.

'Little choice there is there,' said Baker. 'He opens his mouth then he'll get charged and convicted by association.'

'But how do we get out of here without Smith?' queried Martin.

'Easy,' replied Smith. 'You know the goods yard near Botchergate I think? It's a ten minute walk straight along there.' Smith indicated the direction in which they had been walking.

'Yes.'

'Well when you get to that, you just turn right and keep going. That's the main line south, and the most direct route out of Carlisle.'

'That'll do for us. Alright pal, thanks for your help.'

Somewhat unwillingly Smith put his gloved hand into Rudge's and allowed a handshake, though it was plain that Rudge was stronger by far, and his grip was painful. Martin also shook hands, but Baker was almost effusive in his thanks, taking both of Smith's hands and shaking them. They were evidently good friends.

'I hope to see you soon Smith, and under happier circumstances.'

'I'm sure that we'll meet again before too long James; until then, take care of yourself.'

With that, Rudge, Martin and Baker set off once again down the tracks. When they had gone about fifty yards, Baker looked back. They had left PC Fortune lying across the tracks where a train could run over him. Smith was struggling to roll the unconscious policeman off the tracks. Baker gave a slight snort, then ran back and helped Smith to drag the policeman off the rails and roll him a little way down a bank to where he lay making a snoring noise in his throat. Rudge looked back at this scene and took a few paces towards Smith, his mouth open as if to say something, his face uncertain, but stayed mute. Smith and Baker nodded at each other, their expressions unfathomable.

'You could come with me,' whispered Smith. 'Lie low; those two don't like you all that much.'

'No. They're my mates and I'll stand by them.'
Smith felt in his pocket and brought out an object wrapped in cloth.

'You'd better take this then at least. Just in case.'

'No!' said Baker.

'I think you might need it. take it!'

Reluctantly Baker took the small bundled object from Smith and then ran off to rejoin his companions leading south-east out of Carlisle. Smith watched him go with an unreadable expression, then turned back to retrace his steps across the railway bridge that spanned the River Caldew. Halfway over the bridge he stopped, sighed with some regret, and took off his light coloured coat which he then threw over the parapet into the water. Shivering with cold, and adjusting his clothes, he then made his way down Denton Street, and shortly afterwards was safe in bed.

13

A Long Walk

Christopher Fortune was alive, more by luck than judgement; if James Baker had been a stronger man, then Fortune's head would have been stoved in. When Smith and Baker rolled his body down a slope, he had been conscious, though inert, but had passed out shortly afterwards. Regaining his senses a few minutes later, he found that when he tried to get up, there was so much pain and dizziness in his head, that he couldn't walk. He was in a dreadful state and knew that his wounds were such that if he did not get help, then he might die. There was also his duty to consider, and what had happened had to be reported to the station. Sobbing with the effort of what he did, fighting the pain at every move, he began to crawl. Such was his determination that fifteen minutes after he had been rolled down the embankment, he reached the steps of the Rome Street signal box and began to haul himself up to the cabin.

Thomas Evans, on duty in the box, heard Fortune and opened his door to see a man, apparently wearing a red mask, all bloody and bruised, crawling up towards him. Horrified, Evans recognised Fortune and helped him into the warmth of the cabin.

'Good gracious! What's up? Have you got run down with an engine?'

'No. Four men set upon me.'

'Where are they? Where did they set upon you?'

'At the signal just over there.'

'I never knew such a thing in my life. Sit down now.'

'What time is it?'

'It is ten minutes to three.'

'What shall I do?' asked Fortune, his wits wandering for a moment. 'Will you get me something to drink please?'

Evans had a jug of hot tea and gave Fortune two cups of this.

'I am very sorry for your trouble. Let me bind your head; I have a clean handkerchief and it will help to stem the bleeding.'

Fortune sat passively whilst Evans bound up his head.

Now,' said Evans, 'The best thing you can do is go as quick as you can to the station and send someone.'

'But how?'

'I can help you out of the window; it's on a level with the parapet of the Rome Street Bridge.'

'Can you come with me?'

'I cannot leave the box; we are so thronged at this time of morning that it is not possible.'

Evans helped Fortune out of the signal box window and assisted him to clamber over the parapet onto Rome Street. The signalman watched as the indomitable Fortune pulled himself upright and began to walk slowly, but with purpose, down towards the Carlisle police station in Earl Street. Some fifteen minutes later, with an almost superhuman effort of will, he staggered, fainting, into Earl Street and the hunt was on.

Rudge was quite correct; such a murderous attack upon a policeman would be met with a quick response, and the word went out to all officers to watch out for the four culprits, suspected of being the same men who had carried out the outrage at Kingstown. The news of the assault was relayed to Inspector Sempill, and the thinly stretched county force were also put on alert. As the police surgeon, Dr Walker, arrived to tend eighteen wounds on Fortune's head, the great question in the mind of every officer was; where were the villains who had done this? They were also placed under strict orders not to approach the men on their own.

To the south-east, Rudge, Martin and Baker continued to walk fast along the railway line in a determined, but surely manic fashion. Any three men marching down a railway line, a place where no trespassers are allowed, are going to attract attention. All around them was Carlisle, a place full of sportsmen, many of whom would be returning for the final day of the Netherby Coursing in the morning. They could easily have split up and faded into this flashily dressed crew, but they did not. The problem was that their leader was not thinking straight. By now the gang had been up for over twenty hours. The last food and drink they had taken was eight and a half hours ago. During the day they had walked round the Netherby estate coursing sites; then two miles out to Netherby Hall; then twelve miles into Carlisle and a few through the city via the railways. In all, they must have covered seventeen miles, and their night was not over. Spurring them on was the thought that they had killed two men; yet unknown to them Johnstone was still alive, and so was Fortune. They had no energy to talk and all their thought was to keep walking in a morose silence, and God help anyone who got in their way. A kind of animal instinct had developed in them; savage, brutal and vicious; kill or be killed. At present, all that mattered was to get away; it would soon be replaced with other needs, but all care was thrown to the winds.

They passed men on the railway line; employees about their business or on their way to work, but they did not care; they did not attempt to conceal themselves, and no-one challenged them. Something about them now told ordinary men to keep clear, because they projected danger in the manner that a skunk projects stink; it protected them. Every time a train was heard, they had to take themselves off the track and flatten themselves to the sides, their dark hats and coats making it very unlikely they would be seen by anyone in the passing carriages and engines. To make matters worse, the night was freezing, a hard frost descending; anyone sleeping in the open would probably not wake up in the morning.

They were out of Carlisle by now, open country around them, and still they trudged, dazed with effort and lack of sleep. Seeing a station ahead they left the railway, took the lane through Southwaite village, and rejoined the track to the south of the houses. No-one saw them. It was Martin who broke the silence.

'I can't go on much further Anthony. Honest to God, I'm gonna drop soon. I'm as dry as a bone, and my stomach thinks my throat's been cut.'

Rudge focused his tired brain to form an answer.

'We couldn't stop before; they'd have nicked us. But we can now. What's the time?'

To answer his own question, he fumbled his watch out with frozen fingers and peered at the dial by the light of the moon, now lower in the sky.

'It's after five; be light in less than two hours. We have to get under cover because we can't walk along the rails in daylight for sure. I have an idea; let's keep walking. Can't be much further.'

Too tired to ask, the other two men followed Rudge along the track until, in the middle of nowhere, he stopped, pointed and said 'That's it.'

'What is it?' asked James Baker.

'Plate layers' hut. They have them every two or three miles. We'll go in there.'

'To sleep?' asked Baker longingly.

'Yes. And to stay until it gets dark.'

'What if some plate layers come along and want to use their hut?'

'Very unlikely,' replied Rudge. 'But if they do, there will be choices to be made won't there?'

Martin nodded. The door to the plate layers' hut was locked, but within a few seconds it was open. Inside, seen by the light of a match, were cobwebs and a few old and rusty cans of oil.

'This place ain't been used for months, maybe even years,' said Baker.

'There's some cups there; enamel mugs.' observed Rudge.

'So?'

'There's a river just over there and I think I could drink it.'

In the freezing cold air, frosty mist descending on the river, the three men drank grateful draughts of water, then returned to the hut with full cups to sip during the long day ahead. The far end of the hut had a small fireplace.

'Don't even think about it,' said Rudge. 'Last thing we want is smoke and attention.'

'What about food?' ventured Baker.

'We ain't got any James. Now, if you cast your mind back to the distant days of your childhood, you might remember that to the likes of us, this is nothing new.'

'So what do we do about it?'

'Do? Why we tighten our belts and don't whine about it. Now there's some old sacks over there. I suggest we wrap ourselves up, make things as comfortable as we can, and get some kip because God knows, we need it.'

They needed no further prompting. Within five minutes all three were asleep, and they stayed that way for many hours, not even being disturbed by the goods trains and expresses thundering past at fairly frequent intervals.

....

The Cumberland county police force was small for the area it covered. It was also underfunded and not particularly well equipped. Nevertheless, when word came that two of its officers had been shot, the news spread like wildfire. PC Tomer and his colleagues had come down the road from Longtown and arrived at Kingstown at more or less the same time as Superintendent Sempill in his gig. They had found Roche faint with loss of blood, and Johnstone, to all intents and appearances, about to breathe his last. The nearest doctor had been sent for to see to Johnstone, and as luck would have it, it was Dr Lediard, who was a qualified surgeon. Johnstone was in good hands. The superintendent then headed back into Carlisle to set about marshalling his forces to find the culprits.

Sempill hardly needed to order his men to keep an eye on all the roads leading into Carlisle. The indignation and outrage felt by all officers at the atrocious gunning down of two of their colleagues was palpable and there was not a man among them who did not burn to see the perpetrators arrested. News spread by word of mouth, but the arrival of PC Fortune at Carlisle Police Station with his head a mass of blood and in a state of collapse acted as a spur to its propagation.

When Fortune arrived at the police station, the Chief Constable of the Carlisle City Police, George MacKay, was in his office. When told of a seriously injured officer he came and took one look, and sent for Dr Walker, the official police surgeon. The doctor cleaned and dressed Fortune's wounds, but after the unfortunate officer had been sent home and put to bed,

Walker opined to MacKay that he doubted that the injured man would ever be the same again. MacKay immediately set men to go down the railway line, and although they met several railway employees who had seen three men in long coats, they could not be found. It was ascertained that a goods train had left the Crown Street goods yard at 3.30 am heading for Tebay, where there was a marshalling yard, and a telegram was sent ahead to have it searched. This was done, but there was nobody hiding on the train.

The reaction of the Chief Constable of Cumberland was immediate. Roused from sleep at his house in Wetheral, five miles outside Carlisle, John Dunne immediately donned his uniform, put on his cocked hat, and was driven into the city to marshal his forces for a manhunt. Somewhat inclined to be stout, barrel chested and with a formidable full beard, he was a man of great determination with a redoubtable reputation as a thief taker. It was not long before he was conferring with MacKay and Sempill.

'So where do you think they are now?'

'There are, to my mind sir, three possibilities. Either they hopped onto a train and got away, they are somewhere south of Carlisle, having left the train, or they are in the city.'

MacKay interjected, 'They could have walked out of Carlisle along the main line, in which case they might still be doing that.'

'I thought of that,' said Sempill, 'but I rejected it as implausible.'

'Why so?' asked Dunne.

'Because of the stupidity of it sir. They will know that we are looking for a group of four men. They know they are dressed distinctively and that many people can identify them. People who see them will know immediately that they are the men that the police forces are looking for. Logic says they should split up. There are so many sporting types in town that we'd never find them.'

'There is another thing John,' said MacKay. 'They'll be as tired as dogs. I don't know what food or drink they have about them, but if they did the Netherby job then they have been walking all night. They'll need to go to ground. There is nowhere south of Carlisle where it is possible for a group of men to stay where they would not be recognised as wanted.'

'Unless they slept out,' said Dunne.

'In this frost? They'd be frozen corpses if they did that,' replied MacKay.

'Perhaps they caught another train?'

'We have checked that sir,' said Sempill. 'The most likely one was the three-thirty goods, but there was no-one there. We have men looking into every train south at Penrith, Shap and Tebay. If they try that way, they cannot go unseen.'

'We had men watching at Citadel Station did we not?'

'We had sir.'

'So how did the villains get past? I mean, they were bypassing the station when they attacked Fortune weren't they?'

'We think they entered Carlisle along the canal line sir; we did not watch that one; not enough men. It seemed an unlikely route for them to take.'

'Which implies a certain local knowledge,' mused Dunne. 'Do we have any characters in our usual suspects who are capable of such a thing?'

'Not on this level sir.'

'Which implies in turn a local guide without a criminal record. Someone knows their way around, Sempill, and that means that they could be hiding anywhere in the area.'

'Indeed they could sir.'

'I assume that all rural officers have also been informed?'

'They have sir, and instructions given not to approach these men alone.'

'You incline to think they are still in Carlisle then Sempill?'

'I do sir. It makes sense. If they were attending the coursing, then chances are that they've been staying in the city. The place is full of sportsmen at the moment and the sensible thing for them to do is to blend in with others of their kind. It would be hard to spot them.'

'That does make a lot of sense. Very well, I want every possible man out looking for these criminals. I take it that your's already are George?'

'They are. If they are in Carlisle we have a fair chance of getting them. I'm sending men round the lodging houses and every man who has an informant will seek them out. Someone, somewhere will talk.'

'They are armed sir.'

'Yes' said Dunne. 'That's my next call. We do not have any firearms I take it?'

'Not one sir. We have never received funding for them. It was not deemed necessary by the Home Office you may recall.'

'That's an omission we must make good in future I think. Have we any officers who have used pistols before?'

'I can enquire among the men sir,' said Sempill, raising an eyebrow.

'Do so. I want a telegram sent as soon as the office opens, to General Goodenough, Commander of the Northern District. There are weapons enough in the garrison for our purpose. If he would be so kind as to lend us some pistols then I should be most obliged to him. Sign it per and pro.'

'Armed police? The public will not like it.'

'You think not George?' said Dunne. 'I fancy that the newspapers will be howling for it before too many hours have gone by. It's all very well to rely on policing by consent, but officers have been shot, and attempted murder done in the centre of Carlisle. I think the public will demand that these men be taken, and quickly too.'

'Sadly, I think you are right,' replied MacKay. 'After the shooting of poor Simmons down in Essex, they have a squad of men standing by with revolvers in case they are needed, and officers on night patrol are armed already. There is a disturbing tendency among the criminal fraternity now to go about with pistols now. What chance do officers armed with sticks have against criminals armed with guns?'

'You'd better have some pistols for your chaps then too.'

'How many shall you ask for?'

'I was thinking perhaps ten.'

'Make it fifteen if you will, and the city shall have five.'

Carlisle was no great industrial hub like Bradford, Huddersfield, or Manchester. Its population stood at around forty thousand, so that by any standards it was classed as a small provincial city. Life, for most people, consisted of hard work, interaction with a community in which a lot of people knew each other, and was played out with respect for the law.

It is true that there was crime, but by the standards of most cities, it was, by and large, very small beer. The main problems consisted of drunkenness and fights between drunks, with the occasional burglary. On the morning of Thursday 29 October 1885 Carlisle woke up to news of shooting and savagery, and it would be difficult to overstate the wave of revulsion that swept over the city. A small crowd gathered outside the police station hoping for news, as accounts of what had happened the previous night swept from mouth to mouth, growing in horror with each telling. In boarding and lodging houses, landlords and ladies looked at their tenants closely to discern if anything about them made them suspect. Strangest of all, and although the weapons could not be seen, armed policemen patrolled the town. A great anger came into being in people's minds against the men who had done these awful things in the midst of their community. It was not a placid feeling either, for if Rudge, Martin and Baker had appeared on the streets, known as the culprits, then they would have been lucky to get away with their lives.

A few miles to the south, in a cold hut made of old sleepers, and set into the side of an embankment, three men woke up in the early afternoon hungry and without a crumb of food. They had slept like the dead.

'I can't remember the last time I was this hungry,' said Rudge. 'I think I have been, but it was when I was a nipper.'

'Then let's go now and find a place where we can eat something,' said Martin.

Rudge looked at him pityingly.

'Are you really that stupid John?'

'Who you calling stupid?'

'A man who wants to go out looking for food when all the coppers in Carlisle and all round are looking for him. You go out there and I bet you get nabbed within an hour. Then you're done pal; trussed and roasted.'

'Roasted! Don't say that,' pleaded Baker.

'Yeah; sorry about that,' said Rudge. 'We are right in it now pals, but we can't go out; not yet anyway.'

'What? Stay here all day?'

'Yes John. No-one's been in here for a long time and the chances are no-one will come in here today. We need to get from here as quick as we can, but not in daylight.'

'We could jump on a train.'

'The trains that go past at about sixty miles an hour John? After you…'

'Well we need to get where we can get on a train.'

'We do, and that will be after dark.'

'What do we do till then? Starve?'

'Tighten your belt another notch John. It does help, as you may remember.' Rudge smiled faintly in the cold air and fished in his pocket. 'This'll keep us occupied a bit until the light goes.'

He started to deal cards onto the top of an oil drum that he dragged between the three of them, and so they settled to while away the remaining hours until it became dark enough to venture outside.

14

Fugitives

Police Constable Joseph Byrnes had good reason to be happy with his lot. He had been born into a poor home in Ireland, and seeking employment, like so many young Irish folk, he had headed to England. For a few years he had worked as a miner in the Millom haematite mines, but the work never suited him because he was over five feet ten inches tall, and big with it. The best miners had a smaller physique and young Byrnes found mining an uncomfortable profession to follow; he began to think of finding a job more congenial to his physique. To his surprise, over his time in Cumberland, he found that a large number of policemen on the beat were Irishmen, and that he was just the sort of man the force were looking for. At the age of twenty-one he joined the Cumberland and Westmorland Constabulary, and served four years of duty at Alston and then was sent to Harrington. At the age of twenty-four he was posted to Whitehaven and fell passionately in love with Eleanor Bertram, the daughter of his inspector. If rumour was correct, they married quickly and for good reason; the first child came rather fewer than nine months into the marriage. The austere morality of the police force did not countenance that sort of thing in their ranks, and it is perhaps a measure of disapproval that in the eleven years of his marriage, Byrnes had not progressed beyond constable.

That did not matter much to Joseph Byrnes. He had been posted to the rural hamlet of Plumpton where he and Eleanor now had four children, the last born just a week ago. It was a real love match and the couple lived in a police house just a few yards from the Packhorse Inn. Over the road was the vicarage, but apart from a few small cottages, all about were green and lush pastures, and views of the fells not too far away. Byrnes had integrated well into the local community and was respected as a good and conscientious man, popular with everyone because he kept the peace in his manor.

Byrnes's chief was Superintendent Fowler, based at Penrith Police Station. At about eight o'clock on the morning of Thursday 29 October Fowler received a letter from Superintendent Sempill in Carlisle, informing him of the night's events in that city and details of the men who were wanted for questioning. He immediately put men to watch the railway line and every road leading into Penrith, and sent out word to all rural officers to be on their guard. He also gave strict instructions that these wanted men were not to be approached. Constable Byrnes received these orders by way of a telegram sent to Plumpton Station, and although he did not really expect to see anything in his quiet area, he spent several hours patrolling the lanes round Plumpton on the lookout for four men in long coats, walking south from Carlisle.

Fowler was a very energetic officer, efficient and intelligent; he did not want any of his men shot, and knew that the four men who carried out the attacks in Carlisle were desperate and dangerous. Penrith Police had no guns available, and no permission to carry them. He also had an idea that the men might be walking south from Carlisle, which would be foolish of them, but possible. The immediate problem was that he and his officers had no way of tackling the men head on, so he set his net with limited resources. The strategy was to watch, and to report. If the fugitives were spotted, they would be walking; if Fowler heard of this, he could concentrate a group of his constables in ambush. They should, at the right place, be able to rush the supposed villains, overwhelming them by numbers before they could pull their guns out and use them. It was, he knew, the only chance he had of apprehending the suspects but it did not curb his anxiety about the danger to his men, hence the explicit instruction that they were not to tackle the fugitives. Because of this, and very unusually, he undertook to drive his own gig round the rural beats to see every officer to the north of Penrith. He repeated his instruction about non contact to every man he met on his round that day, and at three o'clock in the afternoon, he said it to PC Joseph Byrnes at his house in Plumpton. The police house was a very short distance from the crossroads on the main Carlisle to Penrith road, where the Packhorse Inn stood. Constable Byrnes was having a short rest after several hours of patrolling the lanes. He had walked the two and a half miles from Plumpton to Calthwaite Station, the next up the line to warn staff about the police wanting to interview four men who might be walking down the line. The station master there, John Hayes asked him what he should do if he saw them, and Byrnes replied, 'Nothing. Just let us know. It would be pure folly for one man to tackle three armed men.'

For the moment, Joseph Byrnes had done all he could. He went home for a cup of tea and a bite to eat. The knock on the door came as a surprise; Superintendent Fowler stood there.

'Good afternoon Byrnes. I'm just doing my rounds to see how things are. I take it that you've seen nothing here?'

'Of the four men sir? No. Not a sign of them.'

'We are a long way from Carlisle here, but it is conceivable that the villains who shot two officers up there are coming down this way.'

Byrnes was impressed with the gravity of the situation because the rounds of rural constables were usually carried out by a sergeant, often Sergeant Bremner from Penrith, or an inspector. For the superintendent himself to be doing this was, in his experience, unique.

'I'd like you to show me to the station and introduce me to the station master there. I want to impress upon him how serious this matter is.'

'Right away sir.'

On Fowler's gig, the two men drove the scant mile down to the station, an austere brick building where Byrnes introduced the superintendent to William Gornall, the station master.

'You'll have heard that we are looking for four men in connection with some serious crimes, and that they may be coming this way?'

'I have. There has been no sign of any people like that here though.'

'If anyone answering those descriptions does show up here Mr Gornall, you must be sure to let me know, either by telegram or by train or any other method. It is vitally important that I know of their approach.'

'You may be sure Superintendent, that if they come this way, I shall let you know as soon as is humanly possible.'

'Above all Mr Gornall, do not attempt to do anything yourself. These men are armed and dangerous.'

When this was done, Fowler drove Byrnes back to the police house and dropped him at home, repeating his warning.

....

Some miles to the north, all was not well.

'Can we not go now Anthony? I can't think of when I was ever as hungry as this?'

'You can go anywhere you like John. Off you go.'

'On my own?'

'Well I ain't going out there; and if James has got any sense he ain't neither. Just be a good chap and when they nick you, don't tell them where we are eh?'

'I'm not going out until it gets dark,' said Baker.

'That's that then!' snapped Martin. 'I got to stay here too ain't I?'

'Unless you fancy a rope cravat, yes.'

'Until dark?'

'It's the only thing that makes sense. About the only thing that does. I wasn't thinking straight last night. We should have split up. I bet every copper in the area is looking for a group of men.'

'We could split up now.'

'It's too late. Any one of us on our own would stick out like a sore thumb round here, just from the way we're dressed.'

'Could pretend we're tramps.'

'You don't look like no tramp to me James. You look like a flash little city boy. No; we got to get out of here fast when we can, and for now there's safety in numbers.'

'So what now?'

'What now John? We sit. We wait. And I don't know about you but I'm fit for the knackers and need more kip.'

Try as they might, with daylight outside, and the possibility of rail workers coming to their hideout, none of them could sleep any more. It was not long before the cards came out and they whiled away the remaining hours of daylight with talk as passenger trains and goods wagons thundered past at frequent intervals. There was no walking the railway line while the sun was up. They did not know it, but fifty yards away, up the bank, was a road and along it passed Superintendent Sempill and his driver in the middle of the afternoon. They were unarmed; neither party knew how close they had come until some weeks later.

'I've been thinking,' said Rudge.

'Seems to me Anthony, that you do over much of that,' retorted Martin.

'That's as may be, but someone's got to, and frankly my old pal, it ain't you is it? At least not normally. Truth be told John, you are often a bit hasty.'

'Least I get things done.'

'You do. It is true, but often mate, you are inclined to be a bit like a bull in a china shop and get yourself into more trouble. I remember you getting yourself more slaps from the screws in Portland than you needed to simply because you could not stop yourself answering the bastards back.'

'They was out of order.'

'Yes. Maybe, but to save yourself a lot of pain all you had to do was keep your mouth shut, and a lot of the time my old China, you don't, on account of the fact that you act before you get your brain in gear. Now I suggest you shut up and listen.'

Martin opened his mouth to say something, thought better of it, then closed it again.

'Exactly!' said Rudge. 'Now then, the situation for us right now is pretty bad ain't it?'

'I should say so,' said Baker.

'I shot a copper. You beat another to death with a crowbar. John here, though he thinks we don't know, has reasons for not going back to London, and if he's caught, could end up being strung up. Am I right?'

Rudge looked Martin in the eye, but he said nothing, just glared. Sometimes Rudge was too sharp for his own good.

'The fact is,' continued Rudge, 'that this country is not safe for us, because if we stay, there is a very good chance of us getting topped before the next six months are out. Am I wrong?'

The other two did not answer, just looked at him glumly.

'There is one sensible answer to this,' said Rudge. 'We must get out of this country.'

'All of us?' said Martin in surprise. 'Not just me?'

'Why not John. We're mates. I've been to America before so it don't bother me. The three of us could do very well over there. Afresh start for all of us.'

'But what about Nellie?' asked James Baker. 'I'm not leaving Nellie.'

'I'm pretty sure that your Nellie would rather have you alive in America than dead on some gallows James. Our choices are a little limited right now. Perhaps you might have thought the situation through before smashing that copper's head in.'

'He might not be dead.'

'Do me a favour! You went berserk and done for him. You can send for Nellie once we get somewhere to live. Might only be a few weeks James. Come on; be sensible. She can sell up your stuff and come over quick enough. Once you're over there the rozzers can't get you and you can get yourself a nice little place with Nellie.'

'And live 'appily ever after,' growled Martin.

'You are a cynical bastard John, and you may scoff, but can you deny the truth of what I have said?'

'No,' admitted Martin.

'Then we all head for Liverpool. We have a contact from the Nabob who could get you onto a ship. In exchange for some of what I have in my pocket, he can get all three of us on, and off we go. Fair enough?'

'Alright by me,' said Martin. 'I'll be glad of the company.'

'James?'

Baker hesitated, his face working in indecision. Finally, 'Yes,' he said.

'Good!' said Rudge. 'That's settled. Now, whose deal is it?'

At four-thirty in the afternoon, the light was beginning to fail, and a train roared past. Martin stuck his head out of the door.

'It'll be dark in about ten minutes I should think. Shall we get going then?'

'Not yet,' said Rudge.

'Why not?'

'Going home time. Lots of farms stop when it gets dark. Just give them a little while longer to get home for their dinners and there'll be less people about. Remember; we are creatures of the night.'

Their muscles were still tired from the long walk the previous day, and they had no exercise during the day, so when they ventured out into the darkness, they felt stiffness in their legs and a little sore; as city men they were not used to the amount of exercise they had taken in such a short time. Nonetheless, they had no choice if they wanted to leave the area quickly and were soon into their stride as the weariness wore off. In all of their stomachs was a void and a gnawing feeling of emptiness, and an abnormal sort of heat to their heads, because they had eaten nothing now for something like twenty-four hours, and each mile they marched wore off more and more of their energy reserves.

At about six-twenty, in the dark, they met a law breaker. John Johnstone, a farmer, from Petteril Bank was walking north along the railway line, using it as a short cut. He could not see them properly but they were walking south in single file on the same side of the tracks as him and he brushed against two of them as they passed. They looked at him, but merely nodded and walked on, saying nothing; they should not have been there, but neither should he.

By just after 7.20 pm on the Thursday night, they approached the small rural station of Calthwaite and walked up onto the end of the platform. Bill Milburn, the porter, saw them coming and alerted John Hayes, the station master, to the presence of the men they had been asked to look out for. In the night air, they could hear the men having a hurried discussion.

'If all three of us go, it looks odd. I think you should go and ask John.'

'Me? I ain't going. You go. I'm happy to wait for a train.'

'There might not be one. James, you are a fairly well spoken sort of chap. You go and find out.'

'Alright; I'll go. Give me the money then. I'll ask that bloke there.'

James Jackson, a farm labourer, was surprised to be asked the train times, and knew nothing of wanted men.

'I'm sorry pal. I don't work here and I don't know. They'll be able to tell you ovver thyere.'

He indicated the station building.

James Baker then approached the station house and came into the ticket office.

'My friends and myself would like to buy tickets for the next train to Penrith. Can you tell me when it is please?'

John Hayes did not have to lie; if the men had left their hideout earlier then they could have got a train, but the last one that night had left at seven.

'I'm sorry sir, but there are no more passenger trains tonight.'

Baker looked disappointed and Hayes decided to be helpful.

'It's about seven and a half miles to Penrith from here sir. You might do it in a couple of hours on the road at a smart pace. It's straight down that way.'

'I see. Well that is what we shall have to do then unless there are any lodgings here. Thank you.'

'There are no lodgings round here sir.'

Baker nodded and returned to his companions with the bad news.

'It's worse than you think,' grunted Rudge.

'What do you mean?' said Baker.

'You just went and asked two blokes about a train. I didn't see that you had that poking out of your pocket.'

'What?'

Baker looked down his coat. Sticking out of his pocket was his jemmy. It had dried blood on it and a few hairs stuck in it.

'Oh.'

'Yes. Oh. Let's hope they didn't notice, but whatever else, it was bloody stupid James. You'll have to get rid of that pretty sharpish.'

'I don't want to; I've had this one a long time.'

'Ditch it James. It's enough to hang you, and us as well. Alright?'

Baker nodded, but he was not too happy about it. Rudge was right though; Jackson had noticed it.

Glumly, they set off down the road towards Penrith.

'I tell you Anthony, I got to eat something,' said John Martin plaintively. 'It's been too long. I'm bloody famished.'

'Pity this place ain't got a pub.'

'I'm wondering if that bloke was telling the truth,' mused Rudge.

'What do you mean Anthony?'

'I mean John, that if he's been warned to look out for a group of men, he might have put us off so that we did not catch a train. I think we should ask again at the next station.'

'Won't they say the same?'

'Not if we ask to see a timetable. Then we'll know for sure.'

'Where is the next station?'

'I haven't a clue. Makes no difference really. But I hope that the village has a pub, that's all.'

As soon as they were gone, John Hayes was on the telegraph informing Mr Gornall at Plumpton, the next station down, that three suspicious looking men were on their way. He repeated the message to Penrith Station from where it was passed on to the police. Superintendent Fowler now knew definitely that the men were coming down the road from the north and set up an ambush for them on the road they must come down, at Raiselands, just north of Penrith. His quarry marched inexorably towards him; the trap was closing and the three men would soon be in the net.

15

The Packhorse

The station was dimly lit in the cold night air, and a frost was forming fast in the fields surrounding it. Down the platforms dim oil lamps provided illumination in a soft yellow gleam, especially by the signs that read "Plumpton". Inside the station, paraffin lamps gave a brighter light, the smell drifting out of the half open door and across the area outside. A soft tick-tock came from the clock in the small waiting room, and William Gornall, sitting in the ticket office, was thinking that excursion trains were a nuisance, because otherwise he would have closed up and taken it easy for the night. There was a special due later and he had to be there to see it off.

A few minutes before, a telegram had come down the line to him from Calthwaite asking him to inform PC Byrnes that three suspicious looking men had been asking about trains south. Seeing the urgency of it, he buttonholed a lad who hung around the station to look at trains, and gave him the message in an envelope.

'Now young Bill, you get that to Joe Byrnes as fast as you can; he'll want to see that quick.'

Master Bill Lowthian took to his heels, but not along the road. There was a footpath across the fields that he thought a quicker route than the road, even in the pitch black and he arrived at the police house a few scant minutes later.

A few minutes after Bill had set off on his errand, Gornall was startled when a man appeared at his window; it was about fifteen minutes before eight o'clock.

'Excuse me mate; can I buy a ticket for the next train south please?'

'I can sell you a ticket sir, but there are no more trains tonight. The next one is at just after seven in the morning. There is an excursion train due later between eleven and twelve; you could probably get on that.'

'Oh I see. May I buy a timetable then please?'

'I have none for sale here sir, but you can borrow mine to look at.'

James Baker took the timetable, looked it over, and then handed it back.

'Thank you. Can you tell me if there is an inn or pub in this village?'

'There is sir. If you go down the lane and under the bridge on the left, keep going just about half a mile and you'll come to it; the Packhorse Inn.'

'I may ask about accommodation then, but might be back later for the excursion.'

Just outside the station was a gate leading to a goods yard, and there waited Rudge and Martin.

'There is no regular train, but there is a pub just up the road. And there's an excursion train later, after eleven, which we could get.'

'Yeah,' growled Martin. 'There was some geezer passed us a few minutes ago and we asked him; just up the road.'

'That at least is some sort of silver lining,' said Rudge. 'We have sufficient to get some food, some drink and have a bit of a warm.'

'What then?'

'What then James? I am not inclined to hang around here because I have no doubt that our presence will be noted. It is still better for us that we get the hell out of here as quick as we can. I say, food, drink to numb our feet, and then we'll catch that excursion special.'

'Funny thing really,' ventured Baker.

'What is?' asked Rudge.

'The excursion. It's probably one of the special trains from Netherby Coursing. Full of sportsmen. We'll blend right in.'

'Oh now that is an excellent thought!' exclaimed Rudge. 'I love it! Some grub, some rum, and then home free on a train load of blokes dressed like us.'

'Well come on then!' shouted Martin. 'What the hell are we waiting for?'

As the three fugitives set off down the road in a high optimistic mood towards Plumpton village, William Gornall was tapping furiously at his telegraph key informing Penrith Station that three suspicious looking men were in the village; message to be relayed to Inspector Fowler. There was delay, for Fowler was not at the station, but waiting in ambush on the road north of the town.

Joe Byrnes was relaxing at home, and holding his new baby in his arms when the knock came on the door. It was his wife who opened it and saw the lad Bill Lowthian there with an envelope.

'Message for the constable, Missis.'

'Come in then Bill and we'll see what it is.'

Byrnes read the note from William Gornall, then passed his wife the baby.

'I have to go out Nell. There's been a suspicious looking man seen at the station.'

'It's dark and cold Joe. Do you have to go? Everyone's on the alert about this shooting business and people have been reporting suspicious characters all over the place. It's probably nothing.'

Byrnes laughed, 'Now then my Lady, you're a policeman's daughter and wife to another. You know better than that.'

'You have to go.'

'I have to go. We are always on duty.'

'You'll be careful Joe. I know you and I know that you have no fear. You'll not do anything foolish will you?'

'I'll be careful. It would be foolish to tackle three armed men on my own so I will not do it you may be sure. If Gornall has telegraphed to Penrith, then there might be some officers on the 8.10 to Carlisle. Now give me a kiss my girl; duty calls.'

He had not taken his uniform off, but put on a comfortable slouch hat against the cold, dragged on a good warm dark coat and went out with Bill Lowthian.

'Right lead on Billy boy. Which way do you favour?'

'Across the fields.'

'Then across the fields it is; forward; march!'

Rudge, Martin and Baker knew nothing of shortcuts across fields, but marched on towards the village along the road in very high spirits. Coming towards them was Miss Fanny Lowthian. It being pitch black so that you could hardly see five yards in front of you, all the three men saw was the outline of a young woman. As they passed her, Rudge lifted his hat, 'It's a very fine night Miss.'

'It is indeed,' replied Fanny, and passed on her way.

It was just after eight-twenty when Robert Nicholson and Thomas Simpson were standing outside the vicarage and having a good old crack, when three men marched briskly out of the darkness.

'Excuse me mate. Can you tell us how far we are from the pub?'

'Yes; it's about one hundred yards up there.'

'Thanks pal.'

Just outside the Packhorse Inn, Rudge stopped.

'I don't think we should all go in.'

'Why not?' asked Baker.

'Firstly, the rozzers will be looking for a group of men. Not two men; three or four men. If we go in there we'll attract attention.'

'Alright,' said Baker. 'What's second?'

'I think one of us should stay out here and keep watch.'

'What for,' grunted Martin.

'All these villages have a copper. If he comes we'd be trapped in the pub. If one of us is outside, we'd have some warning.'

'You're over thinking again Anthony,' returned Martin.

'Maybe,' replied Rudge. 'You got any dosh?'

'No. You've got it all.'

'That's right pal. And we need the man outside to have a gun. James ain't got one; I'm going in. That means you stay out here.'

'What?'

Martin was too late; Baker and Rudge entered the Packhorse, Rudge calling back over his shoulder, 'Don't worry pal; I'll see you right.'

Rudge walked into the Packhorse and up to the bar where stood the landlady, Mrs Ann Griffiths.

There were perhaps six men in the bar apart from thirteen year old Margaret Murray who had popped in to chat to Mrs Griffiths, her aunt.

'Two gills of beer please, and have you got any food?'

Mrs Griffiths was too polite to raise an eyebrow at Rudge ordering two quarter pints; these men must really be short of cash.

'We have no cooked food at this time gentlemen, but I could do you some bread and cheese.'

'And do you have a bottle of rum?'

'Not as such sir, but I do have a bottle you can have, and we can draw you some rum from a cask.'

Two gills of beer were brought by Margaret Murray, and the landlady bustled into the back to put the rum into a bottle. Rudge quickly went to the door with a beer.

'Get that down you quick.'

'Bloody beer!' said Martin, grabbing at the glass and draining it at one go. 'Didn't touch the sides. Any grub?'

'Coming up.'

Rudge went back to the bar just before Mrs Griffiths returned with a large bottle of rum.

'There you are sir; oh that was quick. You must have been thirsty.'

'I am,' replied Rudge. 'We've come a long way; been riding all day. Two more please.'

'I'll get it now then. There's the bread and cheese.'

The beer was strong. If they had been remotely interested in such details, it was nearly eight per cent ABV but since they were not brewers, such a thing did not occur to them. Although they did not have much, it was heady stuff and that is what they wanted. On their empty stomachs it went straight to their heads and began the process of removing rational thought from their minds. The cheese was a large wedge and had been cut from a roll that had been coated in wax. The outer rind had been stamped with the name of the maker; it made no difference to the taste. They ate some bread and cheese, but not much. Rudge drew a large handkerchief from his pocket and spread it out, putting the bread and cheese into it.

'There's a train later; a special, and we do not want to miss it. If you don't mind Missis, we shall take this with us.'

'I don't mind sir. That'll be three shillings please.'

PC Joseph Byrnes had reached the station across the fields and went into the ticket office to see William Gornall.

'Where are these three men that you saw?'

'They left a few minutes ago. I think they were heading for the Packhorse.'

'The Packhorse you say? Well I think I might go and have a drink and keep an eye on them.'

'You're not going to tackle them are you?'

'Not at all. There are strict orders that we must not. I will do nothing to provoke them, but it will do no harm at all to keep an eye on them. You sent word down the line?'

'I did. I asked Penrith to pass the message on to Superintendent Fowler.'

'He's a man of action that one. I would think there will be some men coming on the next train. When is it?'

'Just a few minutes. 8.12 it will be here.'

'If any arrive, then send them up to the Packhorse will you.'

'I'm not sure you should do this Joe.'

'It will do no harm to go and have a drink now will it? Sure, I will not be provoking them at all, especially with them carrying guns.'

'Shall I come with you sir?'

'No need Billy; but your brother Thomas is a good man in a corner. I'd be obliged if you'd step over to his house and ask him to come up to the pub. If it comes to blows he's a fine chap to have on your side.'

'If it comes to blows!'

'Stop worrying William,' said PC Byrnes. 'I will not even speak to them. You know well that Mrs Griffiths puts a glass of rum on the shelf for me every night. If I don't go, I'll be missed!'

So saying, Joseph Byrnes headed down the dark lane and turned up towards the village. Bill Lowthian sped off to his brother's house to ask Thomas to go to the Packhorse to meet PC Byrnes, but Thomas was not in. Byrnes walked at a steady pace. In the gloom of the lane he met Thomas Simpson.

'Good evening Thomas. I don't suppose you have seen three strangers have you?'

'I have. They asked the way to the Packhorse. I've just come from there myself and they were in the bar.'

'Thank you; I'll go and have a look at them.'

Before too long Byrnes was outside the vicarage; he would be passing his own house soon, and the pub lay just beyond.

Rudge and Baker left the Packhorse; Martin was standing outside.

'All quiet out here. You got anything for me to eat? I'm bloody starving.'

'We have food John but we'll eat it at the station.'

'What's wrong with eating it here?'

'It struck me that there's not many in the pub but there might be later. Blokes might be at home having their dinner and come for a pint after. We don't need that sort of crowd.'

'Alright, fair enough, but that special's not due till between eleven and twelve.'

'Did I imagine it?' asked Rudge, 'but was there not a nice little waiting room there with a nice little fire?'

'There was,' said Baker, 'but won't that station master get suspicious? He might have been warned to look out for us.'

'Did he look that way?' asked Rudge. 'Did he seem over bright to you? He did not strike me as the sharpest pencil. Anyway, given the choice of being stared at by a rural station master for a couple of hours, and a pub full of blokes for the same time, our odds are better with one bloke I think.'

'Fair enough,' said Martin. 'But have you got any booze?'

'I have John. Have a swig of this.'

Martin took a long pull at the bottle, then handed it back wiping his mouth.

'By God that's the good stuff.'

'So it is. Certainly keeps the cold out,' replied Rudge, also taking a long swig then passing it to Baker.

In the cold, alcohol on an empty stomach has a very quick effect; senses heightened and spirits high, the three men set off down the road towards the station. After a couple of minutes brisk walking, they were outside the vicarage when they saw the figure of a well built and tall man in a dark coat coming towards them.

Joseph Byrnes had walked briskly across the fields to the station. Then he had walked at a lively pace from the station to the village. His uniform tunic and trousers were made of good thick wool, and with a thick wool coat on the top, he had become hot. Unsurprisingly he opened the front of his coat to cool down a bit. As he approached the three figures that he now saw coming towards him on the dark road, all they could see was a man in a coat wearing a slouch hat, but down his front was the faint metallic gleam of uniform buttons. For a moment his hat threw them because it was his comfortable slouch hat, his helmet being at his house, and the alcohol in their bloodstreams made it hard for them to think clearly. It also removed their inhibitions.

'Are you a copper?' called out one of them.

Byrnes, taken aback because he had not seen the three approach in the pitch black until they were almost on him replied.

'I am a policeman.'

The Irish voice rang proudly in the night air, for Byrnes spoke for law.

There was no thought and no time for him to react; the animal instincts took over. Two of the men launched themselves forward before Byrnes had even time to think about what was happening. The policeman found himself gripped hard, each arm held by a man who was not disposed to be gentle. The impetus of their rush drove him back against a field wall, and at this point, realising that he was being attacked, he began to fight back. He could not move either arm, so attempted to kick out at his assailants, but it only made them grip him harder with all their strength; he could feel their fingers digging into him like pincers.

'Hold the bastard; I'm just coming,' said the third man loudly, pulling a pistol from his pocket. 'Hold him steady.'

He took two paces forward, aiming his pistol carefully so as not to wound his companions, and fired. The bullet entered Joseph Byrnes's left eye and came out above his left ear.

The constable immediately slumped, his head pouring blood, a dead weight between the men who had his arms; now they had difficulty holding him up. It had all happened in seconds.

'He's done for,' gasped Rudge. 'We got to get him off the road so he's not seen.'

Baker's face was a study in astonishment.

'Over the wall?'

'Yes John. Give me a hand.'

Wheezing with the effort, the three men picked Byrnes up and got his body onto the top of the wall. Then they rolled him into the field.

'What now Anthony?' asked Baker.

'What now? We get the fuck out of here! That's what's now!'

'Are we still going to the station?'

Rudge looked at him wildly, but his expression could not be seen in the darkness.

'That station just down there? Where we sit and wait for the next two and a half hours with a dead copper just over the wall? You not think he'll be missed? Eh?'

'We have to go.'

'Damn right we have to go. There's something else. Your hands all sticky?'

Baker and Martin had not given any attention to this, and realised that they both had sticky hands.

'Head wounds bleed,' said Rudge. 'We are covered in the stuff; our clothes as well. Not only have we got to get away; we cannot be seen.'

'Back down the railway?'

'Yes John. Down the railway to Penrith. Jump a goods train and get the hell out of this place.'

Inside the vicarage Elizabeth Irving, housekeeper for the vicar Mr Kennedy, heard a shot at exactly 8.34 by the kitchen clock, as did her daughter Margaret. Across the frosty fields Robert Lunson heard the shot at his signal box at Broclemoor. Although unusual none of them thought to investigate; shots were not unheard of in an area with a population containing many farmers and gamekeepers.

Eleanor Byrnes thought her husband was out late on duty and, being engaged with four children, did not hear a shot. Joe was often out late; he would be back when his duty was done for the day.

Down at the railway line three murderers walked as fast as they could, their hands still wet with the blood of their victim. To get away as quickly as possible was almost the uppermost thing in their minds, but there was one need that overcame even that.

'For God's sake Anthony, give me some bloody food,' snarled John Martin.

'Eat as we walk?'

'Just eat. Yes; as we walk.'

Rudge felt in his pocket and pulled out the handkerchief that contained their bread and cheese.

'Fuck!'

'What's up?' gasped Baker as he marched as fast as he could to keep up with the other two.

'He bled into my pocket.'

'Onto the food?'

'Yes.'

'I don't care,' shouted Martin. 'Give me some bloody food now!'

For a split second, the hardened Rudge stared aghast, wondering if Martin realised what he had said, then wordlessly he handed Martin some bread and cheese, covered in the blood of the man they had shot. Martin didn't even baulk but crammed chunks of it into his mouth and chewed.

'How is it?' asked James Baker.

'It's food.' snapped Martin. 'Apart from that I don't give a shit.'

'I don't either. Give me some food Anthony.'

Rudge handed over some more of the contents of his handkerchief to Baker who rubbed it on the sleeve of his coat to try to get the blood off. Did Rudge hesitate a moment? He dipped his hand back into the food, picked up a chunk of bread, peered at it and then and bit into it.

'Don't say a word,' snarled Martin. 'Not a fucking word.'

Chewing their unholy meal the three men, new energy in their limbs, marched on down the railway tracks heading to Penrith. When they were done eating they washed the taste away with rum.

16

Flight

Mr Benjamin Scott, Mayor of Carlisle, was not a happy man that evening.

'There is great consternation in the town Mr Dunne, and it's not to be wondered at. You tell me that there are four desperadoes loose in Carlisle, running round with loaded guns. I hope you shall soon have them safely under lock and key!'

'I am doing my best Mr Scott, but we are not used to having to deal with events on such a scale as this in Cumberland.'

'I'm sure you are right, but you must have every man available to search for them. Every corner must be examined. Feelings in the community are running very high Mr Dunne.'

'I assure you sir that I have every available officer out looking for them.'

'How many is that?'

Dunne hesitated. 'All told, about thirty men. That includes officers who have volunteered to do extra duty.'

'That's not many! Have you asked Mr MacKay for some city men?'

'That includes the city men.'

'Well you must fetch some more in from elsewhere in the county Chief Constable. I'm surprised you have not done so already.'

'As a matter of fact Mr Scott, I have done just that. I think we might be able to get another ten men.'

'Ten? I was thinking a few more than that! Can't you bring in some more from elsewhere?'

'From the Cumberland and Westmorland Force? I fear not. I just do not see how it can be done.'

'Why not? You are the Chief Constable after all. Just order them in and they will come.'

'It's not quite as simple as that. It's a question of numbers.'

'Quite so. We need more policemen to look for these villains so fetch them in from other spots like Whitehaven, Penrith or Workington.'

'That's where I have been combing men from Mr Scott, but if I take more then I think it will have a bad effect over the two counties.'

'How do you mean?'

'I mean, that including myself, I have a total of two hundred and twelve officers of all ranks at my disposal and they are spread very thin.'

'But that's excellent! Bring them in to search for these swine.'

'You misunderstand me. That number is the entire force for Cumberland, and Westmorland; the entirety of the roll. If I bring them in as you say, then which areas shall I leave without policemen? Consider that at any particular time, since a man cannot be on duty for twenty-four hours, half those men are off duty; they have to eat, sleep, see their families and so on.'

'Which means that at any one time you have about one hundred and six men on duty in the whole of the two counties?'

'Exactly so. And imagine Whitehaven, or Workington, or Maryport without sufficient police on duty on Friday or Saturday night.'

The mayor looked nonplussed and blew out his cheeks.

'I can see that it is quite a problem. Keeping a balance between catching these men and policing across two large counties must be quite difficult. Can you not bring in men from other forces like Northumberland?'

'I imagine that the Chief Constable of Northumberland would be responsive to such a request, but it is, in the end, a question of funds. They would have to be paid for.'

'And your budget does not stretch to that?'

'Not really, but I have no authorisation to send money in that direction. I'd have to apply to the council.'

'And that takes time. Alright Mr Dunne, I see your problem. I shall tell people that you are doing all that you can with the resources that you have.'

'You might mention an increase in the budget too Mr Scott.'

'Aye; I'll do that, but things like this do not happen all that often. I wouldn't get your hopes up; they are very parsimonious with ratepayers' money.'

'I would not worry too much. We will get them. Carlisle is on the alert, though they may have slipped past us, and if they are heading south, Mr Fowler has Penrith looking out for them. Northumberland police have been warned.'

'You have eyes everywhere Mr Dunne.'

'I like to think so Mr Scott. It's only a matter of time. We have missed them on several occasions, almost by accident.'

'Oh really?'

'Yes. The men I have at Longtown, including PC Tomer, who I have a high opinion of, were waiting for them after the burglary, but they slipped past him. What happened at Kingstown you know about, but when Superintendent Sempill was returning back to Carlisle as fast as he could, I think he must have crossed the road bridge as they were crossing the railway bridge. He put men on watch at the station you know.'

'But they bypassed that.'

'Yes. Then there was poor PC Fortune. If only we had put more men on the railway lines; we did search for them but they had gone. They escaped by the skin of their teeth to heaven knows where.'

'Perhaps it's a good job. More men might have been shot.'

'Two can play at that game now. I have armed men patrolling the streets and the marshalling yards.'

'They won't get away will they?'

'No. They won't get away.'

Far to the south and about ten o'clock at night, three figures approached Penrith down the railway line. They had walked in silence from Plumpton, for once again, they were very tired, but it was their lack of noise that stood them in good stead when it came to the police ambush. Superintendent Fowler and his band of determined men were just under three hundred yards away at Raiselands Farm, positioned to watch where two roads from the north came together. Fowler only had enough men for one ambush, but had set officers to watch the other ways into town. So it was that Police Constable Patterson, cold and fed up with watching the line from the north for several hours, felt a thrill pass through his heart as he saw three figures approaching in the dark. Obedient to his instructions, he crouched down behind the parapet and waited as the men's footsteps crunched on the track bed below him, then let them walk away towards the town. Then, stealthily at first, and then with increasing speed, he ran as fast as he could go, about a quarter of a mile towards where Fowler was waiting.

The superintendent was not in a good mood, waving a piece of paper he had just received from the police station.

'Why the hell was this not given to me before? It was sent from Plumpton just after eight. It is now just after ten. Two hours for me to be informed that our suspects have been seen in Plumpton!'

'I don't think anyone knew it was urgent sir. It was delivered in an envelope.'

'I can see that we shall have to have a good look at our procedures tomorrow morning,' said Fowler, waving the telegram at the unfortunate constable. 'But you are only the messenger so I won't shoot you.'

'Thank you sir.'

'Sergeant Bremner; I want five men now; I am going to Plumpton. The rest stay here with you and keep watch. Our suspects are very near.'

It was then that Patterson arrived with the news that three men had passed along the railway line and must by now be at Penrith Station.

'Good God! They have got past us. Quickly now; everyone to the station; stay together; no man is to face them alone.'

Most of Penrith's police force now pounded along the road heading back into town.

In the marshalling yard of Penrith was a goods train, evidently about to depart.

'That'll do us,' breathed Rudge. 'Get on there and we will be miles from here by morning.'

'What then?' whispered Baker.

'We ditch these coats for a start. We can't do it now or we'll freeze to death, but when the sun comes up, shivers or no shivers, these coats go.'

'And then?' asked Martin. 'We are completely skint.'

'No we ain't you mug. Not with what I got in my pocket. All we have to do is get to Liverpool. There's a bloke there who will fence this lot and we'll be in funds again. I tell you mates, we'll be out of this yet.'

Christopher Gaddes had never regretted leaving the employ of Sir James Graham at Netherby Hall. Life as a second coachman had been quiet and uneventful, but at twenty-six years old, Gaddes wanted something a little more varied. Employment as a railway guard offered more money, travel and a greater diet of experience. It was pure coincidence that he happened to be the guard this night, on a goods train about to leave Penrith, heading for Lancaster. Railway staff were always well up-to-date on news and what was going on in the country. This was not only because of the speed of the trains, but also because of the telegraph which sent messages in morse up and down the length and breadth of the land. Gaddes knew of the Netherby burglary, and he knew of the shootings at Kingstown the previous day, as well as the bludgeoning of poor PC Fortune. The indignation among rail staff mirrored that in the country at large; some dangerous villains were on the loose and had to be apprehended. Gaddes of course, felt that he had a personal stake in the matter as he liked his old employer and did not appreciate the violation of his home and Lady Hermione's jewels. Thus he also knew that three or four men were on the run, and railway staff had been asked to keep an eye open for them.

As the train began its clanking progress out of the dark yard, heading south, Gaddes walked back along the track beside the slowly moving wagons, then, as his guard's van approached him, he swung himself up onto the platform at the back, holding onto the handrail, a practiced move that he had done many times before. As he did so, he thought he saw movement out of the corner of his left eye, and when he had steadied himself he turned to look in that direction. Three men had run out from among the wagons in the goods yard and as he watched, they sprinted over to his train. Each of them hauled himself up and dropped down into the second wagon down from him. He took his bullseye lantern and shone it at them;

they knew he had seen them. He said nothing; neither did they. They ducked down into the wagon, and hid under the tarpaulin covering it. Gaddes knew immediately that they had to be the men the police wanted to apprehend.

Hurriedly he wrote a note, and as his van passed Penrith South signal box he threw the note out towards the platform of the box and shouted. He was not heard and the note; as he saw, fell short. Undeterred, he wrote another note, and waited his chance.

That he was worried was undeniable. There were three wanted men on his train. If they conferred and thought that he was a problem, then they might come back and attack him. It could be very bad for him, especially as they had guns. Gaddes was no coward though, even though his pulse was raised and he had a sweat; it would have been very easy for him to have just pretended he had seen nothing, but this was not in him; he had to do what was right.

In the wagon, there was little conversation about any dilemma.

'He saw us.'

'Yes John,' said Rudge, 'He saw us.'

'Ain't you worried he might give us up?'

'What for? All he saw was three geezers hitching a ride on his train. He won't mind; he'll have seen it many times before now.' Rudge now remembered something. 'Oh yes; James, give me your jemmy please, and that little bag you think I don't know about.'

'What for?'

'Never mind; just give me it like a good lad eh?'

Reluctantly Baker handed over his favourite tool together with a small alpaca bag that he had taken from Lady Graham's room.

'That's for Nellie,' he said.

'Excellent!' said Rudge, popping his head out of the wagon. They were just passing a line of stationary wagons and he threw the jemmy and bag into one of them.

'Oi! That's mine! Why did'ye do that?'

'Don't cry James. I'll get you another when we are safely away. Evidence that was. Now it's gone, along with a very identifiable bag. Get caught with that, and we were done for.'

'Get caught with the jewels and it's the same.'

'I can always ditch them as well, if need be.'

'Did the guard see you do that?'

'I don't think so John.'

'He's supposed to stop us being here ain't he? He's a guard.'

'I'm sure some of them have seen hard times John. He won't mind a few poor chaps down on their luck having a free ride home.'

'I hope you're right.'

'Of course I'm right. Anyway there's little option now is there. Now let's get some kip.'

Under the tarpaulin the cold was not so bad, and the three men lay close together for warmth. It was not too long before they were fast asleep, the click of the wheels on the rails ticking the miles away hypnotically.

South of Penrith is Shap, a long slow upwards climb to a summit which required two engines for passenger trains or loaded goods trains. Gaddes was guard on an unloaded train, so it was not double headed; progress up Shap was thus slow. As the long line of empty goods wagons was drawn at walking pace up towards the summit, Gaddes saw, not too far ahead, a light goods train waiting on a loop, that he knew to be northbound from Liverpool. As his train chuffed its way slowly upwards, Gaddes shouted and threw his note onto the footplate of the Liverpool engine. The driver picked it up and read it immediately. As Gaddes drew away heading south, the driver leaned out and gave him the thumbs up. His message was understood. Gaddes's next stop would be at Tebay, eighteen miles to the south, and the other side of Shap; but a warning would go ahead.

Back at Penrith Superintendent Fowler had divided his force into two groups, a faster group being sent panting to the south of the marshalling yards; there they turned and headed north towards Fowler leading his party south. The police stormed the marshalling yard, looking everywhere, joined by railway staff, enthusiastic to catch the villains.

'Have any trains left for the south lately?'

'One has,' replied Mr Scott, the Penrith station master, 'But it is very unlikely that they got it from what you say. It left just after ten. They'd have had to have been greased lightning to get it that quick.'

'That's as may be,' said Fowler, 'but I fear they have escaped us. We shall continue our search of the yard and the town but you'll oblige me by telegraphing all stations south to be on the lookout.'

Fowler's iron trap had closed, but the quarry it was meant to catch had escaped by the skin of its teeth.

Just after nine-twenty that evening in Plumpton, Bill Lowthian and a couple of friends had passed the vicarage. In the darkness they heard a low noise that sounded like growling coming from a field opposite the vicarage. They thought it was a dog, and passed on without thinking about it any further.

Thomas Lowthian had spent a few hours in the Packhorse and had seen the strangers come and go; they were only in the pub for five minutes. Just after ten o'clock he left the pub to go home and walked down the lane towards the cottage where he lived, near the station. Just as he passed the vicarage he heard a peculiar noise coming from over the wall of the field opposite; it was a low moaning such as might be made by an animal. Knowing that there were no beasts supposed to be in that field currently, he went to look over the wall, but in the pitch blackness, could see nothing. As the field was rented out to Mr Griffiths, landlord of the Packhorse, he decided to return to the pub, and walked up to the bar.

'Back already Tom? Not had enough for tonight then?' laughed the landlord when Lowthian reentered the pub. William Griffiths's expression changed when he saw that Tom Lowthian had a puzzled look on his face.

'Have you got any cattle in that field opposite the vicarage Bill?'

'Nothing at all,' replied Griffiths. 'I had a few sheep in there but they've cut the grass so close I moved them to another place to let it grow.'

'Well there's something in there now, and it's making a very strange noise.'

'There shouldn't be! What sort of noise?'

'A sort of moaning noise.'

'In my field?'

'What sort of moaning noise?' asked James Tinkler, another customer.

'Like I said; a low moaning like an animal that's been hurt.'

'Maybe that's it,' interjected James Nicholson, setting his pint down. 'If there's a hurt animal we should probably go and look at it.'

'Too right!' said Mr Griffiths. 'And I shall ask it what it's doing in my field!'

That raised a laugh; Mr Griffiths found a lanthorn and the four of them set out down the lane.

In the dim light of the lanthorn and just outside the vicarage, they found a pool of something dark and wet on the road. As they looked at it, a low moan came from over the wall opposite. Hurrying over to the wall they peered down to where they could see PC Joseph Byrnes lying twisted over a scattering of stones that he had fallen onto after they had been dislodged from the wall. His head was a mass of blood and from him came, every now and then a low moaning sound quite unlike anything they had ever heard before.

'Oh my God! We must get him from here as soon as we can.' said Mr Griffiths taking the lead. 'To the Packhorse with him.'

As tenderly as they could the four men lifted the stricken constable over the wall and carried him to the pub where they laid him onto a table.

'We need a doctor at once,' snapped out Mr Griffiths, and one was sent for. Mrs Griffiths was despatched to the police house to break the news to Mrs Byrnes, who was soon at her husband's side.

The doctor who was sent for did not arrive at the Packhorse until twenty-five to one on the Friday morning, and in the event he was not a doctor. He was William Matthews, an articled student with Dr Montgomery of Penrith, but even had the doctor been present, there was nothing he could have done. Matthews was beside PC Byrnes for fifteen minutes, cleaning up his wounds, when at ten minutes to one the constable died without regaining consciousness. The men who had killed him were now murderers on the run.

17

Tebay

The London and North Western Railway met the North Eastern Railway at Tebay, which made it a very important junction. It also lay below Shap, and sixteen engines were based there permanently in the sheds, which also contained engineering facilities and a depot with all kinds of railway equipment such as snowploughs, and a repair shop. What had once been a tiny hamlet had grown into a settlement of over a thousand people, and the area round the station and marshalling yards employed about one hundred and seventy men. When Christopher Gaddes arrived there at eleven-thirty on Thursday night, he hoped and expected to find a reception party waiting for him, but to his chagrin, there was nobody. There was also no sign from the men stowed away in the wagon two down from the guards van. Quickly he made his way down the train and advised the driver and the footplate man of what was going on; then he went to the station office where he found that the warning he had sent was just being written down. Since he had now arrived in person, it was irrelevant, and he set himself the task of gathering men.

Over the next few minutes he was joined by drivers, yardsmen, wagon greasers, porters, and railway servants of all kinds, who armed themselves, mostly with sprags.

Now a sprag is a prop of metal or heavy wood that is used to wedge between the wheels of a wagon to stop it from rolling; as such it is a very formidable club. The men holding them were angry because the place had been buzzing with the news of shootings near Carlisle all day; such things did not happen in Cumberland and Westmorland. That the villains were escaping justice by using the railway struck each man almost as a personal insult. Gaddes had some difficulty in keeping them quiet; he could not see how many of them there were in the dark but he thought there were at least twenty men.

'Quiet please. We don't want to warn them that we are coming do we?'

'True enough,' said George Beattie, one of the yard foremen. 'We must keep the noise down. Which wagon are they in though?'

'I believe that they are in the wagon second down from my van, unless they have shifted.'

'How can we find out?' asked Beattie.

'If I jump into a few wagons, like I am looking for something, they might not be alarmed. My only worry is that they see you and run away.'

'Right chaps. Quiet as mice alright?' snapped Beattie.

In the darkness beyond the station lights, it was difficult to see, but the gang of men slowly moved, many on tiptoe, and in absolute silence, back along the train towards the guard's van. Gaddes went into several wagons, in a leisurely fashion, making sure that he could be seen by anyone at the back, and that he was not looking for anything in particular. As it was, they saw nothing, and Gaddes miscounted the wagons, and eventually sprang into the one where Rudge, Martin and Baker lay fast asleep under the tarpaulin. He landed right on the slumbering Rudge and all hell broke loose, along with a fair share of panic.

Taken completely aback, Gaddes scrambled out of the wagon as fast as he could. John Martin jumped to his feet and shouted, 'Get back or I'll put a bullet through your fucking brain!'

Then he jumped out of the wagon as Rudge and Baker jumped out of the other side. Martin faced George Beattie and his expression was full of manic fury as he grabbed at his coat, seeking to pull something from an inside pocket. He did not have time. Beattie felled him to the ground with one blow from a sprag three inches thick, where he lay groping at his coat, still trying to pull something out.

He shouted at Beattie, 'What do you mean? I am one of the men in search of the robbers.'

Then he got up. Beattie was having none of it and hit him again. William Parker, an engine driver, now threw himself onto Martin, pressing him back onto the ground and punching him; Beattie joined him and the two men went for his pockets. Beattie pulled out a revolver, which Martin had been groping for, whilst Parker found a short length of rope in another pocket. This was very handy, for they twisted Martin's hands behind his back and tied him up with his own rope.

Rudge was being chased by a yelling mob, and he headed under a bridge which took the railway over the River Lune; one of the arches was dry. Temporarily and in the shadow of the bridge, he dove a hand into his pocket and pulled out a leather tobacco pouch which he threw into darkness over the river, not seeing where it fell; he did not have time to make sure it was closed as a railwayman called Mason was in hot pursuit. Emerging onto the other side of the bridge he ran straight into Robert Willis, foreman of the locomotive shed. Rudge's hand darted towards his pocket, but his coat was buttoned up and Willis was not a man to waste time. He hit Rudge very very hard with an iron jack bar and knocked him to the floor. Within seconds, Willis and his brother, along with Mr Brunskill, had him and frogmarched him up onto Tebay Station where they tied him to a pillar. William Parker came up and asked, 'Have you got his revolver?' When they searched him, they found a large calibre pistol.

Baker had got away.

The railwaymen searched high and low for him but there was no sign anywhere, and eventually they gave up looking. They had two captives tied to pillars in the station, and Rudge and Martin dared say nothing for the men's blood was up and they feared the consequences. Telegrams were sent to the police, and further south to watch out for the third man who had escaped. The local constable, PC Branford was sent for and arrived at the station at 12.10 am. From the moment they had been captured, Rudge and Martin had said not a word.

James Baker was a frightened man. He could not stay in the area because when daylight came there would be people looking for him; he had to escape, and there was only one way for him to do this quickly. He had run away very fast from Tebay station, heading for Shap and the railwaymen had not been fast enough to catch him. When he saw that the pursuit had given up, he took to the fields and circled back towards the railway. He arrived back at the tracks about two hundred and fifty yards south of the station; the night was as black as his hat. At midnight, Thomas Matley, the driver of a goods train leaving Tebay and heading south for Lancaster, was coasting his engine out of the yard and slowly gathering speed. He liked driving in the dark for, as he often said, he had excellent night vision; Baker did not. If he had, then he would have concealed himself better. Matley saw the figure of a man crouching down beside the railway tracks in the darkness. Looking back, straining to see, he saw the man leap onto the fourth wagon along and climb into it. This was quite an athletic feat, for the only footholds were the axle boxes.

Matley turned to his fireman who was sweating and shovelling coal into the firebox, 'Looks like we have a passenger Ted.'

'You reckon it's one of them blokes the police were after?'

'More than just likely. Our lads got two of them and it looks like we've got the third.'

'What do you want to do?'

'Nowt until we reach Oxenholme. Then you nip off to the office and see if there's any police about and get some help.'

Baker sweated, and not only with effort. He knew that he would be hunted and the only possibility for him to escape would be to get to a large centre of population where he could melt into the background crowds and disappear. Every train would be searched, and probably at every station. This meant that he would have to get off the train at every halt, and then get back onto it unseen when it left. He dared not go to sleep. One slip as he leaped onto the train could put him under the wheels and he would have to do it repeatedly.

When the goods train reached Oxenholme Station, Thomas Matley sent his fireman to the office asking if there were any policemen about. Oxenholme being an important junction, it had an unusual and very new device installed, called a telephone with a link to Kendal police station. Arrangements were made to hold the goods train for a while in a siding; it was not long before two constables and a sergeant arrived in a fast gig from Kendal and together with some railway staff the train was searched. Nothing was found, and after a while the goods train left, heading for Lancaster, two hours to the south.

The night express from Carlisle to London had left the Citadel Station at 12.05 am, and Henry Cooper, the guard, was pleased to find that it was running on time, approaching Lancaster at 2.24 am exactly. He liked precision, was a stickler for detail, and in many ways was the ideal man to be a guard, because the little things were important to him. Like all railway servants he knew about the three or four men that the police wanted to question. He was also a man of great moral courage and resolve. The express drew into Lancaster station and as it stopped, Cooper stepped off his van to look down the platform, watching for people getting on and off, and, eventually, the green flag signalling the train to depart. He had been standing for about a minute when a man approached him on his right hand side. This was a surprise to Cooper, because he was standing by the last carriage, and the man had appeared, apparently from the direction of the goods yard.

'Excuse me please. Is this the train for Crewe way?'

'Crewe way? Where do you want to go to?'

'Liverpool, or anywhere.'

'Have you got your ticket?'

'No. Where can I get one?'

'Where have you come from?'

'Down the yard; past the policeman down there; I spoke to him.'

'It is funny at this time of morning.'

'Oh, I've been gall-ing it.'

Cooper took this to mean that the man had been seeing a sweetheart, but he did not believe it. Superintendent Russell from Carlisle was at that moment in Cooper's guards' van, so he knew very well that this could be one of the fugitives. In addition, the man had blackish specks all over his face and his coat was smeared with something that was not clear in the station lights. He put two and two together and made four, then laid his hand on the man's shoulder.

'You are the man that is wanted!'

'For what?'

The man then tried to break free, but Cooper had a firm strong grip on his coat and whatever else was under it. Right away the man twisted and slipped out of both of his coats, which came off down to his wrists; he almost got away. Cooper let go of his coat and grabbed him round both shoulders grappling with him, shouting for help. By now a ticket inspector and a porter had arrived and they flung themselves onto the man, pinning him down and holding his arms up behind him. Cooper told his suspicions to his fellow workers and said that the man should be secured, as he had to go. He had the satisfaction of seeing the man tied up before he had to reboard his train, heading for London.

James Baker had been caught, and largely by his own foolishness.

Superintendent Russell was at first gleeful, but then subdued because he came across the rules of law enforcement in another county.

'I am sorry Superintendent, but the rules are quite clear. If a suspect is apprehended on any train in Lancashire, then he must be given over to Lancashire police. I know you would very much like to take him back to Carlisle on the next train but you can't. I'm fairly sure that the reverse would apply if we were in Cumberland and Westmorland, but we're not you see.'

Russell had to admit the justice of the station master's position; there was nothing he could do.

'It'll be alright Superintendent. He'll have to go in front of the magistrates anyway, and I'm sure they'll allow your request.'

'What will he be charged with?'

'He was on the platform without a ticket. I expect he'll be charged under the railway's bylaws for travelling without a ticket. The company takes a dim view of such things.'

Back at Tebay, Police Constable Branford had searched Rudge and Martin; he had already been given the revolvers taken from the two men. He found nothing incriminating, as the men had already been searched by William Atkinson, the station master at Tebay. He handed Branford the bottle of rum that he had taken from Rudge; there was not much in it; as he handed it over it slipped and fell onto the floor, the neck breaking. Although Rudge did not say anything, he seemed aggrieved at the breakage of his property. Branford also took custody of two silk handkerchieves. From Superintendent Sempill in Carlisle there came a telegram; Branford had to deliver the men to him by the first available train. As it was not desirable that he should do this on his own, Christopher Gaddes volunteered to accompany him, if a relief guard would take his train down to Lancaster. A willing man was found, so Gaddes and Branford bundled Rudge and Martin onto the guards' van of a northbound goods train at 1.20 am. The captives had still said nothing at all, but it was Rudge who broke the silence.

'Do you think I might have my handkerchief please?'

Branford knew of the Kingstown shootings. He also knew that PC Joseph Byrnes had been murdered by the men in front of him. Here was a monster that had dared to speak to him. One pace took him to Rudge, and he punched him on the ear. Nothing else was said, but murder was in Rudge's eyes; if his hands had been loose then Branford would have had a struggle on his hands. Rudge knew he had nothing to lose now, and one more copper would make no difference to his fate. Branford and Gaddes were both stern men, and any look from either prisoner was met with a stony stare; the unrelenting and merciless gaze of determined men looking at those who had crossed over the borders of human behaviour. The train clacked on, but not into the Citadel Station. Superintendent Sempill, with a squad of men, was waiting at Upperby Junction, just south of Carlisle. Just before 2.00 am he charged them with committing the burglary at Netherby and with the attempted murder of Sergeant Roche, PC Johnstone, and PC Fortune. Such were the vicissitudes of the telegraph at night, that Sempill had not yet heard of the murder of PC Byrnes; he would shortly be informed of this. He cautioned them and gave them an opportunity to make a statement accounting for themselves.

Rudge and Martin said nothing. It was almost as if they had been struck dumb and any observer might have mistaken their attitude for indifference. In reality they were completely spent, dehydrated, dizzy with lack of food, and almost thankful to be bundled down into the cells at Earl Street police station where both immediately fell into an exhausted sleep.

James Baker had not been allowed to get much sleep, though he was glad of the plateful of porridge given to him in Lancaster police cells, and wolfed it down as a man would who had not had a proper meal for over forty-eight hours. He was then brought before Lancaster magistrates on a charge of travelling on the railway without a ticket. When asked if he had indeed been on the platform without a ticket, he answered simply 'yes'. The bench was unanimous in fining him four shillings. Of course he did not have it, but the magistrates, instead of sending him to the cells for a week, remanded him to the custody of Superintendent Russell of Brampton, who wished to take him back to Carlisle for questioning. The delay in setting off for Carlisle was perhaps unfortunate for Baker. Rudge and Martin had been taken through deserted city streets to be lodged in the police cells. Baker on the other hand was put on a train with Superintendent Russell and accompanying officers, which would not arrive in Carlisle until 1.20 pm.

Carlisle woke up on Friday 30 October to the devastating news that the men who had shot Sergeant Roche and PC Johnstone, then battered PC Fortune almost to death, had murdered a police constable in the pursuit of his duty. Whilst the people of Carlisle were pleased that Rudge and Martin were in the police cells, somehow, the news of Baker's capture leaked out. What also leaked out was the fact that he was being brought by train to the Citadel Station and from thence to Earl Street.

Baker could scarcely believe his eyes as his train drew into Carlisle Station. There were thousands of people, a dense crowd, waiting for the train. They had forced their way through the ticket barriers onto the platforms and as the expected train from Lancaster drew into the northbound platform, they set up such a baying, jeering and hooting that could be heard a mile away. Superintendent Russell's reaction was simple, 'Bloody Hell!'

Baker turned pale with fear, for he knew that if the mob could get their hands on him, then his chances of surviving were nil. In addition to the throngs on the platforms there were thousands more outside the station booing, shouting and shaking their fists with rage. Baker had become their monster; a figure of hate and loathing to be destroyed, wiped off the face of the earth, blotted out and crushed like a loathsome insect.

Superintendent Sempill was waiting with a group of policemen, and it was only their uniforms that deterred the crowd, but as the train stopped, the crowd boiled over and groups of men rushed to look into the carriages. It was not long before they found the one that contained James Baker. On the platform were fifteen policemen and they drew their batons in a line facing the crowds whilst a messenger was sent to Earl Street. Before too long, Chief Constable Dunne himself appeared in full uniform with cocked hat and he gave orders for his men to remove the prisoner from the train surrounded by policemen. As Baker left the train his eyes widened as the noise became overwhelming and men struggled with the police in their efforts to get to him. Fists were shaken and people were out of control with rage; pandemonium ensued as the noise inside and outside the station swelled to unbearable levels. For a while the knot of policemen managed to make their way along the platform through the crowd, but the mob, and their indignation became so strong that the police were forced to a halt. People were screaming that Baker should be hauled to the nearest lamp-post and hung, and several men hurled themselves at the police to try to get Baker; they were beaten down with batons. One man managed to get close enough to grab Baker by the hair with a grip so hard that it seemed that his scalp might come off. Baker groaned with the pain of it as officers felled the man with heavy blows. Fighting hard, the police managed to get Baker with his back to the wall near the refreshment rooms where they formed a line around him, striking at all who came near. Many men got close enough to aim blows at him, but most of them were fended off by police batons.

Mr Preston, the Carlisle station master brought in every member of staff that he could find to assist in pushing the crowd back, but their number was legion. Eventually they brought a station trolley for Chief Constable Dunne to stand on, and from this position he shouted at the crowd nearest, who quietened enough to listen, impressed by his uniform.

'I must ask you all to desist at once. The law will take its course and justice will be served; but this is not the way to do it. Please stand back and allow us to remove our prisoner to custody. He will be tried and judged in due course.'

This caused some hesitation in the mob, and the police were able to hustle Baker into the refreshment room and bar the door, which provided some respite. They were not safe though, because the crowds outside the station showed no sign of losing their determination to string Baker up. It was probably the largest demonstration of popular feeling ever seen in Carlisle. People climbed onto the roof of a stationary train at the platform to get a view of the refreshment rooms. They did not wish to be cheated of their prey.

After about half an hour the crowd inside the station had quietened somewhat and Mr Dunne thought that it might be possible to make a rush before the mob could decide what to do. The police formed a determined knot around Baker and Mr Preston and rushed through the crowd barging all out of their way until they reached the hydraulic lift going down into the tunnels under the station. Whilst a determined cordon kept the crowd at bay, Superintendent Sempill, Chief Constable Dunne and a few officers were taken down in the lift to the chambers underneath the station with Baker. There, the crowd could not get at them, so most dispersed over the next half hour. At about two o'clock, forty minutes after his arrival, Baker was again put in the lift and exited the station into a cab. There were still several hundred people about but the dangerous thousands had gone. To a cacophony of booing and hisses, Baker was driven the short distance to Earl Street where he was charged in the same way as the others. Rudge and Martin were then brought up from the cells and all three were charged with the murder of PC Byrnes. Rudge and Martin stayed utterly silent, but Baker protested his innocence. The wheels of justice began to grind.

18

A Nation Aghast

"When beggars die, there are no comets seen;
The heavens themselves blaze forth the death of princes."

When three villains shoot two policemen, batter another, then kill another, it is the newspapers that take the place of comets and the messenger of the gods is not Mercury, but the telegraph. By late Friday afternoon the shocking events in Cumberland had been relayed to all parts of the United Kingdom. On Saturday morning every newspaper in the land was carrying reports of the arrest of the three men who had murdered PC Byrnes, and expressing the hope that justice would be served upon them in due course. The names of Christopher Gaddes, Mr Beattie, William Parker and Robert Willis were on the lips of millions. Overnight they became figures of admiration, national heroes and the very epitome of British pluck. Such heroic assistance in law enforcement should be seen as worthy of reward, prizes and adulation. Such was the demand for knowledge of these men that in a very rare break from the norm, newspapers commissioned artists to supply their likenesses to be shown to their avid readers. The news also served another purpose.

On Saturday 31 October 1885 Detective Sergeant John Rolfe of Scotland Yard, opened the *Morning Post* and read that the Netherby Hall burglars had been caught after a desperate resistance. The hairs on his neck began to prickle when he read on; Police Constable Byrnes had been murdered by a bullet to the temple. His mind flew back to a bright day during the summer on the Commercial Road when he had attempted to arrest John White, alias Martin.

'Take a step closer and I'll put a bullet through your eye.'

'White, you bastard. This is you ain't it?' he whispered to himself.

Always a man to trust his instincts, he took the newspaper to Detective Inspector Shore, his immediate chief.

'So you think it's White?'

'I'd put money on it guvnor.'

'It's more than likely that it is. White's a vicious little sod and shooting to the head seems to be something of an obsession with him. Maybe he's gone and done it this time. We can't act on assumptions though John. You'll need a bit more than gut feeling for us to get permission to go on a jaunt to Carlisle.'

'Shall I telegraph for details and descriptions then sir?'

'It can't do any harm. In the meantime let's just watch the newspapers for what comes out eh? They are banged up safely; we can always look at them in a week or so.'

'Yes sir.'

Rolfe turned to go.

'John.'

He turned back to face Shore.

'You do know you're not going to get him for Simmons don't you?'

Rolfe's face twisted slightly in incomprehension.

'If he's killed a copper up north John, then he'll hang for that.'

'And if he doesn't sir?'

'I would think that very unlikely from what I can see; but yes, if he gets off, then we shall request that he be sent to stand trial for Simmons. But we both know the end of this I think.'

'I know sir, but it's about closing the file; seeing justice done. If he shot Inspector Simmons then people should know it and also see that justice has been done for both murders.'

'I agree with that.'

Inspector Shore leaned his elbows on his desk and put his hands together flexing his fingers as he thought.

'If it really does look like Martin is White then you and I will be taking a trip to Cumberland. I hear that it's a nice part of the world.'

Rolfe nodded. 'Then I look forward to it sir.'

James Brindle on the other hand, was not looking forward to anything. He was standing in the Nabob's private study and blenching under the hail of abuse that he had been receiving. It was just as well that the Nabob's wife and children were out. London's top mobsman's mask of respectability was always very thin, but had his neighbours heard the tirade coming out of his mouth on this particular morning then they would probably have melted in the heat of it. His voice had changed too, all culture washed out from it, and what was left was pure East End.

'What the FUCK are those nutters doing? By God Brindle I've topped a few geezers in my time but this takes the bloody biscuit. A copper for fuck's sake and the man has four kids. Four kids Brindle! I got kids. How do you think that makes me feel?'

'Not very good Mr Walker sir.'

'NOT VERY GOOD? I should bloody cocoa! That's four orphaned children and a young mum left to provide for them.'

Brindle was not sure how to react. One of the most merciless killers that he had ever known, was expressing pity for the wife and children of a policeman. Maybe he'd gone soft? The Nabob continued.

'I sent those idiots north to do a simple job. Just to nick some jewels. NOT TO START A FUCKING WAR! You know what's gonna happen now Brindle? DO YOU FUCKING KNOW WHAT'S GONNA HAPPEN NOW?'

'No Mr Walker sir.'

'Then I'll tell you. Every bloody gutter rag in this nation is gonna be calling for the police to be armed, and the way things are, that is what's gonna happen. And you know what that means for our business doncha? EH?'

'It gets more difficult boss.'

Walker was calming somewhat though his face was working with fury.

'Armed coppers. They'll close us down within six months. We can't let that happen James. We can't.'

'How we going to stop them boss?'

Walker looked at Brindle blankly, then replied softly.

'We don't need no guns James. You know I've given an earth overcoat to more than my share of geezers, but I like to think that every bastard I ever done in deserved it. But you know the weird thing James? I've never used a gun. Knife, axe, jemmy, meathook, garrotte; I've used 'em all. But never a gun. Wanna know why?'

'Why boss?'

''Cos it's too bloody easy. Just pull it out and blow someone away. Other methods; well you have to think. You have to make an effort; you have to assess the situation. Guns is too spur of the moment.'

'What do you want me to do Mr Walker?'

'Put the word out James; from the Nabob; you can say it's from me. Any bastard in London what uses a shooter on a job from this day on better say his prayers because if he does, then he is a fucking dead man. You got that?'

'Yes Boss.'

'And let the rozzers know it too. If we don't use guns then there's no need for the rozzers to have them is there? That's strategy James. It sends a signal to them that this is a what do you call it?... an aberration; a foul play, and that we will not stand for it either.'

'Makes it sound like a game boss.'

'It is a fucking game James. And it's our move. The rozzers think it's open season on rozzers. Unless we signal different, then the rozzers will get tooled up and come after us hard. I am signalling that we in our community, do not approve of events what have taken place recently.'

'Do you think they will get the message boss?'

'I bloody 'ope so James, or life is gonna get a lot harder. We've had it soft my son,' and here the Nabob patted Brindle's cheek familiarly. 'We are going to try to keep it that way. Mutual understanding and respect for the rules. That's what's needed here. Too many dead rozzers lately. I must think of a way to show that we wish to make some amends for the failings of some of our number. Right. Off you trot.'

Far to the north, three different men had made statements to Superintendent John Sempill, and all had tried to maintain some form of plausible defence.

'Your name is Anthony Benjamin Rudge?'

'Yes, it is.'

'Are there any other names that you have gone by?'

'There are others, but I chose this one for myself some years ago and have been known by it ever since.'

'That is my understanding; we do have your other names you know; William Walsh and William Fennell. That last is who you were born as.'

'I regard them as ex names. Previous names; Rudge is who I am and will stay.'

'Very well Mr Rudge, what is your age?'

'Thirty-eight.'

'That is strange. We have information that you are forty five.'

Rudge just shrugged; Sempill let it go at that.

'What is your occupation?'

'I am a dog trainer.'

'A dog trainer?'

'Yes. I train dogs to do all manner of things and people pay me to do it.'

'How do you account for your being caught in the goods wagon of a train in company with Martin?'

'I had to hop on the train because I had no money left to get home. I lost it all betting at Longtown.'

'Is that why you went there? For the coursing?'

'Yes. I have a professional interest in dog events and I like to bet. On a good day it is a considerable supplement to my income.'

'But you did not have a good day?'

'No,' Rudge grinned. 'I just about lost my shirt.'

'When you were arrested you were covered in a considerable amount of blood. Can you account for that?'

'Of course I can. I was fast asleep in a wagon with two blokes I met, and all trying to get home when some bloke jumped on top of me. We all thought we was being attacked and ran for it. Then another bloke hit me over the barnet with an iron bar. I bled like a stuck pig. Head wounds do that you know. It was my own blood on my coat; lots of it. They should be done for assault, and the copper what hit me on the train.'

'When you were taken, you were carrying a large calibre revolver. Why was that?'

'Nothing illegal in that Superintendent. Lots of people carry guns for self defence. I gamble; I deal in money as a bookie's runner and often carry large amounts of cash about. The gun is to protect me from villains and robbers, which of course I am not. Why am I wearing these?'

Here Rudge shook his fetters at the superintendent. By order of Chief Constable Dunne, all three men had been tagged as "dangerous." He had ordered that they be fettered and that their legs be shackled with heavy irons.

'These are damned uncomfortable Superintendent and suited to criminals. But the law of the land says that I am innocent until proven guilty. None of us should be wearing these things.'

'I'm following my orders Mr Rudge. You must take it up with the Chief Constable.'

'Oh you may be quite sure that I shall bring it up in court,' retorted Rudge.

When Sempill interviewed Martin, the conversation was very similar in that Martin also admitted to being known as John White, but he claimed that he did not know Rudge before the evening when they caught the train.

'I met 'im in a pub only a short time before we caught the train. Never set eyes on the geezer before but we was in the same boat; skint and no cash to pay for tickets home. So we jumped on a goods train.'

He also said the blood on his coat was his own, caused by his being bashed to the floor with a sprag at Tebay by over-zealous railwaymen.

James Baker was all naivety and indignation when Sempill interviewed him.

'I was never in any goods train; I don't know what you're talking about. I don't know those other two blokes.'

'Yet you were at Longtown?'

'Yes; I was at Longtown with hundreds of other geezers. I'm quite well known there. I've been going for years.'

'And your real name is James Baker.'

'Yes it is. I am a greengrocer and general dealer in provisions. I have a shop at 106 Montague Street, Bethnal Green. I like to bet on sporting events and I work sometimes as a bookie's runner which is why I was in Longtown.'

'Did you travel south from Carlisle to Lancaster on a goods train?'

'I did not. I was at the coursing on Tuesday and Wednesday, but I left on Wednesday evening and took a train to Newcastle. I spent the night in a brothel there, which I am not proud of, and I'd rather did not come out, for I have a girl waiting for me at home. On Thursday I caught a train back to Carlisle and took a passenger train down to Lancaster.'

'How do you account for the smears of blood on your coat?'

'Some railway employees mistook me for a man the police wanted and they grabbed me using a good deal of violence. Naturally, they not being policemen, I resisted. I got cut during the struggle, and maybe some of them did; that's how the blood got on my coat.'

Sempill described his interviews with the suspects to Mr Dunne and opined that a lot more evidence would be needed for the magistrates to remand his prisoners. Dunne thought not.

'You forget that when Rudge was arrested, he had a bottle of rum on him. We know from witness statements that the men who murdered Byrnes bought a bottle of rum at the Packhorse Inn. I think you need to get Mrs Griffiths to have a look at that bottle.'

'Yes sir, but I have no doubt that there are hundreds of similar bottles. Any defence solicitor will make hay with that. You think they will get off sir?'

'Not if we do our work Mr Sempill. We need something to link those men to the crimes done at Netherby Hall. If we can do that, then life will become simpler.'

Rudge and Martin were men experienced with the law, with courts, and with evidence. They knew that on the face of things, evidence against them was very slim. The blood and the guns they had explained. They were the victims of an attack by over zealous railway employees looking for villains who had committed crimes. They should be released quickly for lack of evidence and apologies should be given to them.

James Baker on the other hand, was twenty-eight. He had Nellie and a shop waiting in London which provided him with an honest livelihood. The prospect of being found guilty of murder and then being hanged had a devastating effect on him. He lay on his bed in a police cell, pale, and occasionally shaking with fear at his own thoughts and dread. It was hard for him to sleep and he could scarcely get food down. He begged that a telegram be sent to Nellie Baker in Bethnal Green explaining that he was in trouble; it was not too long before she caught a train and headed for Carlisle. In his cell she bit her lip, glancing around, because she, and he, knew that they could not speak freely. They did, however, know how to put on a play.

'Have you told them you didn't do anything James? That you're innocent.'

'I have Nellie. I told them that I don't know those other men and never saw them before I was brought here.'

'So where were you after leaving Longtown?'

'I went to Newcastle.'

'Oh yes? And what was you doing there?'

'Just visiting some friends.'

'Oh yes? cried Nellie, indignation in her voice. 'I know the sort of friends you mean! You've been at it again ain't you James?'

'No Nell! I swear I ain't. It's only you Nellie. I don't want any other gals now.'

Outside in the corridor, ears were listening. Did the playacting stiffen Baker's alibi? Probably not. At any rate, the game was about to change.

John Wilson, a young railwayman employed in the Tebay engineering shed, had a very curious mind; and a very sharp pair of eyes. On his lunch break he decided to revisit the scenes of the night's excitement. First he went to where the men had jumped out of the wagon. Martin had been taken close to the tracks, but the other two men ran away. One had disappeared, but the other one had gone under the railway bridge. Wilson followed the path taken by the panic stricken Rudge the previous night, churned up by the feet of the shouting mob that had pursued their quarry under the dry arch of the railway bridge. Under the bridge, Wilson looked into the River Lune, but the water was brown, a couple of feet deep and he could see nothing. He turned to go, but the wintery sun on this cold morning just happened to catch something in the mud at the very edge of the water. Bending down, Wilson picked it up, to find that while all that glisters may not be gold, sometimes it is, and this one had a diamond in it. It was a beautifully made and very expensive ear-drop. Looking more closely at the mud, Wilson also saw, and picked up a small brass watch key. Rudge had not had time to tie his tobacco pouch closed before he threw it towards the river. There was also the remains of a wedge of cheese, the rind of which had some blue lettering on it.

Wilson took what he had found to PC Branford, who had not long been back from Carlisle. Branford immediately telegraphed the news of the find to Superintendent Sempill and was instructed to bring the ear-drop and watch key straight to Carlisle along with the cheese. Perhaps with a small sigh, and a thought that duty must be done, Branford was on the next train north.

Shortly after Branford arrived at Earl Street Police Station, Superintendent Sempill left it to catch a train. Before long he arrived at Longtown where, since he had telegraphed ahead, PC Tomer waited with a gig. Within a few minutes the superintendent was asking Lady Hermione Graham if she recognised the ear-drop and watch key. She did so immediately and without hesitation.

Jewellery stolen from Netherby Hall does not find its way to under a railway bridge at Tebay on its own. Sempill had the first link of a chain with which to bind the hopes of the three men now in the cells back at Earl Street.

Friday morning had brought in a small piece of evidence in the shape of an iron jemmy, some nineteen inches long which had been found in a goods wagon in a sidings at Blencowe, not far from Penrith. On it was what appeared to be caked blood, and there were a few human hairs attached to it. Upon investigation, they matched the colour of the hair on PC Christopher Fortune's head. With the jemmy was a small alpaca bag of quite an expensive kind. Lady Hermione identified this bag also as her own property. How the jemmy and the bag had got into the wagon, was a mystery.

Pieces of a jigsaw were falling into place. Much now depended on the upcoming identity parades.

19

A Question of Identity

On Friday morning, 30 October, Mr Maclean, station master at Gretna, told PC Tomer that three bags left in his charge on the day of the robbery, had been sent on to Carlisle left luggage, to be called for. On being told of this by Tomer, Superintendent Sempill had the bags seized, and opened. Inside were tools very well suited to house breaking, and a sack full of revolver bullets. On the same day, an inquest was opened by the coroner Mr John Carrick, at the Packhorse Inn upon the death of PC Joseph Byrnes. Sergeant Bremner identified the body as being that of PC Byrnes; the inquest was adjourned immediately for one week at the request of Superintendent Fowler to allow the facts to be ascertained.

The name "Baker" had caught the imagination of the public in no uncertain way and a strange sort of hysteria was prevalent. Following information that a Corporal James Baker of the Cumberland Militia bore a resemblance to the man 'Smith', police descended on Carlisle Castle and arrested him. That afternoon he was confronted with Sergeant Roche who had held onto 'Smith' at Kingstown before being shot. Roche, for his courage, was newly promoted to inspector but did not identify the soldier as 'the fourth man', so he was released. Police Constable Johnstone was very ill and unable to attend, but Chief Constable Dunne had been to see him personally and promoted him on the spot to sergeant for his valour. Until then, Doctor Lediard thought that Johnstone had been sinking; after his promotion he rallied and began to improve.

In Manchester, Inspector Caminada of the detective branch thought that a local villain called William Baker was the mysterious fourth man. He was known to frequent sporting events, and was well known at dog fixtures all over the country. Baker made no resistance when arrested, but accompanied the detective to the police station. A telegram was sent to Superintendent Sempill who asked that he be held in custody; Constable Hargreaves was sent from Carlisle to get him. He was seen by Inspector Roche and by Mr Hetherington, who had been at the shooting in Kingstown, but they could not identify him as "Smith" so he was released.

On Saturday afternoon, Rudge, Baker and Martin were brought up before the magistrates at Carlisle. The hearing did not take place in the court but in the superintendent's office in Earl Street Police Station, Mr Horrocks being chairman of the bench.

'What do you want from us at this stage Superintendent?' asked the Chair.

'Sir, I am asking for a remand of the prisoners for a period of one week to allow further investigations to proceed, and evidence to be collected and assessed.'

'I object to that very strongly!' declared Rudge. 'No evidence has been given, yet this man seeks to deprive us of our liberty for another week on his word alone. I do not see how this can be allowed.'

Horrocks was not a man to be browbeaten.

'You three men are remanded for one week on the charge of wilful murder.'

'We have heard no evidence,' protested Rudge.

Mr Horrocks did not reply immediately but consulted Mr Hodgson, Clerk of the Court. Then he spoke to Rudge again.

'In addition to being remanded on the charge of murder, you are also remanded on the charge of robbery and attempted murder.'

'And are we to be remanded on this man's statement and not upon evidence?' cried Rudge, waving his hand at Sempill. 'I should like to hear some evidence.'

'You have heard sufficient evidence today,' replied Horrocks.

'I have heard a statement made, but I have heard no evidence!'

'The statement you have heard is taken as evidence. I should also tell you that whatever you say may be taken down in writing and may be used in evidence against you.'

'If any evidence is to be called as to identity, we ought to be placed among other men.'

'You will be treated in the usual way and no distinction will be made in your case.'

Rudge was firm on this. 'Well the usual way is for the police to place a man among a number of others.'

'The usual way will be adopted with regard to you. You will be placed among others.'

'Sometimes the rule is broken.'

'The rule will not be broken,' said Mr Horrocks firmly.

He then remanded the prisoners for a week. Rudge and Martin were removed and placed into the same cell. Presumably it was hoped that they would converse, and be overheard but they were far too wily for that. Baker was placed in another cell with ordinary prisoners.

Joseph Byrnes had been a Catholic, so the Church of England graveyard at Plumpton was not for him, even though he had been friends with Mr Kennedy the vicar. On Sunday 1 November, his funeral was held at Penrith Cemetery. His body lay at the Packhorse until the hearse came, and a considerable number of villagers followed it four and a half miles to his final resting place. Superintendent Fowler and two sergeants, with five constables, marched in front of their dead colleague whilst six carriages carried other mourners. The crowd at the cemetery was huge, estimated at two thousand people, and the coffin was borne to the burial place on the shoulders of the police escort. Father Meynell of Penrith undertook the burial with a moving sermon, speaking of duty and expressing the hope that PC Byrnes would stand in front of the Almighty and receive the blessing,

'Well done thou good and faithful servant.'

Mrs Byrnes, weeping inconsolably, had received visits from Lady Graham, accompanied by Hilda and Queen Victoria had sent a telegram of sympathy and condolence.

When the ceremonies were over, the police marched two by two back to Penrith police station.

Superintendent Sempill had received a telegram from a Detective Sergeant Rolfe of the Metropolitan Police, requesting descriptions of the arrested men, particularly the one calling himself Martin. The particulars were sent straight back down the line to Scotland Yard, where, as soon as Rolfe read them, he sped into Chief Inspector Shore's office.

'There it is sir. The prisoner Martin has a lump between his eyebrows and when arrested, was wearing a cap with a glazed peak which he uses to hide the blemish.'

'So it's White.'

'Yes sir. No doubts in my mind.'

'Right. I'll telegraph this Superintendent Sempill to let him know we are coming for the purposes of identification. We'd better take Abberline with us as well.'

'Fred sir? What's it to do with him?'

'Word on the street is that White was the bloke that fired at a gamekeeper and shot a gardener in the leg down in Sheffield Park back in February. Abberline's case; he'll want to see the man. Get some rail warrants made out and we'll be off tomorrow; back Tuesday I should think.'

In the event, an assistant commissioner heard of the proposed visit to Carlisle and did not think it was necessary for three officers to go; so it was Shore and Rolfe who made the trip and were shown to Martin's cell in the police station.

Rolfe walked into the room where Martin had been placed, away from Rudge. The murderer was facing the window when the door opened, but he almost jumped out of his skin when a familiar west country voice spoke.

'Well John, you've gone and done it this time haven't you?'

'Rolfe!'

'Sergeant Rolfe to you White. You going to put a bullet through my eye this time?'

Martin stared at him, a look of hatred.

'You think you're gonna provoke me into saying something I shouldn't. I wasn't born yesterday you know.'

Rolfe shrugged. 'Here's another face you know very well.'

Inspector Shore stepped into the cell.

'We have a pretty good idea that it was you that shot Inspector Simmons. You let Adams swing for it and he deserved it for he was there; as was Dredge, though he got off.'

Martin said nothing.

'You let another man hang for what you did White. What sort of coward does that? You could have spoken up and maybe saved him.'

'From what?' said Martin, his voice dripping with contempt. 'Just supposing I did shoot Simmons and Adams was there. Suppose it was me that hanged? What would Adams have got? Twenty years in Portsea or Portland? Dartmoor? If I knew James Adams, he'd rather be dead anyway. We all got to die some day Mr Shore. Don't forget that.'

'We haven't forgotten anything, John,' said Rolfe. 'That's quite a philosophical approach you've got there, but you're forgetting something.'

'What's that?'

'That if they find you guilty at the next Assizes, which is in January I believe, then you will be shuffling off this earth rather earlier than any of us most likely.'

Martin, ever given to temper, almost replied 'Fuck off copper', but choked the words back. Rolfe's reputation as a thief taker was equalled by his reputation for violence. The Wiltshireman did not take back chat and all Martin would get would be a slap to his face.

'I got nothing more to say to you.'

'I'm not worried John. If they let you off what you've done up here, I'll be back to take you down to the Old Bailey and finish the Simmons business. But I don't think that's likely. I think the judge up here is going to make sure you get a nice new overcoat; made of wood. Bon voyage!'

With that, Rolfe was gone. He and Shore identified Rudge and Baker as notorious burglars and gave a wealth of information to Sempill about their past crimes and prison sentences served. Martin was marched back to the cell he shared with Rudge, and momentarily he may have forgotten the listening ears outside the door. He told Rudge that he had seen Sergeant Rolfe, but the conversation finished with him saying to Rudge, 'I suppose I shall be done for the Romford murder now.'

Rudge's eyes widened and he immediately signalled Martin to shut up.

Chief Constable Dunne had received a telegram to the effect that a mystery gentleman had offered five hundred pounds to the Metropolitan and City Police Orphanage if they would accept two of PC Byrnes's children to take care of. He relayed this news to Chief Inspector Shore who blew out his cheeks and replied, 'If that is so then they are very fortunate young men. The orphanage is restricted to children from the Met and the City police forces. If they let them in, then they will be very well taken care of and educated.'

'It's a good place is it?'

'It certainly is; the best facility of its kind in the whole country I should think.'

'It would lessen poor Mrs Byrnes's burden considerably.'

'It would do that.'

'Do you think they will be let in?'

'I do sir. The commissioners are not going to turn down five hundred pounds.'

'Do you have any idea who might have put up this money?'

Shore looked grim.

'I do sir. It may be to salve a guilty conscience, but I think it is more like a signal or even a peace offering. One thing is certain; the commissioners at the orphanage have a lot of thinking to do.'

'A signal you say?'

'Yes. I believe a certain somebody may be sending a message to the effect that he thinks these characters in your cells have gone too far and that he does not approve.'

'Well I will not ask you to explain further, but it is a most generous amount. I myself have started a fund for the relief of Mrs Byrnes and a reward for the brave fellows who risked their lives capturing these villains. Sir Frederick Graham has already subscribed fifty pounds.'

Shore lifted his eyebrows, 'That's not to be sneezed at either sir.'

'No indeed. He and his wife have been the victim of a heinous crime and he did not need to do it; it's very generous. By the way Chief Inspector, have you and Rolfe any objection to delaying your start back tomorrow until the afternoon?'

'Not if it's in the line of duty sir. How may we help you?'

'We have to do some identity parades and I need men whose faces are not known round here.'

'Oh I think we can do that sir.'

Rudge, Martin and Baker were rather unkempt by now and in order that they present a decent appearance in the parades, a barber was called in to shave them and cut their hair on Tuesday morning, 3 November.

'What's all this for then?' Martin asked as he was shaved. 'Are we gonna have a visit from the mayor?'

'You're not that popular,' replied the barber. 'The safest place for you is in here, believe me. There's a lot of folk in Carlisle would like to have words with you.'

'I'll bet,' chortled Rudge. 'They'll change their tune when we get off I think.'

'You think you'll get off?'

'They got nothing on us but a load of circumstantial,' replied Rudge, who was in an ebullient mood. 'The magistrates will have to let us go.'

'We shall see about that,' replied one of the policemen watching them. 'Now come this way; you have an appointment upstairs.'

With leg irons impeding their progress, the three men were ushered into a room and lined up with six other men. Rudge was amused by the sight of two of them and cried out, 'Well Mr Shore and Mr Rolfe! What they doing you for then?'

'You'll be laughing the other side of your face soon enough Rudge,' growled Rolfe.

'Well we shall have to see about that won't we Mr Rolfe? He who laughs last and all that.'

The three prisoners were lined up with the other men, when Rudge shouted, 'Here! This ain't right. We're the only ones wearing leg irons. Let's have leg irons for everyone or take these off!'

'Just shut up Rudge,' said one of the attending officers. 'It's all in hand.'

Some sheets were produced and the feet and ankles of all the men in the parade were covered so that the leg irons could not be seen; then the proceedings began. In came the witnesses; station masters from Gretna, Calthwaite and Plumpton, along with Inspector Roche who had grappled with Baker at Kingstown. A group of witnesses from Plumpton came in and Rudge, Baker and Martin were picked out by most of them as being the men they had seen on the night of the murder. Then came Thomas Lowthian. As one of the men he had seen on the road near Plumpton on the night of the murder, he tapped the shoulder of Detective Sergeant Rolfe. Rudge waited until Lowthian had left the room before exploding with laughter.

'Well they got you bang to rights Mr Rolfe. You done it right enough!'

Rolfe just gave him a stare that would have cut its way through steel. He had already seen the weakest link, and he wanted to interview him before returning to the capital.

'Well James. I confess that this is a surprise to me. I didn't have you down for a murderer. Tealeaf, yes. Portico man, yes. Murderer? No.'

'I ain't killed anyone Mr Rolfe. I don't even know those other two blokes. I never seen them before I was brought here.'

'So you say James. Yet we now have several witnesses identifying you as one of the men seen outside Plumpton station on the night that PC Byrnes was shot to death. What do you say to that?'

'They're all either mistaken or lying Mr Rolfe. You know how it is. People want to look important. I was never there. That's the truth on me mother's life.'

Rolfe wished he'd had a pound for every time he'd heard that in his career; he reflected that there would be a lot of dead mothers about if it came literally true.

'I hope your solicitor can convince the jury of that when this comes to trial James, but I want to know from your own lips now. Did you kill PC Byrnes?'

'I never killed anyone Mr Rolfe. I will probably never see you again in this life, but I want you to know that I never killed no-one. And I ain't got a solicitor.'

'Oh you have. Your dad from what I hear, is very upset. He's on his way up here soon, and he's engaged Mr Moore to take your case.'

'Mr Moore!'

'The same. He's defended more of your type than I've had hot dinners, so if you are innocent then you are in good hands. But if you've been lying to me James, then may God have mercy on your soul. For what it's worth I believe you. You didn't kill the man. But who did?'

'I ain't a grass Mr Rolfe. I don't peach.' Then he added hastily, 'But I wasn't there anyway.'

Rolfe nodded, 'And that James is what's going to kill you. If you named the murderer and turned Queen's evidence you'd get a long stretch, but you wouldn't hang.'

'I told you Mr Rolfe. I wasn't there.'

Rolfe got up to leave. 'You're a fool James. Your loyalty to those men will hang you. I'll leave you now. But your fate is in your own hands laddie. You'll all hang together if this goes the way I think it will.'

Chief Constable Dunne had a different matter on his mind, and had called in to see Mr Joseph Leavers, the governor of Carlisle Prison.

'I think it very likely that there will be some executions in the early part of next year. I understand that the gallows has not been used for some time?'

'It has not. I am having it refurbished.'

'I have had some thoughts on the matter. I am of opinion that since they may all hang for the same crime, they should all be hanged together.'

'At the same time you mean?'

'Exactly so. It would be fitting I think, since they will all hang for the same murder.'

'I see your point, but we would have to build a gallows especially for that one job.'

'Indeed; and it would send a powerful message out to any potential murderers that they may suffer a like fate. You will recall that it has been done before?'

A triple hanging in Carlisle you mean? Yes. Little, Woof and Armstrong back in 1820. A bad business.'

'Hanged for burglary, highway robbery and vicious assaults on many people.'

'Yes. And they died cursing all and every one, denying the existence of God and calling out all sorts of blasphemies. I do recall though Mr Dunne, that it went off badly.'

'Indeed; they did not die instantly. I think we must do better if we are called upon to execute Rudge, Martin and Baker.'

The chief warden stopped for a moment to think.

'Very well. I will put out feelers among the local carpenters to see if there are any who might be able to build us a working triple gallows should it be needed.'

'I rather think it will.'

'*Entre nous,* so do I.'

20

Casting Doubt

On Monday 9 November Mr William Gladstone, the leader of the Liberal Party passed through Carlisle on the train, which stopped for a short time. A large and enthusiastic crowd awaited him and he was about to make an impromptu speech from his carriage window when Mrs Gladstone remonstrated with him. He had to be content to speak to three or four reporters who were allowed onto the train so that they could relay his words to the people of Carlisle. After the usual political and uplifting sentiments for local Liberals, he then expressed his sympathy, his gratitude and admiration for the way in which the police were dealing with the matter of the Netherby burglary and subsequent events. He thought that they had shown intelligence, devotion and gallantry; he was glad that a subscription was being raised and he wished to contribute towards it. He handed the sum of two pounds to Mr Allison, Chairman of the Carlisle Liberal Association, to be given to Mr Dunne. Many of the great and the good would be moved to do the same; it was quite clear that society expected justice to be done upon the wretches who had carried out some appalling crimes. Christopher Gaddes and Henry Cooper both received eight pounds and a handsome letter praising their actions from Mr Dunne.

All this was nothing to the three men who were brought before a full bench of Carlisle magistrates on 11 November with Mr Horrocks once more in the chair. A huge crowd was gathered outside the courts, and the public benches filled up as soon as the doors opened. The prisoners still wore leg irons and had not been shaved for a couple of days, so did not look very fresh. Superintendent Sempill appeared to press the charges whilst Chief Constable Dunne was in attendance. The prisoners had no solicitor, so Rudge leaned forward to Mr Sempill.

'Excuse me, but would it be possible to have paper and pencils to take notes with?'

It was Dunne who replied.

'You shall have paper and pencils, and every facility will be given for you to take notes and to cross examine witnesses.'

'Thank you.'

Mr Dunne then spoke to the court, outlining the events that took place between the burglary at Netherby and the capture of the three prisoners. Following this, witnesses began to make their statements, starting with the staff from Netherby Hall. Rudge, Martin and Baker said nothing at first, just listened and made notes.

Lady Hermione Graham made her statement to silence in the courtroom, but said that the value of the jewellery in her bedroom had been exaggerated. It was no more than about one thousand pounds, and of that about two hundred and fifty pounds worth was taken. It was now that Rudge rose to begin his performance, for this was his theatre and his stage.

'Your Ladyship has been asked a question in reference to a common watch key. Do you think you would have in your possession a common brass watch key, value a penny?'

'That is what might have been in the case, but I really cannot say whether there was or not.'

'I ask the question because my own watch key has been taken from me.'

This caused a murmur in the court room. Rudge had cast doubt on one of the pieces of evidence already.

There followed a number of people who claimed to have seen Rudge, Martin and Baker at Longtown and near Netherby

Hall. Rudge's strategy was to make it seem as if they were misremembering or had been compromised at an identity parade. Another buzz of excitement came when Alexander MacLean, the Gretna station master identified the three men as being those he had seen at his place of work. Rudge stood to cross examine him.

'Do you swear to me as being one of the three men you saw?'

'I swear to you as being one of the prisoners.'

'Where did you gain that knowledge? When we were placed together at the police office? What did you say then?'

'I pointed you out as one of the men.'

'Will you give us the words exactly?'

'I said "That's one" and pointed at you.'

'Was I the first man you pointed out?'

'No sir; you were the second.'

'Can you recognise the third man?'

'Yes. Perfectly. The centre man, Martin. I pointed him out after you.'

'Don't you remember saying "They are very nigh exact; that's like him"?'

'No. I said positively, "That's the one".'

'A bare faced lie!' said Rudge. 'I wish to place Mr Sempill on oath.'

Mr Horrocks said, 'When Mr Sempill is called as witness, you can ask him.'

Rudge sat down reluctantly, and as he did so, repeated again, with some indignation, 'A bare-faced lie.'

It was David Johnstone who rattled Rudge in his campaign to discredit witness testimony. The court listened with great interest to his story of how he peeked through the door at The Graham Arms and saw the prisoners handling skeleton keys.

Rudge stood up and asked 'Do you know the nature of an oath? Do you know when you kiss the book, the penalties that attach to telling a lie; where you go to?'

'Yes.'

'Where?'

'Just where I expect you are going sir.'

The court dissolved into laughter as the chairman angrily banged his gavel for silence; Rudge looked discomfited then retorted; 'You may keep your personal remarks to yourself.'

He continued to question Johnstone, needling him about what he saw, but the witness would not deviate from his story. When Rudge was done, Mr Horrocks asked Martin if he had any questions.

'No. It's no use asking questions.'

Baker asked what Johnstone had first said after he saw the three men handling housebreaking keys.

'Speak a little louder please,' said Johnstone. 'I am a little hard of hearing in this ear.'

Baker looked a little taken aback, then replied, 'Then turn round the other and you'll be able to catch it fast enough.'

Once again the spectators burst into laughter.

Rudge boiled over, jumping up out of turn and shouted at the witness.

'If I was going to take a thief you are the first man I would take! So help me God, he is a liar, and he knows it.'

Then he hurled himself back into his chair.

The real drama of the day came to a hushed and fascinated court when Inspector Roche described his encounter with four men at Kingstown and was rock solid in his identification of Rudge, however much the prisoner tried to shake him. Rudge had fired a revolver at him. It was Martin who came off best from this exchange.

'You say to the best of your belief I am one of the men. Can you swear positively?'

'To the best of my belief, you are one of the men.'

'But can you swear that I am?'

'I will not swear. To the best of my belief, you are one of the men.'

'That will do,' said Martin. 'Thank you.'

Rudge was trying to play to the gallery and get people on his side and it became obvious that the stage had missed out on a great thespian when he questioned Sergeant Handley who said that he heard the moans from half a mile away made by PC Johnstone when he was shot.

'You were half a mile away and heard the moans?'

'Yes.'

'You must have good ears. You say it was quite light and yet you brought a lamp out?'

'Mr Armstrong brought a lamp out. I did not ask him.'

'You may depend upon it that Mr Armstrong is as sensible a man as you are.'

'Yes. Of course.'

'It seems ridiculous that a man should take his lamp out on a moonlight night. What was it for? To look for the moon or what?'

Once again the court laughed loudly. Rudge was winning them over as a comic turn if nothing else, but he went on too long with some fairly pointless questions about the relative positions of people on the night of the shootings. Mr Horrocks decided to intervene.

'This kind of examination will do you no good.'

'If I have transgressed, I hope you will make excuses for my ignorance.'

'Oh no. We don't say you are transgressing. All I say is that you are doing your case no good, but rather the opposite.'

'Well sir, I don't suppose that will be dissatisfactory for you to say that here. It appears to me that you want me to say nothing.'

'If you wish to cross examine do so as long as you like. We are only giving our opinion.'

Despite this warning, Rudge continued to cross examine each witness that came forward, and Baker, obviously encouraged by this, followed his example only to come a cropper when he tried to infer that Mr Armstrong was mistaken in his identification of himself at Kingstown. Armstrong came back strongly.

'You do not need to try to get out of it for I would know you among a thousand. You are the man sir!'

This also caused laughter in the court, but at Baker's expense.

After the first day before the magistrates, the prisoners were taken back to their cells; Rudge and Martin were again in the same room, Baker, for the moment, on his own. The custody sergeant was beginning to worry about Baker and whether or not he would be fit to stand trial if sent to the Assizes. He was pale and shaking much of the time and lay in his bed refusing to eat much food. When Nellie came to see him, he told her repeatedly, 'They won't hang me Nell. I won't let them. I'll kill myself first.'

Nellie did not really know what to say in answer to this sort of remark.

'They have not proved it completely James. And when your solicitor gets here, then he'll do right by you.'

Baker was not hopeful.

'He might, if I'm still alive when he gets here Nell. It's so cold in here I think I'll freeze to death soon.'

It was true; it was November and Baker's cell was unheated; he shivered in the one woollen blanket he was allowed.

The other two were utterly different, each being stoic in the face of what might happen.

'I'll tell you what John,' said Rudge. 'I look on this as a sort of test. I have always said that I would rather die than go back inside for another stretch. If they put us in the frame for this and they hang us, then I shall go to the gallows a cheerful man, because the alternative is unthinkable.'

The listening ears in the corridor heard nothing incriminating.

'That's all very well,' replied Martin, 'but I'm still hoping to get out of this. Lots of them witnesses is very confused.'

'They are,' replied Rudge. 'And I'm working on that. If the magistrates doubt the evidence against us, then they will let us go. It still hangs on identity. After all, the men who shot the policemen are not necessarily the men who burgled Netherby Hall now are they?'

Superintendent Sempill had been thinking exactly the same thing, but he was rather more confident of his case than Rudge. Despite the latter's determined attacks upon the veracity and memories of many witnesses during the day, he had several who were adamant that the three men in the dock were the same three that shot Inspector Roche and Sergeant Johnstone. It was a great shame that Johnstone was still so ill that he could not be moved, though it appeared that he was making great strides towards recovery. One thing Sempill was sure of; the more eyewitnesses held firm as to the identities of the gunmen, the stronger his case would be.

Rudge knew this too, and on the second day spent a long time grilling Mr Hetherington who had stood with Mr Armstrong and Inspector Roche at Kingstown. He tried the same ploys as the day before. Hetherington was mistaken. He could not see properly. He was not in his right senses, implying he was drunk. He was lying. Hetherington did not budge but testified to the presence of Rudge and Martin as the shooters and that there was a fourth man. He could not swear to Baker.

A curious witness was James Hay, a gardener at Stanwix who swore that on the Sunday before the burglary he had been asked questions about the Etterby Road and the Caledonian railway by John Martin. Both Martin and Rudge said they could prove that they had direct alibis to show that they were nowhere near Stanwix on Sunday, but Hay had not named Rudge in his evidence. Rudge thought that Hay's imagination had been worked on, or something more sinister was happening. Mr Ferguson, one of the magistrates told him,

'You are doing yourself no good by cross examining a witness who has never said anything about you.'

Rudge, a fire in his eye, leaned over the rail of the dock and answered emphatically,

'I beg pardon. If these two men sink, I sink with them. I know as much about law as that.'

There followed a series of witnesses about the attack on Constable Fortune, but the man himself could not attend court. Most of them identified Rudge and Martin, though strange to tell, not Baker, until it came to James Jackson who had spoken to Baker at Calthwaite station. Rudge tried to muddy the waters again, but his efforts were wearing very thin now. William Milburn, the porter from Calthwaite also identified Baker as having spoken to him. Rudge's defence, all composed of people who were mistaken, people who were lying, people who had been put up to it, and people whose imaginations were playing tricks on them, was collapsing.

Most extraordinary in this trial was that at the moment none of the men had legal representation, but were left to flounder their way through the first stage of a trial for their lives, on their own.

Friday 13 November saw the examination of the death of PC Byrnes. Dr Montgomery had performed a post mortem upon the dead constable.

'I made a report in writing which was handed to the coroner at the inquest, and appears upon his depositions. There was a bullet wound through the left orbit which made its exit an inch and a half behind the left ear. The bullet had penetrated the brain substance and also the skull. The shot had taken effect from the front. I am perfectly certain that the bullet wound caused the man's death. It was nearly a quarter of an inch in diameter.'

Did Baker wince? The doctor also described considerable bruising round the arms where the constable had been gripped.

Rudge now had a way out of the murder charge. He took it and cross-examined the doctor.

'You say the bullet wound was a little over a quarter of an inch in diameter?'

'I said about that. I did not measure it. I guessed it with the end of my finger.'

'The reason for my asking this is that from the appearance of the muzzles of these revolvers, the smallest one is nearer half an inch than anything else.'

'I say I did not measure it. I do not know the exact measurements of the barrels.'

'No. I do not say that you did.'

The doctor turned peppery in his response.

'I say that the wound is such as would be produced by either of these pistols.'

'If you don't lose your temper sir, I shan't lose mine.'

Superintendent Sempill intervened.

'Just answer his questions.'

'Well I can give no other answer than what I have already said.'

'You are only giving an idea?' said Rudge.

'Yes.'

Rudge pressed the point, stating that if the wound was only a quarter of an inch, then it would not be possible for a bullet from either of the revolvers found on himself or Martin to have caused the injury.'

'You have not measured this wound.'

'No.'

Chief Constable Dunne intervened. 'It will be done.'

'It will be done?' cried Rudge, 'And the man is buried! You are in a hurry to get me to sit down.'

Mrs Griffiths could not swear at first that Rudge had been the man who bought the rum for her on the night of the murder but changed her mind during her testimony, which Rudge was puzzled at.

'Something must have occurred to alter her opinion,' he said to the court.

Mr Horrocks asked Mrs Griffiths why she could identify Rudge now, but not before.

'Because I see now he is the man who was in our house.'

'It is, I suppose,' said Rudge, 'a minute since this woman began to give evidence, and she alters her opinion and says I am the man. Something must have occurred to alter her mind and that something I want to know.'

'I cannot answer that question,' said Mr Horrocks, 'because I don't know anything about her mind.'

'I want her to explain it. Perhaps it may have been a little temper or a little spleen. Ladies are very peculiar and sometimes you don't know when you tread upon their corns.'

Once again the court burst into laughter. Rudge was in his element.

'Can you give any reason?' he asked Mrs Griffiths.

'No. I have told you.'

'You have not told me. It appears Madam you have enough sense to jump from one conclusion to another as a keen lawyer can do, and yet you have not sense enough to know why you have altered your opinion. I daresay if you were to look into your own mind, you would find a reason.'

'She has given you a reason,' said Mr Horrocks.

'I ask any intelligent man,' declaimed Rudge. 'Is that a reason?'

'You must take her answer as she gives it. You can only take the witness's answer.'

There then followed details of the dramatic events at Tebay, and a parade of railwaymen appeared, giving their accounts to an enthralled court. The hearing was adjourned until the following Monday when the remainder of the Tebay evidence was dealt with, as well as accounts from Henry Cooper and other Lancaster men as to the capture of Baker. After this, Rudge, Martin and Baker were further remanded until Monday 23 November. Rudge thought that on the whole it had gone rather well. He had cast doubt on the word of most of the witnesses, shown that some evidence was spurious, and had discounted the watch key as evidence. They might, he thought, get off this yet.

21

Mr Johnson

Rudge had been thinking hard. Back in the relative privacy of his cell he spoke to Martin in a voice full of urgency.

'We are gonna get done because we don't have a legal man to speak for us. There's lots of things wrong with those witnesses, including the bloke who made things up about speaking to you on Sunday. Then there's the people who change their minds about identifying us. I'm pointing these things out, but they ain't hitting hard enough. We need help.'

'I thought you was doing rather well actually Anthony.'

'I ain't been doing bad, but like I said, we need someone with a bit more punch. James's dad is getting him a solicitor. We need one too; otherwise we won't do as well as we could from this.'

'Look,' whispered Martin. 'They got us for the burglary. Finding that ear-drop under the bridge where they copped you was unfortunate.'

'That's as may be,' replied Rudge, 'But like I said, them as did the burglary ain't necessarily them as did the shootings are they?'

'True enough, but we got all those people identifying us,' whispered Martin. 'How do we get out of that?'

'Exactly! We get a solicitor to take them apart. Destroy the identifications and they have no case!'

'Trouble is Anthony, that we got no money.'

'Ah,' said Rudge. 'I meant to tell you about that.'

'About what?'

'I did have some money.'

'You said you was skint, like James and me.'

'Well,' said Rudge. 'I was lying wasn't I?'

Martin thought about this for a moment.

'You're a fucking crook Anthony.'

'Par for the course John. Takes one to know one.'

'So how much you got?'

'Enough to speak to a solicitor, but that ain't all. You and me got gold watches matey.'

'The rozzers have them.'

'Yes they do. But they don't belong to them. Did you nick yours?'

'Nah. I paid for it fair and square; with money from stuff what I nicked.'

'Same here. The watches are legit.'

'We could sell them you mean? Get legal help?'

'Exactly John. Right on the nail.'

'Alright,' said Martin. 'I'm all for it. How do we get a solicitor? We don't know any names here.'

'All we have to do is ask.'

'But ask who?'

'Patience,' said Rudge. 'The young copper who brings our food in seems a decent lad. I'll ask him a question.'

'But he don't like us. They think we killed a copper; one of them.'

'Makes no difference. Just wait.'

The young constable who brought the midday meal into the cell was greeted with a question from Rudge.

'May I ask you a question young sir?'

'That depends what it is,' said the young constable warily. 'Anything within the law I will answer.'

'That's fair enough,' said Rudge. 'I would not ask a policeman to do anything dubious. What I want to know is this.

Who, from your experience, is the most irritable, peppery and bad tempered solicitor in Carlisle?'

'Oh,' said the constable, 'That's easy. Mr Johnson.'

'Makes life difficult in court does he?'

'I should say so! He's a real curmudgeon.'

'And,' said Rudge, 'He cuts quite a figure in court I should think.'

'Oh yes! I've seen him argue hammer and tongs with the magistrates many a time and he does not like Mr Sempill at all.'

'Then he's just the man for me!' declared Rudge.

'What do you mean?' asked the constable nervously.

'I mean that I want to see this Mr Johnson as soon as possible.'

'What for?'

'To instruct him as to our defence. Oh don't worry young man. I won't tell a soul where I got the name from; if I see him within the next few hours. It is my legal right you know.'

So it was that Mr Thomas Johnson stood up before the magistrates on Monday 23 November and addressed the bench.

'I have just been instructed by these prisoners to defend them here today…'

Mr Horrocks interrupted him, 'You have been instructed, did you say?'

'Yes. There is one question I would like to ask. By whose authority are these men placed in irons? The law assumes a man to be innocent until he is found guilty and I think it a very sad thing.'

'That is a matter over which the bench has no control whatsoever.'

'Thank you for that observation,' said Mr Johnson, and sat down.

Superintendent Sempill now gave a deposition to the effect that he had been to Plumpton with a Mr Asquith, a land surveyor, and measured all the distances that had been mentioned by witnesses in the killing of PC Byrnes. There had been some dispute by Rudge over who was where and when they were there. Mr Johnson waited his turn; he and Sempill had crossed blades many times.

Sempill mentioned that on the night of the robbery he had sent word to the City Police in Carlisle, alerting them to the crime. Johnson stood up.

'You say Mr Sempill, that you sent word to the City Police office that this robbery had been committed.'

'I did.'

'Whom did you send?'

'I sent two city policemen.'

'Do you know their names?'

'No I don't.'

'Try. It is very important you know.'

'Well I tell you I don't know the men.'

'Do you swear?'

'I did.'

'Then you decline to give me the names of these two officers?'

'I don't decline. I tell you I do not know them.'

'Don't be angry then.'

'I am not angry.'

'Who gave the description of the men to you?'

'Sergeant Roche did.'

'When?'

'In his house, in bed.'

'Have you got the description he gave of the men while in bed, taken down in writing?'

'I am sure I cannot say.'

'You must have it in writing. Have you not a book for the purpose?'

'This is simply quibbling.'

'It is not quibbling.'

'I took it down upon a piece of paper.'

'I must ask you to produce that piece of paper.'

'Well I don't produce it.'

Mr Johnson spoke to the clerk of the court, 'I must ask you, please to make a note of that. Has a copy of that description been put in?'

Chief Constable Dunne replied tersely, 'No.'

Then Johnson turned back to the fuming Sempill.

'Are you aware if a description was posted about by your authority?'

'I am not aware of it.'

'Do you know, of your own knowledge whether that description was put in the papers?'

'I do not know any such thing.'

'You are remarkably innocent, I must say.'

The cross examination continued and moved on to how the identification of the suspects was carried out. Mr Sempill was asked how it was done.

'The men were placed in my office beside the cells for identification. The three prisoners were there as well as three other persons but I cannot give you their names. There were about thirty different persons altogether. The three men were persons whom the witnesses did not know.'

'We do not know that!' declared Mr Johnson.

'But I am telling you.'

'I am much obliged for the information. There were some very well known characters Mr Sempill. Was there a person called Joe Riley there?'

'I don't remember.'

'Will you swear he was not there?'

'I believe he was there once.'

'Perhaps you will be more sure presently. Was he there?'

'I cannot tax my memory with it, but the men were unknown to the witnesses.'

'But how do you know they were unknown to the witnesses?'

'Well I believe so.'

'You must not settle that as fact!'

The questions continued as to who was at the identity parades and under what circumstances and tempers wore very thin.

'Perhaps you can tell me if these men had irons on?'

'They had, but the irons were not visible.'

'What was visible?'

'If you wait till I have finished my answer, I will tell you.'

'I must have a categorical answer to my question, not a speech.'

Mr Mounsey-Heysham, a magistrate, now butted in.

'All these witnesses have already been examined before us. Therefore your point is not relevant as the witnesses have identified the prisoners in court.'

Mr Johnson was not a man to be browbeaten and came right back at him.

'I am speaking as a lawyer and I say that I am entitled to ask him how these men were identified, and by what means.'

The magistrate replied, 'On a question of committal, this is not admissible.'

'As an advocate I say that in my opinion, it is admissible,' retorted Johnson contemptuously, then turned back to Sempill.

'What was visible?'

There followed some more bad tempered exchanges about conditions at the identity parades, but a most extraordinary exchange took place at the end of Sempill's testimony. Mr Johnson read over the clerk's record of what the superintendent had said, and asked him again if he declined to produce the descriptions he had sent out of the suspects before they were arrested.

'I do not have the description, and if I had it, I would not produce it,' retorted Sempill angrily.

Like Rudge, Mr Johnson had cast the entire identification question into doubt. The proceedings lasted about one and a half hours, at the end of which, acting upon his client's instructions, Mr Johnson reserved their defence. Mr Horrocks thereupon committed the prisoners to take their trials at the next Assizes. Then Mr Johnson stood to speak again.

'…These men have property upon them, or had property on them, and I wish to make an application and ask that you will allow that money to be given up for the purpose of their defence.'

'What is it that you apply for?' asked Mr Horrocks.

'For the money and watch.'

'Your application for the money is granted, but that for the watch is not.'

'I cannot see the distinction. It is not suggested that the watch is part of the property stolen.'

'No. But it could have been stolen from some other place.'

'Oh,' said Mr Johnson, taken aback by the assumption. 'But there is no evidence to that.'

Mr Dunne now interjected, 'If the magistrates wish it, Mr Sempill can be put back into the witness box to prove that applications have been made...'

'Oh no, no,' cried Mr Johnson. 'It is very important that their property be restored to them.'

'It rests with the bench entirely,' said Mr Horrocks, 'to decide as to the disposal of any property. Your application with regard to the money, as I have already said, we grant. With regard to the watches, we refuse to grant it at present. Afterwards we may change our minds.'

Johnson was indignant.

'We can prove where they bought the watches. That is practically denying them the means of defence.'

The proceedings being over, and the magistrates being unmoved, the prisoners were then removed from the dock and taken away. There was now a great change in their circumstance, for until now they had been held in police cells. They were transferred to Carlisle prison and placed in the charge of Mr Joseph Leavers, the Governor. Mr Leavers was a keen naturalist, very intelligent, and as soon as the three men were in his care, their leg irons were removed. Rudge and Martin had separate cells, but Baker's mental condition was a concern to Mr Leavers and he called in his head warder Mr Andrew Johnson to discuss the matter.

'That man Baker is in a very bad way. I am thinking that if placed into solitary confinement, he may do himself some mischief.'

'It is something that we have seen a few times before sir.'

'Indeed it is. I am minded to put him into an association cell. What do you think of that idea?'

'It can do no harm sir, and might do some good. Certainly it would be far more difficult for him to hurt himself if there are other men in the cell with him. But of course the human company and conversation may help to keep his mind on an even keel. Left alone to his own thoughts, considering what he faces, he might run mad.'

'Well then he would not be fit to stand trial at all.'

'Indeed not sir.'

'Who do we have that he could be placed with safely?'

Johnson mused on the matter for a moment.

'Robert Cummings and John Watson sir.'

'They are hardly criminals those two! As I recall they got drunk and were prosecuted for breach of the peace. The only reason they are here is because they could not afford to pay sureties for their good behaviour. The trouble is that they keep doing it.'

'That's right sir,' said Johnson, marvelling yet again at how the governor knew the details of every prisoner in his gaol at any time.

'Apart from that they appear to be very innocuous men. They will not be any threat to him and conversation with them might steady his mind. Very well. Place him in their cell.'

Superintendent Sempill knew very well now what his prisoners' line of defence was going to be. He was exasperated by Thomas Johnson's goading of him. The solicitor had thrown the whole identification process into doubt, and had also cast aspersions on Sempill's professionalism for not following rules on the use of notebooks. Above all, he had insinuated that he, Sempill, had circulated to the public descriptions of the wanted men; this would completely invalidate the use of identity parades altogether. There was a real danger that his case against the suspects would fall apart. He knew more than ever that he was going to have to build a more solid case of evidence against the three men, or a barrister at the assizes would simply tear it apart. As for Mr Dunne saying that the bullet holes in Byrne's skull would be measured when the man was now buried in Penrith Cemetery; he did not know what to think of that! If the police made mistakes then these three men would walk out of court as free men; the mistakes had to stop.

Sempill called in an expert to examine the revolvers taken from Rudge and Martin. Rudge's gun was powerful, expensive, and capable of firing five bullets; it was a "Bulldog" made in Birmingham. Martin's was French and held six bullets, though it was not as big as Rudge's and fired smaller calibre rounds. The bullet extracted from PC Johnstone matched those found in Rudge's pistol. A bullet taken from Inspector Roche's arm matched those in Martin's revolver, as did another bullet found on the road after painstaking searches.

Chief Constable Dunne had taken men away from their normal duties and set them to search the River Lune between Tebay and Lancaster, a distance of over thirty miles. He hoped that they might see something glinting in the water that would prove to be some of the jewellery taken from Netherby Hall. They searched the river in vain for weeks. It was the brain of PC Scott that provided the breakthrough which reinforced the evidence of the ear-drop already found under the bridge at Tebay. Scott was tired of wading the waters of the Lune, especially in late November and early December; it was very cold, but on 12 December a thought struck him. What if the thief who stole the jewellery had not thrown it into the river? What if he had expected to escape? What if he hoped to come back later unobserved and retrieve his loot? He took himself once again up to the dry arch where the ear-drop had been found, and looked into the river. There had been no rain lately and the water was as clear as gin; nothing suspicious could be seen. The other bank, across the river, was steep and overgrown with weeds; no-one would ever go there; there was no access and no path. Scott gritted his teeth and once again waded into the river which was about eighteen inches deep at this point; he crossed to the other side.

The tussocks of grass and nettles were thick, so Scott drew his truncheon and began to part the vegetation, letting light down between thick clumps. It took a few minutes but before too long he saw something gleaming in the winter sun, and stooping, in his gloved hand, he picked up a diamond ear-drop. It was in the open mouth of a small tobacco pouch which also contained three diamond stars and a ring. He knew that two items were still missing; a small enamelled gold watch key, and a silver picture frame. They could not be found, but as the bag was not sealed properly, it was supposed that they had fallen into the river and been swept away. The bag was lying in the vegetation and no attempt had been made to conceal it so it had evidently been thrown across the river from the other side where Rudge had made a desperate dash for freedom chased by a mob of angry railwaymen.

It did not take Superintendent Sempill long to take the jewels to Netherby Hall and have Lady Hermione identify them. The ear-drop originally found had been enough to place the Netherby burglars at Tebay, but this sealed their fate even more than it had been. Whatever happened, Rudge and Martin would be going to prison for a long time for burglary, but if the identification evidence stood up at the Assizes, then they would hang.

James Baker solidly maintained that he was never at Tebay but in Newcastle. This meant that he might escape the burglary charges, however, as with the other two, the shootings, assaults and murder depended on his being identified as present when they were done. A number of witnesses had already done this, but if his lawyers could break that down at the Assizes, he might yet walk free. All of them were going to need a very good barrister if they were to stand any chance of escaping the hangman.

Rudge found that the regime in Carlisle prison was unlike any other that he had stayed in, and remarked on it to Andrew Johnson, the Chief Warder.

'Aye well Mr Leavers has some ideas on the treatment of prisoners which many governors would not agree with. He holds that rehabilitation of men is more likely to occur if they are treated with humanity. You'll not find the silent regime rigidly enforced here, though in theory we do have it.'

'Yes. I already noticed that. Is this a recent thing, the allowing prisoners to speak to each other during exercise?'

'It is; since Mr Leavers's appointment. You can also speak to the warders.'

'It's a new thing to me,' said Rudge. 'I have done a bit of time as you know, and we had to keep our mouths shut. It takes a man's individuality away I think.'

'It's a basic human need,' replied Johnson. 'To talk to others; it's very hard to take it away, like rendering them dumb, and even blind.'

Rudge, who had hated all men in uniform for many years, was surprised at his own reaction to Andrew Johnson. The chief warder was genial, and it was hard not to like him.

Johnson continued. 'There is also the fact that you are not actually convicted of anything Mr Rudge. You are remanded in custody awaiting trial, and until the law proves otherwise, you have to be regarded as innocent. That will also reflect in how you are treated.'

'I wish it reflected in the food,' said Rudge ruefully. 'Quite frankly it's not good. Tasteless slop. I could tuck into a good steak.'

'It is true that the prison fare leaves something to be desired,' admitted Johnson, but you have to remember that the governor is working on a tight budget and that every ounce of food has been calculated by doctors as being right to sustain life. It's very basic, but they were more concerned with nutrition than taste and the Home Office decrees the menus.'

'I wonder if it might be possible to pay for better food to be sent in,' mused Rudge. 'I'll have to ask my solicitor. Do you never get better food sent in for prisoners?'

Johnson paused for a moment, hesitating.

'Spit it out Mr Johnson; words rarely bite.'

'Very well,' said Johnson slowly. 'If they condemn a man, he gets a choice of whatever he wants for his last meal.'

'Oh!' said Rudge. 'I think I would forgo my wish for better grub if that's the condition.'

He ruminated for a moment, then spoke again.

'I met him once you know. Mr Berry.'

'You met the hangman?'

'I did; at Doncaster races a few years ago. I bought him a drink and had a chat. I made him a bet.'

'What bet was that?'

'I bet him thirteen pounds to two that he would never hang me.'

Johnson stared at him for a moment.

'Well Mr Rudge, all I can say to that is that I wish you the best of luck with your bet. That matter hangs on the outcome of the January Assizes.'

'Better that hangs than me,' replied Rudge with a hollow, rather forced laugh. 'If I win, I can't see how I can spend the money anyway.'

22

Careless Talk

When people get excited, they often become garrulous, and James Baker was in a constant state of nervous excitement, which was hardly surprising, considering his plight. His father, Thomas, had left his furniture shop in Bethnal Green in the care of Baker's mother and he journeyed up to Carlisle to see his son. Baker had assured him that he was innocent, that he was not guilty of the Netherby burglary and that he had been nowhere near Tebay when Rudge and Martin were taken. His father was no fool; he hardly could be that after running a business in the East End of London for thirty years. Being a man of some means, he had engaged a solicitor to act for his son, but things had all happened very quickly so that Mr Moore was not available to make the trip to Carlisle to appear in front of the magistrates.

'The thing is Jimmy, that you need a solicitor to do all the leg work of organising the defence. But a solicitor cannot speak for you at the Assizes. It has to be a barrister and the best we can get.'

'What's his name, this barrister?'

'Mr Moore is trying to get a Mr Miles Mattinson. Apparently he's very good but he will need an assistant in a case as serious as this. That will be a junior barrister, a Mr James Lumb.'

'And they believe me to be innocent?'

I think that goes without saying Jimmy. It's nonsense of course that you could do such dreadful things as they say you have been doing, and I hope that will become clear as the trial goes on.'

'What are people saying out there?'

'Oh it's all rubbish. The papers make you out to be some sort of monster, but they always do that don't they. Lies are their stock in trade. People will change their minds quick enough when you're found not guilty. Just wait and see.'

'Will I see this barrister man?'

'No. Mr Moore will be the man you speak to; he will represent you to Mr Mattinson. You will probably see him just before the court opens.'

Rudge and Martin had been having a similar conversation with Thomas Johnson, but Rudge was curious.

'Do you believe our story Mr Johnson? That we murdered no-one?'

Johnson was a man of the world; he had been around the law for many years and spoken to villains of all sorts many times.

'It's not up to me to believe or disbelieve you Mr Rudge. My job is to ensure that you are properly represented in court and that the best case possible is made to establish your innocence.'

'You think us innocent then?'

'That's not what I said. If you are innocent then a properly run court will establish it, provided that all the facts are laid before it. That's my job and that of your barrister. We shall do that to the best of our ability, but if you are guilty then the evidence for it will outweigh anything we can say.'

'Like the scales of justice then?'

'Exactly so Mr Rudge.'

'How likely do you think it is that we shall win our case?'

'On the murder? We have a good chance on the face of things. Superintendent Sempill has fluffed the identification process. The parades were flawed, and the circulating of a description before the parades were held destroys utterly the value of them. What they are left with are the words of Inspector Roche, PC Handley, Mr Hetherington and Mr Armstrong and, as you pointed out, it was dark and none of them has identified all of you. Roche particularly could not swear to you Mr Martin.'

'That's because I wasn't there,' growled Martin.

'That is as may be, but such a flawed process could be enough to throw doubt into the minds of a jury. If there is sufficient doubt then they cannot find you guilty. There was also the farcical situation with the Chief Constable stating in open court that the bullet wounds in Constable Byrnes's skull would be measured when the man lies buried in Penrith cemetery.'

'Then we might walk out of court?'

'I did not say that either Mr Martin. You are forgetting the ear-drop under the bridge at Tebay, and the subsequent finding of the other stolen property from Netherby Hall. If the court decides that you stole them, then you could be going to prison for a long time, even if they find you not guilty of murder. There is also the question of the cheese rind of the sort sold in the Packhorse Inn at Plumpton and identified as such by the landlady.'

'Nothing to do with us Mr Johnson,' said Rudge. 'There was a bloke we met on the train; the one who ran off. My guess is that he dropped that jewellery as he ran; the cheese as well. He must have been one of the burglars, but we didn't know that.'

'The police contend that man was Mr Baker.'

'Neither of us know him. First time we saw him was in the dock in front of the magistrates.'

'So your contention is that the third man in your wagon, whom you did not know, ran off and has not been caught and that he is the burglar?'

'That is correct.'

Mr Johnson's face was expressionless. 'It appears that Mr Sempill is not the only very innocent man around these parts,' he said, making a note in his book. He stood to leave, not offering to shake hands.

'We shall build a case gentlemen. You may have no qualms about that. I shall brief Mr Cavanagh with what you have told me and shall return if he wishes to know more. Good day to you.'

With that, he left.

'Well that all sounds very hopeful John,' remarked Rudge before the warders came to put them back into separate cells. 'All we have to do is stick to our story and we have a good chance of pulling through this.' Then he whispered 'And don't say nothing stupid!'

'Course not! What do you take me for?' came the hoarse whisper back.

James Baker on the other hand, was not a reticent man. He was in fact rather talkative and facing some very serious charges. He was inclined to jabber on at some length about his past to the two men he had been put to share a cell with. There were of course no listening warders because Governor Leavers would never allow such a thing. It was his business, upon receipt of a warrant from the magistrates, to imprison men and to carry out sentences as sanctioned by law. Acting as some sort of mechanism for the incrimination of prisoners in his charge was no part of his job. Baker's mind was never a strong one, and he was cracking under the strain of what he was going through. Having spent some time in prison before, he was used to men of his own class and occupation there. Consciously he might have known that Cummings and Watson were not such, but his subconscious continued to act as if they were, and in time they became, in his eyes at least, his confidantes. The two men were in fact not criminals at all, merely two ordinary working class Carlisle men who were in prison because they could not afford to pay their fines for being drunk and disorderly. Their mouths did not hang open in disbelief at what he was telling them, but their minds certainly did.

'So you went in through the window and the owner of the house was waiting for you with a stick!'

'That's right John. He fetched me a hell of a whack with it and tried to grab hold of me.'

'So how did you escape?'

'Pure luck. I wasn't completely through the window and he was to the side of me. The blow came across my shoulders but by the time he was ready to hit me again I was sliding down the ladder and away.'

'So you are actually a burglar then? No messing?'

'I am,' said Baker proudly. 'No point in denying it. I did time for that job and paid my debt to society so no harm in telling you.'

'Well I'll be jiggered!' said Cummings.

Baker basked in the adulation of men who had no conception of what his life was like; and adulation was what he needed; he fed off it now like a lamb with a bottle. He drew strength from their admiration, and drunk with it, embellished his past misdeeds, invented daring escapades, and occasionally told the truth. Away from Rudge and Martin, he blossomed and bathed in the astonishment of lesser men. He would have done better to keep his mouth shut.

The days in prison wore on in monotonous fashion, for the regime inside the walls was that sanctioned by the Home Office, and silence was the general rule. Mr Leavers, in allowing association cells and limited talking, was further ahead in his thinking than most of his contemporaries in other gaols. For most prisoners, the day was monotonous; Rudge was well used to it. He gazed morosely round the cell that he had been placed into. There was no bed but a wooden plank set into the wall under the window, and no mattress; prisoners were not to sleep comfortably. There was a pillow but it was a coarse sack stuffed with coconut fibre; but Governor Leavers did at least believe in hygiene, and unlike Portland or Parkhurst, the two woollen blankets, were at least clean. Resting on them were a bible, a prayer book and a hymn book. Rudge did not have to look to see that the rest of the cell furniture was present; he knew they would be because an inventory was taken every day. These comprised a wooden plate with spoon, a box for salt, two tin mugs, a metal chamber pot, a wooden bucket with lid, a hand brush, a towel, a piece of soap and a few squares of brown paper. There was also a slate with a piece of chalk, and as soon as he was shown into his cell on his first day there, Rudge grabbed these and wrote, 'May I have pencil and paper please?'

'I'll ask,' grunted the warder.

Rudge nodded his thanks. The prison was as silent as the grave. If you made a noise outside when and where it was allowed, you could be deprived of your food. No-one wanted that.

Separate, and silent.

The words, written down in black and white, sound so innocuous. Rudge had endured years of it. No communication with other human beings; no singing, no speaking. Locked for most of the day in a cell by himself; it sent men round the bend. The loneliest lighthouse keeper in the world was at least relieved after a few weeks. The alone-ness of men was the terror of it. The system had been designed by Christians determined to enforce retreat, reflection and contemplation on criminal minds, somewhat like monks, or the prophets of old in their hermit caves. What they did instead was deprive them of their sanity and confine them into a cold stone box some nine feet long, seven feet high and five feet in width. This was the world for all prisoners after sentence, at least for the first twenty-eight days in prison. Thereafter there was work outside the cell for most, but each night meant being confined into the cell again, each man alone with Hell and his own demons. Rudge had plenty of those. An appalling wall of boring monotony stretched in front of him, even if he escaped the gallows. At times, in Portland, he had wanted to scream his frustration, his howling desperation at the walls, and had to stuff his handkerchief into his mouth to stifle the agony of it.

At night Rudge shivered with the gross intensity of the all pervading cold that seeped into his cell from the winter outside. Two woollen blankets were enough to keep the life in a man but the plank bed he slept on was composed of three lengths, and between each was a gap through which the cold came from underneath. His skin grew dry and his fingers cracked; his slop pail and water froze overnight. It did not help that he knew that this was not an especial punishment. All prisoners went through the same thing; Anthony Benjamin Rudge had no fear of Hell because he had spent fifteen years of his life in this system and nothing he could conceive of could be worse; if anything he might have longed for the biblical Hell as being at least warmer than a prison cell.

To Rudge's surprise, there were two people who made his life in Carlisle more bearable than he had experienced in any other prison, and these were the chief warder and the governor. The governor was required to live at the prison, which had been built on a radial pattern with his house at the centre. Corridors connected his home to the four spokes that spread out from this hub, thus he could visit cells at his leisure. Mr Leavers often did so, and was genuinely interested in what the men in his charge had to say.

'I'm a remand prisoner Mr Leavers. I have been charged with certain things but I have not been convicted. It seems unjust to me that I should have to bear with the treatment of a criminal when I have not been found to be so.'

'I assure you Mr Rudge, that you have the same food and the same provision as anyone else in this prison. The whole is laid down by the Home Office and I have very little leeway in changing the conditions of your imprisonment.'

'I know that sir but it is winter now and very cold.'

'I can hardly let you have a fire in your cell you know.'

Rudge laughed. 'An extra blanket would be a great help.'

To his surprise, Leavers replied, 'I think the extra blanket is a reasonable thing. I shall see that you have it. Anything else?'

'Some reading matter.'

'I agree. You are not undergoing punishment, but awaiting trial. We have a small library and I shall instruct that you are to be allowed access to it.'

'The food is very basic; might I be able to buy my own? I can pay.'

'I am afraid that is very much against regulations, but the food is of good quality; I check it myself. The diet however, is prescribed from above. It may be monotonous, and I agree that it is, but it is devised in the Home Office and is calculated precisely by experts to keep men alive and healthy.'

'No chance of some beer or wine then?'

Leavers laughed. 'Now that really would be extending my brief a little too far. But you knew that. You must be content with the fare you have, and at least you may be comforted by the fact that you eat better than the former residents of this place, even if you drink the same. And they did not have government issue cocoa.'

'What former residents are those sir? And the cocoa, I allow you, is one of the good things about being inside.'

'Yes,' said Leavers dryly. 'Cocoa is seen as a pleasure by most men. The monks who formerly lived in this place did not have that.'

'Monks? In prison?'

'There was a monastery of the Black Friars on this site long before it was a prison,' explained Leavers.

'Well I am not religious,' said Rudge.

'Which is perhaps a pity,' replied the governor. 'You would find it a great solace in your current situation. And perhaps you might not have done some of the things you have done in life.'

Rudge looked thoughtful.

'We had clergy round where I was brought up. Holy Joes we called them, or black boys. Some of them were decent, and some of them were mugs. They used to tell us not to thieve or lie and that sort of stuff.'

'The advice was good I think.'

'With respect sir, that's easy to say. If you followed their advice where I was, then you'd starve to death pretty quick. You soon learned that it's dog eat dog in this world. It's easy for a well fed man to tell a hungry man to behave.'

'Do you have any notions about morality?'

'Oh some,' replied Rudge, with a wry face. 'I don't swear in front of ladies; I don't hit women though there's plenty who do. I despise them for it ain't manly to do that. But as for taking things from people who have; no. I have not that.'

'But why kill?'

'Who says I've killed? That's the very thing I'm denying.'

'But you have met men who have killed other people?'

'I may have.'

'Do you know why they did it?'

'I think so,' replied Rudge, with a certain intensity. 'To avoid coming back to places like this. To avoid being dragged back to Hell. I think a man would do anything to stop that.'

'You blame the prisons for murders?' asked the governor incredulously.

'Yes, I do,' replied Rudge without hesitation. 'You have to understand sir that you are an exception. In other prisons there is no understanding of the effects on a man's mind of what he goes through. Would a man commit murder in order to avoid many years in prison? I think that he might very well do that. I have seen that in others many times.'

'But not in you?'

'Really Mr Leavers; must you try and catch a man so? Of course not in me.'

'Yet you carried a gun.'

'For protection only.'

'That's to be established by the court.'

'The court must establish what it will sir. I have not killed anyone.'

'As you will answer to God?'

'I do not think there is a God Mr Leavers. But if there is, I sometimes think he must rather answer to me for where he has placed me, and what he has made me.'

In chapel, on Sunday, attendance was compulsory. The prisoners stood in boxes, side by side, separate, like coffins stood up, unable to see or communicate with the man next door. Rudge and hundreds of others roared out the hymn:
'ALL PEOPLE THAT ON EARTH DO DWELL;
SING TO THE LORD WITH CHEERFUL VOICE.'

The volume raised the roof. The fervour swelled the heart of the chaplain who felt the men must see God.

Yet this was the only occasion for the inmates of the prison when they were able to fill their lungs and exercise their voices at full volume. They took the most of the opportunity. For perhaps the majority, God did not exist; for some, he was a still small voice of calm; yet for all, he broke the silence of the government's reformatory grave and that was enough to sing his praises until their throats split.

23

An Arrest

The mystery of the identity of the fourth man continued to engage the fascination of the nation, and it might well be that the man who caught him would receive a great deal of kudos. For a policeman this meant a lot; it entailed instant promotion, an increase in salary and much admiration. Small wonder that men in dark blue uniforms across the United Kingdom dreamed of being the chap who brought in the fourth man. PC Westwood of the Metropolitan force was no exception. On Wednesday 23 December he was on patrol in Regent Street; the afternoon was cold but the road was thronged with people shopping for Christmas. Suddenly, among the crowd he saw a man he knew, having arrested him before for burglary, and who had spent some years in prison. Regent Street is a long way from Netherby Hall, but Westwood had been reading descriptions of the wanted fourth man, and was convinced that this man was the fugitive. Placing his hand on the handle of his truncheon, just in case there was trouble, he walked over to the man, who was looking in a shop window, and announced 'James Baker, I am arresting you on suspicion of burglary. You must accompany me to the station.'

'Alright Mr Westwood,' replied the man. 'I'll come quiet, but you are making a mistake.'

Westwood marched his prisoner round the short distance to Marlborough Street police station and the news was quickly relayed to Scotland Yard. Word came back very quickly that two of the Yard's best detectives were on their way to take him in charge, Inspectors Shore and Abberline. So anxious was the Yard to show action in the case of the fourth man, that they sent out a telegram to the news agencies announcing that a man had been arrested and was being taken to Carlisle for purposes of identification. The problem was, that once that was done, there was no going back. The public would simply not understand a mistake in this particular investigation.

Shore and Abberline arrived at Marlborough Street and waited for their prisoner to be brought up from the cells. This was done, and he entered the room. Abberline, as tough as they came and a policeman of more than twenty years service looked at him and swore. 'Fucking Hell.'

'Hello Mr Abberline, Mr Shore. Nice to see you again.'

Abberline turned to Westwood.

'Are you trying to be clever?'

'No sir. He's a known associate of Rudge, Baker and Martin and I think you'll find that he was at Longtown Coursing.'

Shore rounded on the prisoner.

'Is that right? Were you at Longtown?'

'Yes Mr Shore. It was good sport and I made a bit of money on the doggies. There's no crime in that is there?'

'Did you do the Netherby job?'

'Now come on Mr Shore. How could I have done that?'

'Nonetheless, you were at Longtown. You'll have to come with us now.'

'But what for? There's nothing against me; no evidence, nothing.'

'You'll be needed for purposes of identification.'

So it was that two senior detectives bundled "James Baker" onto a train and headed for Carlisle that same evening. Superintendent Sempill waited, all eagerness, to see the fourth man, the solution to the mystery; the man whose capture would tie up all loose ends. As the two London men walked in with

"Baker" in between them, Sempill's face took on a look of astonishment.

'I know. I know,' said Abberline. 'But we are following orders Super; from on high.'

'Has your commissioner seen this man?'

'No sir. He just sent orders that the suspect was to be taken to Carlisle immediately.'

'I see. Very well; the wheels are set in motion and we might as well go through with it. There's a bench sitting especially for this tomorrow morning.'

'It's alright sir,' said "Baker," 'I don't mind a little holiday. Sometimes it's nice to get out of London.'

'Just you shut your mouth,' snarled Shore, who was in no mood for cheek from someone with a record as long as his arm.

Early the next morning "Baker" was brought before Mr Horrocks as Chairman, accompanied by four other magistrates. As the prisoner stepped into the dock, Mr Horrocks's eyebrows shot up towards his hairline and the other magistrates stared. "Baker" was not handcuffed but stood there in the clothes he had been arrested in the previous day, a shabby suit of checked tweed. On his head he had a newish silk hat and round his neck a white muffler; he was the very picture of a minor East End mobsman who had fallen on hard times.

'You must remove your hat in court,' said Mr Horrocks.

'I do apologise sir,' said "Baker" whipping his hat off immediately. 'The police officer told me to put it on.'

'What do we have here Superintendent?'

'The prisoner before the bench is James Baker, alias Smith, alias Johnston.'

'My name is not Baker sir.'

'The prisoner is charged with the Netherby burglary and the attempted murder of Sergeant Roche and PC Johnstone.'

Horrocks looked at Sempill with a somewhat disbelieving eye. 'You ask for a remand for this day week?'

'Yes.'

'That will not be the regular court day.'

Mr Ferguson, another of the magistrates, interjected, 'We could remand him for a week, and one magistrate, on his own if necessary, then renew the remand until Saturday.'

Sempill was satisfied with this.

'I don't think it would be desirable to say more at present than that. I have good reason for thinking that evidence will be forthcoming.'

Mr Horrocks nodded, banishing the doubt from his face.

'That is sufficient to justify a remand.'

The Clerk of the Court, Mr Hodgson asked, 'You have not had time to get up any evidence?'

'No. The prisoner only arrived here yesterday.'

'Excuse me sir,' said "James Baker". 'May I write home please?'

'I do not know what the rules are on that,' replied Mr Horrocks.

'There will be no objection to it,' replied Sempill.

Mr Horrocks nodded and spoke to the prisoner.

'You will be remanded for a week to this station. You said just now that your name is not Baker?'

'My name is Smith sir. That is the name I go by. That is my name, but as you have got it down, it doesn't matter.'

'You say your name is Smith?'

'It is Smith.'

'Just Smith?'

'James Smith sir. My pals call me One-armed Jemmy.'

'Do they? I see. Very well. Take him down,' said Mr Horrocks, nodding to the attending officers.

When he had gone Mr Horrocks waited as the court cleared, motioning Sempill to stay where he was. When the spectators and reporters had all gone, he spoke.

'A one-armed man Superintendent? One of the most notorious burglars in London? A member of the Ladder Gang? A one-armed man? And he looks as if he's fallen on hard times too.'

Sempill looked sheepish.

'He could have been there as a lookout sir, an accomplice. We have to put him through identification just as any other suspect. And I have been told that he sometimes wears a hook.'

'I take it that he lost his arm some time ago?'

'A good many years I think; apparently it was caught in some machinery. It does not appear to handicap him too much.'

'I see that, but I imagine that in the pursuit of burglary, lack of an arm is not an asset, particularly in climbing ladders. I only hope that some of our more lurid newspapers do not pick up on this for it will begin to look as if we are pulling some sort of practical joke.'

'No joke sir. Due process is all.'

'Very well, but try not to be too disappointed if it leads nowhere, as I suspect.'

'No sir.'

'By the way, I have read in the newspapers that Madame Tussauds in London are staging a waxwork tableau of the murder with models of the accused. Can you ask our friends of the Metropolitan Police if this is legal before a trial has taken place?'

'I can sir and I will, but I cannot see how they can get true likenesses of the prisoners if they are locked up. They will say that it is a work of fiction with artists' impressions of the men who did the murder.'

'Find out please if they have actually named our prisoners. If they have then I shall send a strongly worded complaint to the Home Office. We must have no outside prejudice of that sort.'

It is perhaps needless to say that a week passed by and not a scrap of evidence was brought against One-armed Jemmy and thus he was released without charge, the court paying his train fare back to London.

Rudge, Martin and Baker were all losing weight on the prison food; Rudge in particular had a chubby face when he was arrested, but the small helpings of beans and bacon fat that he received all too often in solitary confinement, were stripping the pounds off him, as well as causing great discomfort to his system and bringing on flatulence. He was not alone in this, for the whole night in a prison was punctuated by prolonged farting, and in the morning the smell and fug in the central wells was enough to fell a man. The only relief to this tight diet was on Christmas Day when each prisoner received a generous portion of beef and vegetables with potatoes, followed by some excellent plum pudding.

Outside the walls of the prison, matters were moving ahead. On 29 December, Rudge, Martin and Baker were reunited in the dock at the magistrates' court. There was new evidence which had to be presented before the Assizes began in January. Once again the dryly efficient Mr Horrocks was chairman of the bench.

To Baker's utter horror Mr Dunne the Chief Constable, now had Robert Cummings brought into the room. He was no longer sharing a cell with Baker because he had served his time and been released. Upon his release he had gone straight to Andrew Johnson, the chief warder of the prison and told him what Baker had been boasting about. Mr Dunne told the bench that he wished to bring in this man to give evidence.

Mr Johnson the solicitor almost flew to his feet. He and Dunne had already had some very bad tempered exchanges that morning.

'It will concern Baker alone. I object to it as far as the others are concerned.'

Mr Horrocks drawled, 'Baker's statement will only be evidence against himself.'

Mr Dunne was about to reply when Mr Johnson, his temper sparking the air, almost spat the words at him, 'If you go on like this much longer, I shall ask for you to be put out of the court!'

'If you can!' retorted the Chief Constable.

Mr Horrocks was not pleased. 'This is very irregular Mr Johnson. I wish you would keep quiet.'

'I protest! Mr Dunne hits me with his stick and tells me to keep quiet. I don't think you realise your position sir. Mr Dunne has no right to address himself to me; he must do it to you.'

'You must do the same.'

'Certainly I will; I have always done so.'

Mr Hodgson, the Clerk, thought that Cummings's evidence had better wait for the Assizes. It was a well established rule of law that a statement made by one prisoner could not be received against the others who were not present at the time. Upon hearing this, Mr Horrocks ruled that the evidence be reserved for the Assizes.

PC Fortune, who was now well enough to testify, gave his evidence as to what had happened on the railway line when he had challenged four men on the night he was battered. This time it was Mr MacKay, Chief Constable of Carlisle City

Police who acted as prosecutor. Fortune's testimony gripped the court, speaking of the men who had attacked him until MacKay also stepped over the border of what was allowed.

'Do you see any of the men here?'

Once again Mr Johnson was on his feet like a shot.

'Oh no! No! That won't do!'

MacKay took no notice, but did not repeat the question. When Fortune had finished, Mr Horrocks asked, 'Do you object to that question being put Mr Johnson, as to whether he identifies any of the men?'

'I do.'

'I allow the objection.'

'Thank you sir.'

It was now that James Baker stood up and asserted his right to question Robert Cummings, despite Mr Horrocks having reserved his evidence to the Assizes. Seeing his agitation, Mr Horrocks asked Mr Dunne if he would oppose this, but the Chief Constable did not; Cummings was brought in.

Heads craned forward on necks, expecting legal fireworks and sharp questioning; they were doomed to disappointment. If they had read the police description of Baker they might not have been so, because he was described, as was Martin, as reading and writing imperfectly. What followed was almost embarrassing. Robert Cummings took the stand and Baker asked him a series of inept questions about when he had supposedly confessed to Cummings, and when the witness had made a statement to the governor. He was clearly implying that Cummings had been reading newspapers or had been bribed to make a statement. The witness on the other hand, was quite firm. James Baker had told him and John Watson that he had been at Tebay when the railwaymen caught Rudge and Martin; and that one of his companions had thrown a tobacco pouch containing the stolen jewels into the River Lune. Both Watson and Cummings had made separate statements to the same effect and neither man had any motive to lie about it. When it was over James Baker was pale and shaken, for his own defence had collapsed in a heap of loose bricks; out of his own boastfulness, he was established as being at Tebay and in the company of Martin and Rudge.

Rudge's face was like thunder. If the testimony of Cummings and Watson was believed, and it probably would be, then he and Martin were established as the jewel thieves. By association it also established them as the men who assaulted Roche, Johnstone and Fortune in the course of their escape since Roche and others had identified them. Several times he shouted 'Not true!' and had to be silenced by Mr Johnson the solicitor who now knew that he would have an uphill struggle to save his clients. All that could rescue them from the gallows was if the Crown failed to link the murder of PC Byrnes with the Netherby burglary, and that hinged on identification. Whatever happened, there was now little doubt that if they were not hanged, Rudge, Martin and Baker would be going to prison for a very long time. Rudge was intelligent enough to know this; Baker was not; he also did not realise that if Rudge could have got his hands on him after his examination of Cummings, then he would have been lucky to escape with his life; he had almost put their heads into a noose.

At the end of the proceedings the new witnesses were bound over to appear at the Assizes and notification was sent to John Watson that he too would be required. All now hung on 15 January when the Assizes would open and a game of life and death would be played out under the saturnine gaze of Mr Justice Day.

Nellie Baker visited James in prison when the court proceedings were over. Conditions were such that not a lot could be said. Like all visitors Nellie was shown into a large wooden box which sat in a room. She sat down facing a small opening covered in wire gauze. On the other side of the room was a similar box where James Baker sat facing her. The gap between the boxes was four feet. Behind each box stood a warder, listening to all that was said. Baker was despondent.

'They've done for me Nellie. Those blokes is lying. Every word they said is not true.'

'You think they've been bribed?'

'They must have been! I never said all that stuff.'

'Where do you think they got it from then?'

'They read it in the newspapers and cooked it up to make me out to be bad.'

'Why would they do that?'

'Cos that's what rozzers do ain't it? They got to arrest someone or they look bad. They're just putting me in the frame because they need to hang someone. You'll tell Mr Mattinson won't you?'

'I will tell him, you may be sure.'

Whether Baker's barrister would find this useful or not was debatable, but he would be told.

Conversation in the cages was necessarily stilted.

'How are you in yourself James?'

Baker sobbed, unable to hold back his increasing fear.

'Not good Nellie. I think they're going to hang me.'

'Oh now don't say that James. You ain't done nothing and you've got a lot of good people on your side.'

'I know that Nellie,' said Baker bursting into tears and cupping his face in his hands. 'But I can't stand much more of it. I just feel like ending it all now.'

'That's enough of that talk!' said the warder behind him.

'What's it to you?' shouted Baker. 'You ain't the one facing a rope and I'm an innocent man.'

'We shall see that in a couple of weeks,' replied the warder. 'Now this interview is over and you must go back to your cell.'

'But I've only just got here!' cried Nellie.

'I know Ma'am, but after what Mr Baker said, I have no choice. Suicide is a crime and here is a desperate man. He will be confined, and put on watch so that he does not harm himself.'

'You mean so you can save him for the gallows!' shouted Nellie.

'Shouting at officers is not allowed Ma'am; if you wish to retain visiting privileges, please don't.'

Nellie dabbed a tear away, and the warder relented.

'It ain't my place to save anyone for the gallows as you put it Ma'am, but Mr Baker just threatened to kill himself. That is a crime anyway and we will prevent that at any rate. What happens next is up to judge and jury; everything hinges on that.'

Down in London the Nabob nodded to himself with satisfaction on reading his newspaper. The managers of the Metropolitan and City Police Orphanage had relaxed their rules so that two of the children of PC Byrnes could be admitted there. The oldest boy, being nine years old, could be admitted at once; the other, being only four and a half, would have to wait until he was seven but did have a place. The top mobsman drew deeply on his cigar and felt satisfied. His signal had been understood and his conscience was clear; cheap at the price. He could wash his hands of this business now, with a clear conscience. There had been a couple of men who disregarded his instructions about carrying revolvers while doing work, but

Brindle had broken their legs with a pick-axe handle, and word had got about. The police did not need guns.

On 2 January 1886, a jeweller named Wood was arrested in Liverpool. Not long before, he had been in prison for bigamy. On his release, he married a third woman, a waitress named Jane, and then tried to set up a business in Birmingham where he got heavily into debt with his suppliers. Unable to pay them, he and Jane packed all the jewellery into a suitcase or two and headed for Liverpool. The happy couple were about to board a steamer under assumed names for a new life in America, but unfortunately Mr Wood fitted very well the descriptions of the notorious fourth man. He was seen and arrested, and although it quickly became clear that he was not the fourth man, he had been caught in possession of a lot of jewellery that did not belong to him. It was also found that he was still married to his first wife and that in marrying Jane he had committed bigamy a second time. The hunt for the fourth man continued.

24

Cavanagh

Through a narrow entry off the south side of the Strand, in London, is a cobbled passageway which leads to a very exclusive world, well-named the Inner Temple. It is quaint and old. The area contained in this city block is a rabbit warren of alleys, closes and strange winding stairs. There is a particular silence to the scene and the very stones and bricks reek of ancient law, since it is inhabited largely by barristers, for whom it is a very choice address.

Lurking just the other side of a brick arch was a close by the name of Elm Court. An enterprising builder had at some time erected the conceit of a broken pediment in honeyed stone over the entrance to a flight of time-worn stone steps which led up to apartments such as are desirable to men of the law. One of the denizens of these was Christopher Cavanagh, barrister at law, late of Dublin, author, legal pundit and a man, so it was said, to watch. Mr Cavanagh was staring morosely through the leaded diamond-glassed window of his chambers at a pigeon that appeared to be looking at him from a window ledge opposite.

'Yes,' he said to himself. 'If they could fly, they'd have more chance, and in that respect you have the advantage over them.'

He was speaking of Rudge, Martin and Baker, though only the first two were his concern, for Mr Cavanagh was the Returning Barrister for Cumberland. Barristers are, of course, sole traders, and a man has to make a living, so a lawyer in Mr Cavanagh's trade has to take work where he finds it. Some barristers are overworked, and sometimes have to hand cases to somebody else who administers the "returned" case; this did not happen often in Cumberland. The other aspect of the work was, that as the appointed Returning Barrister for Cumberland, he could be asked to represent murderers in court who could not afford a barrister. Christopher Cavanagh had no choice but to do it, though he knew in this case that he had been handed a poisoned chalice. Still, he would do his best; some day he hoped to be a judge, and a case like this could make a man's name overnight. He must give it his best shot. That might mean some wheeling and dealing, some twisting and turning and perhaps a few tricks. He smiled wryly to himself.

'Very well. In such a case the best defence is to attack. The best general, if he can, chooses his own battlefield.'

It was 11 January before he could begin his campaign, for the calendar of the Queen's Bench did not have an opening until then. Justices Denham and Grantham heard Mr Cavanagh ask to have the trial of Rudge and Martin at the Old Bailey because it was not possible for them to receive a fair trial in Cumberland. There had been hysterical articles printed in the local press about his clients who had already been found guilty in the minds of the Cumbrian public.

News of this reached Cumberland via the newspapers; what the ordinary man and woman in the street saw was a stuck up and uppity London lawyer attacking their good name and the result was that even before Cavanagh had set foot in Carlisle, he was not a popular man. Mr Justice Denham remarked that Cumberland was not alone in its detestation of burglary and murder. If Mr Cavanagh got what he wanted it would make a rule that burglars never be tried where their crimes were committed. Cavanagh was not put off by this.

'My Lord, it is not just the newspapers that have prejudiced the public against my clients. Mr Rudge points out that during the Coroner's Inquest, all the prisoners were shackled. This is not usual practice and must convey an impression of guilt to the general public. They had no legal representative at the start of the process and they were attacked by a mob before appearing before the magistrates. My clients have also been represented in a waxworks as carrying out the murder of PC Byrnes. None of this is fitting or appropriate to a fair judicial process.'

Denham replied, 'I think that the effigies in Madam Tussauds a most improper thing, but they are in London, not in Carlisle, so will not prejudice a Cumbrian jury. As to the rest, it is my opinion that your clients will receive as fair a trial in Carlisle as they would in London. Your application, Mr Cavanagh, is an insult to all intelligent people in Cumberland. Your request to move the trial to the Old Bailey is denied.'

Rudge received the news in his cell from his solicitor, Mr Johnson.

'It is most unfortunate. I myself swore an affidavit testifying to all the irregularities that have taken place since your arrest. Procedures have not been followed very well, and I do not think that their lordships have appreciated how much public opinion has been affected by the actions of the police.'

'Will they get away with it?' asked Rudge? 'I mean I'd be happier if the trial was in London after all that's been going on.'

'I do not believe that Mr Cavanagh will allow them to get away with it. He will attack them for what they have done, and in particular the process of identification.'

'You think there is hope for us then?'

'Oh there is always hope Mr Rudge, until there is none. I am afraid however that Mr Baker's loose tongue has landed you in some hot water. If you do escape the murder charge, I think it would be only fair to warn you that the burglary charge may stick and that will mean a very severe sentence.'

'We ain't going to walk then are we?'

'In the lap of the gods; whatever else, Mr Cavanagh, Mr Lumb and myself will do our best to mitigate it.'

Johnson left, shaking his head as he walked out of the prison gates. He did not know what to make of Rudge. The man was clearly intelligent and well read. Despite the East End accent he was very sharp and his defence in the magistrates' court had foreshadowed what his barrister had to do. It was very hard to reconcile in his mind the murderer and burglar he was supposed to be, with the man in the cell who quoted Thackeray, Dickens and Shakespeare at him. What might he have been if his feet had gone down another path when he was young? Martin was easier to categorise; the man was a thug, not very bright, and Johnson, despite the professional barrier in his head, had a strong suspicion that if any of these three men had killed the police officer, then it was Martin.

Mr Cavanagh, full of the law, was not finished with London, for his indignation knew no bounds, his case appearing to him to be obvious. He submitted his request for the trial to be moved to London to the Court of Appeal in the Exchequer Chamber, and he thought his argument was completely watertight. William Palmer, the Rugeley poisoner had been tried in London for murdering a man with strychnine. It had been clear that if he had been tried in Staffordshire he would not have been found guilty, for public opinion was on his side. Tried at the Old Bailey, Palmer had hanged and Parliament passed an act allowing for trials to be moved to the Central Criminal Court where the public had been prejudiced one way or another. The case for moving the trial of Rudge and Martin was surely even more obvious than it had been with Palmer.

The Master of the Rolls himself, Lord Esher heard the appeal along with two other judges; Mr Cavanagh was buoyant as he faced the bench, only to have his hopes deflated at once by Lord Esher.

'I cannot hear your appeal Mr Cavanagh. This court is for decisions in civil cases. Yours is a criminal case and not under the jurisdiction of the court of appeal.'

Mr Cavanagh was not to be put off, even by the second most important law officer in England and Wales.

'My Lord, section three of the Palmer Act gives this court jurisdiction.'

The Master of the Rolls was not a man who liked to be contradicted; he decided to swat this insect.

'You are bringing your case very shortly and very conclusively; only unfortunately for you it is the wrong way. There are some things which I cannot listen to with any deference at all. To tell one as old as one is that any question in a criminal case could be heard before the Exchequer Chamber is sticking one full in the eye!'

The spectators in the court dissolved into laughter and Mr Cavanagh turned red. He was now a clown and could do little to recover, though he tried.

'A grave responsibility rests upon me in this matter. The application is not because I have not a great confidence in the intelligence and fairness of a Cumbrian jury, but in a case of this description it seemed proper that the court, if they entertained the matter at all, should give their opinion as to the paragraphs which have appeared in the papers and which have been of a very serious character.'

The Master of the Rolls listened impassively to Cavanagh's lame excuse, then knocked his arguments ruthlessly on the head.

'It is quite plain that this court is for appeals on civil matters, not criminal. It has no jurisdiction in a criminal matter.'

And that was that; all was reported in the newspapers with a certain amount of glee. Mr Cavanagh's line of attack had fallen flat on its face because he had been barking up the wrong tree, and all he could do now was to pack his bags and head for Carlisle, hoping that he could do better. He had not high hopes; in the eyes of the public he now had a lot of egg on his face. He would be appearing before Mr Justice Day, and he knew him from past experience to be a man of firm opinions and quick temper; there could be sparks flying, if not fireworks.

In Carlisle the excitement mounted as the time for the Assizes approached. The question was over who would be allowed into the court to hear the most important trial that had taken place in the city for many a long year. The Grand Jury box would, of course, be reserved for magistrates and local dignitaries. In deference to the victims of the crimes that the suspects were accused of, the high sheriff's bench was reserved for Lady Hermione Graham and such of her society friends who might wish to accompany her like the Duchess of Roxburgh. The ladies' gallery would be absolutely crammed full of what the *Carlisle Patriot* described as "Fair and Gentle beings", or at least those fortunate enough to obtain tickets from the high sheriff's office; they were in great demand.

Mr Littler, QC, of London, had been instructed for the prosecution and he came with a formidable reputation.

Quietly, discreetly, the digging of a pit and the building of a new gallows, able to hang three men at once, went ahead in Carlisle Prison. This is not to say that the three prisoners were prejudged as guilty, but it was as well to be prepared. Mr James Berry, the public hangman had been contacted and had pencilled some provisional dates in his diary. He in turn alerted his new "assistant" that he might be needed. His new assistant was to work with him under a false name.

When James Adams had been hanged for the shooting of Inspector Simmons in Essex, one of the witnesses had been Sir Claude Champion de Crespigny, a newly appointed magistrate. Sir Claude was a member of a very old and aristocratic family and took his public duties seriously. If he was to be an administrator of the law, then he determined that he would learn the whole process, up to and including hanging, so that he would be completely proficient in his magisterial duties. He had an idea that he might end up as high sheriff of Essex, responsible for carrying out all executions in that county. James Berry thought at first that he was dealing with a fool, but the passage of a few coins and personal acquaintance soon showed him that Sir Claude was completely serious. Thus he agreed to take the aristocrat on as his assistant for the next hanging, and it looked like this was going to be Carlisle. Berry was, of course, sworn to secrecy and Sir Claude assumed the name Charles Maldon for his new job.

Christopher Gaddes and other railwaymen from Tebay were now national heroes. Several of them had received substantial cash payments from the reward fund set up by Chief Constable Dunne. This had increased Gaddes's savings considerably so that he felt able to proceed with something he had been wanting to do for a very long time, but had not been able to for lack of funds. On 20 December 1885 he married Catherine Hodgson at the church in Longtown and there were crowds of people to see off the five foot nine inch, blue eyed and brown haired champion with his bride; as a signal mark of favour the marriage ceremony was attended by Sir James and Lady Graham. The rumour was going round that the stalwart Gaddes had impressed the Chief Constable of Cumberland so much that Mr Dunne had invited him to enrol in the police force where his rise was certain.

Theories were being voiced. Great amusement was caused by the Birmingham Daily Mail which asserted that James Baker had married a girl from Carlisle in 1881 at St Cuthbert's Church during race week. According to the reporter, the fourth man that everyone was hunting for was in fact this woman dressed as a man. Nobody took this very seriously of course because it was common knowledge by now that James Baker already had a wife so unless he was to be accused of bigamy, he could not have married another. For the moment, Eliza Baker was keeping very quiet, but of course, despite the fact that Baker had been living with Nellie for some time, Eliza was his legal spouse. If he was found guilty and hanged, all that was his came to her, by law.

By now, several newspapers were in agreement that the Netherby burglary and subsequent shootings were the result of planning by some criminal mastermind, probably in London. The men who were about to go on trial clearly could not have been operating on their own. In Portsmouth the news of the shadowy mastermind was read by a young doctor attempting to set up a practice, called Arthur Conan Doyle.

An anonymous letter appeared in several newspapers which laid the blame for the murders squarely at the feet of the prison system.

'I am convinced that the men who murdered the policeman at Plumpton, and are known to be returned convicts...whom the brutal and degrading treatment they received in our convict system has turned into fiends. Nothing is more common than to hear a convict say "I'd rather be topped than do another lagging." I have in mind the case of Thomas Fury who was brought from prison and hanged on his own evidence for a murder in Sunderland. Prisons are veritable hells. The warders are as brutal as the convicts they guard. Only places like Chatham and Portland can turn out such finished monsters.'

This was read by Rudge in his cell, for Andrew Johnson, the chief warder, seeing a man desperate for brain food, had been giving him some newspapers. This puzzled Rudge, for he had hated all warders; he did not hate Johnson because the man was kind to him. He was starting to like this particular warder and so felt able to ask him a favour.

'Do you suppose that the governor would allow me some writing paper and a pencil or two? There's a few things I want to write down.'

He did not add "just in case", but Johnson knew what he meant.

'I'll ask the governor for you this very day,' said the chief warder very slowly.

Rudge laughed. 'You needn't worry you know. I ain't the suicidal type and even if I were I certainly won't be killing myself with a pencil.'

'That does not worry me,' replied Johnson. 'I've had some experience in the judging of men and I do not think you are the self destructive sort, but I have seen my men attacked by people in the past with a great variety of implements. You'd be surprised.'

'Somehow,' said Rudge, 'I doubt that. I've seen things in my life that would curl a lot of people's hair Mr Johnson, but I remind you that I am not a convict. I am a remand prisoner and have not been found guilty of anything.'

'Aye that's true enough,' admitted the officer. 'I think you'll have what you need and within the hour too.'

'Why are you being nice to me?' said Rudge, curiously.

'All I am giving you Mr Rudge is the common courtesy that I would give to any other man.'

'No. It's more than that. You could do that in a cold sort of way, but you do it with kindness. Why is that?'

Johnson thought for a moment,

'I believe in a God Mr Rudge, and I read my bible. In the Kirk I have often heard the minister tell my congregation that we should not judge people lest we be judged. It was something I bore in mind when I joined the prison service. As a member of the Free Church of Scotland I am also enjoined to treat others as I would wish to be treated. You are not religious I think, so perhaps you do not understand.'

'Oh I do. I may not be religious, but I do know kindness when I see it. I can be kind too you know; prisoners are still human beings.'

'Aye, that is true and something that many people forget. But you do not believe in God I think? You told Mr Leavers that.'

Rudge's reply was slow.

'I said to Mr Leavers that I did not think there was a God.'

'Ah, so you've left room for doubt.'

'Maybe, Mr Johnson. I dunno. I've seen a lot of men in prison suddenly "get" God when they're in trouble. I always said I'd never go down that path.'

'Because it's cowardly?'

'Something like that.'

'You were brought up a Catholic I believe. Would you like to talk to the priest?'

Rudge mulled this one over.

'It would do no harm I suppose. Alright; yes please.'

'I shall speak to Canon Waterton.' Johnson smiled, 'It's conversation at least. It breaks the silence.'

'And I won't get into trouble for it. Fair enough sir. Talking is good. Send him along please.'

25

Trial

On Friday 15 January the Cumberland Assizes opened and a Grand Jury found a true bill of robbery, murder and assault against Rudge, Martin and Baker. They would be tried before a judge and jury starting on Monday 18 January. Baker was by now in what the warders called a "blue funk." He spent his time in a solitary cell, pale and sometimes shaking with the terrors conjured up by his own mind. He was also watched all the time now. His grasp on the world was slipping away, and although Nellie had visited him more than once, her presence seemed to almost distress him more in reminding him of what he was losing. The only person who could get through the wall of fear with which he had surrounded himself was James Wilson, the prison chaplain to whom he repeatedly declared his innocence.

John Martin was indifferent, maintaining a mask of toughness which slipped only when he asked to see a priest. Like Rudge, he was never religious, but now, facing what might be the end of his life, he was glad to talk to Father Thompson. Canon Waterton, who was now having conversations with Rudge felt that dealing with saving the soul of one probable murderer was enough for one cleric to manage, especially as Rudge could talk nineteen to the dozen on so many topics it made his head whirl. Thompson was having a hard time actually making conversation, and had led something of a sheltered life. John Martin had scraped together all that he could remember of his childhood religion and understood that the priest was bound by the confessional, so he grew to trust him. The priest listened with impassive face but horrified mind to what sounded like an upbringing from Hell. Martin was simply the greatest sinner he had ever met. During all his time in prison, Martin had not a single visitor. He was about to face someone who had met many sinners in his lifetime and was well used to dealing with them.

In his private life Mr Justice Day was considered to be a kindly man, but he came to Carlisle with a fearsome reputation for severe sentences. As he swept into court at ten o'clock in his full panoply of robes and wig, the personification of the majesty of the law, the room fell quiet and, packed as it was, you could have heard a pin drop among the three hundred or so people in the chamber. A considerable crowd had gathered outside and during the trial several attempts were made to storm the gates and get in, only to be stopped by a line of police with their truncheons drawn. The awful list of charges was read and then the jury was ordered in. Mr Mattinson, defending Baker thought that the jury was too much alike in age and immediately asserted himself by challenging six jurors, who were replaced. Finally, twelve men sat in the box and the hearing got under way.

Mr Littler did not waste time and opened the prosecution immediately, speaking for over an hour and outlining all that had taken place when the various crimes were committed. Then began a long parade of witnesses attesting to what they had seen. For the moment Mr Mattinson held his fire, but Mr Cavanagh questioned each witness, his line of attack being plain. He was attempting to cast doubt on the identification of the suspects, but was over eager to cause the witnesses to say the wrong thing. Inspector Roche, describing when he was shot indicated that the fourth man was in a light coloured coat and was about five feet and seven inches tall. James Baker immediately sat up to take notice.

'Have you identified the fourth man?' asked Mr Cavanagh.

'I have not seen him sir,' replied Roche as the court dissolved into laughter.

Then Mr Cavanagh made a great mistake. He was cross examining Sergeant Johnstone as to what happened when he was shot.

'Was the man who shot you nearer to you than the two men who were backing away from Sergeant Roche?'

'He was nearer sir.'

'I must ask your Lordship to take that down,' said Mr Cavanagh to the judge.

The judge exploded with rage.

'You may ask what you like! Only I object to be told what I take down!'

'I do not tell your Lordship; I only asked you,' ventured Cavanagh.

'I shall take down what I think fit and I shall take down nothing which I do not understand. I shall certainly not take anything down at your dictation!'

'I do not think of dictating to your Lordship but I have a terrible responsibility resting upon me and I ask your Lordship to take a note of this.'

'I will take down everything that is material, but I will not take down anything I do not understand. When I get an answer I understand, I will take it down in the discharge of my duty.'

Cavanagh gave it up and continued questioning Roche, to be followed by Mr Mattinson. Nonetheless, he was not finished arguing with the judge.

PC Fortune had still not identified the men in the dock at an identity parade and was asked by Mr Littler if the men who attacked him were in the court. He replied that three of them were, and indicated Rudge, Martin and Baker. Mr Cavanagh waited his time, then stood to say, 'This witness has never identified the men at all.'

Mr Justice Day came straight back at him, 'He has identified them now.'

'He has never identified them with other men. They were not put with strangers when he saw them.'

'As a matter of fact, he says these three men are the men he saw. I am very much surprised that such an objection should have been allowed (by the magistrates).'

Mr Littler chimed in, 'It only shows the extreme fairness with which these cases are conducted in Cumberland.'

'Extreme fairness' said the judge. 'Or something else.'

On the Tuesday morning Mr Cavanagh asked that all the witnesses who had given evidence should not be allowed to sit in court in case they were recalled. He also asked that the medical men who were due to give evidence should not remain in the court. Mr Justice Day said that they might remain after they had given evidence. Mr Cavanagh looked at Mr Justice Day and the judge looked back at him. Day did not like Cavanagh and over the next few hours took several opportunities to poke jibes at him and at his expense, causing much amusement in the court.

It was in the afternoon of Tuesday when Mr Cavanagh attempted to pull a little trick to undermine the credibility of Superintendent Russell as a witness, that he came badly unstuck. During questioning he asked Russell to hand over the revolvers and bullets taken from the prisoners, along with the key to one of their suitcases; that of Baker. After looking at the exhibits for a moment, Cavanagh handed Russell a key.

'You say that is the key?'

'I don't say so.'

'You don't say so?'

'It has no label on it.'

'Oh,' said Mr Cavanagh to the court, 'Unfortunately I have handed him my own key. The two are so very much alike.'

Gales of laughter swept the court, but it was at his expense.

'I am too old to be done that way!' said Russell, provoking yet more laughter.

Mr Cavanagh was making a very good job of undermining his own credibility; he was now seen as a player of silly tricks. Rudge however, seemed to be enjoying himself, though at times he was indignant, once calling out in protest 'This is like murdering men' when Fortune did his *ad hoc* identification. When the court laughed, he laughed; he made copious notes and occasionally leaned forward to whisper in Mr Johnson the solicitor's ear. Martin sat sluggish and uncomprehending, saying nothing. Baker slouched, a pool of depression, twitching and silent.

Then they called John Watson a weaver from Wigton who had shared a cell with Baker and Robert Cummings. He related how Baker had told him what happened at Plumpton.

'He said the policeman came up to them and they told him to stand back. The policeman insisted on arresting one of them and they fired and shot him through the head and he fell. They lifted him up and pitched him over a wall and then proceeded on the line and got into a railway truck at Penrith. He said they then went on to Tebay and got out. The jewellery, he said, was found near the river. That is all I have to say.'

The effect on the court was as if a bomb had gone off; it was devastating. Now a hush descended on the room. Watson admitted that Baker had newspapers in the cell which contained full accounts of the burglary and murder, but he had not read them; Baker had kept them and said that he was not allowed to read out to them either. At any rate Baker had told his tale before any of the newspapers were allowed into the cell. He learned the tale from Baker's own lips. not the papers.

The weight of the witness evidence had been considerable, but Watson could not be moved from what he said; soon the case for the prosecution was over. Mr Cavanagh and Mr Mattinson did not call any witnesses. Mr Littler now summed up the case for the prosecution and it was damning; again he spoke for an hour. His comprehensive presentation ended by saying that the evidence was sufficient to justify the jury convicting all the prisoners.

Mr Cavanagh now stood to appeal to the jury's good sense. He said that there was not one tittle of evidence to show that any of the men accused had ever been in the grounds of Netherby Hall. There was strong evidence that the robbery had been committed by someone with local knowledge. The only thing connecting the prisoners with the robbery was that the jewels were found near to their place of arrest. All that could be proven from that was that they had received stolen property, which was not even a felony.

He then went into some extraordinary mental athletics to show that the three men had all been in the Packhorse at the time the shot was fired that killed PC Byrnes. The missing fourth man was the real murderer. Rudge, Martin and Baker might have left the Packhorse without seeing the fourth man at all. They might have seen Constable Byrnes lying apparently dead on the road and pitched his body over the wall. Maybe the fourth man dragged the body of the constable over the wall, which would account for the discolouration of the dead man's wrists. If this was the case then they were not guilty of the murder; it was the fourth man and they were only guilty by association.

The blood on their coats could have been got when they passed through the cattle pens at Penrith. And in any case all the policemen had not been wearing proper uniform but coats over the top. Perhaps Rudge, Martin and Baker had been defending themselves from attack, not knowing the men they shot and attacked were policemen. All the evidence against his clients was circumstantial. His final appeal to the jury was that one day they too would stand before a tribunal and would have to justify on the day of judgment for what they had done. There was reasonable doubt and he beseeched the jury to find his clients not guilty.

When he was done, there was a disbelieving silence in the court. Mr Mattinson stood to defend his client with a raised eyebrow. He did not mince his words but gave a very sober and close argument in which he cast doubt on the statement of John Watson. Why on earth should Baker have made a confidante of the stranger in his cell? He demonstrated that judging by the times of the shooting given by various witnesses in Plumpton, Baker, and probably Rudge, were still in the Packhorse Inn when the murder took place. Baker also had no revolver, unlike the other two. This implied that Baker was not guilty of the murder; suspicion thus fell on Martin. He asked the jury that if they entertained the slightest doubt about this, then they should give him his life. It might be passed in a prison's gloom, but at least it would give him time to find salvation and mercy from God.

It was ably done, and realistic.

The jury retired at twelve minutes after seven and returned at twenty minutes past eight. The atmosphere in the court was taut and electric as in dead silence the Clerk of Arraigns stood and asked the foreman.

Gentlemen of the jury, have you agreed upon your verdict?'

'We have.'

'Do you find Anthony Benjamin Rudge guilty or not guilty?'

'Guilty.'

'Do you find John Martin guilty or not guilty?'

'Guilty.'

'Do you find James Baker guilty or not guilty?'

'Guilty.'

You say that all the three prisoners are guilty of wilful murder? You say that is your verdict?'

'Yes.'

A gasp when round the room as the foreman finished speaking, and the clerk turned to face the dock.

'Anthony Benjamin Rudge, you have been found guilty of wilful murder. Have you anything to say why the court should not proceed to pass sentence of death?'

'I have sir. I don't know that it will be of any use now. I proffered it to the learned counsel, but he thought it had gone too far. The evidence of the prosecution, the evidence of the experts settled that the wound in the skull of the deceased was three eighths of an inch, and the prosecution tell you that it was impossible for a bullet coming from the smaller revolver to cause that wound. If the hole in the skull is but three eighths of an inch, the bullet that came from my revolver - I call it mine, as it was taken from me - my revolver being over half an inch, it was impossible to say that it caused the wound, when the experts tell you that. Because it is not like flesh; the bone does not contract. One revolver, they tell you, is too small, it only being three eighths of an inch. My revolver is over half an inch... a hole which does not contract could not be made by a bullet half an inch in size.'

John Martin was then asked the same question.

'What is the good of saying anything?'

Rudge chimed in, 'It is all settled, of course.'

Baker said that the evidence proved he was in the pub at the time the fatal shot was fired.

Rudge butted in and told him not to rely too much on that. The wound was the thing; he then went on at length about the size of the wound until he paused and continued more slowly. Rudge, put off his stride at first, now found it.

'... had they not found me guilty of murder but only found me guilty of any of the minor charges, I knew that my former character would have compelled you to sentence me to a long period of penal servitude. I thank the jury. I will now say something, not for myself, but I speak for the prisoner Martin. I confess to the murder myself.'

There was a sensation of exclamations, gasps of horror, and excited chatter in the court.

'I own it. Although I say I own it, you cannot prove it. No-one else was there but myself, not a soul, and yet a bullet that came from my pistol did not do it. The prisoner Martin, and the prisoner Baker are both equally innocent of this ... you have had some evidence here that is utterly false.'

Rudge then went on to condemn some of the witnesses as liars, but finally came down to what he really felt.

'In passing death upon me, you are passing the sentence that I want, that I absolutely want. I prefer it to going into the living death of penal servitude. I know what it is. I have been through it, where a man is thrust into himself and the iron, as it were is forced into his soul and has no outcome. I have met with only one exception and that is in this gaol here. If there were more governors like the governor in this prison, there would not be so many desperadoes; not so many men who would be willing to draw the trigger rather than go back again. I am telling you what is absolutely true and what I am stating now, I state as a dying man ... I say take me. If you hang these two men,' and here Rudge thumped the desk in front of him with some passion, 'then you are committing judicial murder ... but the jury have come to their verdict, whatever I may say, and the law says, I suppose, that three men must be hanged.' Now he shouted with vehemence, 'I say again, it is judicial murder.'

Mr Justice Day, his voice trembling with emotion, and black cap upon his head, now condemned the three men to death, begging them to seek forgiveness from God in the time they had left. When he was done, Rudge asked a question.

'Does your Lordship have any influence with the Howard Society? If so I wish to make some statements concerning the treatment of convicts.'

'I have no jurisdiction over the matter but I do not doubt that any reasonable request will be favourably entertained by the officers of that society.'

'It will perhaps come with a better grace from your Lordship than from me. I can give information as to the treatment in convict prisons.'

The Clerk of the Court called out, 'Remove the prisoners please.'

'My Lord, asked Rudge. 'May I ask that my property be given to my friends?'

'Any application of that kind must be made to the proper authorities.'

As Rudge was led down the steps he spoke to Martin.

'Well they've done for us properly John,' and laughed. He appeared to be completely at ease with what had happened.

After a glowing tribute from the judge to the police and the people responsible for the arrests of the murderers, the court adjourned at nine o'clock. All that remained now was to set the time for the execution; it would not be long in coming. It was exactly one year since Inspector Simmons had been shot dead in Essex.

26

Waiting

Rudge had shot at Inspector Roche and Sergeant Johnstone, and it was by merest chance that they had not died. He had been saying for years that he would rather kill than go back inside, and he had attempted to do so. The great irony for him was that he had not actually killed anyone and had tried to point the court in the right direction. To him it was clear; if the bullet hole in Joseph Byrnes's skull was a quarter of an inch in diameter then he could not have been killed with either of the pistols confiscated at Tebay, both of which would have left an entry wound twice as large. This pointed clearly to the wound being inflicted by another gun, but there was no other gun found.

Rudge sighed. He actually did prefer to die than go back to prison, and if he had not been hanged, he knew that he would go to prison for many years; he would rather be dead. A strong part of him knew that he was deserving of death under the law, for he knew what had really taken place and had not said. The policeman was dead and the law said that the men found guilty of a common purpose in carrying out such a crime were equally so. Very well. It was time to set his affairs in order and put his thoughts to rest on a couple of things.

He now had his pen and paper and settled down to write what he had in his mind; a letter to the woman who might or might not be his daughter. The possibility of her existence, especially as he had no other children that he knew of, was something he wished to come to terms with, before what might be his end.

'*For the Attention of Rebecca Jewson.*

Dear Rebecca,

I am writing this letter in the full knowledge that you may never read it, because you do not know that I exist. You have been brought up with the 'knowledge' that another man is your father, and once such a thing is planted into someone's mind, it is almost impossible to shift.

However what we know is sometimes not correct. This applies to me as much as anyone else and what I think may be wrong, but I suspect that I may be your father. If you ever read this then it will be because you suspect or know that what you have been told is not true. The only way that I can see this happening is if your mother has told you that there is a possibility that I am your father, and so you have come looking for me.

I am closer to death than I like so I want to say a couple of things before I go.

Firstly, despite my suspicions, I have not contacted you with them because you have a life and are happy. It would be a selfish thing for me to burst in upon that with nothing but suspicions. Certainly it would not be the act of a father who cared; better that you live serenely than with a troubled mind. With no actual proof other than a family resemblance that I may be imagining, as much as I would like to know, I will not act for the idea is hateful to me that you would be distressed with no cause.

Secondly, and most importantly, I want you to know that if I am your father then you were conceived, not as a by-blow or a one night pleasure. You exist because I loved your mother. I asked her to marry me more than once, but she would not, which is her privilege. I can quite understand why she would not want me, or a man like me in her life. It was her right to choose and her decision, and probably for the best.

Lastly, if what I suspect is true, then you have, though I am dead, your father's love. You may ask how that can be, because I do not know you, or you me, but I love the idea of you, and that is sufficient. Remember; you were loved and wanted by the man who may be responsible for your existence.

That is enough; I will give this letter to my brother Thomas, sealed and never to be read except by you, if you ever come looking. The only other person who knows what is in here is Canon Waterton, and he cannot tell, being a priest.
You have your father's blessing; goodbye dear girl.

William Fennell'

Canon Waterton read this last with a surprised eye.
'Are you using a pen name Anthony?'
'No Father. That's what I was baptised. Anthony Benjamin Rudge will be hanged for murder soon enough. It's better for a girl to be related to Bill Fennell I think.'
'You have a point.'
'Can I ask you Father, when it happens, to give that to my brother Thomas?'
'I will give him the letter; I am not bound by the prison regulations to hand them in, but as the letter is in effect a dying wish, only to be delivered after your death, then I regard it as under confessional seal. Tell me though, do you really think she is your daughter?'
'Dunno Father. I never will, but writing that sets me at ease.'
'Then it's a good thing.'
With the shadow of death hanging over them, the rules were relaxed for the three men with prison staff treating them as

kindly as possible. They could choose between tea and cocoa for their drinks in the morning and afternoons. Pudding and porridge gave way to fish and meat, while they were allowed to smoke, though Baker did not. None of them was ever left alone now so that they could do nothing to cheat the gallows.

Rudge, perhaps for his writing, and a governor sympathetic to intelligence, had been moved to a cell with a fireplace with a fire, where he spent hours scribbling. When the news was brought to him that the high sheriff had fixed the date of execution as Monday 8 February, he merely shrugged and smiled; he had gone past worrying about it.

'After all,' he said to Canon Waterton, 'It is not given to many to know the exact date and time of their death. It could be seen as a fortunate thing.'

'You think so? Why? Because you have time to prepare?'

'Yes, that, but also because I know when it all ends. I've had enough Father and I want out. If this is the way it ends, then so be it. I'm not going to waste time grumbling about it.'

'You value yourself so lightly?'

Rudge laughed. 'No, it's not even that. My life has not been like yours or that of any man with sufficient opportunity or money. I chose my path aiming to live a life at a better level than what I was born to. I knew the risks, and I have been breaking the laws all of my life. I suppose that in a way I deserve this fate. Think of it as my way of making amends, though truth to tell I don't think I have all that much to make amends for.'

'You have enjoyed a life of crime?'

'It has its moments, but no, that's not what I meant. I came into this world poor. I did not make this place where some are very rich and have more than they will ever need. I was born into poverty, and unfortunately I was given a brain, and that means that I read a lot. Sooner or later you have to ask why this world is the way it is; then you see that it does not have to be this way.'

'So you stole from people who had more than you.'

'Yes, because the dice are loaded for people like me and it's not going to get any better. I'll tell you frankly Father, this world is a sewer, and I shan't be sorry to leave it. If there is a next world as you believe, then I hope it's better organised than this one.'

'May I ask you something?'

'Ask away Father. I may not answer, but asking does not hurt.'

'Was there actually a fourth man?'

Rudge laughed loudly and openly.

'The question that the whole nation has been asking! Alright Father, there was a fourth man. He was just some young chap who had attached himself to us along the way. He left us at Carlisle where I think he had lodgings, and from what I read in the newspapers he very sensibly ditched his coat and got away.'

'Does that make you glad?'

'Of course. He'd done nothing bad. You'll get no name from me or the others though, so don't bother asking.'

Martin and Baker had no fireplaces and complained a lot about the cold.

The work on the new scaffold was pressing ahead under Mr George Black, a master joiner, and banging and sawing could be heard all over the prison. It was being built in the old treadmill shed, the governor having decided that the treadmill was something he had no use for in his prison. Rudge's brother visited him, the usual restrictions applying, and asked if the noise bothered him.

'Oh you needn't bother about that. It wouldn't bother me if they were putting it up at my bed head.'

To Rudge now, leaving the world was no more than a formality, and not a very interesting one.

Baker's family had been pressing for a reprieve for their son, but the Home Secretary showed no inclination to do it for villains who looked and acted as if they had come straight from the pages of a penny dreadful magazine. The public expected justice, therefore justice would be done. Hearing that Queen Victoria was in residence at Osborne House on the Isle of Wight, Baker's mother and father took the train and ferry down there to plead for mercy; they could not get through the gate.

John Martin had also accepted what was going to happen. He was a professional thief and had been in prison with hard labour before. He killed in order to avoid going back and he took this as being understood in his class of people. It was a hazard of the job and he had been caught, so must pay the penalty. His mouth was closed; he did not grass. Inspector Rolfe visited him and asked him if he could throw light on a number of unsolved cases in the London area. Martin just smiled at him with contempt.

'I ain't letting you know any more about it. I'm not a grass and I don't peach.'

The only person he really spoke to was Father Thompson, taking increasing comfort from religion and the life after this one; as it turned out, this was significant.

Baker received a string of visitors; in turn he saw his mother, his father, both his sisters and his brother in law, and of course Nellie. He especially asked to see his three year old nephew, which was allowed. However a conversation with Nellie caught the attention of a warder, who, had he been more imaginative, might have read more into it than he did. Baker knew that the game was up and the lies had stopped; he was speaking of what happened at Tebay.

'You ran under the bridge and Rudge came after?'

'That's right Nell. They was hard after him and I could see we was going to get nabbed. But I got away and he didn't.'

'Did you throw it in the river?'

'Yes. It seemed the best thing to do.'

There was a pause. The warder listened, interested, because this was the first time he had heard Baker admit that he had been at Tebay; not that it mattered any more, but it was an interesting titbit. The reporters outside paid a few bob for snippets like this. Had he been sharper he might have remembered that it was Rudge who threw the jewels over the river.

'Best place for it then,' said Nellie, after a pause. 'Quick thinking James. Well done.'

Baker, who really did love her and especially now that she had stuck to him so loyally, began to cry, but as she knew, that was not unusual now. So did she.

Rudge's manuscript was nearing completion, and it was very long. He expanded on what he had said at the trial and had believed for a very long time. His descriptions of the prison system, the silent routine, the bread and water, the punishments, the turn-screw, the treadmill, the oakum, the rock breaking and so on, were lurid and detailed. He spoke of man's injustice to man and repeatedly stated his belief that minor criminals were turned into monsters by the very system that was supposed to reform them; the term "Reformatory" when used to describe a prison, was an obscene joke.

Of the police and especially of prison warders, he was bitter and abusive.

'It is a strange thing to me that with rare exceptions, police officers and warders are drawn from the very class of society that produces criminals. The very desperation that drives men into a life of crime, drives other men with the same background, into selling their souls to become sheepdogs, putting on a uniform because it provides a wage, a house and a family. Yet the values held by these men are the same as those held by the safe cracker, the pick pocket and the ladder man, because they come from the same slums, have the same poverty, and are bred in the same ignorance. The brutality displayed by the criminal in the course of what he does, is echoed in the brutality of the uniformed watch dogs who are set to watch over their fellows. Their morality and their prejudices are exactly the same as those of the downtrodden poor and criminal, for that is whence they spring. You deplore the violence and outrageous behaviour of a thief, yet in the prisons the same brutal behaviour is exhibited every day towards the unfortunate inmates. Blows are common; gangs of warders beating prisoners unconscious is common. Bribery, corruption and venality stalk the corridors, and the same is true of the police. The whole criminal justice system is staffed by men who, if they were not in uniform, would probably be thieves and murderers themselves. They call men like me "monsters" but they forget, or cannot imagine, that monsters like me are not born. They are made.'

There were, according to Rudge, three great causes of crime.

'The first is heredity. If you are born into a poor family, then in this country as so ordered, you are going to stay poor. It may be true that there are avenues out of poverty for some of these unfortunates, but for most, life offers nothing more than rags, a scramble to find the next crumb to go into your mouth, life in a hovel, and an early death. The easiest way out is to turn to crime, and so is created a great under class of people who can only subsist from one day to another because they steal. They did not create this situation; they were born into it and it is their prison from the day they are born until the day they die...'

Warming to his theme, he came to the second cause.

'Locality is a key to understanding how criminals are made. I was born in Bethnal Green where it is not uncommon to find whole families of ten or more people crammed into a single stinking room in a rookery where filth and disease are endemic. Such was my upbringing. Do not imagine that the people who inhabit these festering slums are there by choice. Not a mile away from where these people live, there are banks, restaurants, mansions full of unimaginable wealth. Even the merest fraction of that, spent well, could improve the lot of thousands, even millions of dirty, half starved wretches who eke out a living in the dank and decrepit streets of East London. You are not brought up in such a place. You learn how to survive, and the law is that of the jungle. There are places in the East End where every family is engaged in criminal activity, because that is how their world is and the only way it can exist. It does not have to be this way, and I am convinced that it is deliberate. The people who have ordered things in this country, the Crown, the government, the lords and ladies, the bankers and the businessmen; they have made it this way, and it is done on purpose. We are supposed to be a rich country with a huge and powerful empire. It does not show in the places I describe where surely the conditions are worse than the worst slums we hear of in Calcutta and Benares. Life for many is as Hobbes described; solitary, poor, nasty, brutal and short. I have, through my own efforts, learned to read and have now a level of education above many of my fellows. I can only imagine what I might have been had this happened when I was a child, and not when my feet were already set upon the path described by so called 'respectable' society as villainous.'

For his third cause, he came back to the police.

'The police system is actually a cause of crime, for we see the actions of policemen who turn a blind eye, who take bribes; who ask for 'favours' and some of whom are as violent and corrupt as any burglar. But it is more than that, because the police are not just supposed to be the guardians of law and order. They act as an army on the street to keep people down and oppress them. Mark my words, the East End is a simmering pot of discontent and soon there will be riots, if not revolution. There are many who see a police officer's or a prison warder's uniform as little more than the mark of a traitor, and hold them in contempt. They would use violence against them with no more compunction than they would at killing a dog.'

The manuscript was bitter, detailed and very one-sided, though perhaps that is understandable. When it was done Rudge, proud of his work, which he thought a frank exposition of what he believed, gave it to the governor, asking him to forward it to the Howard League, the organisation dedicated to the reform of the criminal justice system. Governor Leavers took it, and read it, his eyebrows lifting up towards his hairline. On 9 February he sent it to London, but not to the Howard League. He addressed it to the Home Secretary.

'I doubt very much,' he told Andrew Johnson, 'that it will ever see the light of day, but Rudge could hardly grumble. I have placed it into the hands of the one man in England who actually has the power to do something with it.'

'Maybe it will help to bring change sir?' ventured Johnson.

'I have my doubts on that,' replied Leavers. 'It is long overdue and one day it will happen, but I fear no time soon.'

The document did not matter to Rudge once he had handed it over to Leavers. He had said his piece. Now he could wait for his next assignment when he had an appointment to meet a Mr James Berry.

27

Berry

James Berry was going to be very careful in Carlisle, because, as he well knew, he had blotted his copybook badly in 1885. The hanging of Rudge, Martin and Baker was going to be his first after the end of what had been a horrible year. If he botched this one then he might well be out of a job because he knew that the Home Secretary, Lord Cross, his ultimate employer, was not happy with him.

On 23 February he had tried to hang John Lee three times at Exeter prison, but three times the trapdoor of the gallows had failed to open. Amid the panic, the stamping on the trap, the white faces and shaking of all witnesses, when the execution failed for the third time, the chaplain walked out declaring that it was an act of God and he would have nothing more to do with the procedure. Since by law, he had to be present, Lee lived, and his sentence was commuted.

'Wasn't my fault,' Berry repeated to himself whenever he thought of it. 'How could I have picked up on the warping of the doors? They worked perfectly with a dummy.'

Of course James Berry had to have a tough personality, but he had determined that whatever happened, he would do the job properly next time, and he did. The trouble was that Berry could actually think, believed in what he was doing, and wanted to do it right. Much of the trade and craft in being a hangman was passed on from one hangman to another until William Marwood came along. Marwood had developed the technique known as the long drop where prisoners died instantly, their necks being broken. This was so effective that it had become the standard method of execution in Britain, replacing the slow strangulation that had taken place before. The trouble was that each prisoner had to be calculated individually or the execution could go wrong. Marwood had left only very sketchy notes on his techniques and calculations when he died in 1883. Berry was having to feel his way and learn as he went, but at least he did it intelligently.

After Marwood's death Berry, an ex-policeman, had applied for the job of public hangman but lost out to Bartholemew Binns. He turned out to be the most horrendous drunk who turned up to every execution absolutely sozzled and bungled them all. He lasted less than a year, botched the deaths of nine people, and was sacked; then they sent for James Berry. By and large he was a vast improvement, but his table of calculations was not yet complete, much depending on lessons learned from experience.

Berry sighed at the memory of 30 November when he had executed Robert Goodale at Norwich. He got his figures wrong when working out the drop. In front of the horrified witnesses Goodale disappeared down the trapdoor and the rope went slack. When they looked into the pit they found his body lying completely decapitated with the head lying beside it. James Berry had come in for a good deal of criticism in the press for this, but, as he told himself, no-one could complain that death had not been instantaneous.

'I say Berry, is it necessary that I stay in the prison tonight?'

Berry winced as he and his new assistant walked across the footbridge at Carlisle Station. He was not a man who was particularly comfortable with the aristocracy, but Sir Claude had paid him handsomely to be allowed to be his assistant in the upcoming execution.

'No Sir Claude. It is usual for the executioner to sleep in the prison the night before a job, but that's tomorrow night, so no.

You do not have to sleep in the prison, though I do say that they make you comfortable enough.'

'Ah,' said Sir Claude. 'If that's the case then I shall stay in the County Hotel tonight.'

'*Of course he would*,' thought Berry. 'If you want to stay incognito sir, you'd better keep your voice down.'

'Oh,' said Sir Claude, his voice dropping to a stage whisper. 'Why is that then?'

Berry looked at him for a long moment before deciding that he was actually serious.

'Three reasons sir. Firstly, if you'll forgive my saying so, by the standards of an executioner's apprentice, you do have a very posh voice. If someone hears you they might smell a big fat rat.'

'You mean they would suspect that I was not as I appear?'

'That you are not a working class chap called Charles Maldon. Yes sir.'

'Good point. What was the second reason?'

'If you are staying at the County Hotel, the best in town and are known to be my assistant, then it might be thought odd that you are staying there and I, your employer, am not. It's probably best that we part company and pretend that we are not acquainted as we leave the station. And I'd better stop calling you sir, in public at least. I'll call you Charlie as I am supposed to be the boss.'

'Fair enough. How shall I find the prison tomorrow?'

'That's easy enough. Turn left out of the station and walk down a couple of hundred yards and it's right there. If you turn up about say ten o'clock, we shall conduct our business with the governor.'

'Dashed early!'

Berry's face went wooden.

'And what about divine service? Shall we attend in the prison?'

'I think that might be considered bad form; the executioners at the same service as prisoners; not that I think our men will be there. If you wish to observe the Sabbath then I suggest an afternoon service at the Cathedral. We should be through our business by then.'

'What was your other reason? The third one?'

'That should be fairly obvious. You are rather well known Sir Claude. Sportsman, steeple chaser, boxer, soldier, balloonist. It might be well to keep your collar up and your hat on; there will be a lot of reporters from national newspapers in town this weekend and you might be recognised.'

'Yes! Excellent point. You are right. I'll see you tomorrow Berry.'

With that, Sir Claude, carrying his own case as a working man should, walked out of the station, across the road and into the swanky County Hotel.

The secrecy was too late of course. Sir Claude was an extrovert character and his first remarks had been loud enough to be heard. On the station was a reporter for the *Carlisle Patriot* with sharp ears. Sir Claude was 'rumbled' but for the moment his presence went unannounced. The editor of the *Patriot* was of the Conservative persuasion, and had a healthy regard for old aristocracy. He decided to respect Sir Claude's pseudonym and wait on events; there was nothing here that would not keep.

More interesting was the rumour that Rudge's brother Thomas had been heard declaring in a pub that his brother would never live to hang. This in turn led to another rumour sweeping the city that an attempt was made to smuggle poison to the condemned man. On this very Saturday Thomas had visited Rudge and taken with him, his three year old son. Mr Leavers had all visitors searched for poison, but the little boy had an orange which he rolled round the cell, unpeeled. This was the only time during his wait in a condemned cell, that Rudge expressed any form of regret.

'It would have been nice to have had a nipper or two Tom, but that ain't going to happen now.'

'From what you told me there might be one walking round that could have called you Dad.'

'Yes, but I don't actually know that. You look after this one eh, and try to keep his feet on the straight and narrow. He'll have a better chance than I had. At least he gets to go to school properly. He likes that stuff though don't he just?'

Looking forward to the visit of his young nephew, Rudge had requested and received some extra sugar, butter, lemon juice and bicarbonate of soda. During the night he had made some toffee over his fire, and now the little boy chewed it with enthusiasm.'

'I'd like you to have this Tom and register it with the patents office. I think it might be worth a bob or two.'

'What is it?'

'The plans for a new sort of key ring. I have been filling my time in writing and I also designed this. If the family can profit by it, then that's a good thing.'

As Thomas's time ran out and he prepared to leave, Rudge said, looking at his nephew. 'I'd give him a penny, but I haven't got one.'

Mr Johnson, on duty in the cell, felt in his pocket. 'You have one now.'

'Thank you Mr Johnson; you are a decent man.'

Rudge bent to give the penny to his nephew. 'There you are son; spend it well.'

'Goodbye Will,' said Thomas, who had never used Rudge's new name. 'God bless you.'

'I doubt he'll do that where they all think I'm going,' said Rudge, grasping Thomas's hand firmly. 'Goodbye Tom. My love to all and tell them I'm sorry about this, but for me it's for the best.'

With that, Thomas was gone, and Rudge had received his last visitor.

John Martin had been very stoic and uncommunicative all the time in his cell, but as the time of his death approached, he opened up more to Father Thomas, disregarding the warder who was now with him all the time. Some of what he said was surprising.

'I was sorry to see what Lady Graham said about the photo I nicked was of her dead father in law and of sentimental value to her. I'd like to think that she can get it back.'

'Where is it?' asked the priest.

'I didn't need it and it was too easy to identify so I slid it out of the frame and threw it into a hedge along the roadside into Longtown. It's probably still there.'

'I shall tell them and a search can be made.'

'Yeah; you do that and tell her I'm sorry.'

On another occasion Martin was speaking of how the trio had escaped along the railway line.

'We never really did trust Baker you know. He never carried a gun and that made him different to us.'

'You mean his heart was not fully in it?'

'That's right. Rudge and me figured that if someone did get shot then he could always say that it wasn't him and blame us. I never liked him, but Rudge nearly done for him that night.'

'What do you mean? That he might have killed him?'

'That's right.'

'But why? What had he done?'

'He went back to help lift PC Fortune. We thought he might have decided to leave us and turn Queen's evidence.'

'He would give you away?'

'That's right. He'd grass on us, but he came back so that was that.'

Martin saw Canon Waterton as being of a higher rank than Father Thomas, and by this time the Canon was speaking to both him and Rudge. To him, Martin made two further statements.

'You can tell Rolfe that he was right. I was there when Inspector Simmons got shot down in Essex, but it wasn't me. He hanged the right man. As to the shooting of Constable Byrnes, that was me. I didn't intend to kill him but to disable him so that we could get away, but I aimed wrong.'

The Canon relayed this news to the police and to Mr Leavers, but the governor was not sure how much it could be believed.

'After all, Rudge confessed in court that he did the shooting, perhaps in an attempt to get the other two off at the eleventh hour. Martin could be doing the same, for Baker is still hoping for a reprieve. Such a confession might save Baker; I doubt it but I shall pass it to the Home Secretary anyway.'

'You think it an attempt to save Baker?'

'It is possible. Martin may calculate that if his last act is to save life, then it might in some way weigh against the sins he has committed.'

'And avoid punishment in the hereafter?'

'Quite. You said yourself that he has become more receptive to religion in the last two weeks.'

'Well if it is that, then the impulse is noble, but the matter itself is academic I think.'

'Yes. Baker will hang. He was there and in law, all are guilty.'

Baker himself clung to the idea of being saved by a last minute reprieve, but no word came, though he knew his family were clamouring for one. He remained pale, often shaking and frightened. The only time he showed any brightness at all was when a familiar face showed itself at the door; Captain Wilson, Her Majesty's Inspector of Prisons was making his annual rounds of Carlisle.

'Oh hello Mr Wilson,' said Baker brightly, perhaps believing that the inspector had news.

'Hullo Baker. I'm sorry to see you like this.'

They had met before in other prisons, and Wilson now asked the question he always asked. 'Any complaints?'

'Oh. No Mr Wilson. No complaints,' came the deflated reply.

Rudge did complain to the inspector. His view was that before they were convicted they should have had better food, and since they were condemned, he should have liked to have had some wine, if not beer.

Berry and Sir Claude had received the information they needed about the height and weight of the three men, and had peeked through the eyeholes of the cell doors, sizing up the physiques of the men they were to hang. Berry then sat with Sir Claude calculating the drop needed for each man before inspecting the new gallows. He was very pleased. It was built of substantial timbers with a cross beam that would bear a weight of sixteen tons. Three collars were on the beam, each with a loop for a rope, and large trapdoors that would swing open into a deep pit underneath.

On Sunday, with the assistance of Sir Claude, the hangman placed ropes of the correct length into the loops, then tested the whole mechanism with weighted dummies.

'That'll do it; it'll work as nice as ninepence!' declared Berry.

The stage was set for the final act.

At 6.30 am on Monday 8 February 1886 Emma Leavers, the governor's wife, brought the three men a hot mug of tea in their cells, for which they thanked her; she would be the last woman they ever saw. None of them wanted to eat, but spent the next hour or so praying with the three priests, asking for God's forgiveness, and in James Baker's case, still hoping to be saved by the Home Secretary. He was given holy communion by Reverend Wilson. A very large crowd of around three thousand people had assembled outside the prison and the bell began to toll at 7.45. At five minutes to eight Berry went into Martin's cell and quickly pinioned him with a looped leather strap in front of him which secured his arms. Sir Claude entered Baker's chamber and did the same with him; Berry then secured Rudge. There was no resistance or protest, and when it was done, all three men rose and walked to the place of execution. Rudge seemed to be quite cheerful, the outcome being the one he preferred to any other, except acquittal. Martin looked calm and collected. Baker on the other hand looked, according to one of the two reporters allowed in the room, dazed, like a man not looking at what was in front of him but something beyond. He staggered as he walked, his legs weak, and had to be supported by the chaplain and the warders. When the three men were together Rudge looked glad to see the other two and walked up to them and, as best he could with his tied arms, took each of them by the hand. 'Goodbye old pal,' he said. For the first time Martin's face showed emotion; 'Goodbye,' was all he could choke out.

Rudge, who bore the warders at Carlisle no ill will, also shook hands with them, saying 'God bless you,' and several of them returned the greeting.

On the gallows trapdoor their names had been written in chalk and each walked obediently to his place, Martin in the centre with Baker on the left and Rudge on the right. Sir Claude strapped their legs together as Berry fitted and adjusted the nooses. Then Berry placed white hoods over each man's head. At this point the men were all heard to mutter 'Lord Jesus receive my soul.'

As Berry moved towards the lever that would open the trapdoor, Baker yelled out 'Nellie; keep straight. I die an innocent man, but I forgive everybody.'

The trap swung open and the men dropped through into the ten foot deep pit. Baker and Martin disappeared from view, but Rudge, being a heavy man, had only been given a short drop as sufficient to break his neck; his head stayed bobbing above the level of the trap almost as if taunting his executioners. There, by law, they hung for the next hour before being taken down.

The black flag was hoisted over the prison and a huge cry of satisfaction that justice had been served upon the murderers went up from the thousands gathered there.

Berry was ravenous, having had no breakfast. He left the prison and went over to the restaurant in the County Hotel with Sir Claude, at his invitation, where he ate a good breakfast with obvious relish. However, Sir Claude was not the only notable person in town. There is a curious hypocrisy in law-abiding citizens in that although they want murderers to be hanged, they detest the hangman. Berry was recognised and many of the hotel guests objected to his presence as they ate breakfast, especially as he came "reeking of the gallows". One gentleman was so outraged that he summoned the manager who explained that Berry was a recognised officer of the law and could not be prevented from being there. Another gentleman, a kilted Scottish landowner, was so disgusted that he left his breakfast and stalked off.

Berry replied to people's ire by calling out, 'You want justice done? It's been done. If the judge, or the prosecuting barristers had been here you canting hypocrites would invite them to your table and make much of them. But the man who carries out your will, you despise; well I don't give a damn.'

'How dare you sir! I'd like to give you a good thrashing!'

'You could try,' offered Berry. 'I wouldn't mind giving you a six foot drop and a squeeze!'

The man's eyes widened in horror, remembering who he was speaking to, and he left the room in haste.

Berry finished his breakfast before going back to the prison, followed by a small crowd. Sir Claude did not accompany him. Dr Lediard, the very man who had attended to Roche and Johnstone after they were shot, had been the surgeon attending the execution. When the bodies were taken down he noted that death had most likely been instantaneous with Rudge and Martin, but Baker may have lingered a while. In his official report of the affair he wrote that the executions had gone off "In a very satisfactory manner."

28

Nellie

Nellie Baker gazed almost hungrily over the ship's rail as the low flat banks of the Mersey estuary slipped by. She was not quite sure why she stored up the view so intensely, because she knew she would never be back. Britain had given her nothing, and ultimately, had taken away the man she loved. Yes, he had been a villain but she knew that James was no murderer, though she also knew that he had killed PC Byrnes without meaning to. She had thought of starting her new life under her maiden name, because of course she had never married James legally; she could not, because he was already married to Eliza. That bitch! Looking back, the last few months had been interesting, to say the least.

No matter what had happened, she thought she had earned the name Baker, and Blumson, though her official surname, had not been the way she saw herself for a long time. She would take of James all she had left, and in Canada, she would be Baker.

James would have divorced Eliza if he could, but there was no easy way that a working class man could get a divorce because it was so expensive a process; only the rich could do it. Eliza had run off with another man when James was doing time in Portsea prison, but legally she was still his wife. The moment he had been hanged, she had come crawling out of the woodwork and claimed everything he had. She had taken the contents of the shop, the furniture, household goods and money. Nellie, who had helped build up the shop and run it, was left destitute. It was ironic that the last of her money had been spent on a return ticket to Carlisle to see James just before he had been hanged. There had been no funeral expenses of course because executed prisoners were buried inside the walls of the prison in which they were hanged. On her return from London, Eliza had been waiting and Nellie had no home; the only thing she had left was the clothing she stood in because Eliza claimed that James had bought the rest of it; it had been sold to a second hand slop shop. In despair she had gone to see James's parents, but they had never approved of her, their son's mistress as they called her, an immoral woman, and they told her to go away and never come back. Part of her thought that they blamed her for what James became, thinking that if he had not needed money to support her, then he would never have turned to crime. It was nonsense of course, but it gave them something to cling to. The only family she had, even if she had money for a train ticket, was her old aunt in Carlisle but she did not want to scrounge off her; she was poor anyway. There was no chance of her getting a respectable post, for she had no references from previous employers, and if they got wind of who she was, she would never be trusted anyway; she was, to all intents and purposes unemployable. Yet she had to live; she needed food and shelter, and that was why she went to Mary Jones.

Mrs Jones followed a rather specialised profession; she trained thieves and had a dazzling local reputation as a shop lifter. Her reward was to take a cut in whatever her graduates stole.

'So you've got nothing left at all dearie?'

'Nothing at all.'

'And you've no mind to go on the game?'

'No thank you. There are better ways to make a living, as I well know.'

Mrs Jones looked at her slyly.

'"Nellie keep straight", he said.'

What James had cried out as the gallows opened had been in every newspaper in the land.

'That's all very well,' said Nellie. 'That wife of his has nicked everything I had, so keeping straight is hardly an option for me. I know what's what, and I need your help.'

There was a long pause, and then the older woman said 'I think you do. Alright. I teach you, I lodge you, I feed you and I clothe you. In return I want sixty per cent of what you get.

Nellie pulled a face. 'That's a lot.'

'Look my girl, I know you're not a fool but it's market forces ain't it? You haven't got a lot of options right now. Anyway,' and here Mrs Jones grew kinder. 'You'd be an investment and I'd need a return on my investment. Who's to say that if you turn out to be a profitable concern, we can't reduce that in time. Do we have a bargain?'

'We do,' said Nellie. 'Like you said, I've not got a lot of choice.'

Nellie found herself lodged in a dingy room on James Street in Hoxton, not far from the market; Mrs Jones paid her rent. She was fed in Mary Jones's kitchen, and, to her surprise, was dressed respectably in clothes befitting a middle class lady.

'Why?' said Mary Jones, in return to her question. 'Because, my girl, you're well spoken enough and you have to look the part when we go out. You're the daughter and I'm the mama! You come out with me and we go shopping. I'm the fussy cow who insists on being shown everything. You are the quiet little mouse who goes round the shop and nicks what she can by hiding it under your coat. You might take a careful look at that coat.'

Nellie looked; inside the coat on both left and right, had been sewn very large pockets.

'Yes. You can get quite a lot in those. Just be careful not to let it bulge.'

So Nellie was able to keep body and soul together during Spring and Summer of 1886. She made quite a nice living, sallying forth into different parts of London, and to her surprise it was really easy, and though her heart pounded with the fear of discovery the first few times, it became something really slick. All sorts of items went into her coat pockets, to be transferred, once they had left the establishment they were visiting, into Mrs Jones's shopping bag so that they could go into another shop with Nellie's pockets empty. At the end of the day Mary Jones would take the day's pickings to a particular shop in Shoreditch High Street and sell them.

'We are doing very nicely Nellie. I have to say you are very good at this; best partner I ever had. Carry on like this my girl and we might try the West End. That'd be something wouldn't it? Oxford Street? Mayfair?'

All had gone smoothly in her new career until September, about seven months after James had been hanged, calling on her to be straight. On this occasion they did not operate as mother and daughter, but entered Edward Rowell's draper's shop in Hackney High Street as separate customers, Nellie going in two minutes after Mrs Jones. Seeing that Mrs Jones had the assistant completely distracted in conversation, Nellie took a ladies' jacket, value twelve shillings and sixpence, and stuffed it into her inner coat pocket. Unfortunately for her, Hackney High Street shop keepers were well used to the ways of the large criminal class that haunted the East End. Another assistant, a young man named Crane, was watching as Nellie tried to leave the shop in haste.

'Hey you! Stop right there,' was what she heard as a young man grabbed hold of her arm. Mary Jones, seeing that the game was up, attempted to leave. Nellie pulled herself free and ran out onto the pavement, but both women were now caught and held by the shop assistants shouting 'stop thief!'

Mrs Jones shrieked at them. 'You let me go! I don't even know this young woman! How dare you lay your hands on me. I'll get my husband along here directly and he'll give you a good hiding sure enough!'

'What's happening here?' came the dread voice of the law as the local beat officer walked up to the shouting group.

'This woman stole a coat; she's got it under her own coat right now!' said one of the assistants.

'Open your coat,' commanded the officer, not bothering with manners. He was not to be argued with; coppers in the East End usually are not. Nellie opened her coat with a slightly shamed face.

'You are under arrest. Now what about the other one?'

'I never saw this young person in all my life. I just came in here to look at some pillow slips in the window and now I have been called a thief. I'm a respectable married woman.'

'Do you know this woman?' the constable asked Nellie.

'No,' she muttered, with her eyes downcast.

'Right.' The officer looked at Mrs Jones. 'Hop it.' A relieved look on her face, Mary Jones scuttled off down the road, while Nellie found herself marched down to Worship Street Police Station and locked in the cells. It was there that she met Detective Sergeant Robinson, a rising star in the Metropolitan Police; he knew who she was. Nellie gave her address.

'James Street? You working for old Ma Jones?'

Nellie said nothing.

'Oh you don't have to say anything Nellie. This is one of the places she uses. I know how this is. Don't worry; I'll soon have her, you may be sure.'

Robinson went straight round to Nellie's room in James Street, taking with him the constable who had arrested her. When they got there they found Mrs Jones. She had just paid the rent which was due, and had taken possession of everything in the room which she was about to have transported back to her own house. As soon as she saw Robinson she knew she was about to be nabbed.

'Is this the woman you let go in the shop when you arrested Ellen Baker?'

'Yes sir,' replied the constable.

'I don't know why you did that, but take note of her face. She's one of the worst shop lifters in the East End and has done time with penal servitude more than once. You're on ticket of leave now ain't you Mary?'

'Yes.' The answer came between clenched teeth.

'Well it looks like you'll be back inside for the winter don't it? Turn out your pockets now.'

The pockets revealed several pawn tickets.

'They ain't mine. They're Nellie's.'

'See?' said Robinson. 'This is how it works. Everything that Nellie's got, she has put into pawn. When Nellie comes out she wants her stuff back. To get it she has to work for this old sponge. One of the oldest tricks in the book. Right, you come along with us quietly now. You know the alternative.'

In the Worship Street Magistrate's Court the next day, Mrs Jones pretended to cry for sympathy, denied that she was on ticket of leave, and said she had been trying to earn an honest living for four years. The magistrate did not believe a word of it and sent her for trial at the local Assizes. Now it was Nellie's turn.

'I understand that you are the widow of the man Baker who was hanged at Carlisle in February. Is that true?

'It is sir.'

'I take it that he was your means of support. Have you fallen into bad times following his death?'

'I have sir. It is very hard to make ends meet.'

'I understand that and I am sorry for it. The fact remains however that you have committed a crime and the law must be upheld. I am inclined to give you a choice in the matter because of these circumstances. I can send you for trial at the Assizes, or I can sentence you myself now to six weeks in prison with hard labour. What course do you prefer?'

'I plead guilty sir, and I prefer your sentence rather than the Assizes.'

'Very well. Holloway for six weeks. It is my fervent hope that when you come out, you may find a better form of subsistence than that which has brought you before me. Take her down.'

In the court sat a Mr Wheatley, a Christian missionary; the East End was seen as a place full of heathens needing God, so Mr Wheatley had begun his crusade some years before, and his particular vocation told him to save fallen women from sin. He needed very little imagination to understand why Nellie had become a thief, and he determined that he was going to save her. He had a very well developed channel for rescuing women and starting them in a new life, but in this case, he needed help. Fortunately his missionary work relied on donations from devout Christians, and some of them occupied very important posts in the government. One of these prominent people was Mr Charles Stuart Wortley, member of Parliament for Sheffield and under secretary at the Home Office. Wheatley was given permission to speak to Nellie in her cell and ask questions; then he went round to Wortley's house to explain matters to him.

'You mean to tell me that after Baker was hanged, this young woman received no help at all from anyone? No money, no house, nothing?'

'That is exactly the case.'

'And you are prepared to use your connections to give her a new life?'

'I am. But I need immediate help Charles. I am sending a batch off tomorrow, so she must be on a train to Liverpool this very day if she is to be with them. The next opportunity will not be for six months.'

'Then I'd better get my hat and a few papers.'

It did not take long for Wortley and Wheatley to ride in a cab to Holloway where Nellie was given another choice.

'There is a ship leaving Liverpool tomorrow evening for Canada. It is a young nation and because of the nature of the work of developing it, there are large areas where the population is thin and there is a shortage of women. This means that there are opportunities of all kinds for young women to carve out an honest life for themselves. Would you like that?'

'I should,' said Nellie. 'But I have nothing. How can I do such a thing?'

'Your passage would be paid,' said Wheatley. 'You will be clothed and fed. On arrival in Canada you will be met by Christians who will help you to find honest work and accommodation. You need never steal again and can live a respectable life.'

'Or you can stay here and finish your six weeks hard labour then back out to work for the likes of Mrs Jones,' said Wortley.

'Only you have to decide now,' said Wheatley. 'The ship leaves tomorrow. What do you think?'

'There is nothing to think about. I accept.'

'I thought you might,' said Wortley. 'I have here a paper commuting your sentence. You will be released immediately and you must come with us.'

'You have that power sir?' asked Nellie, somewhat awed.

'The only man above me is the Home Secretary in this affair. Believe me,' snorted Wortley, 'I have the power.'

So it was that Nellie found herself with a hastily packed bag on a train that very evening, with a volunteer to accompany her to her ship. With a feeling of disbelief and acting almost in a dream state, astonished that things could have turned round so quickly, she boarded the SS Sarnia lying in the Mersey on 17 September 1886, heading for Quebec via Belfast. She was one of twelve in a group added after the initial tally of passengers was made. Wheatley had evidently persuaded some of the shipping companies to use spare berths for his women in search of new lives. At the age of twenty-four and nobody's fool, she had a chance to make good, and every intention of using it.

Now, as the Sarnia slid down the muddy waters of the Mersey towards the sea, Nellie felt the need to make a break from her past; a farewell gesture. She had managed to keep only a few things of her past life, but one of them was a rather battered man's hat. It had been seen by Mary Jones, and the police, and the missionaries, and none of them had commented on it, believing it to be a sentimental souvenir of James Baker; but it wasn't. It was far more significant. It was too small for Baker's head; on the other hand it fitted Nellie very well.

Now, a wistful look on her face, she threw the hat down into the water where it washed away in the foam of the ship's wake.

'Goodbye Smith' she muttered.

Handsome, rather than pretty, with the hat, the false beard and a big coat, it had not been too hard for her to be Smith. Having once been a housemaid at Netherby it had been easy for her to guide James and his companions to the Hall and back. She had not liked Rudge and Martin, for she knew they looked down on James for not carrying a gun. It was funny that Martin thought she was a "nancy boy". She had sharp ears and had heard that; sound carries at night. If Martin had been brighter he might have rumbled her. For a while she thought Rudge suspected who she was, but soon realised that he was hearing what he wanted to hear and accepted Smith as a bloke who was helping them in exchange for cash.

James knew of course, and that was why he had gone berserk when the policeman grabbed hold of her. He was protecting his woman, so he'd hit the policeman, which she thought a stupid thing to do. It had all escalated from there, but she had been shocked at James battering PC Fortune so badly. It was vexing that he had not come with her to aunty's house which was a few minutes away, but Rudge and Martin would probably have shot them both if they thought they were being betrayed.

James had not liked to carry a gun, but Nellie knew that carrying one gave you status among mobsmen. She, as Smith, carried a pistol; she had persuaded James to get her a ladies' pocket revolver 'For protection' as she put it. To her dismay, instead of what she wanted, he had bought her a single shot parlour pistol. It fired only a .22 round at low velocity. This was what she handed James, wrapped in a cloth, when they parted after rolling PC Fortune off the railway line. To her disgust James had purchased it second hand from a man at a fairground who had been using it as a 'plink' gun. It fired rounds made not from solid lead, but pressed lead powder. In the fairground, when you fired it at pipes or tins it hit the target with a 'plink' noise and the pellet dissolved instantly into powder without penetrating. The power of the .22 cartridge was limited and was supposed to be used for indoor target practice; if it hit someone it would hurt like hell; up close it would wound. It might even knock someone out. For the trip north, and unknown to James, Nellie had obtained some proper .22 solid lead bullets and loaded one into her gun. James never knew that when he shot PC Byrnes, though he realised it afterwards. She really should have told him; Byrnes might not have died. Rudge, Martin and James need not have died. Rudge of course could not grass on James, though he knew full well who fired the shot. This was why he drew attention to the different calibers at his trial compared to the wound in PC Byrnes's head which he knew to be caused by a .22 bullet from a gun he had not known James had, until he used it. The prosecution had suggested that James did the shooting with a gun that had never been found, but they could not prove it. James disposed of the gun in the River Lune as he ran away at Tebay; it was probably still there and would remain so for ever.

James of course had realised after he shot PC Byrnes that Nellie had put a solid bullet into her pistol. Most people missed the significance of his final words and concentrated on how he told her to 'keep straight.' The most important bit for her was the second part, 'I forgive everybody.' That was for her, and she alone knew it.

When she left James on that awful night, she had thrown 'Smith's' light coloured coat into the river and peeled off her false beard which had also gone into the water. Smith, as might have been observed, was rather paunchy round the middle. This was Nellie's skirt, rolled up and held in place with a piece of string. There was no-one about and all she had to do was pull one end of the knot and "Smith" vanished as a young woman came out of the shadows and walked to her aunty's house. She had even seen a policeman on her way there; he had nodded at her, perhaps mistaking her for a lady of the night, but certainly not for a desperate robber.

Now the 'fourth man' who the entire country would like to see caught and put on trial, sailed out of the Mersey with the government's blessing, and towards a new world and a new life in Quebec. All that remained were ghosts of what had been; in the killing of Joseph Byrnes they had acted together, and all were guilty. Let the dead bury the dead. As for Nellie, her spirits rose with every turn of the ship's screw. For her the prospects looked a lot brighter and more hopeful than anything she had left behind.

Miscellany

- Carlisle prison was closed in 1922 and knocked down some years later. All the bodies of condemned criminals were exhumed and reburied in Carlisle Cemetery in the Dalston Road. There were nine altogether and the 1886 skeletons were apparently 'in good order' and still wearing their boots. Not far inside the gate from a busy road is a small black marker stone bearing the words 'Rudge, Martin and Baker.'
- A Nellie Baker did leave the UK bound for Canada on 17 September 1886. This was two days after being jailed at Worship Street Magistrates' Court. Mr Wortley MP did intervene to save her, and it was reported in national newspapers that she had settled into a new life in Canada. She arrived in Quebec on 27 September on the *Sarnia* a steamship which also had sails, of the Dominion Shipping line. We are allowed to hope that she enjoyed a long and happy life there, perhaps with many descendants.
- James Berry was paid a retainer of £1 a week, and received £10 for each execution; £5 if the prisoner was reprieved. He used to hand out business cards where he thought appropriate. He resigned as hangman in 1892, having got wind that the Home Secretary was going to sack him. After his resignation he went to America but found that tough as he might be, his demons came to torment him as he grew older and he thought of all the people he had hanged. He became a Christian and spent the latter part of his life campaigning against the death penalty. In 1893, giving a lecture on his career, he said that he had hanged 193 people. When he hanged the Plumpton murderers he had drunk a whole bottle of brandy beforehand and it did not make the slightest bit of difference in dulling the thoughts he was having. The people

he hanged were all working class. No aristocrats were ever hung. Berry made his living mostly as a poultry farmer just outside Bradford.
- Where PC Byrnes died, Chief Constable Dunne caused a memorial to be erected in red sandstone. On it is a cross surrounded by the words 'Do or die.' Underneath is the inscription "Here Constable Joseph Byrnes fell on the night of October 29, 1885, shot by the three Netherby burglars whom he singlehanded endeavoured to arrest." Now, as time progresses, the memorial backs onto a modern housing estate on a road named after him. His grave in Penrith cemetery was found to be unmarked and in 2012, Brian Parnaby, one of his descendants, persuaded Cumbria Police Force to erect a headstone. A memorial service was held with appropriate ceremony, 120 years after Byrnes's death.
- Sergeant Johnstone, who Rudge shot through the body, when he was recovering, received a gift from Dr Lediard, who attended him. It was the bullet that was taken from him, beautifully mounted in a wooden case lined with velvet. Johnstone was much taken with it. In later years he was promoted to the rank of inspector, and based at Penrith.
- Christopher Gaddes, the brave railway guard was invited by Chief Constable Dunne to join the police force. He did so in 1887 and was shown a lot of preference. For whatever reason he did not get on well with his new career, stationed at Workington. In 1892 he was allowed to resign and he became a shop-keeper in Longtown.
- James Baker's widow took over his grocery shop in Bethnal Green and appears to have kept it in business until 1912. His parents closed their furniture shop for a while after his execution but reopened it after a decent interval, They never ceased to mourn him.

- Superintendent Sempill continued a distinguished career in the police force by becoming Chief Constable of Stirlingshire in 1890.
- Mr Dunne continued as Chief Constable of Cumberland on a salary of £140.12.6d per quarter. When he eventually retired as Sir John Dunne he enjoyed a pension of £350 a year.
- One of the reporters who saw the execution and the face of Baker afterwards was so disturbed that he left and walked alone on the fells for three days because he could not come to terms with it.
- Dr Lediard said after the executions that Rudge had asked for leeches to be placed on his head as he was 'suffering an overflow of blood.' When this request was refused he asked Dr Lediard to carry out a post mortem after he had been executed, and dissect his head because he thought there was something wrong with his brain. Permission was not given for this.
- Hysteria over the identity of 'The Fourth Man' continued after the executions. Among others, James Muirhead was arrested in August 1886 by Detective Cox in London, and forced to go to Carlisle where he was released after not being identified. It turned out that he had been arrested before, suspected of being the fourth man, but had been released.
- Mr Cavanagh never become a judge. In October 1915 he was back in Carlisle and suffered a seizure while engaged in a case at the court. He was removed to a nursing home and died soon afterwards.
- The ring that was stolen from Lady Hermione Graham was lost from the family some years later; probably when some of the estate was sold off just before and after the First World War. Subsequently, and decades later, the ring turned up and was given to Sir Charles Graham, Lord Lieutenant of

Cumbria. Inside it, and in very small engraving were the words 'This ring cost four men their lives. The Netherby Burglars 1885.' Who did it and where the ring had been, remains a mystery.

- There was no right of appeal for convicted felons. All that could be hoped for was that relatives or friends might appeal to the Home Secretary, which sometimes succeeded. Similarly, defendants had no right to speak in their own defence in court; it was the job of the barrister to do that. The only time they could speak was after the verdict had been announced.
- Many years after the murder a story or rumour was circulating that a man called Summers, who had emigrated to Canada, had fallen ill whilst employed on the Canadian Pacific Railway. He was supposed to have confessed before dying to being the fourth man. Seeing that his companions were prepared to murder people, he had left them at Carlisle, because he was not. This story may be apocryphal because there is no evidence extant to support it.
- Three years after the murder of PC Byrnes, his widow married again. Her new marriage, to a man some years younger than her, appears to have been happy; she had three more children. In addition to the £500 donated to send two of her boys to the police orphanage, a further £500, raised by public subscription, had been invested for her support. Another £500 was divided among the railway staff and police officers who caught the murderers.
- Sir Claude Champion de Crespigny never became high sheriff of Essex. There were many who felt that he had been over zealous and displayed too much fondness in the role of executioner. It was clear that he was not fitted to occupy the

office of high sheriff. He died in 1935 at the age of 88, active in sports and walking long distances right to the end.
- In February 1890 a man named Barrett, a known associate of Rudge, Martin and Baker, was reported to have been arrested in the United States, supposedly as the missing fourth man. A detective was to be sent to New York to fetch him back to London but Barrett committed suicide in an American police cell.
- Inspector Roche continued in the police force until 1892, rising to the rank of Superintendent. In that year he resigned and took over the Dock Hotel in Wallsend which he ran for sixteen years until his death in 1908.
- Sergeant Johnstone recovered from his wound and eventually reach the rank of Superintendent at Penrith. At one point he had a great row with Chief Constable Dunne and was reduced to sergeant. Nonetheless, he was a good officer and worked his way up to superintendent again. He retired from the force in 1907 and died in 1933.
- Jimmy Dyer the Cumberland Bard, whose statue now sits in The Lanes shopping centre in Carlisle, wrote songs about the trial of the murderers, and played them and sang in the streets.
- In 1938 Miss Eva Elwes wrote a play entitled 'Rudge, Martin and Baker' which was performed at Her Majesty's Theatre Carlisle.
- On the day that Rudge, Martin and Baker were hanged, an enormous riot broke out in London as thousands of people rampaged through the West End, smashing, looting and destroying. The police lost control for a while and had to bring large reinforcements in to quell the rioters.

- From the *Arrarat Advertiser* Australia, September 1908:

'Anthony Rudge, one of the Netherby Hall burglars and murderers, invented, during the time period that elapsed between his arrest and his execution, a key-ring on an altogether novel principle. The idea was sold by his executors for £500.'